THE
FORGOTTEN
MOUNTAIN

HEATHER LYONS

"Deserving to be a new classic for the modern day, **The Collectors' Society** should be on your must read list."—*The Paisley Reader*

"If you love classic literature, and you love fantasy and fairy tales, this is a must read book for you."—*Book Briefs*

"This is one of those books where you have to sit back and question an author's sanity because how the hell did they ever come up with this amazingly insane and totally unique idea if not for a bit of insanity on their parts. All I can say is thank goodness for Heather Lyons and her crazy thoughts, **Collectors' Society** is. . . . . . I can't even explain it, just know that it IS . . ."—*Reads All The Books*

" . . . A unique tale that will leave you breathless, enthralled and begging for more. If you thought you knew classic fairy tales, think again!"—*Resch Reads and Reviews*

"I'm finding it almost impossible to put down in words the love I feel for this story. It was nothing like I expected and yet everything I wanted."–*The Book Hookup*

"I'm not exaggerating when I say that **The Hidden Library** has everything you could possibly want or need in a book: laughter, heartache, romance, action, adventure, mystery, suspense—the list goes on and on. If I could've dreamed up a book that would satisfy my not-so-secret love of fairy tales as well as my never-ending search to find exciting and inventive storylines, I wouldn't have come close to dreaming up **The Hidden Library** because it's completely and delightfully unique. Not only does it have a nostalgic feel that beckons my inner book lover, but it's also refreshing in a way that kept me guessing as to where the narrative would go next. "–*Nose Stuck in a Book*

"Beautifully crafted settings, gripping plots, and enough emotion to satisfy even the coldest of hearts, Lyons has taken elements from some of the greatest novels in history and fashioned them together to create *herself* a spot on the shelf of future "Great American Classics." Heather Lyons has woven together a story that transforms history, bringing a new-found love of classical literature to a whole new generation of readers."–*One Guy's Guide to Great Reads*

"**The Hidden Library** has it all: intrigue, romance, danger, hope, passion, and despair. The wide range of emotions you feel while reading this story will leave you breathless and begging for more."–*Typical Distractions Book Blog*

"I was completely entranced with the first book of this series, **The Collectors Society,** and **The Hidden Library** is no different. This is a highly entertaining and well-written series that I hope doesn't go away any time soon. "–*Books She Reads*

"This series keeps getting better and is a must read. A rare 6 star rating from this picky reader!"–*A Literary Perusal*

"I've never, never, never EVER read a book with such extraordinary characters in the fantasy genre." -*Melissa Reads Books*

"A mystically fantastic read that takes you on a magical fun journey. . . . Start this series now!!!" -*TSK TSK What to Read*

"This book has everything, everything. A beautiful romance. Wonderful friendships. Some love sacrifices. Broken hearts. An evil genius." -*Lost in a Book Blog*

"Sequels don't always live up to the original books but let me tell you Heather has knocked it out of the park with **The Hidden Library** . . ." -*Book Starlets*

*This one is dedicated to
Andrea Johnston and Jessica Mangicaro,
two special friends who have been with these
books & characters since the beginning.*

THE GIRL WITH THE RED CLOAK

ALICE

THE DOOR TO MY flat is wide open yet entirely sealed with webbing. I know this silk, have valued its strength in the past. I also know better than to attempt to tear it apart with bare hands, so I redirect to the flat next to mine. That particular door is unlocked—rarely do Society members lock their doors against one another—and when I enter, I sternly remind myself to remain levelheaded and calm.

Even though his smell is so utterly alluring and strong in here.

I locate what I desire in less than a minute: a pair of daggers left behind weeks ago, whilst I was too lazy or forgetful to bring them the scant distance back to my flat. I proceed to carefully check every single room, ensuring my focus remains on the task at hand rather than the memories clamoring to consume me. And yet, the muscle inside my chest squeezes, demanding notice.

Once satisfied the flat is secure, I return to my own. It takes several swipes of the daggers to slice through the tensile, and by the time I finally enter my quarters, sticky silk clings to my hair and clothes. This matters little, though. I have much graver concerns than whether or not my appearance is up to snuff.

Before me, the sitting area is in disarray, the few extraneous items I've allowed myself since my induction into the Society spread haphazardly across the room. The sole casualty of extreme violence appears to be a lamp in pieces upon the rug. Although it's been hours since Lygari was within the walls of the Institute, my fingers curl tightly around my blades as I quietly make my way toward the bedroom.

Within, I discover a body of a child prone upon the floor next to the case securing my crown from Wonderland. Her eyes are darkened wide in shock, or perhaps even terror, as she gazes blankly at the ceiling. She has turned a mottled purple and is riddled with burst blisters. Yellowish pus crusts across the visible bits of skin, leaving her a ghastly sight to behold. And still, a smile curves my lips as my eyes fall upon a forgotten set of pan pipes nearby.

My grip loosens on the blades. "Are there any more I ought to be aware of?"

Not more than a second passes before a welcome sight scuttles out from behind the case. Larger than my hand, covered with prickly hair and adorned with lovely yet vicious fangs, the arachnid leaps upon a nearby dresser. "This is the only fiend to breach these quarters, Your Majesty."

"You have my gratitude, Grymsdyke."

He lowers himself down upon two legs. "I live to serve the Queen of Diamonds."

I side skirt the body and sit upon the edge of my bed. "I would ask for your report."

My most deadly assassin coughs as he straightens his body. "Shortly prior to your departure last night, His Majesty the White King of Wonderland convened the Cheshire-Cat, myself, and the Five of Diamonds. After I reassured His Majesty I would remain at this Institute, he bade me to ensure that, if I was not in active service to my liege, I might keep an eye on the Diamonds' crown. Although assured by the proprietors within these walls of its safety, His Majesty is, as he has always been, greatly concerned about your safety. I was glad to offer this small bit of service toward the Diamonds' throne."

Another bow is offered; I incline my head.

"The White King and the Cheshire-Cat did not feel comfortable remaining behind whilst you hunted a foe. His Majesty stated he would accompany you to the gala, and once he departed, the Cheshire-Cat and the Five of Diamonds retired to their quarters to discuss matters back home. I came straightaway to your chambers. Soon after, this child arrived, playing dissonant music on her instrument. As I did not recognize her, there was no hesitation to attack."

My eyes fall once more upon the child's body. Dressed in a dirty red cloak, she cannot be more than ten, perhaps twelve years of age at the most. And still, I cannot muster the proper amount of grief one ought to feel at the demise of one so young.

Youth or no, she possessed a set of pipes like Gabriel Lygari's.

"None other dared enter my chambers?"

"None, my lady."

"The music did not affect you?"

Grymsdyke's body tilts. "It was most unpleasant. The child was a terrible musician. I have done the world a favor."

"Indeed you have." I rise. "Unfortunately, there are more unpleasant tasks ahead of us in the coming days."

"I am yours to command, my lady."

"I suppose I must go inform someone that there is a body to dispose of." I bend down and retrieve the pipes. They are wooden, the barrels nearly gleaming, they've been used so much. "Ensure there are no more stray musicians lingering about within the Institute."

I'm offered a final bow before Grymsdyke scurries up the wall and out the door.

MADNESS

ALICE

"**A**RE YOU SURE ABOUT this?"

Despite its connotations, *sure* is a relative, fluid term at best. One can be sure at any given moment and then riddled with doubt seconds later. One can be sure that the leap into the unknown is the best course of action, only to rue it the moment hard, rocky bottom is struck. Is any person completely certain of something? Our names, perhaps. Our selves. Our morals. Exactly how much of our soul we are willing to sell or part with to gain what it is we most desire.

When I tell Marianne Brandon I am sure, I could not be firmer in my convictions. It is hers that are in question. "Are *you* sure your ministrations will prove effective?"

Although, if I am to be honest with myself, my question is better suited for the Society's protections than mine. I am indifferent to the consequences.

"Yes." Our latest technology wizard's smile is grim as she furiously clicks away at her laptop. In the front seat of the van, Jack Dawkins, otherwise known at the Society as the Artful Dodger or the A.D., snaps a clip into his handgun. Across from me, Mary Lennox loads darts into her tranquilizer gun. She is a terrible shot. Perhaps I ought to clarify that she is incompetent with most other weapons, as well. Her estimable skills lie elsewhere, amongst poisons, potions, medicines, and chemistry. Like I, though, there is nothing anyone could say to tempt her away from what we're about to do. Not even the absence of the Collectors' Society's official blessings.

"Chances are," I say to Mary, "it will be as reported."

She holds her weapon out, testing the weight. "They were given ten minutes to search the place." A loud click sounds in the van as she pumps the chamber. "Even for those as skilled at retrievals like Finn and the A.D., ten minutes is nothing. Wendy asked the impossible of them."

My partner's name is a fist to my belly, but rather than leave me desperate to curl into a ball and weep uselessly about the unfairness of life and how I utterly failed Finn by going against my instincts whilst leaving him behind, it only solidifies the cold rage icing my veins.

Vengeance, the Caterpillar once told me, *can be a delicious and fulfilling meal. Be certain it is what you want to eat, though, because as it travels through your body, it will seep into every last part of you. Your stomach may hurt afterward; you may even want to purge the contents. And yet, even if you can, traces of it will always remain.*

My former Grand Advisor, whose head was struck from his body by the Queen of Hearts and whose body was fashioned into a gruesome clutch to sate twisted, vile needs, consistently proffered excellent advice. There were many I wished to wreak vengeance upon over the years, yet typically practiced restraint per his wise words.

He is dead. The man I am in love with is missing—believed to be dead by most. Mary's love is also missing and assumed dead. Millions of souls have perished at the hands of villains through the destruction of catalysts. There has been too much devastation. Too much loss.

I am ready to eat that meal now.

We are parked alongside the highway just before the gates leading to an estate belonging to a book collector named Gabriel Pfeifer—the same man who once introduced himself to me as Gabe Lygari. I'd spent a portion of an evening inside his mansion alongside Finn a while back. We came to purchase a pair of books for the Librarian, but once Lygari's collection was discovered to be immense and riddled with collectables from authors, we lingered to investigate. Weeks later, Finn was sent back alongside the A.D. to retrieve a catalyst, only to discover that the library and house we'd spent time within no longer existed. In its place was a sterile, empty riddle of a tomb.

Late last night, as the four of us within this van met to discuss this morning's outing, I typed Lygari's name into the Internet search on my cell phone. It was something I never thought to do before, something none of us had. How deliciously, patently spot-on was my find: Lygari translates to *liar*.

It fits the man I now hunt.

The A.D. climbs into the back of the van with the rest of us. We ready ourselves even though chances are the structure is just as abandoned as when Finn searched it the week prior. Bulletproof vests are strapped to our chests; guns slide into holsters. Daggers are strapped to our bodies. Three will go in, and by God, three will come out. There will be no time limit during this search.

Marianne clicks away at her keyboard. The screens bolted to the van's walls waver until new images appear, ones from security cameras inside the house Lygari named Bücherei. *Library.* I want to tear apart this athenaeum. People do not go to the trouble of hiding entire libraries if there is nothing worth protecting within them.

If he thinks he can hide it from me forever, then Lygari is truly a fool.

"The security cameras are now in my control." Marianne's eyes do not stray from her laptop screen as her fingers fly across the letters of her keyboard. "The overall system has been, as well. Viruses were encoded into them to ensure they stay mine."

Despite still being unsure what constitutes a technology virus, I consider this is excellent progress.

The A.D. scratches the back of his neck, his head ducked as to not hit the roof of the van. "However did a Janeite manage to keep such tech skills quiet for so long, luv?"

"I understand the meaning of discreet." Her lips thin. "Let us hope that all present do as well."

Intended or not, these sharp words leave the A.D. stiffening. "Are you saying you found something on your witch hunt to implicate me, too? Maybe me old mate Fagin has been pickin' secrets out of me pockets whilst playing merry tunes?"

"She's not saying that, you fool." Mary slaps her hand upon the van's wall. "We have a common enemy right now—several of them, actually, now that Sweeney Todd, Rosemary Lovett, and F.K. Jenkins are all missing from the Society's custody. Our focus must remain upon them, not finding blame or fault within each other." Heat crawls up her neck, blotching her fair skin. "You know what else? I'm *glad* Marianne uncovered Wendy's treachery with Peter Pan or whoever the hell he is." She jabs a finger against the A.D.'s shoulder. "And you should be, too!"

He winces before sighing. "I know. I am. I'm sorry, Marianne. You were just doing your job. It's just . . ."

"Wendy is your friend." Marianne spares a small yet sympathetic glance. "For what it's worth, I believe she was coerced whilst under the guise of a compulsion trance."

The A.D. grunts quietly. Our focus returns to the screens. Upon them are nothing but empty rooms, just as Finn reported. A sane person would let this go to turn down more fruitful avenues. I am not sane, though. Not fully. As the Cheshire-Cat reminded me all too recently, I believe in the impossible.

The A.D.'s cell phone trills to life. He removes it from his pocket and slides it onto the console next to Marianne. Neither Abraham Van Brunt, the leader of the Collectors' Society, nor the Librarian was officially briefed on our plan outside of an email sent en route. Van Brunt is in mourning; he, unlike Mary or myself, believes the worst by eschewing hope. Although at first I rashly considered him a coward for doing so, I now do not begrudge him such feelings. It is not the first time he lost family members to villainy. His wife Katrina, Finn and Victor's adoptive mother, perished when Sweeney Todd destroyed the catalyst for 1820IRV-SGC. Now it is assumed by most that his sons lost their lives in the same manner, only at the hands of Gabriel Lygari/Pfeifer rather than Todd. Van Brunt is entitled to feel as he must.

Once the shock of last night's deadly events morphed into rage, I left behind the doctors and nurses tending my wounds at the hospital the Librarian sent me to and caught a cab back to the Institute. I obtained some of Victor's mysterious yet miraculous healing spray he and Mary commandeered in a futuristic Timeline and mended the superficial cuts rendered by broken glass. That these medicines were not proffered after the attack only proves the shock felt by the Society over the tragic events. And that was when I made my way to my flat and was briefed by Grymsdyke.

The Society was besieged last night in more ways than one. Whilst Finn and I were at a gala for the New York Public Library, searching for Lygari and discovering the Queen of Hearts instead, the Institute was infiltrated by villains. Security footage viewed in the wee hours of the morning showed Lygari and a dozen children roaming the halls, pipes to their lips mere minutes after our departure. Nearly everyone, save my assassin spider, was affected by whatever tune echoed from the wooden instruments. Even the Cheshire-Cat was not spared. Each soul stopped what they were doing, swayed, and proceeded to slump to the ground. Some slept where they were, others stared dazedly, focused on nothing in particular. None moved. Worse yet, Lygari went to the medical wing of the Institute and roused Sweeney Todd, freeing him from his straps. The murderous fiend was gifted a pen and two books and then was sent on his way. His amorous partner in crime, Rosemary, and colleague, F.K. Jenkins, were similarly freed, although they departed separately from Todd into a different doorway. Lygari and his musical children lay in wait until Van Brunt and the others also attending the gala returned. It was then they met the same fates as the rest of our colleagues.

The Institute, in chaos, had no sleep as its residents scrambled to make sense of the turn of events. Word spread quickly, and once it did, calls and communiqués from various Timelines poured in, requiring Van Brunt to stamp out fires left and right. As if that weren't stressful enough, he is also overseeing the cleanup of the Institute whilst figuring out the directions of its agents.

This small group here in the van wasted no time leaping into action, especially when, shortly after two o'clock in the morning, I also discovered via my cell phone's search functions that *Pfeifer* translates to *piper.* There is much still to research, yet one thing is certain: *Lygari is a lying piper.*

I suppose there is a benefit to such wretched pieces of machinery after all.

Somehow, Mary and the White King were spared from such treachery when they returned from 1905/06Sōs-IAAC. Their stay at the Institute was brief before Mary edited into my original Timeline, allowing Jace to hunt the Queen of Hearts in familiar territory. She related how they'd found the Five of Diamonds and the Cheshire-Cat sleeping in their flat; when roused, both were disoriented. These states were attributed, at least in her mind, to being awoken in a land strange and far away from one's own. During the time she was in the Institute, Mary saw no others than the Wonderlanders—and whilst strange, she did not question this too much, as they departed so quickly afterward. I have no idea how or why she and the White King were spared, but that matters little right now.

What does is finding Lygari.

The A.D. returns to the driver's seat, switching on the ignition. The road leading into Bücherei is rough and unpaved, yet despite the uncomfortable ride, Marianne continues to tend to her computers and monitors.

Mary taps her tranquilizer gun against the van floor. "Victor doesn't have his medications with him."

And a flying boy stabbed Finn with a glowing blade, a situation entirely unacceptable to me. It has been nearly sixteen hours since the 1905/06Sōs-IAAC's catalyst was destroyed, and that is too long already. Every moment, every second counts. If Finn and Victor are alive, as we here in the van hope and pray, they must be found quickly.

Bücherei comes into view, tall and inconsistent about how it wishes to look: frosted glass, rough wood, and burnished metal both appears old fashioned and futuristic all at once. Imposing hedge mazes wrap around the building, and in the gloomy light of a dreary late morning on the verge of snow, the darkened leaves leer sinisterly to any wishing to come too close.

And close we come. The A.D. parks the van directly in front of the small stone path leading to the door. There will be no subterfuge today. If anything, I want Lygari to know I've been here. That I can, and will, appear as I wish. If he foolishly believes he has brought me, Wonderland's Queen of Diamonds, to her knees, I wish for him to feel bitter, frustrating pangs of disappointment.

I do not play by his rules. I play by mine and mine alone.

"Keep the door locked," I inform Marianne. She will stay in the van, monitoring the security system. As excellent as she is with her technology, she is not prepared to brandish a gun or a blade, nor would I wish her to. Selfishly, I am well aware of my need for her expertise in the coming days.

Another phone rings. It's mine—and like the A.D.'s, it's placed on Marianne's console. It is her choice whether or not to update them as she sees fit. I rather like Marianne Brandon. She is in possession of a quick mind, a large heart, and much-appreciated loyalty. Although I was ready to do what it took to compel her, she did not hesitate in agreeing to accompany us today.

I adjust the earpiece that links the team's ability to converse with one another during assignments. "I desire as much recorded as possible," I tell both Marianne and Mary. "If we do not readily uncover anything relevant, it will behoove us to thoroughly examine any footage for subtleties missed."

"I have already begun doing so." Marianne points to the second screen on the left. "I packed several cameras in your bag, Mary. There are fresh batteries if needed."

Mary bites her lip as she stares down at Marianne. The two women haven't had the easiest of times being gracious to one another over the last few weeks for reasons still unclear to me, but temperaments have thawed somewhat in the past few days. For that I am glad, as we cannot have a house divided in this war we fight.

The A.D. clears his throat. "There's no time like the present, ladies."

I grab hold of a war hammer I commandeered from the weapons wall in the Institute. It feels good in my hand. Familiar. The only thing better would be my vorpal blade, but the White King of Wonderland now wields it in my stead as he defends our lands.

Outside, a hint of snow tinges the air. The wind picks up, rattling like mournful ghosts through the still-green leaves of Lygari's hedge maze. It is a dreary day, one best suited to fires, soft blankets, and warm drinks. I have yet to spend such a day with Finn Van Brunt, where we read in companionable, contented silence, my head against his shoulder and his arms around me whilst losing ourselves within such a cocoon. And this loss, as irrational as it may be, only adds fuel to my blazing desire for justice.

The van door behind us slides shut. A click signals Marianne's adherence to my wishes, and then we three descend upon the front door, the crunch of dead leaves and twigs beneath our feet cutting through the uneasy silence the gloom sunrise has brought. In a surprising show of gentlemanly manners, the A.D. moves to open the door. When the handle does not depress, a half smile curves his lips. "It's locked. But no worries. I can have it picked open in no time."

"There is no need."

Darkish-blonde brows scrunch together. "But—"

"Stand to the side, please."

When he fails to move at my thinly veiled order, Mary not so gently yanks our companion away.

The door before us is thick. The handle is ornate. It is a beautiful door, no doubt chosen specifically to adorn a building as fine as Bücherei. It takes me three strong, measured swings of my war hammer against the handle and its surrounding area to break it apart and permanently scar its beauty. Picking a lock is kind, respectful even. A picked lock can be relocked. I do not wish this door to close behind me. I do not wish to be respectful of Bücherei.

The time for genteel manners is gone.

The A.D. is in danger of catching flies with his mouth as he ogles the door's remnants. For someone who professes to be so clever, he certainly underestimates ladies far too often.

Stale darkness, oppressive and opaque all at once, looms before us. I am unafraid, though. I am not even taken aback. I believe in the impossible, after all. I have seen, *lived* the impossible.

I step past the wreckage into the house. On the drive here, I poured over Finn's report. It was hastily written, and I fear I am to blame for his lack of thoroughness. I'd been paralyzed, languishing at the Institute while he was sent under protest on a fruitless mission. Attached to his notes, though, are schematics associated with the building. I memorized the paths he took and the general layout. What I find before me is neither the library-based residence I toured nor the mansion Finn described. Not even the rooms upon Marianne's screens in the van appear before us.

"Mother of God," Mary whispers as she crosses the darkened threshold. Her breath is a crystalized cloud in frigid air, illuminated by sunlight streaming in the cave before us.

This is not a house, nor is it a library. There are no man-made walls, no man-made floors. There are no ceilings, no windows, no light fixtures, no pools, no bookshelves. There are no stairs, no kitchen, no bathrooms, no stray, dilapidated couch. There is only rough stone laced with ribbons of quartz and packed, rocky dirt disappearing into a blanketed tunnel of darkness whose end I cannot see. Behind me, when I look upon the door, I see the lip of a rock blocking part of the entrance as a door would.

Well, well. How very curious.

"This . . ." The A.D. shakes his head, eyes wide and filled with alarm I am certain he would deny with his last breath. "What the bloody hell is this?"

I press on my earpiece. "MDB, are our visages shown upon your screens?"

Marianne's voice fills my ear, as clear as if she stood next to me. "Affirmative, ALR."

"Describe what you see, MDB."

There is no hesitation. "You, ML, and JD are standing within a foyer that lays just beyond the entrance."

Curiouser and curiouser. "Describe the foyer, MDB."

"I estimate it to be twelve to fifteen feet wide and stretch thirty to fifty feet before emptying into . . ." She pauses. "What appears to be a sitting room. According to the schematics, there ought to be a hallway intersecting the foyer within twenty feet of where you stand."

For the first time in our acquaintance, true fear cowers in Mary's eyes. It's pale and she's doing her best to hide it here in this dark tunnel of a cave, but it's there all the same.

"How far am I from the nearest wall, MDB?"

A moment passes. "Perhaps a foot at the most, ALR."

"Which direction?"

Confusion tinges Marianne's answer. "It is to your right."

I thrust the war hammer out in a straight line to my right. It, along with my extended arm, goes well past the estimated distance between self and wall to touch upon rock.

I turn to the right and face the supposed wall, the one I'd once passed by before turning up ahead into another hallway in order to reach the massive, ornately carved doors leading to Lygari's library. Ribboned quartz through stone reflects back at me.

"MDB, report what you are seeing right now."

"You now face the door, and are staring up at the security camera mounted above."

The A.D. swears quietly. A strangled noise emerges from Mary. There is no security camera in this cave, and there is most certainly nothing mounted upon the rock's lip.

"I must say," Marianne continues, "your smile is most unpleasant right now. It's very un-Alice-like."

Hmm. "And the A.D. and Mary?" I inquire. I face my colleagues, still standing in the shafts of pale light filtering through the entrance. Behind them, pieces of the broken door litter the ground. "What is it they are doing?"

"They are standing directly behind you, hands upon your shoulders, staring up at the camera. ALR, is there a problem?"

The A.D. is the one to answer. "Yes, there's a bloody problem! This is not the house I was in last week. And you clearly are not seeing us!"

"JD, please clarify?" Marianne asks.

Mary whispers, "I don't understand what is happening. This is impossible. This is—"

"Take out your camera, Mary."

Her wide eyes fly to me. Thin beams of dulled sunlight illuminate her face, leaving her appearing as if she was more ghost than vengeful woman.

"It is clear that Marianne's equipment will not serve us any good in this moment. Bring out your camera, so we might effectively record the truth."

"But—"

"Your hesitation is of no help to our purposes, Mary."

Ah. There. Steel fortifies her spine. Determination and anger fill the spaces fear so recently occupied within her eyes.

"What is going on?" Marianne asks, but no one responds. "Whatever do you mean, my equipment is not effective? I checked it thrice prior to departure."

Mary tugs out the small video camera out of the bag Marianne packed for her.

"Alice, I mean no disrespect, but . . ." The A.D. shuffles his feet. "How in the hell are we going to search for anything when we can't see? We didn't bring flashlights, no external lighting. Our cellphones are back in the van, so it's not like we can even use the flashlight functions on those." He motions toward the looming inkiness. "I'm good in a fight, but I have no experience going up against things I can't see."

"Are you afraid of the dark?"

His eyebrows shoot up at my question. "I'm no child!"

"No one claimed you were. I merely inquired whether or not you feared the dark. Many people do, even though the dark is nothing but the absence of light. What lies within, though, is what you ought to consider whether or not to fear."

He's offended, but his spine straightens, too. A gun now rests in his hand.

"Fear aids none of us right now. Fear only holds a soldier back."

The A.D. grunts once more. Thankfully, his overly inflated ego will not allow fear to dominate him, not when I call him out on such matters as I have.

"I must insist you report back and inform me if everything is all right, ALR." Marianne's voice fills my ear. "Why are you three simply standing within the foyer, staring up at the camera? Do you see something I cannot?"

Marianne's fear is of no use, either. "We are merely contemplating our next move, MDB."

"Is that what we're doing?" Mary's camera is held aloft, panning the darkness surrounding us. It's nearly tangible, this black: cold and sharp and unexpectedly aware.

Before I can answer her question, though, the floor beneath us trembles. Rubble drizzles and then pours like angry water from the ceilings and walls. Gusts of wind shoot at us like arrows from the darkness, meant to knock us off our feet.

I dig my heels in. The urge to laugh maniacally tickles the back of my throat. He thinks to scare me with a show?

In the din, the A.D. does not see these attacks for what they really are. Scrambling to grab hold of Mary, as she is just mere feet away from him, he shouts, "Earthquake!" Together they lurch toward the doorway beyond the mouth of the cave, toward what they view as safety. "Alice! We need to get out of here before the whole bloody place collapses!"

I do not retreat. As rubble turns to rocks, and rocks into boulders that mean to build an imposing wall of defense before me, I widen my stance to stay afoot. Lygari assumes he is clever then, does he? He thinks he can surprise me, terrify me with the impossible. Silly, insipid man. He ought to have tried that on a girl who has spent her life in the safety of the known rather than a woman who grew up amongst the inconceivable.

My name is repeatedly shouted from beyond the door. Lygari roars at me with his rocks and wind.

I angle my war hammer in front of me, pointing into the distance. A boulder slams onto the ground not an inch from its tip, and still, I refuse to flinch. This is nothing. This is a puppet show for children compared to what I've seen before. I shout, "Is this the best you can do?"

The winds turn cruel and lashing. Shards of rocks tear at my skirt, my arms and cheeks, and still I stand. He has no idea that my fury, my vengeance, will always supersede his now. Knowingly or not, he's deftly assured that.

Pain is irrelevant. Achievement of purpose is all that matters.

"Hear me now: I am coming for you. If you think I will not hunt you down and extract payment for your sins, then you do not know my story well enough."

The winds howl incoherently about me.

"Your head," I shout, my voice loud and clear in the insanity of the crumbling cave, "IS MINE!"

An explosion sounds. The wind twists until my skirt whips around my legs and my hair stands on end. Blood trickles down my cheeks, down my arms, down my neck. Droplets swirl in the vortex around me. And still, I refuse to back down. I stay there, my hammer readied in defiance, my clothes tattering, until the last rock crumbles into place and the air stills.

Silence descends in the filled tunnel. My colleagues shout my name again, more fearfully than before.

"You and I are not done yet." My voice grows until it slips through the cracks and crevices in the fresh wall looming before me. "But when we are, I want you to remember that you brought this upon yourself. There will be no mercy shown. No clemency. In those last moments, when I turn your severed head to face your stricken body, you will rue the day you came against me and my own."

My hammer swings and strikes stone. In the pale light angling beyond the lip, I watch how the cold gray of stone weeps red.

And Marianne thought the smile upon my face in whatever trick

Lygari played upon her was unpleasant. She would undoubtedly be horrified at the one curving my lips now. I finally give in to my impulse, and I laugh.

Madness—that old, dear friend of mine—has come home for a visit. And I welcome its return with open arms.

THE RARE BOOKS DIVISION

ALICE

ABRAHAM VAN BRUNT'S ARMS are folded as he watches Mary apply some of her miraculous healing spray on the remnants of Lygari's tantrum. We are convened within the medical ward of the Institute, and I am wholly indifferent to her ministrations, eager instead to resume my search. Lygari must be afforded no rest, no time to regroup. I desire the fiend to be scrambling on the defensive rather than continuing upon the underhanded offensive he's waged against Timelines and the Society.

The time for niceties and civility has passed. If he wants brute force, I am willing to offer it freely.

The Society's leader has been quiet thus far, simply listening to my team's report. The moment we returned home, he was waiting in the parking garage beneath the Institute, the Librarian standing beside him. I'd had Marianne apprise them of our situation as soon as we began the journey home. And there they were, their faces serious, the muscles in their bodies taut as they awaited our reports.

I met the Librarian directly in the eye, but she quickly looked away. Her mannerisms indicated it was to cough and then murmur something to Van Brunt, but I cannot help but think it was more than that. And now she stands quietly off to the side here in the medical ward, listening intently to the events of the morning, and I suspect I am the only in the room to see the discomfort and lack of surprise haunting her eerily bright eyes.

"Our attacks must be multi-pronged." My tone is cool. Efficient. "Whilst some within the Society continue researching the clues Lygari has left us, others must be on the front lines, actively searching for the liar." My gaze returns to the Librarian. "Unless, of course, there are those within our ranks who would prefer sharing the information they already know?"

"Ms. Reeve," Van Brunt says brusquely, "that will be enough of that."

Since the moment she sent me to the hospital to examine my injuries caused by the destruction of 1905/06Sōs-IAAC's catalyst, the Librarian has not spoken another word to me. But as I was loaded into an ambulance, she murmured something that has viciously played on loop in my mind. *"I am so sorry, Alice. More than you can imagine. I failed. Remember to trust your instincts."*

She claimed she failed. Failed at what? Figuring out who Lygari/ Pfeifer is? Not determining the masterminds behind the catalyst destructions quickly enough? The challenge I offer her now is silent yet patently clear, and still, it remains unanswered.

Our colleagues are now the ones to wear discomfort and surprise as they witness this hushed standoff. The A.D. is the first to attempt to redirect the conversation. "You act as if this is war, and we are in the midst of battle."

"It is astounding to me that there are still those of you who do not see that that is exactly what is occurring." I wave off Mary. "And if you continue to remain blind to such facts, you might as well offer yourself up to Lygari's machinations now."

"No one is going to do such a thing." There's anguish stewing in Van Brunt's eyes, frustration and fury in every line of his body. "Ms. Reeve, a word in my office."

Minutes later, we are ensconced in the warm room, and I am once more staring up at the plaque that bears the Society's motto. *In paginis mundūs invenimus. In verbis vitam invenimus. In pages, we find worlds. In words, we find life.*

How unnervingly true it all has become.

Van Brunt's chair squeaks as he lowers his large frame into it. Hands folded before him, he regards me warily. "I would think that, as a queen, you would know that one of the more useful tactics in war is to brew discord amongst a group in order to unsettle and unfocus them. It seems reasonable to assume this is what Pfeifer is now doing."

I bristle at his insinuations. "In war, it is also important to remember that those on the battlefield often need to know pertinent facts. To send soldiers onto the battlefield blind is to demand them to risk more than is already being asked for."

He sighs quietly, grief coloring the sleeves he wears.

"The Librarian knows more than she tells."

His regard is bemused, if not exasperated. "And how have you arrived at this determination?"

"Via her own advice, during which she reminded me to trust my instincts. Those, which have rarely failed me, insist there are secrets she holds back that might very well be pertinent."

"Secrets are often just so for a reason, Ms. Reeve."

He knows them then. Or at least some of the things she hides.

"That said, I have worked alongside the Librarian for many years now, and she has only ever been a valuable asset to our goals."

His tone stringently informs me there is no room to further argue the point. Fine. There are other important matters at hand.

"You should have informed me as to where you went today," he is saying.

"I did. Marianne sent an email to you of our objectives and destination."

"En route, yes," he allows. "The point I am making is that you should have informed me *prior* to leaving."

Before we left, his door was closed and both his cell and office phones rang constantly. Had I even knocked, I do not think he would have heard. Still, what's done is done. "Each second we afford Lygari is another step he gains away from us. I could not risk him moving beyond our reach."

"Did you fear I would reject such a mission?"

"No." It's honest. "I must admit, I did not think much of chain of command at all. I found the need for action to be far more pressing than bureaucracy, and did not wish anything to slow me down."

"Ms. Reeve—"

No. The sorrow in his voice, the quietness, are contextual clues I do not wish to be illuminated. I shake my head, hold out my hand, but he says it anyway.

"None of this will bring them back."

The breath that fills my lungs stings.

"You must know how much I desire to find this Gabriel Pfeifer or Lygari or whatever his name is. My wife is . . ." His deep voice is tremulous. "Dead. My sons—"

I am out of my chair. "You give up too easily, sir."

He stares up at me, as if it were me who was the one acting irrational. Somewhere in one of his pockets, a cell phone chimes, but he does nothing to answer it. "The Timeline destroyed—"

"1905/06Sōs-IAAC. I am well aware of its identity."

He nods slowly. "While you were gone this morning, multiple attempts were made to contact it."

"Was there a liaison?"

His forefingers come together to form a tent. "Yes. Unfortunately, all attempts at communication failed. We also tried to edit, but were unable to do that, either. We cannot deny that 1905/06Sōs-IAAC has been destroyed."

"What if that was not the Timeline we were in?"

"Believe me, Ms. Reeve. You would be hard pressed to find any other person so desirous of such a reality, but based on what you told us last night, there is little doubt as to the Timeline's identity. We questioned Mr. Holgrave in depth this morning about his travels to 1905/06Sōs-IAAC, as it was on his caseload. Everything you reported corroborates with what he's seen and experienced. The Librarian spent many hours poring over Japanese literature, hoping for a different outcome. This is the best fit. Anything different would be like someone claiming they'd seen a white rabbit with a pocket watch in 1925FIT-GG."

"I do not know that Timeline, sir."

He does not elaborate. There is no need to, not when his message is so stark. My chest aches. Van Brunt would not lie to me, not about this. And still, I cannot do what it is he wishes. Instinct insists I would know if Finn perished. I would feel it. My gravity would shift, a hole in my heart would form. If the man I loved ceased to exist, I would know.

I cannot give up searching for him, not even if I am alone on this quest. To find Finn, I must find Lygari. The fiend must pay for what he's done—and not because he's simply wronged me, but because he has wronged far too many.

I clear my throat. Force my fingers to loosen from the bunches of shirt fabric they'd twisted between. "Obviously, Bücherei is out of the question until we have the proper tools to overcome whatever enchantments Lygari protects it with. I believe your assistant mentioned prior to our outing that there is a flat registered to a Gabriel Pfeifer in Manhattan. I'll be heading there within the hour."

His office phone is the one to trill now. Van Brunt purses his lips for a quiet moment. "Before you do, I would like you to go speak with a Miss Bianca Jones at the New York Public Library."

Remembering my first interaction with Bianca Jones, I let out a soft groan.

"I have a research team working around the clock on all the puzzle pieces here. Minutes before your return, one reminded me of the connection between Ms. Jones and Pfeifer."

We'd gone to the library's gala because Lygari/Pfeifer was a patron. "Send someone else to question her."

His pointer fingers tap one another. "Our resources are stretched thin as it is, Ms. Reeve. I am not arguing your need to be in the field—you have my full support in your endeavors whether or not you wish for them. But as you cautioned us earlier, we must not remain blind in the coming days. We simply cannot start poking sticks into each rabbit hole we uncover. Such rash actions will only slow us down." Hands press down against the desk as Van Brunt pushes himself up, ignoring how the phone continues to yell out its desires to be attended. "Surely, spending a few minutes with an asset who has had multiple dealings with Pfeifer can only aid, not hinder, our efforts. All I ask is that you or Ms. Lennox keep me apprised of critical updates or plans."

"Who said I planned on taking Mary with me?"

A faint smile cracks his lips. "I would very much like to see you attempt to leave her behind. Please make sure you get the proper equipment from Marianne before you go. I want recordings of every conversation, minor or important, that relates to Lygari/Pfeifer. And now, if you will excuse me, I must deal with more of that bureaucracy you mentioned before."

As I leave, I am quite thankful there were no telephones in Wonderland.

I find Mary lounging on a bench at the end of the hallway. When she sees me, she rises to her feet. "Where to next?"

I nearly chuckle at how soon Van Brunt's words to me come true, but there is no playfulness on Mary's face, no humor in her tone. She is just as serious about this quest as I am. "The New York Public Library. There's . . ." I attempt delicacy, "an overly zealous librarian we are to question."

"It sounds as if you've had dealings with this person before."

A self-professed fan of the books hailing from my Timeline, Bianca Jones' enthusiasm for all things Wonderland was most distressing. "More importantly, *she's* had dealings with the man we hunt—as Pfeifer, not Lygari."

Mary's lips curl in distaste. "That monster has too many names."

That he does.

"We'll find them, Alice. We'll find our men."

The coldness in her words pleases me. "I expect no other outcome."

She nods, and then we are off.

Marianne fits us with small earpieces and special recording devices that appear as tubes of lip rouge. This delights Mary, who informs me she now feels like a proper spy. "The only thing that could make this better is if we had lipstick that allows us to sedate anyone we kissed."

I hold back my smile. "Are you planning on kissing anyone today?"

"One never knows when such activities may be required."

My snort is entirely unladylike. "How would one wear such lip rouge safely? Would it not put its wearer to sleep, as well, considering it would touch her skin, too?"

Mary slips the tube into her purse. "Who would have guessed you would be such a wet blanket?" She turns to Marianne. "Surely you can see the benefit to such a thing?"

Marianne wisely says nothing.

Soon enough, we are in a taxi on our way to the library. Mary pulls up the profile of the librarian we're heading toward on her cell phone. "Bianca Jones, thirty-five years of age, born in Atlanta, Georgia. Currently married to lawyer, she resides in Queens. Holds a Masters of Library and Information Science from Louisiana State University in Baton Rouge. Has been employed by the New York Public Library system for the past five years. Contact with the Society first occurred four years ago, at the suggestion of Daisy Wickershim. Wickershim, just to let you know, served as a local liaison for the Society for nearly a decade prior to her retirement. Jones has expressed interest in serving as more than a liaison; she's applied to become an active field agent. A notation from Brom on her file states there was some concern over the psychological test results, though."

A horn blares nearby, and our driver releases a string of expletives from his open window. I ask, "What psychological test?"

"Most agents go through a battery of tests to determine if they are a good fit for our line of work." She peers down at her phone. "Brom's comments claim Bianca Jones is too . . ." A low chuckle rumbles from her chest. "Naive. He was concerned she might not be able to pull the metaphorical trigger if need be."

"I took no such tests."

"Unfortunately, you were the only person we could find that had been to Wonderland, so no other could do. It's not to say that you weren't observed during your initial weeks of training, though. They obtained the data they needed. And obviously, you proved your mettle fairly quickly."

"Did you take such tests?"

"I did. Finn didn't, if it's any consolation. Nor did Victor. Granted, their cases reek of pure nepotism, if one wants to put a fine point on it."

I wish I could laugh, but the syllables of the one I love's name once more serve as a fist to my belly.

"Are there any agents who hail locally?"

"One of the techs, I believe. There are also a few who help the Librarian with research." She pauses. "Oh! How could I forget? There was one who was a field agent about five years ago."

"Was?" I prompt.

She lowers her voice. "He met a girl in one of the Timelines he'd been sent into and fell hopelessly in love at first sight." A grimace twists her lips. "Refused to come back. Sent the catalyst with his partner instead. Utterly unprofessional, right?"

When we arrive at the library, the sun has already begun to set. People mill about, many lounging upon the steps, reading or chatting with others. Shadows chase the stone lions guarding the building, and I cannot help but recall the time when I stood by one not too long ago, conversing with Lygari.

Our situation would be so very different if only I'd known who he was then.

Inside, we proceed to the information desk so Bianca Jones might be paged. The library is quiet; lamps glow upon reading tables, and the few that are here are deeply immersed in their readings. Mary and I do not break the peace until the librarian we are to question appears. And when she does, I find myself desperately not insisting upon personal space and decorum when she throws her arms around me. "Ohmygod! I am so, so glad to see you. I was hoping we would get to work together again!"

I offer an awkward pat of her back before she releases me. "Hello, Ms. Jones."

"Don't be silly! Call me Bianca, remember?" Her dark eyes turn curiously to Mary.

"Bianca, this is Mary Lennox. She—"

"SHUT. UP."

Both Mary and I startle at Bianca's shout. So do a number of patrons whose glares redden the librarian's cheeks. Her voice lowers significantly. "Ohmygod. Mary Lennox. Here! With Alice in Wonderland!"

The look Mary angles at me indicates she finds my description of *overly zealous* to be mild, at best. Selfishly, and perhaps a bit sadistically, I am delighted the librarian's focused interest switches from myself to Mary. Yet when Bianca does little else but ogle my colleague, I find myself needing to prompt her. "Perhaps we might go to your office so we may converse?"

The woman blinks several times, as if she snaps out of a daze. "Right. Of course! Please come this way." Whilst we wander through the labyrinth to her office, she chatters nonstop. "I love *The Secret Garden*. Like, seriously love it. I don't think there's a girl out there who hasn't wished for her own garden to find and tend once she's read it, you know?"

"Hmmm . . ." is all Mary offers.

"I loved all the symbolism in it. When I was younger, I found it quite romantic!"

As I haven't read Mary's story, I ask, "How so?"

Mary kindly jabs a pointy elbow into my ribs.

"Well, it was a bit like a young love triangle, really—"

Mary is so startled I have a very hard time not giggling.

"And obviously, I had my favorite—"

Now Mary's eyes narrow dangerously.

"And of course, I can't think of a little girl who wouldn't want the attention of two dreamy boys like that." She stops before her office. Splotches of pink stain her dark cheeks when she motions toward Mary. "Listen to me, babbling like that. To you of all people, no less! I'm so sorry."

"I find it delightful," I say drolly. "Who was your pick for Mary's childhood beau?"

Bianca unlocks her door and switches on the light before ushering us in. "I know everyone always says Dickon. And I do love how symbolic he was, how he stood for the story's heart and love of nature. But I really loved the relationship between Mary and Colin. How he inspired your kindness and eventually, through friendship and the garden, he overcame his illness and was able to walk again."

Mary's response is swift and tight. "He is my cousin, and a brat to boot!"

Bianca's eyes widen significantly. "Oh, I mean—yes, I knew that. Of course. Well, not the brat part. I mean, yes, he was demanding, but . . . your personalities were really alike, and it's just . . ." More timidly, "A lot of stories have cousins becoming romantically involved and all."

As much as I find her needling of Mary a fine turn of events, considering Mary's proclivity toward doing the same to others, there are still questions that must be answered. "We appreciate your willingness toward meeting with us today, Bianca."

With Mary's cold gaze frosting the room, the librarian's voice is more subdued. "I'm more than happy to help the Society in any way I can."

Mary pulls out her tube of lip rouge Marianne provided. "Do you mind if we record the conversation?"

Bianca eagerly eyes the sophisticated piece of technology. "Go right ahead. I have nothing to hide."

"Obviously," Mary mutters beneath her breath.

Bianca's face falls even further. I discreetly kick Mary's ankle, and she has grace enough to cease her complaining.

"Do you know of a Mr. Gabriel Pfeifer?"

There is no pause. "Oh yes. Mr. Pfeifer donates quite a bit of money to the library, as well as gifting us copies for our rare books collection. He is a godsend for us."

I cannot help but bristle at such a description, even though Bianca Jones clearly does not know the man's true character. Pfeifer obviously sees himself as a godlike figure, considering he has taken it upon himself to decide whether or not worlds exist or are to be destroyed. "Have you personally interacted with him much?"

"Well, not a ton. I mean, probably a handful of times, and most of those at social functions for donors. If there's anyone who he would talk to on a regular basis, it'd be our rare book specialist."

"Who would that be?" I inquire.

"Her name is Jenn Ammer." Bianca scratches a pen across a small slip of paper. "Here's her phone number, just in case." She passes me the note. "She's in today if you want to go see her. Or I can call her up."

The paper has a drawing of an absurd-looking man holding a teacup and wearing a tall hat with a label that says: *In this style 10/6*. Again, with the romanticism of the Hatter! What utter nonsense.

I fold the note neatly and tuck it with my bag. "Please, do not bother. We will simply visit her once we're done here."

Bianca glances at the watch strapped to her wrist. "Just to let you know, her shift ends at six. If you're going to go down there, I'll need to send word. She'll be in the Brooke Russell Astor Reading Room, and you'll be required to show proper ID to be granted access." Her fingers dance across the keyboard on her desk. "I really shouldn't be doing this, but I'll add you into the database so you'll be able to go in with little problem."

Before I can tell her her actions are much appreciated, Mary demands to know what Bianca knows about Gabriel Pfeifer.

The librarian leans back in her chair, her face thoughtful. "Well, he's always very polite. Charming, too. Dresses well and is very attentive to detail. His knowledge of books is astounding, really, and outshines even a lot of us here in the library. He and Jenn have worked together quite a bit toward efforts to bolster the rare book collection."

This is not enough for Mary, though. "Do you see him often?"

"At least once every few months," Bianca admits. "Some months more, some months less. He's a busy man."

Mary leans forward. "Does anyone ever accompany him?"

"Outside of Jenn?" She's thoughtful once more. "Maybe. I really haven't noticed, though."

How very interesting it is that this Jenn Ammer and Lygari seem to be so close.

"How long has he been associated with the museum?" I ask.

Bianca's brows furrow. "At least as long as I have. Hold on. Let me check." Her fingers clack away at the keyboard once more on her desk. "It says here in his file that his first donation came approximately twenty years ago. Huh. He's aging pretty well, isn't he?" Her eyes widen before squinting at the screen.

"Have you discovered something else?" I prompt.

"Do you remember the books you came in here for the other month?"

The Society's Librarian had sent me here to fetch a number of books. It was also the day Lygari found me upon the steps out front.

"I wasn't able to give you several of them. It turns out it was Gabriel Pfeifer who checked them out ahead of time. What a funny coincidence!"

Funny, no. Interesting, oh, yes.

"May we have a printout of his file?" When the librarian hesitates, I add, "It would help us very much, Bianca."

She bites her lip. "We're not normally allowed to do this. I mean, yes, I fudged and allowed you access into the rare books division, but . . . to give you printed, confidential information on our donors?" More quietly, "Has Mr. Pfeifer done something wrong? Because, he's always been so good to the library. I can't imagine that he—"

"You've applied to work at the Society, have you not?"

Bianca's attention turns to Mary. "Yes, I've—"

"Then I would think you, of all people, would understand the importance of our work."

The woman flinches, as if she's been stung.

"All we're asking is that you give us a file on a donor. Nothing else."

After a moment, Bianca returns to her computer and types in a command. With her attention focused elsewhere, I mouth the words *tact* and then *asset* to Mary. The whirl of a printer starts shortly after.

Mary huffs out a tiny, exasperated sigh. "I apologize if I am coming off as short. Works has been . . . stressful lately."

That is putting it kindly. Work has been devastating.

"I get it. You guys do important work." Bianca's smile is tremulous but genuine. "I hope someday I'll be able to help, too."

"You are helping us greatly today." I rise to my feet, proffering my hand, but Bianca Jones leaves it untouched as she rounds her desk. Once more, she throws her arms around me, hugging me until I very nearly squeak. A moment later, she offers the same to a bewildered Mary.

"You guys are awesome," she whispers. "Ohmygod. Alice in Wonderland and Mary Lennox in my office! Can we do a selfie before you leave?"

Bianca's phone is extracted and the shot is taken before Mary and I even have the ability to regain our composure or pose. But in the final product, the librarian's smile nearly glows, it is so wide.

In the hallway, Mary's indignance resurges. "Colin, indeed."

"It is surreal how so many people know our stories, that they have their own opinions and thoughts of them, is it not?"

"It's annoying, is what it is." She tucks strands of hair behind her ears. "Interesting about the rare book librarian and Pfeifer though, isn't it?"

A nearby sign informs us we are heading in the correct direction. "If I'm not mistaken, we have a pair of scenarios ahead of us. One, this Jenn Ammer is an innocent who has coincidentally worked with the fiend over the past twenty years. Two, she is an ally of his along the lines of Todd, Rosemary, or Jenkins."

"With Jenkins, he had a minion at a bookstore. This Armmer—"

"I believe it is Ammer."

"Fine. Ammer would be an in to a massive library collection. Who knows how many other assets he has in the literary world? There are other collections, some much larger or more important than that here at the New York Public Library. You have places like the Huntington Library in California, which has an astounding collection of important works. The Librarian has cultivated quite a good relationship with the director and several of the curators there. The British Library in London is also phenomenal, as is the Library of Congress here in the U.S. And those are only just a few of the important libraries that we also have liaisons with or contacts within. There are many others filled with priceless books *here*. Who knows how many other libraries, in other Timelines, Pfeifer might have connections with? It'll be nearly impossible to try to track them all down, especially if he's using multiple aliases."

"We know he has a relationship with this library, using Pfeifer. Let us start with this Jenn Ammer and go from there."

Mary's strong fingers grip my forearm. "I want his head, Alice."

As do I.

A bit later, we find ourselves in a room filled with books hidden behind glass cases, wooden tables, and bronzed lamps, along with a woman with multi-colored hair and glasses. No one else is present; the sound of a pin dropping would be utterly deafening as long as no speech accompanied it. Identification presented is carefully scrutinized, paperwork is filled out, and signatures are required before she introduces herself as the Jenn Ammer we've come to see.

"How very curious it is," she says as she passes back our small rectangles of identification, "that I received a message from Bianca Jones not a half hour before, requesting admission for the two of you into the reading room."

"Yes, well—" Mary begins, but the librarian cuts her off.

"It's against regulations. Visitors must be vetted before coming in here, and a list of reading materials must be submitted beforehand. The books in here are quite valuable."

I force myself to remember manners. "We would like to discuss with you one of the library's donors."

Her lips thin as she stares at us from across her desk. "Isn't this more of a question for the director or public relations?"

Her enunciation is formal, much more so than Bianca Jones. I extract my tube of lip rouge and apply a quick coat, ensuring I activate the recording mechanism.

Mary's irritation is quite evident. "As my colleague was saying, we would like to ask you some questions about a Mr. Gabriel Pfeifer. We understand you two have worked together frequently, especially as he has gifted the library numerous rare books."

"Mr. Pfeifer has been incredibly generous with the New York Public Library."

"How well would you say you know the gentleman?" Mary asks.

Several long seconds tick by, during which Jenn Ammer merely regards us as if we were bugs to be squashed. I cannot help but stiffen at her rudeness. We simply do not have time to humor such a woman.

Finally, she says, with much derision in her tone, "Well enough, I suppose." And then, with suspicion, "Who did you say you work for again?"

Mary taps on the paperwork we recently filled out. "The Literary Preservation Institute."

Ammer's eyes narrow until they are nothing more than slits. A chill overtakes my spine. Her muscles are too taut, the lines of her face too drawn. Disdain no longer colors her face—cold calculation does.

One hand slowly reaches beneath the desk.

Dammit.

I grab Mary and whip her back, kicking a table over just as Ammer pulls out a small gun tipped with what Finn explained to me is a silencer. Mary drops behind the fallen desk a split second before a quiet bullet rips above us.

"What the *hell!*" Mary shouts.

I kick out at the table behind us, knocking it over. A second bullet explodes into the wood shielding us; Mary jumps and scoots to the side. Another kick to the desk knocks one of the legs free.

Footsteps sound; she's left her position behind the desk. If I'm correct, her gun has five to ten bullets left if fully loaded.

I motion to Mary: *You, to the left. Me, to the right.* And then I hold up three fingers. She nods, and I tuck away the fingers one at a time. The cock of the gun matches the end of the countdown. Another bullet splinters the wood, missing Mary by millimeters. She springs toward the left, wrenching one of the lamps from the tables. The cord connecting the light to the table snaps a second before she hurls it at Ammer. The diversion allows me enough time to swipe the broken table leg and dart to the right. The librarian is taken off-guard, stumbling back into her desk when the metal lamp strikes her arm. The gun flies from her fingers, skittering across polished floors. As she scrambles for it, I leap toward her, the wood in my hand swinging.

Contact is made, right across her knee. She roars, buckling to the ground.

Mary wrenches another lamp off a table as I swing once more, striking the librarian's lower back. She sprawls before me, face smacking against the floor. Just as I try to pin her, though, she manages to twist and grab hold of me.

She's strong. Incredibly so.

Eyes bloodshot, she hisses something in a language I do not know before landing a rather inglorious head butt against my forehead. I reel back, giving her enough time to push out from beneath me. She's not only strong, but she's quick, too, and even though I am able to grab hold of a pant's cuff, she's reclaimed her weapon.

"Say goodbye, you nosy little bitch!"

I roll away just in time, the bullet grazing my shoulder. Another bullet flies by, and then a third. Glass shatters on one of the cabinets behind me, causing the enraged woman to swear up a filthy storm.

Mary sends the lamp in her hands soaring toward Ammer. This time, the librarian is able to duck the attack. Another pair of bullets is sent toward a yelping Mary and then me as I do my best to sprint across the room. Yet another cabinet's glass is fractured.

Paper flies out from the shelving, raining down upon me like rain.

And then, as she fires at Mary, who is now ducking behind a table, Ammer begins to sing an unfortunately familiar song.

"Carry on, beyond the skies,
beyond tumultuous sea,

to the heart of the mountain
lies wondrous future for ye."

I reclaim the wooden leg just in time to miss yet another bullet in my direction. Across the room, Mary sends a chair soaring toward Ammer.

Amazingly, the woman does not miss a note in her song. Instead, she charges me, a berserker come to life.

"Sing, sing, little children!
Spill blood graciously."

I leap over a fallen table, swinging. My makeshift staff strikes her across the shoulder, sending her backward into another table. She must feel no pain, though, because she automatically pushes herself up, reminding me of how Rosemary was more machine than woman in battle. Blood trickles from the librarian's lips as she wastes no time pointing her gun toward me.

"Rest assured, in the end . . ."

I barely miss a bullet as I dart toward her.

"Treasure and glory await thee!"

My staff strikes her across the head. I spin and kick out, my foot landing directly in her chest. Once more, she slams into a table, breaking it into smaller pieces. The gun lands a few feet away.

Bloody teeth gnash at me, fingers fumble toward the fallen weapon. Her song is less firm now, the effort it takes to sing more difficult.
"Fear not the blade of death . . ."

I smack the wood deftly across her kneecaps. She gasps, her fumbling growing weaker. And still, she continues to fight me with all she has.

"Fear not the hole of time—"

I grab hold of her head and slam it against the larger of the table pieces once, twice. Her eyes are impossibly open for such a strike, her lips moving, albeit no more singing.

I squat down before her, using the stick to push the gun farther out of reach. "Why did you attack us?"

The bloody smile that grows before my eyes is chilling, to say the least.

"Does this have to do with Pfeifer?"

She says, "You're going to die, little Alice in Wonderland. You, too, Miss Secret Garden." She licks blood from her lips. "You're all going to die. None of you are worthy enough to be inscribed."

I drive my fist across her temple so hard her eyes finally close.

"I cannot believe this!" Mary runs her fingers through messy hair. "What just happened?"

I sag back off her body, drawing my knees up toward my chest. "I'd say we have proof that this woman is more than just someone who works for the library." I wipe sweat off my brow with the back of my hand. "Rosemary sang that song to us, remember? When we first used your truth serum on her. It cannot be coincidence."

Mary peers down at the fallen woman. "Is she out?"

I shrug. "If it were anyone else than someone associated with Lygari, I'd say yes. But unfortunately, it seems his colleagues are a bit harder to bring down."

"This room is . . ." She whistles. "It's pretty much destroyed. The woman is a librarian; these are rare books and documents! I cannot believe she would destroy them so willingly. It's a miracle nobody heard the ruckus."

"She knew our true identities, Mary."

My friend squats down next to me, her fingers flying across the cell phone in her hand. "Should we take her back to the Institute for further questioning?"

Before I can answer, the doors crash open. There stand a pair of security guards, weapons drawn.

Mary jerks up, extending her hands and phone. "Thank God! My friend and I were here to look at some books for research, and the woman at the desk went crazy! She started shooting at us!" She waves the phone. "I was just calling 911!"

One of the men pulls out what I think is called a walkie talkie and issues a statement for backup. The other guard inches forward, his gun pointed unsteadily at us.

I could knock it out of his hands with a single kick. How utterly annoying. Even still, I reluctantly hold my hands up, slowly, purposely rising to my feet.

Mary's voice turns shrill. "What kind of library is this? Since when do librarians carry guns with silencers? Look at that thing." She motions toward the weapon, now several feet behind us. "Somebody better call the police! I want this woman arrested—you better believe I'm going to press charges!"

The security guard stares down at Jenn Ammer, his brow wrinkled. It's then that she mumbles, "Kill . . . you filthy . . . little pigs . . ."

"See?" Mary screeches.

What I see is further proof that Lygari's associates are terrifying in their ability to keep on going when others would fall or yield.

"My God," the security guard whispers. "Miss Ammer has lost her damn mind. What were you two doing that set her off?"

"Nothing!" Mary's eyes are comically wide. "We asked her about a donor, that's all. And she pulled out a gun and shot at us . . . a bunch of times! Thank goodness Alice here has a black belt in karate, or who knows what would have happened to us?" She promptly bursts into tears.

Well, now. Mary is a much better actress than I think I've given her credit for.

"Ma'am?" The security guard lowers his gun, tucking it in his belt. "Are you all right? Your shoulder is bleeding."

I glance down at my arm. "One of her bullets grazed me."

The other security guard says from across the room, "What a fucking nightmare." And then, when Mary wails louder, "Pardon my French, ladies."

The police are summoned. We give our statements. The Society is notified and a barrister is sent to assist us. An ambulance arrives to tend my wounds. Thankfully, an examination of the silent security footage proves our story—Jenn Ammer attacked us, unprovoked. A long-time employee of the library willfully destroyed priceless property.

Her ass, as Mary mutters gleefully later, is grass, whatever that means.

I am commended by a supervising police sergeant for my quick thinking and ability to subdue our assailant. A library administer who listened in on our questioning and recollection of events apologizes profusely. The Society's barrister threatens legal action, and before long, we are escorted home in a police car.

By the time we arrive, it is well after midnight. My blood boils at all the wasted minutes spent trying to explain yet cover up Ammer's true motives. It is now well over twenty-four hours since Finn and Victor disappeared, since 1905/06Sōs-IAAC was destroyed within our walls.

Sleep and I, I grimly decide, will not be friends for some time.

APARTMENT 1202

ALICE

"**Y**OU SHOULD GET SOME rest."

I glance up from strapping a pair of daggers to a holster strapped to my thighs to find the A.D. leaning against the doorframe of the weapons room. I tug my hem of my dress down before I respond. "What have you learned about Jenn Ammer?"

He sighs quietly at my change of subject. In his hands is a tablet. "We've got someone still looking into it, but the basic gist is that, until today, her life has been uneventful. I mean, almost like she hasn't even existed until just recently. She has no police record, not even a parking ticket to her name. I can't even find a birth certificate. She's unmarried and tends to keep to herself according to those who know her. Her colleagues are in shock right now. Nobody can believe that she shot up part of the library."

I slip a small blade inside the sole of a special pair of boots Kip, the Society's trainer and weapons specialist, gifted me recently. "How long has she been with the New York Public Library?"

"Almost a decade—and she nabbed the rare book's specialist position as her first job. Other employees were pretty surprised that someone so green got such a specialized position."

I tug on a coat. "Where's Van Brunt?"

"He's coordinating with an asset we have inside the NYPD so we can question Ammer under the radar."

Good. I slip the straps of my bag over my head so it crosses over my body. "And Mary?"

Van Brunt's assistant is more subdued than normal as he warily regards me. "She said to let you know she'll meet us downstairs."

"Us?"

"I'm going with." He straightens. "Can't let you ladies have all the fun, can I?"

Just when I was worried he'd gone and matured, he says something like this. "Don't get in my way."

"Wouldn't dream about it, Your Majesty." A flourished bow is offered before he swipes across his tablet. "Marianne says that the apartment building has a fairly standard yet highly dependable security system. Every floor has cameras, and there is a doorman in the main entrance and a security guard on duty. Now, the guard has a specific route he takes throughout the building every evening. He isn't scheduled to come back to his office until four-thirty a.m., and typically monitors floors three and four during the three o'clock hour. All other entrances are locked at all times except for emergencies. According to the file you and Mary brought back from your trashing of the museum—"

I heave out a disgruntled sigh as I push past him, into the hallway.

"—Gabriel Pfeifer lives on the twelfth floor, in 1202. Schematics show it's an average apartment for the building."

"Meaning?"

He hurries to catch up with me. "Meaning, when there are several penthouses in the upper floors, Pfeifer's digs aren't as splashy as they could be. Current property values show his to be worth around one-point-two million dollars, as opposed to ten million plus for the swanky ones. You'd think a dude who has a place like Bücherei could afford a better apartment."

I head toward the elevator. "What else do the blueprints show?"

"It's a standard three bedrooms, two baths, just under two thousand square feet. Pfeifer paid cash for it about twenty years ago and owns it free and clear. No renovation permits have been filed since purchase."

A ding sounds; the elevator doors open. I step inside and press the button for the lobby. "Anything else?"

The A.D. glances down at the tablet. "Marianne says that there is an additional security system installed within his unit, one similar to that found at Bücherei. Since she's already figured out the coding to override it, we'll have no trouble tripping anything once we're inside. She can deal with it remotely. It's just getting into the building that's going to be a challenge."

"I'm sure you have an idea about how to overcome such odds, don't you, Master Thief?"

Another flourished bow is offered. "Of course. Marianne has made us a little bomb of sorts."

"As much as I want Lygari's head," I say coldly, "I will not risk innocents."

He titters nervously. "You're always so literal, Your Majesty! Marianne has whipped up a virus that we can install into the building's security system that will render the monitors useless for approximately fifteen minutes. It ought to give us enough time to get up there and have a look around. I've got a flash drive with it in my pocket right now."

I watch the lights on the buttons count down. "Fifteen minutes is not much time."

"Fifteen minutes," he says, "is more than zero."

"How will we get this virus into the security system?"

"Leave it to me." He clicks off his tablet and tucks it beneath his arm. "All you and Mary need to do is take care of the doorman while I do the rest."

The elevator dings once more, announcing our arrival. As the door slides open and I step into the hallway, I ask, "Anything else I ought to know?"

"Just that the Society lawyer who was at the library with you guys advises against this. He thinks you two ought to lay low, especially as you were asking about Pfeifer at the library."

"And Van Brunt?"

"The boss man trusts you to do what it takes."

The Librarian is with Mary when we enter the battered lobby. Whilst most of the rubble has been swept away, there are still holes in the walls and white powder coating the paint. I make sure to look at every blemish, at every gap and every space where art once stood, to remind myself what Gabriel Lygari/Pfeifer is capable of.

It is nearly three o'clock in the morning. A debriefing with the barrister (whose name I honestly did not care to remember or notice), Van Brunt, and a handful of others took longer than I'd hoped. Exhaustion thrashes my bones and muscles, but the determination burning in my veins is much stronger. Every minute I allow Lygari/Pfeifer to get away makes it all the more difficult to find him.

I have not seen Finn in well over a day. He was stabbed. Hurt.

I must close my eyes at the last image I have of him. An explosion sent my beloved flying back against a wall and the door before me winking away before I could do anything to help. His pen came with me, breaking upon contact. He and Victor had no way to edit, no way out.

He cannot be dead. He cannot.

When I open my eyes, I focus on the Librarian. "Did you know Jenn Ammer?"

"Yes," she says simply.

"Have you met her face to face?"

Her lips twist ruefully. "No. We've spoken over the telephone before, though."

"Did you consider her to be an asset?"

"No."

"Why?" Before she can answer, I press, "One would think that you would want to cultivate a relationship with the head of the Rare Books Division."

"I did not need her as an asset because there are other assets within the organization who were more useful."

Mary scoffs. "You mean Bianca Jones?"

"Bianca Jones," the Librarian says, "has great promise. But no, she is not who I speak of."

I wait, but she offers no further clarification. Mary, instead, makes a pointed comment beneath her breath about what *great promise* means.

I have not the temperament for the Librarian and her riddles at this moment. I turn toward the door, but she stays me with a hand. "Alice, a brief word before you go?" She nods at both the A.D. and Mary, who then exit the building quickly.

I'm curt. "Yes?"

"You must trust your instincts."

My eyebrows lift upward. "So you keep saying."

Her bright eyes are somber as she tilts her head, studying me. A delicate hand reaches out and gently smoothes a wrinkle on the sleeve of my coat before patting my arm. Without another word, she turns around and walks away.

She's simply, utterly creepy.

I emerge from the building to find the A.D. and Mary huddled close together. Tiny flakes of white fall from the sky, sticking to the sidewalk and our hair and coats. Frabjous. It would have to go and start snowing.

"Ready?" the A.D. asks.

A sleek black vehicle rests at the curb before the Institute. Inside is a sleepy older agent whose name I believe might be C. Auguste Dupin.

"Best not to rouse suspicion with cabs," the A.D. explains. And then he adds to my pleasant surprise by holding the door open for us.

Mary pats his cheek before she slips in.

Dupin doesn't say a word or even acknowledge us when he begins driving. The ride to the building is not long at all, not at this hour. Music fills the space between us, melodies far too upbeat for such an hour. And still, it helps keep my eyes open, my senses alert.

It's at times like this I wish I'd given coffee a better try.

Once we arrive, Dupin shuts off the car and pulls out a book, silently dismissing us. The building in front of us isn't as tall as many others in this city, but it is beautiful. Graceful arches and carved stone decorate the face; above us, gargoyles perch as mute sentries.

Van Brunt's assistant turns to Mary. "You're a sloppy drunk, okay?"

She shows him a finger that is rather all too impolite.

It doesn't faze him one whit. Chuckling, he presses a button outside the door, underneath an awning. A sleepy voice cackles over a speaker next to it. "Hello?"

"Um yes, hi." The A.D. sounds entirely unlike himself and more American than anything else. "We're here to go to Kristina Floreatetona's apartment, number 1204?"

The speaker hisses quietly as we wait. Seconds later, the voice says, "I'm afraid Miss Floreatetona is not in residence right now."

"Yeah. Yeah! She's on a cruise right now, down in the Bahamas, lucky girl." The A.D. titters a bit more. "We work with her at Smith and Peterson. She's asked us to feed her fish while she was gone. We just got out of a nightclub, and it's late, but . . . even fish need to eat, right?"

"I have no such—" The speaker falls silent. "Oh. I see here. Miss Floreatetona left a note about this. Hold, please."

A buzzing sounds, and then a click. The A.D. offers us an impish smile as he holds the door open. I whisper as we pass, "How did you know all that?"

He whispers right back, "It's called the internet."

The lobby of Pfeifer's building is delightfully warm. It's clean, with decent artwork on the walls and comfortable-appearing furniture mixed amongst plants. A man in a suit and nametag perches upon a stool behind a small stand, proffering a clipboard. "You'll need to sign in before heading up."

Mary takes the clipboard from him. "God, this must be the most boring job ever, right?" Her voice is unnaturally loud and chipper.

A quick glance shows a camera to the right, angled toward the main doorway. Nearby, just to the left of the doorman's post, is a closed door marked SECURITY.

Not even a hint of a smile surfaces on the man's face at Mary's comment.

She stumbles over to the window, peering out. "Can you believe it's snowing? I wish I were with Kristina, on that cruise. I'm utterly over winter, aren't you?"

He watches her without the smallest bit of interest. Behind him, the A.D. quietly makes his way to the marked door. He slips a funny-looking tool out of his pocket, his back angled just right toward the camera so nothing will be caught on film. Leaning against the door, appearing as if he's doing nothing other than waiting, one hand eases a sharp point of the tool into the lock.

Mary promptly drops the clipboard, stumbling. "Oh! Oh!" She laughs merrily. "I might have had a lot to drink tonight."

In the mild chaos, the A.D. briefly wiggles his tool. The door opens quietly.

The doorman steps away from his stand, as if he will pick the clipboard up for her. The moment he bends down, she does, too. Their heads smack together, leaving Mary profusely apologizing and giggling and the poor doorman utterly exasperated with her shenanigans.

I make my way over to them, blocking the direction of the office. "It appears I cannot take you anywhere without you acting the fool, can I?"

Her smile is appropriately disheveled.

The doorman tries once more to pick up the clipboard, and once more, Mary clonks her head to his. She falls to the ground, giggling even harder. "I am so sorry! How embarrassing!" She grapples at the clipboard, only to quickly drop it. "My fingers are a little numb."

"I'm afraid she's drunk," I say to the doorman.

He snorts quietly. "I would have never guessed." And then, a little louder, "Perhaps you ought to be the one to feed Miss Floreatetona's fish. And fill out the form."

Mary passes me the clipboard right when the A.D. slips back out of the office. I cough loudly when he clicks the door shut. "Any day now, ladies. Some of us have to work in a few hours."

Mary is up off the ground within a second. I scrawl three random names upon the sheet and pass the clipboard back to the doorman before we make our way to the elevator.

Inside, we say nothing. It takes well over a minute for us to climb to the twelfth floor, but once the doors open and we find no one in the hallway, we sprint toward 1202. The A.D. has his special tool out once more, jiggling it in the lock. It takes him only moments before we're able to push into the flat.

He flips on the light. Unlike Bücherei's current state, this abode is fully furnished. There are couches and chairs, lamps, and a few framed paintings on the walls. Mary tugs three pairs of special Society-issue glasses out for us that have cameras attached, issuing the instruction we are to document all that we see. The Artful Dodger immediately heads into one of the bedrooms whilst I locate an office. A rather large desk rests against a curtained window. Unfortunately for me, the majority of the drawers are filled with boring items such as pens, scissors, and rubber bands. One drawer has a stack of envelopes within, but a quick scan of the contents presents utility bills nearing their due date.

I fling open the closet; a singular wool coat hangs within. Nothing is in the pockets. A second bedroom is searched: beneath the bed, in the nightstand, in the closet. Only a few suit coats, dress shirts, and slacks folded neatly over hangers are present. A lone pair of highly shined shoes sit on a shelf. The A.D. appears, shaking his head in frustration. He's found nothing, as well. Mary emerges from the third bedroom, also empty-handed. Whilst the A.D. heads to one of the bathrooms, I tackle the sitting room. There is nothing on the coffee table and only a pair of candles upon the end tables. No television, no knickknacks to hide anything beneath. I am close to shouting when Mary announces quietly we have seven minutes left.

It's then my luck changes. Behind one of the paintings on the wall, a tiny, glossy corner peeks out. I slowly tug it out from beneath the brown paper covering the back of the artwork and discover a photograph of a woman with dark hair, her eyes closed as she lays upon a knoll of green grass. I quickly remove all the rest of the paintings in the room, but this is the only item of its kind in the room.

I find Mary rooting through the kitchen. Several bottles of ale and a take-out box sit within the refrigerator. The food in the cupboards consists of individually wrapped pieces of beef jerky.

I hold the photograph out. "This was behind one of the paintings."

Her eyes widen in shock. Before I can ask why, she yells, "Jack! Get in here!"

The A.D. quickly appears, a gun in his hand. When he finds us in the kitchen, he scowls. "Don't scare me like that, Mary! I thought maybe—"

She pays his posturing no heed. "Look at what Alice found."

He edges closer, peering at the photograph. And then, his own eyes widening, he shakes his head. "Impossible."

"What is it?" I ask. "Do either of you know this woman's identity?"

Mary lets out a rather loud breath. "I'd say we do." She takes the photograph from me. "This is Sara Crewe. She used to work at the Society."

Sara Crewe . . ."As in Finn's previous partner?"

She nods warily.

"Why would Sara's picture be here?" the A.D. asks. "This place is wiped clean of anything incriminating. I've searched in all the places I would stash secrets." His frown deepens. "Where did you find this, Alice?"

I motion toward the sitting room. "Behind the painting hanging over the sofa."

We make our way into the room. The A.D. leans forward, staring at the artwork in question. "That's London."

I hadn't even really bothered to pay much attention, but now that I really look at it, he's correct. It's not modern London, however. No, this is a London that Mary, the A.D., and I are more familiar with.

It's—

"Grosvenor Square," Mary announces. "Look at the circle in the middle. And it's not a recent painting, either. That's how it appeared in the nineteenth-century."

She's right. The square patches staring up at me are utterly familiar from the few times I've gone to London with my family.

I glance at the photograph in Mary's hands. "What is Sara Crewe's Timeline?"

It's the A.D. who answers. "1905BUR-LP. Except, it's not really set in the early twentieth-century. The story takes place in the nineteenth-century."

I lift the painting off the wall once more, turning it over. Written in cursive, in faint pencil in the bottom right corner, is *Brook Street*. I carefully peel back the brown paper covering the back to see if any other items are present, and am rewarded with another photograph of the same woman. This one, though, is in black and white. Arms around a man with darkish curly hair in a smart suit with his back to the camera, she's got her head thrown back, laughing assumedly at whatever he is saying.

"Sonofabitch," the A.D. whispers.

Son of a bitch is right. The man's posture is far too similar to Lygari for my comfort.

I flip the painting over, searching the piece for any clues. There is nothing amiss in the scene—just the faint images of people riding and walking through the busy square. The A.D. and Mary quickly peel back the brown paper on the backs of the remaining two canvases in the room, and both are rewarded with a handful of photographs. Many are blurry, others have little to few clear shots of faces. Once we've hung the artwork back up, Mary swears. "We need to go."

We're out the door within a minute, in the elevator before two pass. We step out in the lobby the moment the A.D.'s alarm on his phone sounds. I am pleasantly surprised at how he was right with his estimation. Fifteen minutes did prove to be enough to find something.

The A.D. salutes the doorman. "The fishies are fed." He lowers his voice. "Just don't tell her we had to flush one down the toilet." His rubbery lips twist ruefully. "Whoops!"

The doorman says nothing.

When we are safely in the car once more, I ask wryly, "Does this Kristina even have fish?"

"Her credit card records say she shops at a local pet store that specializes in fish." The A.D. offers me an impish grin. "It was a good assumption."

"You did well tonight, Jack." And he did. Surprisingly so.

The man in question gasps, holding a hand against his chest. "Her Majesty . . . complimenting a poor feller like meself?"

Mary sighs. "Well, this complicates matters."

Feigned outrage reflects back at her. "I actually do know how to do my job, you know."

"No, not that." She pulls the stack of photographs out of her bag. "These."

It's hard to see the details in the dark, especially with so few cars with their headlights on the road. But I can see why her mood is somber. A photograph of Finn and myself had been found in Bücherei, and now another agent, albeit a retired one, is represented in two more found amongst others within another of Lygari's residences.

It cannot be mere happenstance.

When I first arrived at the Institute, I was issued Sara Crewe's old flat. It was still filled with her belongings, and that first night, Finn and Mary helped me box away the multitude of dolls and pillows she'd left behind. Finn had mentioned that Sara was dead, although Mary clarified that, in today's world, she would be, as her Timeline exists in the past.

Sara, then, must exist in the past, in the nineteenth-century. Therefore, I must go there and inquire as to what her connection with Lygari/ Pfeifer is.

BROOK STREET

ALICE

VAN BRUNT STARES AT the two clearest photographs of the stack we discovered, his face devoid of any visible emotion.

"It's Sara." Mary taps on the colored picture, where the woman lounges on a grassy knoll. "Even you have to admit it's the little princess."

The Librarian pulls aside the photograph in which the woman embraces a man. Her head tilts quizzically to the side as she stares at the image. She is wearing a silk, floral robe and matching slippers, her hair in curlers. I have never seen her so informal before, and I must admit, it's a bit jarring despite the hour.

"It does appear so." Exhaustion clings to Van Brunt—but like myself, he will not give in to it yet. There is too much at stake, too much to do. "Are you certain there were no other photographs than these in the apartment?"

"None, boss man." The A.D. cracks his eyes open from where he slumps within a chair. "I checked every room as thoroughly as one can within the time limit. There were just a bunch of bills with Pfeifer's name on them. No other pieces of correspondence, nothing even with his damn signature on it."

"And the other paintings?"

"I've uploaded all the files to the server." Mary does her best to try to hide her burgeoning yawn.

"Could you identify the scenes in the others? Determine if they correspond with the photographs found behind them?"

"Time was pressed, I'm afraid."

"So many of these are unclear." The Society's leader rubs at his temples. "If only there was one that had a decent shot of a face."

"We must find out what Brook Street refers to," I interject.

Van Brunt's blue eyes meet mine. "There is no need, Ms. Reeve, as I already have the answer. It is the street that Mrs. Carrisford resides upon in London."

I ask, "Who is Mrs. Carrisford?" but it obvious everyone else in the room already knows the answer, for knowing looks are shared.

"Sara Crewe married a former beau once she left this Timeline, a Mr. Carrisford."

"Former beau?" Mary snorts. "He's old enough to be her grandfather. She was his ward. The entire relationship between the two of them has always been utterly disturbing." She pretends to gag.

Upon reflection, Finn had told me once that Sara had a boyfriend in her original Timeline, hadn't he?

"They were on a break while she was here," the A.D. pipes up. "Or so she said. Apparently, they'd been banging for a year or so before she joined the Society." He shudders and cackles simultaneously. "Can you even imagine doing such a thing?"

"God, no." Mary clamps a hand over his mouth. "Stop, before I vomit."

Indulging in such salacious gossip will not help us right now, so

I turn the conversation back to where it needs to be. "I was told that when she left, Sara wanted nothing more to do with the Society. Why was that?"

"She had her reasons." The Librarian sets the photograph she'd been studying down upon Van Brunt's desk.

"Since then, there has been no communication with the woman?"

Van Brunt informs me there has not.

"I'm going to go question her." I hold aloft the picture where she embraces a man. "Perhaps she can explain how she has been found to be intimate with Lygari."

"You cannot be certain of his identity, Ms. Reeve," Van Brunt says tiredly. "There are no distinguishing marks to ascertain anything other than Mrs. Carrisford was hugging a man of good height with curly hair."

He is right—there is nothing but a wall of black coat and darkish, curly hair visible. No show of hand, no ring upon a pinky finger. No cleft chin, no eyes to confirm. It could be any man, but instinct insists it is not.

"Nevertheless, I wish to speak to her as quickly as possible."

The Librarian takes the photograph from me, adding it to the neat stack she's recently created. "Let her go."

Van Brunt's eyebrows lift up in the tiniest way, mild surprise reflecting in his eyes.

"You and I both know curiosity always gets the best of our Alice. We should not stand in her way." A sly smile is sent my way.

Mary stifles another yawn. "I'll go, too." To me, more softly, "We're in this together."

Despite the terrible circumstances thrusting us into the position of partnering together, I am grateful it is she who stands by me.

Before the A.D. offers up his service, Van Brunt says, "Mr. Dawkins, I have an assignment I need for you to complete as quickly as possible. Details have been sent to your account."

His assistant mock salutes him. "Aye, aye, o' captain of mine."

The Librarian turns to me. "You'll need to go change first. Sara lives in a rather nice neighborhood, and no one there will desire anything other than propriety."

It's exasperating that she remembers such small details when they slip my mind. Mary and I proceed to head up to the costume room without bothering to rouse Marianne. After all, being so intimately acquainted with the nineteenth-century, she and I know exactly what to look for.

As we help one another with our corsets, Mary gasps as I pull her stays tight. "I'd hoped to never see the wet blanket again."

"No one says you must come."

"I do, as a matter of fact. I loathe these things." She gasps once more. "But they do create an interesting waistline. Make it tighter, will you?"

A good half hour later, both of us struggling to breathe, we're laced in so tight, we're appropriately attired for late nineteenth-century London. Our weapons are artfully hidden within the folds of skirts and bustles. As strange as it may sound, I've rather missed wearing such fashions—although now that I've spent many months corset free, I can appreciation the benefit of burning them all.

Mary writes us into 1905BUR-LP, appropriately close enough to Grosvenor Square. Clouds blanket the sky, but thankfully, there is no rain or snow. We stroll the small distance to Brook Street, gently nodding to those who greet us on our way.

The address Van Brunt provided us is a rather stately, gray abode with stairs that lead up toward a main door. It's a large residence, indicating Sara Crewe went from small flat in New York City to much comfort in London.

I do not hesitate to rap upon the door. In turn, Mary yawns loudly.

"If you keep doing that," I say mildly, "I will start to do so, as well."

She purposely, slowly, exaggeratedly yawns right in my face.

The door finally creaks open, bringing with it an elderly man in smart livery with an upturned nose that appears when I fail to produce a calling card. Nonetheless, I say firmly, "We are here to see Mrs. Carrisford."

"Mrs. Carrisford is unavailable for visitors at this time."

"Is she here, though?" Mary snaps.

Before the butler can answer, a loud crash sounds within the house, followed by an equally loud string of blistering curses.

Everything—absolutely everything: the air, our breaths, our hearts, the birds in the sky, *everything*—goes perfectly, amazingly, impossibly still.

Mary grabs my arm, her eyes wide. Prickles race up and down my arms and spine, because we know that voice. And if Victor is here, then—

I do not bother with formalities anymore. I shove the door the butler's clinging to fully open. Mary bolts into the house. "Victor! Victor! Where are you?"

How is this possible? How is it we came to interrogate Sara Carrisford over photographs found within Lygari's residence and instead found those who we feared lost forever?

The butler is aghast. "Miss! Miss! You cannot just—"

"Where is he?" She's frantic. "Where is my Victor?"

I grab hold of the butler's arm to force his attention. "Are the Misters Van Brunt in residence?"

He gapes at me. Another crash sounds, one loud enough to rattle the walls. Victor's shouting grows even louder. The butler says to Mary, "Miss, please, I beg of you, do not rile the doctor up. He's in fits today as it is! We've only just managed to calm him down—"

A third crash explodes. Mary needs no further explanation before darting down an echoing hallway.

"I will only ask this once more." I grab hold of the sputtering butler. "Are a Mr. Finn Van Brunt and a Mr. Victor Van Brunt in residence?

A deep breath is taken as he straightens his spine. He says nothing, but still. My knees nearly fail me. If Victor is here, Finn must be as well. "I must insist you take me to Mr. Finn Van Brunt immediately."

"Mrs. Carrisford left strict instructions that he not be disturbed without her explicit permission!"

Blessed confirmation, then. Finn is somehow here, at Sara Crewe Carrisford's home in 1905BUR-LP and not in 1905/06Sōs-IAAC as feared. I have no idea how he managed to edit from one Timeline to the other, but I am utterly grateful for it occurring nonetheless. I repress the tears threatening to swallow me whole, knowing I must stay strong and find him. My dagger whips out, angled at the base of the butler's neck. "Is this adequate permission?"

A woman appears at the top of the nearby stairs. "Mr. Groverley! What is this ruckus? I believe I told you—" She stops when she notices our precarious position. I stare up at this delicate, lovely woman—black hair a little too messy, pink dress splotched with dried blood—and there is no doubt in my mind toward her identity.

She thinks to be the guardian at the gates, does she? How ironic, considering. There is no smile upon my face as I curtly greet her. She was in a photograph with Lygari, after all. As of this moment, guardian or no, she is my enemy. "Hello, Sara. Would you be so kind to inform me where Finn is? Your butler seems to have metaphorically lost his tongue. What a shame it would be if he was to lose it for real."

Her mouth snaps open and then shut before she strides calmly down the stairs. She tucks back her hair, and although I'm certain she tries her best to hide it, her hand shakes with the motion. "Mr. Groverley is only following my orders. I beg of you to unhand him so that we might—"

"*We* will do nothing other than immediately go to wherever Finn is."

Steel fortifies her words. "I have no idea what you're talking about."

I consider what I have learned of Sara Carrisford, née Crewe. Finn's former partner at the Society for nearly four years, rumors paint her as exceedingly nice, terrible at hand-to-hand combat, yet at the same time a fairly decent shot. She was neither frighteningly intelligent nor dimwitted, but capable enough. Mary dislikes her immensely, claiming the sugary sweetness of Sara's personality and limitless optimism prior to her retirement were cloying and irritating. Others felt indifferent toward her departure; she has rarely entered conversation since my arrival. That is, until today.

A wicked smile curves my lips. "I think you do."

She lunges at me suddenly, a small knife materializing in her hand. I roughly shove the butler to the side; he collapses upon the ground several feet away. Sara flips over the remaining railing, readying herself.

Well. Perhaps she's a bit better at tactical fighting than I was led to believe.

"You do not want to do this with me, of that I can assure you."

She surprises me with her palm flipped up, tips of fingers motioning toward me to do so. Very well, then.

Desperation colors each of her moves, but I am able to easily counter most of them. She attempts a blow; I parry, sending her blade skittering in a distance. She kicks, I twist her leg and send her sprawling. She does not give up, though, no matter how many times she falls. Her butler even tries to tackle me, but once more, his interference lands him flat on his arse.

Sara truly is not as terrible as she was made out to be, though. By no means is she excellent at hand-to-hand combat, but she has determination and a drive that makes half that battle. She knows how to fall the right way, to get up and not give up. She even manages to land a few decent punches.

I wonder if Finn taught her these moves.

Victor's shouting sounds within the house again. Another crash follows. Sara spins and kicks out at me, but I'm able to deflect her strike and instead grab hold and slam her against a wall. My dagger out and shoved against her neck, I say loudly, "Mr. Groverley, if you approach us without my permission, you will find need to remove your mistress' blood up from the floor."

There's fear in Sara's eyes as she stares at me. There's also more than a bit of defiance. In fact, she spits in my face.

If I hadn't found her picture at Lygari's, I think I might rather have appreciated this woman's spunk. A mimsy she is not.

From between clenched teeth, she hisses, "How long have you been spying on us?"

Wrong yet interesting question. "You and I are set for a very important talk," I say coolly. "And you will answer me truthfully if you value your life. Until that moment, you will do as I say." The tip of my dagger digs into her soft skin. "Is there an understanding between us, Sara Crewe Carrisford?"

The use of her full name surprises her. It also seems to give her incentive to do her best to dislodge me. Like her, I am stronger than I look, though, and whatever defiance she may have, she does not possess one tenth of the determination I have percolating within me.

"I repeat: is there an understanding between us?"

She must rue not having a pistol upon her. *"Yes."*

"Excellent. Let me make myself clear: you are to take me upstairs to wherever Finn Van Brunt is. As there is blood staining your pretty gown, and that is where you came from, I am thinking you have him hidden away up there. But let me promise you, if I find out those stains are from anything you have done to harm him, your life is forfeit."

Her eyes widen before a deep V forms between her eyes. There is suspicion there, apprehension, too—but not toward me, interestingly enough. It appears to be fear of something else. How very curious.

"Is that clear, Mrs. Carrisford?"

"Let me tell you this," she snaps. "If you think to do any harm to him yourself, it will be *your* life that is forfeit. Even if it comes about with my last breath."

I laugh at her threat. She thinks to . . . protect Finn? From me? Who is it she believes I am? Or fears?

I do not loosen my hold on her, but I say more softly, "I vow to you that no harm to him will ever come about from me."

She does not break eye contact. "Then it appears we both are in agreement."

"Fair enough. Now that we've wasted enough time, I ask that you take me to him."

She hesitates. A long, deep breath is taken; the air blown out is shaky. But then, she offers me a small nod of acquiescence.

I angle her body toward the butler, now on his feet and shaking in anger and indecision. "Instruct your man to go ahead of us. We can't have him running off to fetch the authorities, can we?"

She also gives Mr. Groverley a sharp, reluctant nod. He smoothes his waistcoat and ascends the stairs without much hesitation. I keep Sara facing him so that there will be no surprises. But he does as asked, not even turning around once as we climb upward. Sara and I follow, and as we do, I instruct the man to ensure the door is already opened by the time we arrive. He does as asked with this, too, and soon enough, I enter a beautifully arranged room with drawn curtains and the stench of illness hanging in the air.

My heart leaves its place in my chest and crowds my throat. Lying asleep on a bed in the middle of the room is the man I love.

He's here. He's really here. Somehow, he is here.

I instantly release Sara and dart over to his side. "Finn? Finn? It's Alice. I'm here—I'm—" I grab his hand; it's clammy. A thin sheen of perspiration lines his pale forehead. His lips are pallid, his breathing is uneven and shallow all at once.

I rip the bedclothes back and suck in a deep breath. His white shirt is stained dark brown-red. The cotton is gently shoved upward and I peer down at wide swaths of linens circling his waist, their blotches matching those of his shirt.

My eyes fly toward a wary Sara. "Has Victor seen this?"

A nearby drawer is open; a gun is pointed toward me. But that's not what matters—it's that her mouth drops unattractively open as she stares at the scene before her.

I ask the question more harshly.

"Yes, of course Victor has seen it!" Anger and desperation fill her high-pitched voice. The gun in her hand does not waver, though.

"What has he said? Is the wound from the stabbing infected? Has he administered antibiotics?"

She's still gaping.

"Please!" I clutch his hand more tightly. "Tell me what is the matter with him!"

"Nothing Victor's done seems to be helping." Her words are slow, reluctant, as if she's surprised even at herself for answering me. "The wound was thoroughly cleaned and stitched up to the best of Victor's ability with what we had on hand. We've administered pain relief, but there are no antibiotics or laboratories at our disposal."

My gaze falls back to my beloved's face. "How long have they been here?"

Her lips thin into a straight line.

"If I wanted him dead, believe me, I would not be begging you for this information!"

And still, the gun does not lower. "Nearly two days now."

My words are bullets in the room. "Why have you not notified the Society? We would have come to rescue both he and Victor immediately!"

Now, I've truly surprised her, and it's enough for her to lower her weapon just a bit. "I do not have the capabilities to any longer. And we have yet been able to successfully make contact with this Timeline's liaison."

I count to ten, desperate not to lose any more of my raging temper than I already have. I tell her man, "Fetch Dr. Frankenstein Van Brunt immediately. He and Miss Lennox are downstairs."

"Mary's here?" Sara has the audacity to ask.

"Go!" I bark at the butler.

He scurries out of the room.

"Tell me what you know about Finn's condition."

She shows some intelligence by staying on the other side of the room, yet the words that come from her sound as if they're being forcibly torn from her throat. The gun stays down, though. "His fever broke this morning. We were—" She shakes her head, biting her lip. "He's holding on, thank God, but he hasn't woken since they arrived."

I stroke his face gently. "Finn? Love? Can you hear me? I'm here. I'm so sorry it took so long to find you." Angry, helpless tears threaten to crowd my eyes. I lean down and kiss his forehead. "I'm here, love."

His hand in mine twitches. What sounds like a sigh escapes my north star's lips.

"I will fix this." I lift our joined hands and press a kiss on the base of his knuckles. "I promise you that."

Shouting fills the hallway. Sara says flatly, "Fetching Victor will do nothing, I'm afraid."

And then Mary appears with Victor on her heels. And I am stunned.

The Society's doctor looks less put together than I have ever seen before. His hair and clothes are askew, his eyes bright and more than a bit wild appearing. Mary says, "He's in the midst of an episode that came on fast. He—"

"Blimey!" Victor rakes both hands through his hair. "You're here, too, Alice?" A low, majestic bow is offered before he tears himself away from Mary to pace the room, muttering nonsensically beneath his breath.

This is not good. This is not the doctor I know.

"Oh, God," Mary whispers as she stares down at Finn.

Victor wheels around. He juts a finger out, his face turning serious. "The nineteenth-century is a wretched cesspool of blackness when it comes to medicine."

"It is." Mary sounds as if she's attempting to calm a rabid dog. "It's all right, though, darling. We're going home straight away. You will have all the tools and supplies you need there."

He pulls at his hair. "I need you. That's what I need."

She reaches for him. He jerks, but he allows the touch. "You have me, you great idiot. You always have, you always will."

He falls to his knees, kissing her hands before springing back up to pace the room.

She turns to me, her face paler than normal. "I'm afraid it appears both of our boys' situations are dire." As if she's just noticed the other woman in the room, Mary inclines her head. Her voice is frigid when she says, "Sara."

Confusion and wariness line Sara's face. "Mary."

Without warning, Mary pulls out the tranquilizer gun in her bag and shoots Finn's former partner. Our reluctant host quickly crumples to the ground, her revolver dropping uselessly next to her side. A red, feathered dart sticks from her neck. The butler gapes and sputters in shock as he stumbles toward his mistress. Victor, on the other hand, bursts into what I can only term hysterical laughter as he claps a hand over his mouth, and then he proceeds to dance about the room, pretending to be . . . well, I'm not quite sure.

Perhaps I'm not in 1905BUR-LP. Perhaps, instead, I am merely back at the Pleasance, hallucinating once more.

"I think I warned you she was a decent shot," Mary says mildly. She holds up the tranquilizer gun and stares at it. "I'm not, but I suppose I can hold my own with this beauty. In any case, at least now we won't have to listen to any of her sniveling."

I would roll my eyes if I were not so concerned about Finn. "We still must question her, you know."

Mary groans quietly. "Must we? She'll just tell us how we princesses must stick together and all that sugary vomit she likes to spew."

Victor ceases his pacing. "It missed his kidney. His appendix. Went clean through." A finger points at me before he holds both palms out in submission. "Gangan."

"What in the bloody hell is gangan?" Mary sputters. "Do you mean gangrene?"

The butler, now ashen white, takes yet another tremulous step toward his fallen employer. "Mrs. Carrisford?"

"Gangan!" Victor shouts. "Gangan!"

We must get back to the Institute as quickly as possible. While not as badly off as his brother, Victor still is in a precarious state of health, too. I gently place Finn's hand down on the bed so I might root through my bag to find my pen and Society book.

When Groverley practically weeps his employer's name, Mary snaps, "For God's sake. I shot her with a tranquilizer, not a bullet. She's merely sleeping, you oaf."

Victor doubles over in a fresh batch of hilarity, slapping his knees until I am positive bright red splotches stain the skin beneath his pants. I quickly write a doorway to the Society's medical wing. It appears, glowing and bright, in the middle of the room. Groverley promptly faints next to his mistress.

Frabjous.

"Victor?" I snap my fingers, rousing the doctor's attention. "I need you to carry Finn for me through the doorway."

His head lifts. There are tears pouring down his cheeks. "As Your Majesty commands." To Mary, he says solemnly, "My Mary never gives up on anything. I knew that. I was right."

She touches his face, and for an unbearably intimate moment, they simply stare at one another. Victor leans in and kisses her, soft and sweet.

He adds, "It's coming, you know. Saw it outside the window just last night."

A shuddery breath escapes my friend. "Get your arse over to help Alice, but be careful with your brother, okay?"

He does as asked. Whilst I am on agonizing pins and needles at each tiny movement, Victor seems momentarily clearheaded enough to not jostle Finn too much. It is really not a far walk, considering. A hundred feet, perhaps. And still, I am ready to jerk forward if need be to catch Finn.

I follow Mary's warning with a "Be careful," of my own—only mine comes with an unsaid but clear warning.

The look he gives me prior to a quick nod is a familiar one, only to disappear as quickly as it showed itself.

"I suppose we can't have the butler haul Sara's sorry arse back to the Society now," Mary says forlornly.

It is tempting to drag Finn's old partner by her leg, much like I did with the Pan boy. But as I need answers she has, I still require her in fairly decent shape. "Help me lift her up."

Mary's displeasure is loudly voiced, but she does as requested. Together we bring Sara through the glowing doorway and into the Institute.

DESPERATION

ALICE

CHAOS REIGNS SHORTLY AFTER our arrival.

Once the matter of putting Finn down upon a bed I occupied all too recently is finished, whatever control Victor gained is lost once more. He raves about things we cannot see, about a monster that will come to extract payment for his sins and soul. Mary wrestles him the best she can whilst Van Brunt, the A.D., and Marianne burst into the room. Many other agents fill the hallway, desperate for a peek in.

Before our stalwart leader can process the scene before him, Mary shouts, "The protocol, Brom! He's in the midst of a bad episode!"

Van Brunt doesn't hesitate in the task, although I am positive he wishes nothing more than to reach out and touch his sons to verify their presence. He deftly turns and exits the room, the lines of his mouth grim. I am next to Finn, his hand in mine again.

"We're home." I smooth back sweaty hair off of his clammy forehead. "Hold on, love."

"I cannot believe this!" The A.D.'s head whips back and forth between the Van Brunt brothers. "How did you ladies find them?"

Victor rounds on his father's assistant. "He's coming, I tell you. No pity. None. A family's sin is a stain that never washes away. Blood is blood!" He slaps at his arms, rubbing at clean skin below rolled-up sleeves before jutting both out for all to see. *"LOOK AT MY STAINS!"*

Marianne pales at Victor's shouting, but she quickly composes herself. "How may I assist you?"

"Summon the doctor who oversaw me during the boojum infestation. We do not know how long it will take for Victor to be in his right mind."

Marianne swiftly departs.

To the A.D., I ask, "Did you happen to see a woman in the other room?"

He darts to the door. "You brought Sara back to the Institute? What happened to questioning her?"

"Obviously, that did not happen. Place her in the interrogation room we readied for Rosemary. I'll deal with her shortly. And be quick about it. I have no idea how much time we've bought ourselves with Mary's tranquilizers."

"A half hour at the most," Mary wheezes as she does her best to force Victor into a chair. "Perhaps even less."

Once the A.D. leaves, I gently place Finn's hand back down and march over to where his brother now sits. "Mary, please move to the side."

Her brow crinkles, but she does as asked.

"Do not impede what I'm about to do," I warn her. And then I slap a muttering, rocking Victor as hard as I can across the face.

He reels back, stunned. Mary is equally so, livid even. But I now hold his singular attention.

"How dare you!" she barks. "That was totally unnecessary!"

"You have allowed madness to consume you, Victor." My words

are harsh. "I assure you I understand it just as well as you, but for now, your head must do its best to clear and your thoughts and purposes focus on the task at hand. You had a goal for two days, doctor. Do you remember this goal?"

He blinks, his eyes refocusing slightly. "My brother is . . ." His gaze leaves me to settle on Finn. "Oh, God. He's not doing well."

Mary grabs hold of his hand protectively, still glaring daggers at me.

"What specifically ails him?" I press. "Does it stem from the stab wound?"

He moves toward the bed, face falling. "It's—poison. Perhaps magic. I can't be sure. I can't . . ." Words turn soft, hard to hear. "I didn't have antibiotics. I know nothing of Neverlandian metals or poisons, if that's even what was used. My Mary doesn't even have any in her stock, and she collects poisons the way some ladies hoard jewels."

"It's true," she tells me. There is less hostility in her voice now than I thought there would be, as if she now understands my urgency.

But if Mary does not have such an answer, there may be someone who might know. "Fetch Wendy, please. If anyone gives you trouble—"

Her smile is chilly as she heads to the door. "Nobody will give me trouble. Victor, I will be right back. Listen to Alice, okay?"

He waves her off, his focus still on his brother. Finn's shirt is peeled back to reveal the blood-stained bandaging circling the better part of his chest. "It isn't right. The colors aren't right. None of it is right. I've never seen such a thing, in any Timeline or any hospital. Watch the door, Alice. Do not let it take me. Not now. Not yet. He needs me."

"What colors?"

Van Brunt bursts into the room, syringe in hand. Victor doesn't even glance up when his father jabs the needle into his neck. He merely twitches irritably, as if a bee stung him. "Scissors. I need scissors."

Van Brunt pulls a pocketknife from his coat. Victor wordlessly takes it and gently cuts the wide swath of bandages free.

It is a good thing I am a lady with a strong constitution and have lived through many a terrible atrocity on the battlefield, because had I not had such experience, I might very well have fallen prey to those vapors Finn teased me about when I first joined the Society.

"Mother of God," Van Brunt whispers.

Surrounding a neat row of stitches is a vivid starburst of colors ranging from silver to blue to faint purple. These are no normal bruises, nor are they like anything I have ever laid eyes upon in the entirety of my life. These colors form a purposeful yet oddly mesmerizing and beautiful pattern.

What does it all mean?

"Not right," Victor murmurs. "Each hour it becomes more intricate, like . . ." He traces a finger lightly across the space just above the lines. "Like it's perfecting itself." His head jerks up sharply and turns toward his father, eyes widening as if he's just noticed the family patriarch is present. "Antibiotics. Saline, too. He's refused food and water. A drip will do." And then, more softly, "I—I failed him. Didn't have enough tools. Tried leeches. They all died within minutes."

His father takes a deep breath and then nods just once before exiting the room again.

To me, Victor whispers, "Turned black and shriveled up before exploding." His fingers expand as a burst of breath leaves his lips.

My own fingers curl so tightly inward my palms ache. "That will not happen to Finn, Victor. Do you understand me? You did not fail him. You most likely saved his life."

Eyes bright and shiny regard me sadly.

"Neither of us will allow him to perish, will we?"

"Don't let it take me." And then, "You need to understand." He gently peels back one of Finn's eyelids and stands to the side.

If my heart had grown legs and dove down deep inside my chest in order to escape, I would not be surprised in the least. Finn's eye— no, both eyes, as Victor further shows me—are solid black. There is no white, none of the beautiful blue-gray.

My nails dig so strongly into my palms I draw blood.

Mary peeks her head in. "Alice? I've got Wendy out here. She's awake, but not by much."

It goes against everything inside me to walk away from Finn right now, but I do. But first, I offer him my promise. I kiss his cheek, my words for his ear only. "Hold on, love. Even if it requires me moving heaven and earth, I will find a way to fix this. All I ask of you is to hold on."

His head, ever so slightly, shifts toward me. I tell him again that I love him. This time, it is his face to brush up against mine.

I pray our gravitational force is strong enough to keep him afloat.

Van Brunt is already back, shoving a cart filled with a jumble of carelessly organized medical items. Victor rifles through them, muttering nonsense the entire while. Van Brunt says to me, "Whatever you need, Ms. Reeve, you will have it."

I nod and then step beyond the door. Wendy is resting in a wheelchair, Mary standing guard. Green hair a tangled mess around her head, eyes flat and sad all at once, the Society's once-formidable technology expert is nothing more than a shade of her former self. Even the plethora of silver hoops that once adorned her ears and the colorful rings decorating her fingers are gone.

I drag a chair over so I might sit before her. "Wendy, we must talk, you and I." I lean forward, taking her cold hands in mine. She flinches, just a little, as one does with a bit of static shock. "I do not have much time. We must discuss what you know about Neverlandian magic."

Confusion wrinkles her brows.

"There was a boy here, one who flew. I'm told there is a video that shows you talking with him."

Now, those bright eyes of hers turn glassy, racked with fear.

"That same person stabbed Finn, Wendy. With a sword shining with a cerulean glow. And now, Finn is in that room behind us, unresponsive and fighting for his life."

Her head jerks in the direction I indicate, dislodging a pair of tears.

"Around the wound, a strange pattern has developed. Have you ever heard of this before?"

Lips move but only whispers emerge.

"Do you know if—"

"He kills people." Her voice is barely perceptible. I lean in closer, as does Mary. "He—he kills his followers. His boys, the lost ones. When they grow up against his wishes, he thins them out. In battles, he will even switch sides." She blinks slowly. "Funny how people overlook that part. I have never been to Neverland. London wasn't—there wasn't magic in the orphanage." She licks her cracked lips. "Pixie dust is a Neverland thing. So is—*he* is."

I squeeze her hands. "What about his sword? What makes it glow blue? Is it magic? Poison?"

Green hair goes flying when she shakes her head over and over again. "I—I don't know—he—" Wendy's eyes roll back until they are nothing more than whites a split second before convulsions wrack her body.

Mary quickly steadies her head before it lashes against the back of the wheelchair. "Victor couldn't find a reason for these, except that they occur any time she speaks of Pan."

The seizure lasts for approximately half a minute, leaving in its wake a limp Wendy, frothy spittle decorating her chin. Mary gently wipes the mess away, murmuring assurances neither of us can truly uphold: *It will be okay, you are okay, everything's okay.*

Everything is most assuredly not okay.

Wendy's eyes droop, her mouth moving like a puppet's. No further words emerge.

The urge to pluck strands from my hair grows, yet I force my hands to stay at my sides. "Who is the liaison for 1911BAR-PW?"

Mary glances up from tending Wendy. "If I'm not mistaken, it's one of the directors at the orphanage Wendy was found in." Her nose scrunches. "I don't recall her name, though. I've never talked to her—naturally, she was on this one's caseload."

"Her name is Miss Margaret Smith."

We both look toward the door; the A.D. has returned.

"Does she know of Neverland?" I ask him.

"I believe so." Pained eyes linger on Wendy. "Just to let you know, Sara's in the interrogation room. Give her a few minutes, and she'll be right as rain. You should have taken the extra-strength tranqs, Mary."

She shrugs. "I was in a hurry."

I turn to Mary. "Will you contact this Miss Smith and inquire about Neverlandian poisons and magic? I think it's time that Sara and I finally talk." I cannot shake the feeling the former agent knows something. I motion to the A.D. "Perhaps you might ensure Wendy's comfort?"

"Of course." He bends down before his friend. "How about we head up to your apartment and put on a movie? That might be nice, right, Wen?"

Her head lolls to the side; unfocused eyes merely stare up at the A.D. whilst her lips continue to move without rhyme, sound, or reason.

Just as I turn away, Mary stays me with a hand. "Keep in mind that Sara and Finn were close. He would not have gone to her home if he did not still trust her, Alice. I may have always thought her a pathetic cow, but she means something to him."

And yet, Sara Carrisford did nothing to contact the Society once Finn and Victor arrived—not even after learning of her former partner's injuries. Her excuses ring hollow, even if she tried to protect him.

"I'm just saying," Mary continues, "that Finn has always been . . . protective of her, if you will."

Nearby, as he takes hold of Wendy's chair, the A.D. interjects his agreement.

"It is a shame, then," I say coldly, "that Finn is not the one to be able to question her."

It is enough to silence their suggestions.

Before we leave, though, the both of us cannot help but check on Finn and Victor once more. The doctor and Van Brunt are quietly talking as they stand guard next to my love's bed, the father's arm around the son's shoulders. Part of me knows I ought to leave, that this is a moment meant for the Van Brunt family, but whether or not they realize it, they have also become my family, too.

Finn is my family. He is my heart, my north star.

The sound of the door clicking shut has Van Brunt withdrawing his arm from his son. Mary walks over the Victor, murmuring quietly.

"Were you able to learn anything from Ms. Darling?"

I shake my head. "Before she could tell me much, another seizure took hold. Mary is off to contact the liaison for 1911BAR-PW to inquire if they know anything of merit."

"I'm off now." Mary squeezes Victor's hand. "Let me know if you need me, all right, love?"

After another brief kiss, she departs. I must admit, I'm a bit taken aback at how demonstrative they are. Although outspoken about many things, Mary has always been publicly guarded with her intimate affections. But I suppose love will do that to a person, and when it is risked or threatened, one cannot help but reach out and hold it as tightly as possible.

Victor's attention returns to his brother. A pair of liquid-filled bags attached to a silver stand next to the bed are adjusted; thin tubes snake from the sacs down to an IV attached to Finn's hand. "The antibiotics will need time to work, but I'm hoping we'll see a difference by nightfall."

Aches sincerely erupt throughout my chest as I stare down upon my beloved's pale face. Huckleberry Finn Van Brunt is smart and strong and brave and deserves better than he has received. He did not give up on me. I will not give up on him. This is not how it will end for him, let alone for us. A prophecy might have torn me away from my first love, a prophecy I both respect and resent, but there is no prophecy at work here. Wonderland is not at risk. My people, my lands (which I have always put above my own wants, needs, and desires once I embraced my crown) have nothing to do with my relationship with this man.

He is alive. He will remain so, even if I have to go to the ends of the earth and beyond to make it so.

I tell Van Brunt, "The gloves come off from here on out."

It is a phrase I'd heard on a television program, early on during my stay here at the Institute. I'd had to look it up on my cell phone, but once I comprehended its meaning, I rather liked it. And here it is, fully applicable.

The Society's leader's smile is faint as he regards me. Much still haunts his eyes: fear, relief, fury, helplessness. I am positive he finds the same in my own, only I know there to be cold resolve present, as well.

"I would have it no other way, Ms. Reeve."

I allow my fingers to fall upon Finn's shoulder, to have this small connection with him. "I will be interrogating Sara Carrisford shortly. If there is a change—"

"You'll be the first to know." Victor's eyes are still bright, but the set of his mouth is less frightful. There is no further talk of monsters—at least, the kinds that haunt a mad mind, rather than the ones I now hunt.

Neither Van Brunt nor Victor sees fit to offer any warnings over my plans. Instead, Van Brunt rounds the bed and lays a gentle hand against my back. "You have my undying gratitude, Alice."

Alice.

Nearly a year after my induction into the Society, and Van Brunt finally calls me by my given name.

Emotions long buried threaten to swallow me. A lump crawls up my throat, my eyes sting once more. "Whilst I'm gone, I would ask that he is never left alone."

His attention returns to his stricken son. "That I can promise you."

"Please send word to Grymsdyke to stand guard in the room."

When I left Wonderland, it was only under the influence of a strong drug the Caterpillar obtained for me. It offered clarity and conviction in the face of madness, and even then, I'd wanted to tear my skin off because I desperately did not want to go. But I did. I put my people's needs above my own. I walked away from my home, my love, my Court, my people, my lands, my duties, and my dreams. Today, I have no drug to act as my crutch. I am to walk away from this man I love, this man I never believed I would ever find. I am to walk away and ready myself for battle, because from here on out, there is nothing I will not do, nothing I will not try. I will save Finn. I will save him and then I will go even farther, because I am no longer solely championing the people inhabiting the Diamonds' lands. I am now fighting for trillions of souls who do not know I exist, who do not call me their queen. I will fight for them even so. And they need Finn to fight for them, too. He has always been one of their best, their strongest of champions.

Gabriel Lygari, I am coming for you. And I will have my vengeance.

A LOVE STORY GONE WRONG

ALICE

THERE IS NO GUARD posted outside the interrogation room, nor is Sara Carrisford restrained when I enter. That is of no matter, though.

I do not bother locking the door behind me. This woman, this former agent at the Society, had more than one opportunity to overtake me at her home in London and yet was unable to do so.

I have no fear of her, but I can practically taste her fear on my tongue.

She is on her feet, body angled just so toward the door that she must foolishly harbor hopes she can get past me. If she feels the effects of Mary's tranquilizers, she does not show them.

Good girl.

"Where is Finn?"

Her voice is cold and tight, not at all like how I'd imagined it to be after hearing's Mary's characterizations. The woman before me is not sweet.

Even better.

I choose not to answer her question. "Explain to me why I found a pair of photographs of yourself in a Mister Gabriel Pfeifer's flat in Manhattan."

Her eyes widen, but she does not let up on her defensive position. "I do not know what you are talking about."

"This again?" I tsk. "Mrs. Carrisford, let me be clear with you. From here on out, I will only ever ask you a question once. I assure you, you will not desire the consequences of refusing to properly answer."

She says, each word crisp in rebellion, "I do not know what you are talking about."

I am across the room before she can even blink, a forearm across her throat as I throw her up against a wall, one of her own arms pinned behind her. "I rather think you do."

Even as she spits, "Where. Is. Finn?" she cannot hide her pain behind defiance.

My arm jerks up, slamming her head back against the wall. For a good pair of seconds, the whites of her eyes shine. But then she spits out between clenched teeth, "Where is he?"

The next slam of black hair against wall and fist against ribs extracts a cry. "I would have thought you had learned your lesson earlier today. How unfortunate for you that you did not."

A gasp hisses between us. "I want to talk to Brom!"

A knee slams against her thigh, buckling her stance. Another cry is torn from her lips.

"It is critical you understand that I will go as far as it takes to get what I want, Sara Crewe Carrisford." My arm against her throat pushes harder until wheezing reaches my ears. "What I currently want is for you to answer any and all questions I have. If you think there is a single person within these walls who will come to your aid, I must assure you that you are quite mistaken."

Her greenish-gray eyes are utterly wide now, but I believe she rapidly understands our current situation. "At least grant me the knowledge of your full name!"

That I can give. "Alice Reeve."

"How do you know Finn?"

I press harder against her throat. Softly, difficultly, she manages, "I don't know why photos of me were found in some flat."

Not good enough. The fingers of my free hand now dig painfully into the spaces between her ribs. "There was one where you were in a man's arms, laughing. He has curly hair, a dark suit."

Yet another cry surfaces. "I'm telling the truth!"

"You have been gone from the Society for well over a year. From what others have informed me, the pictures in question must be at least two years old. One is thought to be Central Park. The other appears to be at a party." I twist my fingers until tears swell in her eyes. "In the first, you were wearing a yellow dress, your hair in a loose bun."

"I went there to relax sometimes," she gasps. "Like a lot of people."

I wait, unrelenting with the pressure I place upon her. Her free hand grapples uselessly against me.

"I don't know a Gabriel Pfeifer!"

"What about a Gabriel Lygari?"

Her slim brows furrow as she weakly struggles against me. She is not so good an actor to hide this truth, I think. She's genuinely confused by the names I offer.

"Shall I make it easier for you? Were there any Gabriels in your acquaintance here in New York?"

"I . . ." Her body twitches below mine, sincere fear now attacking all her muscles. "I know—*knew*—a Gabe Koppenberg."

Ah. There it is. "Describe this Gabe Koppenberg to me."

"I can't . . . *breathe!*"

My smile is vicious, I'm certain of it. "Of course you can. If you couldn't, you'd have passed out by now. Yet here you are, telling me about Gabe Koppenberg."

She tries to strike at my kidneys with a weak fist, sweeping at my footing with clumsy feet. If I weren't so enraged, I might very well chortle at her pathetic attempts. Soon enough, though, she weakens into submission. Raspy now, barely voiced, she informs me that Gabe Koppenberg was tall and good looking, his hair curly and dark, and his chin indented.

Well now. Is seems the man with two names now adds a third. "Did he wear a lapis ring?"

Fear is replaced by terror. "If you value your life, the lives of those you love and work with here, you must allow me go home immediately."

I increase pressure against her windpipe.

"Yes!" She coughs, sputtering. "The man I knew wore that ring!"

My God. Lygari/Pfeifer was in league with a Society agent.

"How is it you came to know this Gabe Koppenberg?"

"Don't do this," she rasps. "I beg of you. Not here!"

"Do what?" My tone is cold. "Inquire as to why photographs of you have been discovered within the lair of a psychotic murderer, one whom many within these walls feared had erased the lives of the two men I found in your home?"

She has the astounding audacity to hush me, all the while shaking like a leaf beneath my grip. She mouths, "He'll hear you, you must—"

"I must *what?*"

Her wide eyes flit about the room. Louder now, yet still a whisper: "Send me back to my Timeline before it is too late."

I stare at her, our faces so close it would take nothing to head butt or even kiss her. Her breath trembles between us, her heart jackrabbits beneath my hold. Tiny beads of perspiration decorate her hairline until several take the risk to fall toward her chin.

Defiance, terror, agony, shame, and bitter, bitter guilt stare back at me.

Perhaps I am a fool, because I murmur, "Is there something here which ties your tongue?"

Her breath quakes out a nearly inaudible confirmation.

I mouth now: "This room or the Institute as a whole?"

She mouths in return: "Whole."

I lean close. "If you attempt to flee from my hold or even step a toe out of line, I will not hesitate to ensure it is the last thing you ever do. Is that clear?"

I hear, rather than see her swallow. "Yes."

I carefully release her; she sags against the wall, coughing and trembling. Before I can change my mind, I unceremoniously yank her upright. "Into the hall."

She lurches forward, cradling the wrist of the arm I'd pinned behind her. On the other side of the door, we find the A.D. pacing. Or eavesdropping, as he's ever so prone to doing.

I clamp a steely hand down upon Sara's shoulder. "Is there news?"

He quickly shakes his head, eyes narrowing on the woman next to me. There's anger there, disappointment, too.

"Do you have any books upon your person?"

His eyes fly back to meet mine. "Huh?"

"It does not matter which. Do you have one or not?"

He pats his trouser pockets and then those of the long knit sweater he wears. "I have—"

"Write a doorway."

It's not often that the A.D. is taken so aback. "But—"

"Now. Do not tell me which." To Sara, I instruct, "Close your eyes."

She does so with alacrity.

The A.D. tugs out a slim book and his pen. I crowd closer, ensuring Sara's body is a shield blocking any view of what he holds. "Alice, I don't—"

"Jack." Sara's whisper is hoarse. "Do as she says."

Within seconds, a door appears. "You'll have to come with," I tell the A.D.

He nods, holding out a hand to allow us go to first. I shove Sara forward, leading us through the glowing doorway and into a rainy, filthy alleyway—a modern one, though, from the looks of it. Not too far away is a pair of crushed soda cans. The shaking woman keeps her eyes closed, tears leaking out as raindrops splatter against us until the

A.D. announces the portal closed. She drops to the ground, not caring that there is a revolting puddle beneath her and heaven knows what else (I suspect it to be a mixture of rat droppings and decomposing food). Sobs wrack her shoulders as she covers her face in her hands.

The A.D. whistles. "What in the bloody hell did you do to her, Your Majesty?"

I ignore him. "Time is limited here, Mrs. Carrisford. I am needed back at the Institute."

"Oh, God." She's desolate. "How did it all come to this?"

"Well," the A.D. says, "I think it was because you chose to sit before looking."

All right. I cannot help but roll my eyes at his efforts toward bringing levity to the situation.

"First, please tell me how Finn is doing." His former partner's wet face turns toward me. "I just want to know if he's all right."

"You hold no cards here," I remind her. "You do not get to dictate how this goes. Instead, explain why it is you were certain we were overheard at the Institute. Whilst you're at it, stand up. You cannot be comfortable in such filth."

She slowly rises, her chest shuddering.

"Perhaps we ought to find somewhere a bit drier?" the A.D. offers.

I do not move, nor does Sara agree with him. She instead takes a deep breath and smoothes the wet strands of black hair from her face. And still, her words are unsteady when she speaks. "It is because the Institute is bugged."

"What?!" The A.D. jerks forward. "That's fucking impossible! We—we would have known that! Wendy would have—" He bites his words back, swearing softly. "Marianne would have discovered that during the overhaul of the security system."

I just cannot seem to keep up with the words of the twenty-first century, can I? "What does this mean? *Bugged?*"

The A.D. rounds on me. "She's saying that somebody has either been surreptitiously watching us or listening in on our activities without any of us knowing."

I ask Sara, "How would you know this?"

Her lip quivers just as surely as her chest. "It's because I put them there."

"WHAT. THE. FUCK?!" The A.D. shoves her against one of the nearby walls. "Tell me I heard that wrong, Sara. Because there is no bloody fucking way one of our own would ever do that! Not even you, who ran away with her tail tucked between her legs!"

She doesn't fight back. She doesn't even try to defend herself except to say, "I didn't—I tried to—" Black strands whip around her face. "It doesn't matter. You're right. I put them there."

He jerks away from her, raindrops splattering his glasses. "How many are there?"

Her breath in escapes as a shudder. "Dozens. Each floor, each main workroom is bugged except the Museum. Auditory ones, not video, as far as I know. All the size of quarters but slimmer, stuck beneath common objects such as tables, desks, and chairs."

I throw out an arm to prohibit the Artful Dodger's lurch forward. "Why would you do such a thing?"

Long lashes sweep her wet cheeks when she closes her eyes. "I have no good reason other than I felt a strong, irresistible need to do so, one I could not ignore." She swallows. "I cannot be sure, but in the time since, I've come to believe he made me."

"*He* who?"

"The man you asked me about." Her chin juts defiantly upward. "Gabe Koppenberg."

The A.D. pushes away from me, releasing a roar as he crosses the width of the alley.

"He was my lover, in case you were wondering. Or boyfriend, if you wish for a more colloquial term. At least I thought he was." And then Sara Carrisford tells me a most curious story.

She met Gabe Koppenberg at the New York Public Library during a visit on behalf of the Librarian. Smitten with his looks and flattered by his attention, they spent several hours talking. For the next several weeks, they serendipitously ran into one another all over town, often at the most surprising of places. A coffee shop, a bakery. On a crowded subway train, in Central Park. Slowly, over the course of many months, she found herself falling prey to his charms. A discreet dinner once a week eventually evolved into a trio of nights spent together when she wasn't on assignment. They would regularly meet for lunch or for coffee. After he kissed her during a trip to a bagel shop, she believed herself in love. One thing led to another, and before she knew it, kisses transitioned into something more.

It was heady, she tells us. She began to crave Gabe, often resorting to anger or tears when they weren't together. And yet, she never told anyone about him or their attachment—he was her secret, she claimed. He had nothing to do with books or stories or expectations.

"Finn wasn't aware of this relationship?"

She won't look me in the eye when she tells me he did not. But that one word is filled with regret and sadness that I do not need to see in her eyes. "I suppose it doesn't matter anymore." A bitter laugh soaks into the chilly air between us. "Early on during my tenure at the Society, I found myself developing intense feelings toward . . . a colleague. He was always so kind, so charming. So intelligent, so *good.* Not that he ever indicated reciprocal feelings, but it happened all the same. I was already skittish, having embarked upon an inappropriate relationship before." She shakes her head. "I was determined to overcome my feelings, so when I met Gabe . . ." She bites her lip. "It was lovely in the beginning. The answer I thought I was looking for."

"Are you fucking kidding me with this?" The A.D. tugs at his wet, greasy strands. "You're saying that you basically screwed the devil because you had an unrequited crush on some guy at the Society?"

"No!" Her fists curl at her sides. "No, Jack. It's not—" She lets out a frustrated sigh. "I'm merely attempting to explain the frame of mind I was in where I suppose I found it . . . flattering, alluring, if you will, that there was a good-looking, wealthy, charming, intelligent man, who was interested in me. One I would not risk losing everything over if we were to become intimate. I'd . . . made a mistake with Carrisford. Mistaking gratitude for love, allowing it to go too far, too fast, for far too long. I felt I owed him this, tricked myself into believing it was right." She shakes her head, rubbing at her temples. "When I came to the Society, I wanted to erase it all, move on. But I couldn't do it there, not with . . ." Her breath shudders. "It doesn't matter. I traded one mistake for another, even though it was what I feared most. Once more, I moved too fast without thinking of the consequences."

"You're shitting me!" He juts a finger toward her. "She's shitting us, Alice. Goody-two-shoes reputation aside . . . What is this? We're not in grade school, sweetheart!"

"I know that!" Her voice rings in the alley. "Believe me, *I know that!*"

Once more, it appears I must be the voice of reason. "As titillating as all this may be, I demand you both to table such pettiness until a different occasion. Sara, how is it that Koppenberg got you to betray your allegiance to the Society?"

"I don't know." She sags back against the wall, wincing as she continues to rub her forehead. "I really wish I did. It . . . it was a slow transition. Not the relationship, but my changing feelings toward work. He and I would have dinner, and afterward, when I came home, I would harbor irrational bitterness toward my job and not know why. I began to lose time outside of assignments. There were hours I could not recall. Feelings changed without reason. Resentments stirred. I would occasionally wake up in places I had no idea ever going to—in the basement, in the labs, one time even in . . ." A quivering breath escapes her lips as she squints in what appears to be pain. "Even in Brom's office. I was frightened. I wanted to discuss it with Finn, but every time I opened my mouth to do so, nothing would come out. I'd get headaches if I tried, terrible ones that left me in tears."

The A.D. picks up one of the crushed cans and throws it against the wall near Sara's head. I'll give it to her, she doesn't even flinch when he bellows, "That's shite, Sara! It's not as if you have a headache right now, do you?"

"Actually," she says plainly, "I do."

"Did he play music for you?"

Her attention swivels back to me, brows knitting.

"On pipes," I clarify.

"I don't specifically remember that." She chews on her bottom lip. "But we did listen to music often together—in his car, in his apartment. He took me once to a concert at a private school he was a bene-factor to." If I'm not mistaken, her eyes are now significantly redder, and not from tears. "There might have been pipes in that . . . but those were children. Not him."

Children. How very, very interesting she says this. Even the A.D. goes still as this processes. He's seen the surveillance footage. He knows who attacked the institute.

I step closer. "Tell me about this school and these children."

Sara offers a tiny, confused shake of her head. "It was just a school. An elite one, secluded . . . I think it had boarders. I could be wrong." Her greenish-gray eyes meet mine; they are so bloodshot the whites have turned pink. "It's in Connecticut. Gabe said he was an alumni—it was all grade levels, I think. I wasn't there for very long, just for the concert." Her brow knits once more. "Well, it was more like a dress rehearsal, really. We were the only two in the theatre at the time. I thought it . . . sweet, to be honest. To know he supported children and their education."

A long whistle trills from the A.D.'s lips. "Well, isn't that a nice bit of connect-the-dots." He holds a hand up for me, but I do not smack it.

I share his sentiment, though.

I press, "Do you remember the name of this school?"

"It was a pair of biblical names." Her rubbing of her forehead turns vigorous, eyes squinting until tears leak out. "J—John—" Both hands press against temples as she falls silent, rocking, her mouth open in a wordless scream. A not-so-thin stream of blood trickles from one nostril.

"Sara." I lay a hand on her raised arm. "You must push past the pain. Do not let it, or *him,* win."

Shudders wrack her shoulders, tears mixing with rain. But she blurts, wails as if she's physically tearing the word from her mouth, "John . . . and . . . Paul!" And then she doubles over, a cry of anguish ripping from her.

The A.D. mutters, softer now, "Sonofabitch," before dropping down to lay a comforting hand upon her arm.

I do not allow myself to feel pity yet. I cannot dare to lower my defenses. There may be time in the future, but in this moment, in the heat of war, pity is a weakness I cannot bear to embrace. "You claimed Koppenberg made you install surveillance at the Institute? What was his reasoning?"

"I don't remember." Her voice cracks repeatedly. "I woke to discover the equipment in my bedroom. It took me . . ." A choking sound surfaces. "Weeks. He never mentioned it, but somehow . . . there was a sensation within my chest that it was for him. When I was done, I loathed myself, even though there was an urge to discover if he was proud of my accomplishments." Wide, pleading eyes look up at me. The pink is gone, replaced by bright splotches of red. It is as if her eyes are bleeding, or have filled with plasma. "I didn't speak to him, though. Instead, I immediately resigned from the Society. Couldn't tell anyone there, even Finn. He was so worried about me—always asking questions, always trying to get me to talk. I pushed him away so many times. I told everyone I was done with the Society, that I wanted to go home. That I missed Carrisford and what we had, that the entire time I was in New York, I pined for him. I was utterly fearful I would wake one day and realize I'd done something even worse to people I cherished. I refused a pen or any form of communication—it's why I could not contact anyone when Victor and Finn arrived at my home. I purposely cut ties with the liaison assigned to my Timeline; I even departed without a single word to Gabe. I went right back to Carrisford, right back to the relationship I'd run away from. My new husband was a sick man, requiring much tending." Much quieter, "I rarely left the house unless absolutely necessarily. I trained in secret, ensuring I could defend myself and others if need be. But as the weeks and months passed, the urge to find Gabe grew to be nearly irresistible. Terrible dreams plagued me. I imagined I heard music playing when I knew no one else to be around. The sensation, the *knowledge,* that my insidious actions were somehow connected to the man I dated steadily solidified." Her face falls. "I have no proof, just a gut feeling. There were times I hid away in rooms rarely used. A maid I trusted would restrain me until the urges went away."

Muffled sobs tremor throughout her body, the blood streaming from her nose now more forceful. The A.D. squats next to her, his arm half-heartedly around her shoulders, appearing as frustrated and lost as I believe Sara must feel.

She whispers brokenly, "An unsigned note was delivered yesterday morning, saying, 'You've been a bad girl, Sara.' It only seemed reasonable that it had to do with Finn and Victor, as I'd never received such a note before. I couldn't be sure, as I no longer had anything to compare it with, but I was certain it was Gabe's handwriting. I instructed Groverley to refuse entry to anyone. We had no medicines except for what my trusted staff could fetch." She wipes at her face; blood streaks alongside rainwater. "I didn't know what else to do. I feared we were under surveillance. It was clear Victor wasn't on his protocol and was spiraling faster than I'd ever seen him, so I couldn't count on him to protect us. And Finn—" Another choking sound erupts from her chest. "He passed out the moment they arrived. I kept my gun with me the entire time, even though I feared I would wake one day to find I'd used it. I was hearing ghostly music daily by this point. When you arrived, I truly feared you might be associated with him."

"How long was your relationship with this Gabe Koppenberg?"

She glances up at me, and it takes much control to not wince at the sight of such bloody eyes. "Half a year, maybe more." Fists press against her temples. "I did this. I provided him access to the Institute."

"You indicated you visited his home?"

"In Brooklyn, yes."

The A.D. says, "You mean Manhattan."

She shakes her head. "Brooklyn. It was an old, lovely brownstone."

I ask, "Do you remember the address?"

"Not specifically, but . . ." Her nose scrunches. "I do remember the whereabouts."

"Take down the details," I instruct the A.D. "Also, where is our current location?"

He tugs his cell phone out and types what Sara relates. "I thought Your Majesty didn't care about such names."

I say nothing, but there is no doubt my stare is meaningful.

"Fine." He rises before helping Sara to her feet. "It's my Timeline, just in the present. I like to keep my book close, if you know what I mean. I added a few recent pictures to make it more accessible."

"Edit me back into the Institute. Before you return, locate a safe yet discreet location here for Mrs. Carrisford to recuperate within. It sounds as if it is in her best interest to remain out of sight for the time being."

She is smart enough to not argue with me.

"I hope you will understand I simply cannot have you in a position to where you might further endanger those at the Institute or anywhere else. If you remain here, in a Timeline where your resources are severely lacking, you will be safe."

Sara wearily offers her understanding.

"To answer your earlier question," I tell her, "Finn is indeed at the Institute and is, as you may well imagine, not doing well. His brother has administered antibiotics and is closely monitoring the situation."

Her gratitude is softly offered.

"I must return to check on him." To the A.D., I say, "I expect you back shortly. It appears our hunting grounds have expanded."

His nod is uncharacteristically solemn before he pulls out his pen and Institute book.

"What has Gabe done?" Sara asks quietly.

I do not soften the blow. "We believe he is the mastermind behind the destruction of far too many catalysts."

Horror, so much horror, fills those bloody eyes of hers. The list of payments I must obtain from the fiend grows.

I am close to crossing the threshold of the glowing doorway he's written me when I find myself unable to resist the urge to turn back momentarily. Compassion has demanded notice from me anyway. "If it is any consolation, I do not believe you acted of your own accord whilst betraying your colleagues. It appears your Gabe Koppenberg is talented in ways no man ought to be."

"Wait." Although she smoothes her skirt, standing a bit taller, she is still a terrible mess. And still, there's a painful earnestness in her composure as she regards me. "Do you love him?"

I know whom she means. "Yes."

"Why does Jack keep calling you Your Majesty?"

"Because I am a queen."

"The Queen of Diamonds, to be more specific." The A.D. smirks when he tells his former colleague this. "Otherwise known as the infamous Alice Liddell from Wonderland you searched years for."

Her pale, bloody lips form a perfect circle right before the door closes behind me.

BLACKENED TEETH

ALICE

"**T**HERE ARE NO STORIES with glowing blue swords," Mary tells me. "At least, none we can readily find."

I wipe my damp forehead as I stare down at my beloved. Still pale, still unconscious, the only change from when I left with Sara and the A.D. is the temperature of his skin. Not as clammy as before, he is now merely cool.

I cannot bear to see him as such, yet loathe the thought I must once more leave if I am to discover anything behind the truth of his illness.

"We've been scouring various databases with keywords, but there are little to no hits. The Librarian is wading through her stacks of books, but so far . . ." Her shrug is morose, her touch on my arm gentle. "Everyone is obviously still looking."

I turn to face the spider hanging in the corner of the room. "Anything to report?"

"Only that a doctor other than Frankenstein came to visit, Your Majesty." He coughs his strange little spider cough. "More blood was taken. This one was just as baffled as the last. No one seems to know what might ail His Highness outside of the wound from the sword."

I ask Mary, "How did your talk with the liaison for 1911BAR-PW go?"

"Margaret Smith is a very nice woman, but her age is creeping upon her. She knows even less of Neverland than Wendy, and what she does know comes *from* Wendy. She claims no one there really believes in Peter Pan outside of what most people here do. He is a bit of a bedtime story legend and nothing else. She has no idea of anything to do with swords, let alone ones that glow blue, and isn't aware of any poisons specific to her Timeline that differ from ours. Her London is similar to the one we're familiar with, I'm afraid. That said, Brom sent Henry Fleming to investigate further. "

Fleming is a former military man, and one I've come to respect during my tenure at the Society. He's fairly adept at interrogations himself, so if there is something to be found in 1911BAR-PW, I trust him to do so, especially as I cannot be there myself. I have children to hunt, as distasteful as it sounds.

Children who might know of swords with blue blades and the terrible effects they wreak.

"Also, why are you soaking wet?" Mary frowns as her eyes trace a line from my head to my feet. "You appear as if you've been standing in a downpour for the better part of an hour."

I'd immediately come to Finn's room. Van Brunt was no longer present, nor was Victor. Mary was standing guard, and although I know her to not be one of the finest physical fighters in the Society, I also trust her more than most within these walls.

"Do I?" I ask mildly, glancing about the room. "What a pity."

There's not much within these walls: the bed upon Finn lies, a pair of chairs on either side, and the rolling cart Brom brought with him upon Victor's request. There is a window covered in wooden, slatted blinds and a singular door leading out to the main part of Victor's infirmary. I shut the door and begin my search.

"What in the world are you doing?" Mary asks as I run my hands along the doorframe.

"I would hate to think of it being dusty in here." I move over to the window, examining every slat.

"Have you gone even more mad? You're thinking of dust at a time like—"

"You have such a lovely singing voice," I tell her when I move onto the chairs on either side of Finn's bed. "Might you sing a song? I learned in the Pleasance Asylum that music is quite restorative."

Mary has, in fact, a cringe-worthy signing voice and is not at all ashamed to admit such a thing to polite company. And although the quirk of her lips tells me she thinks I've gone bonkers, she does as asked. A truly terrible, off-key version of *Scarborough Fair* fills my ears, and I do my best to not cringe. Grymsdyke, on the other hand, has no such manners.

"If I had ears," he says gravely, "they would bleed at such caterwauling."

I urge Mary to continue. One chair is examined, then the other. Nothing.

She moves onto the second stanza of the song. I quickly check the rolling cart, but once more, everything is as it ought to be. If there is a so-called *bug* in this room, that leaves the bed.

I check the entire frame before running my hands as gently as possible beneath the mattress. When I find nothing, I drop to my knees and peer into the darkness beneath. It's there I finally find what I've been searching for. The size of a modern quarter, a small disk clings to the underbelly of the bed's frame.

Thank you, Sara.

It doesn't take much to pry the small bit off, just a few scrapes of nail against metal. I gingerly hold the piece up for a still-singing Mary to see, pointing to my ear. Her eyes go wide and then narrow as she continues to sing.

He dares to listen to us.

I drop the piece to the ground and smash it with the heel of my boot. The song abruptly ends. Grymsdyke leaps to the ground and scuttles over to where the pieces lay.

"The entire Institute is infested with these." I motion to the mess. "From what I'm told, there are dozens of them."

My assassin shoves at one of the bits of wires and metal with one of his hairy legs. Mary, on the other hand, asks, "How did you know that was there?"

"I would ask you to fetch Van Brunt, as well as Marianne, and bring them here so we might have a conversation. Say nothing until they are safely behind this door."

I do not have to ask twice. "Grymsdyke, might you accompany me?"

The spider glances up at me. I nod, and he scurries up her arm to settle upon her shoulder. The remaining strains of *Scarborough Fair* assault my ears as she shuts the door.

I could have asked her to send a text, but I want—no, need—this small moment alone with Finn. I carefully crawl onto the mattress, inserting myself into the space between his side and the edge of the bed. My head on his shoulder, his hand in mine, I am tempted to give in to the terror and grief demanding to be acknowledged, but there are still miles to walk ahead of me.

In Wonderland, the battles I faced seemed impossible at times, and yet, I was always able to face them head on. But now . . . now, Finn lies in this bed, stricken by a blue sword no one has heard of, with a bizarrely beautiful pattern developing across his skin. His eyes, once so expressively blue-gray, are now black. We no longer have any of Lygari's associates within our grasp. He and they have disappeared into the vastness of Timelines unknown.

I fear I am running in that caucus race from long ago. And yet, run I will and must, until sooner or later I will either stumble or discover what it is I need. I can only pray it is at a children's school in Connecticut, wherever that is.

Finn's heartbeat is uneven against my ear. Worse yet, it is entirely too gentle. Panic blooms within my veins, sharp and clear and terrifying. *Tick-tock, tick-tock,* Rosemary used to chant. Such nonsense was bothersome at the time, and yet now, it's all I can hear or feel. *Tick-tock, tick-tock.*

Tick-tock.

But I cannot allow this to solely be Rosemary's battle cry, because it is also the song of Finn's heartbeat, of the war drums that seem to follow each and every step I take.

I hold onto his hand tighter, wiling his to return the pressure. I do my best to memorize each and everything thing I can about him—the way his skin feels beneath mine, the lingering smell that is wholly Finn despite the illness' best attempts to mask it, the way his hair falls against his forehead and over his ears, the way his soft breath sounds.

I lift our joined hands and kiss the back of his before pressing it against my cheek. Foolishly, I want to berate him, order that he simply cannot let go because I am selfish enough to desire his presence in my life, but instead all I can do is offer a barely audible chant of my own, set in time to his heartbeat, one that tells him the depth of my feelings in three small words.

And then . . .

Then his fingers tighten against mine.

I go still, our hands still pressed against my cheek. My own heart has ceased beating. Could it be . . . ?

I gently squeeze once more. Callou, callay, he offers one of his own in response.

I jerk upright up in the bed, staring down at his face in wonder. "Finn? Can you hear me?"

There is no response. No change in his breathing, no motion of eyes beneath lids. Nothing to indicate the pressure I'd just been gifted not once, but twice.

I kiss his hand again, twice for good measure. A nice clean, even number. Hope has come to bless me, and I must hold onto it with both hands. As I wait for the others, I allow my eyes to drift shut.

Sleep granted at his side is miniscule. When Van Brunt and the others arrive, I reluctantly remove myself from his bed, ensuring I tuck his sheets around him. We wait until the door closes before Mary whispers harshly, pointing to the mess still on the floor, "That was a bloody bug, wasn't it?"

Marianne squats down to scoop up the bits. I must stifle a yawn when I answer Mary. "Yes."

Van Brunt peers down at the mangled mess in Marianne's hand. "How did you know it was there?"

I spend the next few minutes relaying Sara Carrisford's story. To say the others are shocked by her duplicity would be an understatement, even when it is obvious to all that the source of her actions stems from Lygari/Pfeifer/Koppenberg. "They seem, in a lot of ways, to mimic those of Wendy's," I say. "Missing time periods, the inability to recollect events. Sara is plagued by headaches each and every time she tries to speak of such matters; both Jack and I witnessed her bleeding whilst struggling to give us the pertinent details. I cannot imagine the level of pain she was in. Even her eyes appeared to bleed, as if too much pressure was placed against her brain."

The others are momentarily rendered into silence, even Grymsdyke, who perches on Mary's shoulder.

"The blood vessels probably burst," Mary says thoughtfully. "From the strain—or pain."

"Good lord." Marianne covers her mouth with a hand.

"Wendy, on the other hand," I continue, "falls prey to seizures, effectively silencing her during any attempt to converse with us about the boy who'd been visiting her. It's curious, don't you think, that those who have been in regular contact with Lygari or his associates are now paying terrible prices to ensure their silence?"

The door swings open, bringing with it a sopping wet A.D. "There you all are!"

"Shut the door please, Mr. Dawkins."

Van Brunt's assistant does as his employer requests. I ask, "Is everything situated?"

He mock salutes me. "I found a nice lil' hotel not too far from where we were talking, and paid upfront for a few days. While Sara was getting the lay of the land in her new digs, I nicked her a few pieces of clothing, considering her other one was covered in blood, and some food to tide her over. She's got a nice telly to keep her occupied, and some cash for incidentals." He pauses. "You owe me for that."

So far, Van Brunt has remained mostly silent, listening to what we had to report. But now as I take him in, I find his cultured, elegant veneer close to shattering. His body is trembling in rage, his fists curling tight, his lips nearly white from tension. I cannot help but think this a very, very good thing.

"Ms. Brandon, I want the entire Institute swept and debugged by nightfall. Send an encoded text to each and every agent within these walls to begin searching immediately. All assignments, until this is completed, are on temporary hold starting now. I expect every bug you find to be destroyed save a pair for you to study. I want to know where the signal is originating from. At that point, I expect the Institute's security system to be overhauled so that there are no more leaks." He pulls out his phone and furiously types away at it. Marianne quickly excuses herself to get to work.

Once the door shuts behind her, he continues, "Ms. Lennox, please begin an in-depth search on Gabe Koppenberg. I want to know everything about this newly discovered alias of Pfeifer's, including the address in Brooklyn mentioned to Ms. Reeve. From here on out, it is best we keep Mrs. Carrisford out of the loop unless absolutely necessary." He pauses, still beating against his cell phone with his thumbs. "I also expect an address for this John and Paul School in Connecticut within the hour."

"I'll try my best," Mary says.

He looks up from the screen, his bright blue eyes darkening with cold fury. "I cannot accept efforts right now, Ms. Lennox. From here on out, we must simply *do.* The stakes are too high now for anything else." To me, he says, "The Librarian is currently looking into what might be ailing my son. She—"

"I do not trust her."

The other agents in the room all stare at me, agog, but all I can think is: *There. I've said it.*

"I can assure you that—"

"You can assure me nothing. You do not even know her given name."

He surprises me—no, all of us present—by saying, "There you are wrong, Ms. Reeve. I have always known her name."

Mary and the A.D. immediately, voraciously press for its reveal, but Van Brunt's attention remains on me.

He knows, yet will not tell us.

"As I said," he continues, his fingers still flying across the glass of the cell phone, "she will be researching into what might be behind this ailment while we go to Connecticut to search for answers of our own."

I ask mildly, "We?"

He does not bother looking up. "Mr. Dawkins, your expertise will also be required. I have sent a list of items we will be bringing; please go and fetch them immediately. As for you, Ms. Reeve, I naturally assumed you'd want to go with."

He assumed correctly.

The A.D. yanks out his phone before spinning on his heel. Once the door is behind him, Van Brunt says, "Any and all question once we depart will go through Victor."

Mary is surprised. "Do you think that wise? He'd been off his protocol for days."

"He will, as always, rise to the occasion, Ms. Lennox. I would think that you of all people would know this about him."

She sucks in a deep breath, blowing it out from between her lips. "I'll have that address for you shortly."

He nods, and then she departs, as well. Grymsdyke stays behind, once more ascending to his massive web in the corner of the room.

"You ought to know that I will not be gentle in my quest to find Pfeifer and to undo what has been done to Finn."

"I would never wish you to, Ms. Reeve." His phone beeps continually beneath his fingers. "But I suppose that is one of the prices one must pay during war."

I am no longer simply Alice.

"I wish for us to bring the truth serum along to this school in Connecticut. If necessary, I will utilize it against a child."

He nods gravely. "I already sent word to Victor to have him ready some for Mr. Dawkins." And then, more softly, "Before we depart, there is something I must share with you. Something that I feel is important for us to keep in mind as we search for these ever-alarming truths." He motions to the chair on the right side of Finn's bed before bringing the other round. A minute of silence fills the space between us as he types away on his phone.

And then, he holds it out to me, the screen facing upward.

"Do you remember the child you found in your apartment? The one," he turns to motion toward Grymsdyke, "he poisoned?"

I take the phone from him, bringing the picture up to eye level. Before me is a document marked CLASSIFIED across the top. "Of course. She appeared to desire my crown."

"The child's blood was foul," Grymsdyke adds. "It tasted old."

"It's funny you mention that," Van Brunt murmurs to the spider. And then, to me, "It was decided that it would be best if an autopsy was performed upon the body. While we knew the cause of death, there was much . . . curiosity, if you will, over a girl in a red cloak who appeared to have the ability to lull others in a trance with a set of pipes."

I scan the document in my hands. There is a name of Jane Doe, a listing of weight and height alongside color of hair. A smattering of distinguishing marks upon her body are listed, including freckles, moles, and an oddly shaped birthmark shaped like a rat upon her left shoulder. A quick swipe of screen shows the mark, alongside a ruler that shows the entire thing to be less than half an inch long and tall altogether. Her teeth, according to the report, were in terrible shape: worn, filled with cavities, more rotting than not. Another quick swipe of screen shows a close up of the blackened shards littering her mouth.

But those were not the most interesting characteristics of the girl. No, what immediately draws my attention is the notation on how one eye is brown, whilst the other is entirely black. A photo with both eyes opened is attached to the document, and when I stare down into the blackened one, a chill waltzes up my spine.

It is nearly identical to what Finn's appears like: flat, dead, lifeless.

I quickly scan to see if there is a record of a pattern other than the rat marking on her body, but there is none. But there is still a pair of surprises left for me, on the last page of the report, starting with the presence of lesions riddling her brain and ending with the impossible.

Age, based on appearance, height, weight, and maturity of sexual organs, is estimated at eleven years, give or take one or two on either side. However, analysis of teeth and bones puts Jane Doe at approximately 731 years of age. Additional testing is needed.

My eyes fly up to meet Van Brunt's.

"Once the initial autopsy was finished, samples were sent to seven different coroners in seven different Timelines. No other information was given other than a request for age determination. Each follow-up report corroborated the initial findings."

"Why is this the first I'm hearing of it?"

He strokes his beard. "Because it wasn't until just this morning did I receive the last of the test results."

I swipe the screen until I reach the full-body photograph of the girl. She looks exactly as a young girl would. Baby fat still rounds her cheeks. Bruises litter her knees and legs like any other young, active child's. Her hair is stringy and matted, her nose small and pert. Her body is still that of a youth's, with only the barest signs of puberty.

"How can this be?"

"That is a question I would very much like to find the answer to," Finn's father says.

I return the phone, leaning forward in the chair. "That Pan-child, the one who stabbed Finn . . . His teeth are similar to this girl's. As are Todd's, with Rosemary's at a lesser degree."

"It is very interesting coincidence, is it not?"

Todd and Rosemary both confirmed that they originated from 1846/47RYM/PEC-SP. But at the same time, Rosemary told me herself, under influence of truth serum, the earliest memory she could recall placed her at eight years of age.

She and Todd, associates of Lygari, were recruited as children— teenagers, but still. Pan is a child. This girl in the red cloak is a child.

Lygari, as Koppenberg, is (or was) a benefactor at a school full of children.

Coincidences, the Caterpillar used to tell me, *are never really co-incidental at all.*

"How long will it take us to reach this Connecticut?"

"It depends on where in the state this school is, of course, but I would estimate a few hours in a car." He also leans forward. "A few hours is not what we have, though. Mr. Dawkins will fly us in to whatever location it is Ms. Lennox determines we must go; from there, we will obtain a car." Now he stands. "Before then, though, there is one more vital piece of information you must hear that comes from the Librarian's research. I myself only heard it shortly before you returned from interrogating Mrs. Carrisford."

"Grymsdyke, I would ask you to stay."

The web quivers as the spider bows. "As you wish, Your Majesty."

Van Brunt opens the door; standing outside is another agent, ready to take my place at Finn's side. "Tick-tock, Ms. Reeve."

Tick-tock, indeed.

THE TRUTH REVEALED

ALICE

THE INSTITUTE'S CONFERENCE ROOM stands empty. We
meet instead within the Librarian's domain, deep below the basement in the Museum, as Sara claimed it was free of her bugs.
Metal folding chairs have been shoved within the tiny office, and with
Mary and the A.D. clicking away frantically on their laptops, the space
seems even more claustrophobic than ever. There are only a handful of us down here, though; the rest of the agents within the Society
are scouring the floors above for Sara's bugs alongside Marianne, although they have all been outfitted with earpieces that allow them to
hear what is being said without the surveillance being able to overhear.

Van Brunt wants the entire Society on the same page, and for this
I am glad.

I cannot see the majority's faces while he flatly yet concisely lays out what Sara related to the A.D. and myself, but there is no doubt shock reverberating within the Society. Mary herself is enraged at Sara's duplicity, despite the circumstances; Victor nearly equally so as he mutters angrily beneath his breath. As Van Brunt talks, though, I stare down at the polished table of rock and quartz before me. Copies of *Children's and Household Tales, One Thousand and One Nights, Fairy Tales for Children. First Edition, Norwegian Folktales,* two volumes entitled *Duetsche Sagen,* and *Mother Goose Tales* are spread out across the glassy surface alongside a number of file folders. I pick up one of the books just before Van Brunt concludes with, "This corroboration, along with research the Librarian has conducted, leaves no doubt in my mind over the identity of the man we now hunt."

Well, now. He certainly has my attention. Or rather, the Librarian does, because she says, "Alice, you must wear special gloves to hold that book. It's a first edition."

I try not to roll my eyes when she passes me a pair sitting on her desk.

As I slip them on, she continues. "As many of you know, our active field agents have had little to no contact with any Timelines that directly associate with fairy tales. For one, most of these Timelines are associated with multiple stories—some dozens, some even hundreds—and almost all have some kind of magic within, making catalyst identification and retrieval difficult at best. Not too many of us are so willing to go up against clever witches, sorcerers, giants, genies, or the like, are we?"

A quiet tittering fills the room.

"Furthermore, a number of tales associated with the collected tomes of fairy tales are told in other places, leaving the question of whether or not they truly belong to singular Timelines or in fact have roots within many. A story can have its origins hundreds of years earlier but will have found popularity within a collection of a later date. Or a story can be featured in not one, but two or more famous collections. Which Timeline do we then search? Are they connected somehow?" She shrugs, her dark hair tumbling about her shoulders.

"I'll admit we never concerned ourselves much with locating catalysts from these sorts of stories. There was no evidence that any were in danger. Not once in all the years we've hunted our culprits has a single collection of fairy tales been deleted, at least to our knowledge. And none appeared on the wall in the Ex Libris bookstore that revealed targets."

I glance down at the book in my hands, nearly afraid to open it, it appears so fragile. Finn had asked me about fairy tales before, hadn't he? I'd told him I'd never given these much credence. My parents, scholars who preferred the classics, shied away from providing such books to my siblings and me. I've read many a Wonderlandian fairy tale and enjoyed them immensely, though, but I do not think they are quite the same as what the Librarian now talks about.

"It now appears to be for good reason," she is saying, "for I am certain that this Gabriel Lygari, or Pfeifer, or Koppenberg is, himself, from a fairy tale."

The A.D. head snaps up sharply from where it'd been hovering over his computer. "Like . . . Cinderella? Or Snow White? Or one of the princes?"

The Librarian's smile is faint yet tight. "You are thinking of heroes and heroines, Jack. I meant more along the lines of a fairy tale villain. The Pied Piper of Hamelin, to be precise."

Piper.

Pfeifer is German for piper. Lygari means liar in Icelandic. *A lying piper.*

"His story, though, is a difficult one to pin down." She walks the scant distance over to the table. "It is featured in 1816/18GRIM-GT," she picks up the pair of volumes titled *Duetsche Sagen* and holds them aloft, "and received great popularity there, as with many other fairy tales made famous by the Grimm brothers, but it is also found in much earlier texts, dating all the way back, if rumors are correct, to the fourteenth- and fifteenth-century. And even then, there are tales of how his story was told in stained glass dating back to circa 1300, except that window has long since been destroyed. His true name is not known, except that he is universally referred to as the Piper."

And then she tells us a story.

A long time ago, Hamelin, a town in Germany, was plagued by a terrible rodent infestation. They contracted the services of a man who promised he could, for a fee, rid them of their problems. Pipes in hand, music floating through the town, he led the entirety of the town's dazed rats to a nearby river and drowned them all. When it came time for Hamelin to uphold its end of the bargain and pay for services rendered, they reneged. Angered, the Piper then used his magical pipes to lure the townsfolk's children away, never to be seen again.

A stone drops into the pit of my stomach as I listen to her tale. Puzzle pieces slide into place.

I set the book down and strip the gloves off. "What happened to the children he kidnapped?"

"No one knows." Not a trace of familiar amusement is to be found on her lovely face. "Some versions claim he drowned them as he did the rats. Others say he led them to a mountain and hid them away in it."

My fingers beat against my knee, I'm so agitated. "What mountain? Where did this story take place?"

She's uncharacteristically serious as she regards me. "Hamelin is a German city, now called Hameln, and that piece of the tale has never wavered amongst the various versions. As for the mountain . . ." She shrugs. "Some scholars believe it could be Koppelberg Hill. Or Koppenberg Mountain. Or perhaps the forests of Coppenbrügge, or even Poppenberg Mountain. Interestingly enough, there is a Koppenberg Mountain here, but it is a hill, and located in Belgium, nearly three hundred miles away."

Koppenberg.

The A.D. and I exchange startled yet wary glances. At the same time, Mary snaps her fingers. "When Victor interrogated Todd, he claimed his contact's names changed. He said those words, those names: *Koppenberg. Koppelberg.* And . . . and . . ." She smacks her forehead with a palm. "Bunting! Todd also used Bunting!"

The Librarian smiles, as if Mary was in the middle of an exam and spouted the correct answer. "Bunting is occasionally mentioned as the name of the Piper in some of the tales. It refers to his clothes, as does *pied.*"

The A.D. flips his computer screen around for us to see. "You're never going to believe this, but . . . remember that lady that attacked Alice and Mary at the library?"

"You say that as if it were forever ago," Mary says. "It was just yesterday."

He ignores her pointed remark. "Her name was Jenn Ammer."

Mary waves a hand, as if she's hurrying him along. "Believe me, we already know that."

"But did you know that, just like Pfeifer is German, Ammer is, too? It means . . ." He pauses dramatically. "Bunting. Or at least it does according to this search engine's translator."

It all comes back to the legend, doesn't it? To him. To the Piper of Hamelin.

"Don't you speak German?" Mary asks the A.D.

"Yes, but it's not like I learned the word for bunting, you know. Who talks about bunting nowadays?"

I turn to the Librarian. "How many children?"

She glances away from the bickering pair, back to me and my harshly voiced question. When she does not readily answer, I ask once more, "How many children is he said to have stolen?"

Sadness reflects in her blue eyes. "The accounts vary, of course, but it is somewhere around one hundred and thirty."

One hundred and thirty children missing, stolen by a man with magical pipes, over seven hundred years ago, if one takes into account a destroyed stained glass window.

A child, one thought to be impossibly 731 years old, was found dead in my flat.

"Why Gabriel—or Gabe?" Victor is asking. He's jumpy, as if he can barely hold himself still. "Is there any reference to that name in all of these fairy tales and legends?"

She shakes her head. "Not that I can find. I do not know why that is the commonality in all the aliases he uses. I wish I could tell you all what Timeline you could hunt him in, but I cannot. I can provide you with a list of all the texts he's mentioned in, though. We must pray that they are enough."

"He's using them." My fingers twist tightly in the cotton of the Victorian dress I still wear as I offer this firm assurance. "He's using the children he stole. He's transformed them, somehow. Enchanted them to become his minions. Those children we saw on the surveillance video are the same he'd stolen all those years ago, or at least some of them are. Who knows if he's kidnapped others?"

Bleakness fills the room as the wheels in my head spin at frightening rates. We've been so blind. So very, very blind.

I turn to Van Brunt. "The teeth—they're all the same. What if Todd and Rosemary are not who they think they are, but two of these children now grown? Rosemary claimed she could not remember anything prior to her eighth year. We know that the tales told within books, while subject to interpretation, have events that are unchangeable. Sweeney Todd died in *String of Pearls.* So did Mrs. Lovett. What if these two were made to *believe* they were people they were not? What if they were actively encouraged to become like characters from other stories?"

"Like an army." Victor smacks his hands together, eyes gleaming. "His own army of storybook villains. My God, it's a terrifying thought. The list of villains is endless!"

"What kind of magic does he possess?" I ask the Librarian. "What do the tales you've read say?"

"There is no clarification beyond his ability to mesmerize people and animals alike with his music."

Mary reaches over and settles one of Victor's bouncing knees with a hand. "Which he's doing. He did it to Alice and me, although I was mostly unconscious for that bit. All of the surveillance footage shows the children using pipes." She snaps her fingers twice, then thrice. "Oh! Oh! Pan was playing pipes whenever he visited Wendy—or so we assume, based on the footage we have."

"Meaning the boy we thought to be Peter Pan may not be Pan at all!" Victor's voice is unnaturally loud. "What if he was just another one of Hamelin's children, created to be a character from a different fairy tale?"

Mary flies out of her seat, her laptop clattering down onto the metal chair. "He could fly, though! Like the real Pan, only I'm positive Victor is right. I'd bet every last penny I have that he isn't the true Peter Pan. So that means Pfeifer's magic must be more than just pure brainwashing."

Stories, the Librarian and Finn have always told me, are open to interpretation. Mine, for example, was much darker and complex than the children's tale those nowadays see it as. There were no chessboard pieces, there was no silliness.

Pfeifer's story must be much more, too.

"The girl in my room." I round on Van Brunt. "She wore a red cloak. Could she—"

The A.D., Mary, and Victor burst out in unison, "Little Red Riding Hood!"

Well, now. Isn't that a fitting name for the girl? "Did you know this?" I ask Van Brunt.

He strokes his short, dark beard thoughtfully. "It was certainly my first thought when I saw her."

Chances are, though, she was not this Little Red Riding Hood, though. Just as Todd and Rosemary are most likely not the real Sweeney Todd and Mrs. Lovett.

"What about Jenn Ammer?" Mary asks. "Could she possibly believe she is a fairy tale person?"

"We have yet to get proper access to her at the police station," Van Brunt says. "A pit bull of a lawyer appeared, shutting us down. But once we do, we will certainly find the answer to that question." He clears his throat. "We must entertain the notion that he is training them in whatever magical arts he possesses, whether it be through enchanted pipes or true ability. It will be critical for us to study the footage even further and see if we can determine any other assumed characters these children may be. And that, of course, is if they have actually been convinced they are those who they are not. For all we know, there still may be some who have maintained their original persona."

"There were not a hundred and thirty children in the footage," I say. "Not even close. A dozen, perhaps."

Victor's knees are bouncing rapidly, he is so agitated. "Sweeney Todd was known for his blade work; the Todd that we knew was equally adept. The boy we assumed was Pan can fly. I don't think this is a one-stop shop when it comes to training. It looks as if Pfeifer is tailoring each child to specific gifts."

"To do specific parts of his bidding." Mary swears quietly. "Jenn Ammer was, believe it or not, pretty handy with a gun. She was a guardian of sorts, protecting whatever work he was doing at the library."

It's unbearably rude, but I cut off Van Brunt's burgeoning comment to ask, "Victor, what do you mean Todd *was* adept at blade work?"

All eyes turn to him.

He scratches at the back of his neck, eyes darting from side to side. "The dead don't wield weapons, do they?" When quiet shock is his response, he adds fiercely, "Finn killed the bastard after he edited into Sara's Timeline. It's how we got there, actually, considering we didn't have a pen amongst us. We followed him before the door closed, ending up in some alley. Finn shot a bullet right between his eyes. By the time he was done, there was no way Todd was ever going to use his knives on another person, let alone destroy another catalysts."

Mary holds her hands together, staring upward. "Thank God."

Pride fills my bloodthirsty heart.

Van Brunt, though, is silent for a long moment as he stares at his son.

"We knew you wanted to be there." Victor is much more subdued and yet still clearly frantic. "When it was done, but . . . We couldn't risk letting him get away again. Not after what he did to Mom."

"Did he suffer?"

I must admit, it's not the question I thought Van Brunt would ask. Nor would I have guessed there would be so much savage hope in such a request.

Victor's grin is just as savage. "Three shots preceded the one right between his eyes. For good measure, Finn placed one in the bastard's heart, too." The grin curls wickedly. "I might have gotten a shot in afterward, too."

"Did you shoot his dick off, love? Like you'd always said you'd do?" Mary asks.

Across the room, the A.D. cringes, his hand instinctively moving between his legs.

"Yes." The doctor's eyes gleam nearly sadistically, he is so pleased with this confirmation. "I sure as hell did."

"Good," she says. And then, more fervently, "He deserved that and more."

A long moment passes before anyone else speaks. Van Brunt merely folds his hands, draping them over his knees, as his head lowers. Soon enough, though, the emotion he's so desperate to contain disappears and the man who is always in control returns.

"Do you know what this means? We've been going about this all wrong." Victor's out of his chair, attempting to pace between the slim strips of spaces between where we all sit. A finger juts my way. "The sword wasn't Neverlandian, not if that isn't the real Peter Pan. It would be something of the Piper's—something fairy tale-ish."

That bit of news makes me much less happy than it does him. My eyes fall to the pile of books before me. Each tome has multiple stories. There must be hundreds of characters, hundreds of locations.

We don't even know which Timeline to begin in.

The urge to pluck at my hairs is strong once more. *Tick-tock, tick-tock.* Finn is upstairs, fighting for his life. The Piper is out there somewhere, with his murderous horde of enchanted children who very well might die for his cause. We have no idea what they are capable of, where all they wait.

I have seen magic before. Wielded it myself once or twice, although in greatly reduced capacities than what fairy tales spin. I have seen the beauty it can produce and the devastation it can leave in its wake. Magic demands respect. At times, the payment for such can be crippling.

And still, I am ready to face it head-on and pay whatever I must if to do so brings answers and justice.

"Were you able to locate the school?" I ask Mary.

She looks away from a muttering and pacing Victor. "I believe I have. It's a two-and-a-half hour drive from here. It's rural and quite small for being a school that goes from elementary-aged children all the way through high school." Her fingers clack away as she peers down at her laptop. "It's also quite new, just shy of a decade. The Headmistress is named Grethel . . ." She looks up, eyes narrowing. "Bunting."

Jenn Ammer and now Grethel Bunting. What are the chances?

"Grethel sounds quite a bit like Gretel," the A.D. muses.

"Who is this Gretel?" I ask. "Is she from one of these books?"

"They're two different people." Victor tugs at his dark strands. "I remember the name. My mother used to read the Grimm stories to Finn and I, despite us believing we were too old for such tales. We listened, though. It's not the same girl from the Hansel and Gretel story."

A glimmer of pain shines in Van Brunt's eyes at the mention of his late wife, especially in light of recent news.

Victor snatches *Children's and Household Tales* off the table, ignoring the Librarian's pleading for a pair of white gloves. "There was one that had a cook named Grethel. She . . ." He flips through the brittle pages. "If I'm not mistaken, she was greedy and ate a meal that was supposed to be for a guest. Not wanting to get caught, she told the guest that her master wanted to kill him, and then when he fled, she informed her employer that the guest stole the food. In the end, the master chased after the guest with a knife." He forcefully taps on the book. "Yes, here it is! The story is called *The Clever Grethel*."

"Clever?" The A.D. snorts. "More like sadistic."

Mary's laugh is ugly. "That's rich, coming from you."

"I am a thief," he says coolly. "And even thieves have codes. I never set out to have anyone murdered now, have I?"

The Librarian deftly eases the book from Victor's grip, carefully checking the pages for damage.

Mary, though, is rolling her eyes at the A.D.'s comments. "In any case, the question now is: is the original Grethel working with the Piper, if he is, in fact, associated with the school, or is it yet another child he's manipulated? Thanks to Todd and Rosemary, we now know that he's apparently allowed some of the children to age, so we must entertain that possibility."

"I suppose we shall find the answer to that question sooner rather than later," Van Brunt says. "Ms. Reeve, Mr. Dawkins, and I will be heading to this John and Paul school shortly. Until our return, I expect the Institute's security reestablished, with frequent scans to ensure we have no more holes. From here on out, if we are to gain any foothold, we must not allow any more mistakes." He stands up, smoothing his sleek coat. "Ms. Lennox, I expect the report on the Koppenberg alias sent to me the moment you have it done."

"Another note." The Librarian sets the book down. "The day the Piper stole the children of Hamelin was June Twenty-Sixth, otherwise known as the day of Saints John and Paul."

Well, now. Yet another confirmation.

"All assignments have been sent out." Brom nods at the Librarian. "As of this moment, our searches for catalysts are put on hold. We must focus our attention and energies on neutralizing the Piper and his compatriots. Make no mistake. These are not children, if we are indeed correct in our assumptions. Anyone who has lived seven centuries, whether it be in a child's body or an adult's, will have a leg up on us in terms of knowledge and experience. We cannot allow our guard to lower around them."

"Do you think it possible that they could be . . ." The A.D. offers a light shrug. "Deprogramed, or the like?"

"As right now we are only guessing at their true identities, there is no way to answer that," the Librarian offers smoothly. But when her eyes meet mine, I see more than she admits.

Someday, she and I will sit down and have a nice, long talk about secrets and truths. But for now, while everyone stands up and readies themselves for their assignments, we will start small. I make my way over to her. "Do you know more about Finn's condition than you've let on?"

Her eyes flick over toward where Van Brunt stands with the A.D. and Victor. "I wish in this circumstance I did." She reaches out to gently touch my shoulder. "You must be careful, Alice. The road ahead of you is not easy by any means."

I've long learned that it never is.

JOHN AND PAUL

ALICE

T HE HELICOPTER RIDE TO Connecticut was surprisingly yet pleasantly short, although I would not term the actual journey as anything close to enjoyable. I attempted to use the time to sleep, but once the weather changed mid-flight, the turbulence (so-called by the A.D.) left my stomach jumping far more than the contraption I was in. Thankfully, a car was waiting for us once we landed, especially now that the heavens have opened up, spilling tiny, white flakes.

Frabjous. More snow.

The drive to John and Paul School for Gifted Children is also short, and as we wind our way up the road leading to the school, I cannot help but feel as if we've stepped back in time. Dense forests with trees like skeletons loom all around us, and with the piles of snow littering the ground, it appears as if silence has swallowed the country-side whole. At the top of the drive sits a large, foreboding gothic build-ing partially covered in ivy, complete with a pair of peaked towers on either side of the entrance.

As we pull up, the A.D. exclaims from the backseat, "How much do you want to bet that place is haunted?"

I'm afraid I must concur with his assessment. If there ever were to be a building home to spirits, this would be it.

"I'm still not sure this is the wisest course of action," I say to Van Brunt.

The Society's leader parks next to a lone rusted red truck. "Sche-matics of the region show very little covert accessibility." His smile is faint. "Hiking several miles in the snow when a storm is coming in is just not a feasible option right now. We'll start with the Headmistress and go from there."

I grudgingly must admit I am no fan of trudging through snow-storms. Nonetheless, the idea of going back up in a helicopter in such conditions leaves me even more unsettled, as flying through the air is still foreign to me.

The A.D. leans forward, clapping a hand on Van Brunt's shoulder. "I never thought I'd see this day, boss man. Abraham Van Brunt, with-out a proper plan?" A low whistle fills the car.

Van Brunt chooses to ignore this by exiting into the cold air, in-stead.

When we approach to the massive set of doors in front of us, my breath stills within my chest. Carved upon these ornate doors are im-ages eerily similar to those found guarding Bücherei, ones depicting gruesome situations: wolves eating little girls, witches and dragons, coffins, and birds pecking out eyes.

"Bloody hell," the A.D. mutters. "Are they trying to welcome children or scare them to death?"

"This is our confirmation of an association with Lygari/Pfeifer." I stare up at the images. "Those protecting the library at Bücherei were similar."

Van Brunt quietly orders the A.D. to take photographs. As soon as he snaps a few, the doors creak open. Before us is an elderly man, his gaunt, pockmarked face lined by years and his hair wild and gray. His small eyes are sharp, though, narrowing in on us immediately. "What do you want?"

Well, how do you do to you, too? I do my best not to rise to his surliness.

"My wife and I are looking at different schools in the region for our child." Van Brunt wraps an arm around my shoulders. "We hoped to check this fine institution out as a possible candidate."

If anything, the old man's eyes narrow even further as he glances around us toward the rental car. "In this weather?"

"I'm afraid my work schedule does not permit me much time to look." A rueful chuckle falls out of Van Brunt, and I silently marvel at how charming he has suddenly become. "Is there someone we might converse with about the school?"

"No." The doors swing to close, but I thrust out a staying hand.

"Please, sir." I lower my voice, color it with sadness. "We only want what is best for our child. A few minutes are all we ask for."

His eyes now turn to the A.D. "Your *child* is too old for this institution, or perhaps stupid. Either way, we don't accept his kind."

Van Brunt and I both release forced, startled laughs whilst the A.D.'s cheeks color in indignation. "Oh, this is my husband's secretary." I offer a winsome smile. "He is here with us to take notes."

"Mr. Pfriem?" a feminine voice calls out from within the school. "Is there a problem?"

He scowls but steps to the side. "There are some people here wanting to tour the grounds."

A handsome woman of about fifty appears, dressed in all gray to match the building. "In this weather?"

Pfriem scowls. "I said as much, didn't I?"

There are a whole host of things I'd like to say to the both of them.

The woman's head falls to the side as she regards us. "I'm afraid our office hours have ended, and without an appointment—"

"We won't take much of your time." Van Brunt's smile nearly dazzles even me. "I apologize for the lack of prior notice, but it would mean a lot to my wife and I if we could speak with you."

A loud, irritable sigh bursts from her nose, but after a tense moment, she steps to the side. "Very well. Mr. Pfriem, please bring a pot of tea to my office for our visitors."

When he walks away, he does nothing to disguise his prickly, pointed mutterings.

There is no chitchat as we make our way to the woman's office, just edgy silence punctuated by feet against creaky, polished, wooden floors. The walls are unadorned and painted a dreary green, the sconces on the wall antique to even my sensibilities. Every door we pass is shut, with no windows to peer inside. It is unnaturally silent in these halls.

Where are the children? There are no signs of them anywhere. No art on the walls, no signs for grammar or even behavior, no sounds, no anything to indicate that this is a school.

The door marked HEADMISTRESS is also shut, requiring the woman to extract a massive key ring dangling from her belt. A bronze old-fashioned skeleton key is selected, and the sound it makes as it unlocks the door is frightfully loud in such a quiet hallway.

"Well, you might as well have a seat." Her voice is deceptively light despite these rude first words. "Although one of you will have to stand, as there are only two chairs."

The office is quite large yet fairly empty. A singular desk, a total of three chairs, and a filing cabinet are all that inhabit the room. There are no pictures on the walls or desk. In fact, there is nothing upon the oak desk sitting in the middle of the room—no telephone, no computer, no paper, no name plaque, no pens or pencils.

She rounds the desk as Van Brunt and I sit down upon stiff, unyielding chairs set quite a distance from the desk. The A.D. hovers behind us, a pad of paper and a pen now in his hands.

He plays his role surprisingly well.

The woman before us folds her hands neatly upon the gleaming wood before her. "My name is Miss Bunting."

Lygari's associates do not possess even a hint of their employer's charisma, of that I am certain. She makes no offers to take our snow-covered coats, nor does she offer any further pleasantries.

"My name is André Irving," Van Brunt says. "This is my wife, Lo-rina." He pulls a calling card from the inside pocket of his suit coat and passes it to the A.D., who then slips it upon the desk. I am impressed to find the assumed name he has just offered written neatly upon it, alongside the designation *Financial Analyst.* "As we were explaining to Mr. Pfriem, we are currently searching for the perfect school for our child. We—"

Miss Bunting does not bother looking at Van Brunt's card. "Our enrollment is quite limited, and the acceptance process rigorous. We cater to a very specific type of pupil here."

"Which is exactly what we're looking for." I lean forward in my chair. "One must be careful in ensuing the proper placement for a child's education and welfare."

Before she can answer, Van Brunt asks, "How many children are enrolled at John and Paul?"

One of her pinky fingers taps against the desk. "Policy dictates that I cannot disclose information about our population."

Insufferable woman. "Surely sharing how many pupils you have isn't the same as a breach of confidentiality," I say.

Behind me, the A.D. snorts quietly.

Her lips thin as she first regards him and then me. "The safety of my wards is of highest concern."

"Of course." Van Brunt offers yet another winsome smile. "We read online that yours is a school for gifted—"

"We do not have a website."

I can practically feel the heat of Van Brunt's annoyance from where I sit. Miss Bunting is no doubt saved from his sharp tongue by a knock on the door.

Her eyes shift back to the A.D. "Open that, boy."

I must give him credit for keeping his mouth firmly shut and do-ing as she asks. Pfriem comes in with a small silver tray loaded with a teapot and four plain white cups. There are no biscuits, no sugar or milk. He drops it unceremoniously upon the desk, clattering the china and spilling a bit of the tea. "Is there anything else I can do for you, *ma'am?"*

Miss Bunting is either oblivious to his sneering or as unimpressed as I am. "Begin making the rounds."

When he leaves, it's as before with a number of strongly worded opinions not hidden well beneath his breath.

Miss Bunting does not pour the tea nor does she offer us any. Instead, she calmly opens a drawer in her desk and removes a small set of pipes. One that appears eerily familiar to those used when the Institute was breeched.

I am out of my chair in an instant, across the room before she can ever place the pipes to lips. She clambers out of her chair, back to where she thinks she has safety.

"You do not want to do that," I warn.

Apparently she does, because a single note is played before I send both Bunting and the pipes sprawling with a kick to her chest. Thankfully, she does not hit the wall and thereby rouse interest.

"Get the pipes," Van Brunt orders the A.D.

She's a quick thing, because she's on her feet nearly immediately. Bunting growls at me—growls!—, her teeth bared as she charges. Hands out, her long nails pointed toward me like claws, she no longer holds any semblance of propriety. The light in her eyes is all too similar to the crazed sheen of Rosemary's. Growling transitions to hissing.

I cannot allow the ruckus of a brawl to alert anyone of our change in situations. Besides, we're not here to spar. There are questions that must be answered. So when she closes in on me, hands desperate for my neck, I quickly spin and snap back her arms so she is in front of me. Van Brunt wastes no time at the opportunity I've provided. A hypodermic needle is removed from his inner coat pocket as he advances on us.

I head butt the back of Bunting's skull just as she opens her mouth to scream.

"None of that." I twist her arms until I know she must be in agony. "Be a good lady and keep your mouth shut."

Like a wild beast, she lashes in my arms, growling and spitting and hissing. I'm forced to yank us both to the ground so I can wrap my legs around hers, effectively restraining her from any ability to strike out at Van Brunt. I twist us until we're on our sides, so that my head can pin hers down in just such a way shouting is not easy for her. Thankfully, he's able to inject the serum into her fairly quickly. Bunting's struggle against my hold continues for a good minute before she's twitching beneath my body.

I haul her up and slam her into the chair. What the A.D. calls zip ties are taken from his satchel and passed over. Arms and legs are both restrained.

She slurs, "Bitch."

Van Brunt grabs hold of his cell phone and switches on the record function. "What is your name?" There is no longer any agreeableness in his tone nor his words.

She sloppily licks her lips, hatred shining from shrewd eyes. "Grethel."

"Is your name truly Grethel Bunting?"

Ah. There's the frustration I was expecting. She's now coming to the realization she must answer our questions, isn't she? "It is the name I go by now."

"And before? What name did you go by then?"

"Merely Grethel."

"How many children are present in this building? Or should I be more precise and say how many people who appear as children are present?"

"Twenty."

Twenty out of a possible one hundred and thirty or more.

"Where are they?" Van Brunt asks.

"Upstairs."

"Where *specifically* are they?"

Her words hiss from beneath clenched teeth. "In their dormitories."

Van Brunt leans closer. "What Timeline do you originate from?"

His question surprises her, for her eyes widen. Just as quickly, though, they narrow once more into slits. "1812GRI-CHT."

"Bloody hell," the A.D. whispers.

I refuse to ask in front of her what the designation means, but whatever it is, it's clearly unnerved both Van Brunt and the A.D.

Van Brunt's head angles toward his assistant. "Go and see if you can find any of these children."

"Your wish is my command." The A.D. quietly slips out of the door.

"I find it quite interesting that you were able to term your Timeline as such," Van Brunt says, his voice low yet commanding. "One would think that you've spent time studying such things."

As he did not ask a question, she does not offer a free answer. But if looks could maim, he and I would suffer grievous bodily harm.

"Is Mr. Pfriem also from 1812GRI-CHT?"

She is seething now. "Yes."

"And the children here? Or rather the so-called children? Are they also from 1812GRI-CHT?"

"Yes and no."

"Be more specific, Ms. Bunting. Where do your wards here at John and Paul originate from?"

A loud sigh shoots through her nose. "Some are from 1812GRI-CHT. Others are through the connected Timeline 1816/18GRI-GT."

Through a connected Timeline?

She willingly adds, "You two will pay for this."

"Why is it," I muse, "villains always say such things?"

She hisses, lashing against her ties. "You are a cow!"

How very curious it is that her resistance to the Truth Serum is much stronger than Rosemary's.

I bend down, gripping her chin with my fingers. "What do you know about blades that glow blue?"

Ah. We've surprised her again—and frustrated her, because spittle decorates her full lips as she unwillingly admits, "They are enchanted."

"Who enchants them, and what are they enchanted with?"

Astoundingly, she fights desperately to not answer this question. But eventually, once tears streak down her face and sweat lines her brow, she offers her answer in whispered, broken words. "It depends upon the blade."

"It was wielded by a boy who could fly, one who many assumed was Peter Pan."

Grethel Bunting is shaking, she is so livid with what we've done to her. But she tells me what I want to know after another round questioning and resistance, albeit breathily from her efforts. "The thirteenth Wise Woman enchanted his sword with the gift of transformation."

Van Brunt crosses his arms. "What kind of transformation?"

"The best kind," she sneers. "The kind that blesses a soul to become one of the Chosen."

His genteel veneer evaporates. "Who are the Chosen?"

Another struggle leaves her winded. "The Piper's Disciples."

And here is official confirmation of the fiend's identity. Still, my blood runs cold at such a thought, of Finn being transformed into anything other than what he is.

I will not allow it.

I will not.

"Who are you to the Piper?" he demands.

"One of his lieutenants."

Well, now. What a lovely catch we've made.

Van Brunt asks, "How long does the transformation take from this enchanted sword?"

The sheen in her eyes is sadistically gleeful. It appears she has guessed one of ours has been tainted. "A full day."

And yet, it has been more than two days since Finn was stabbed.

"What does the pattern mean?" Van Brunt asks.

She blinks, the glee transitioning to confusion. "I know of no pattern."

He presses, "The one that develops around the wound."

"It is as I said," she spits. "There is no pattern."

"What are the physical effects then?" I ask.

"Eyes that can see the truth."

I am sorely tempted to shake her silly. "Is there a change in the eyes? Do they change color, and if so, what color?"

"Black!" The chair bounces off the ground with her efforts. "They can turn black!"

"Are you one of the Chosen?"

She hisses, "Yes."

"Yet your eyes are not black. Why is that?"

"I am not in rapture!"

Interesting. "How long until the victim wakes up?"

"You are truly a stupid cow! They wake once the transformation is complete—a full day!"

Honestly, this woman is simply ghastly. But still, fresh hope grows within me. Finn has not yet transformed. He has not woken up. He is not someone else.

Van Brunt's phone beeps from its place on the table. He stares down at it before smacking his hand on the desk. "The weather is turning. We must head back."

Grethel's laugh is terrifyingly wicked sounding.

Finn's father digs into his inner coat pocket once more, extracting a small aerosol can. I step far to the side, covering my nose with a handkerchief from my pocket. He mimics me, also holding a cloth to his nose and mouth, as he sprays the woman in her face.

The fight has left her when Grethel Bunting slumps in her chair, unconscious.

Van Brunt pockets the canister. "What an unpleasant woman."

"Indeed." I poke at the woman to see if she truly sleeps. "Was that SleepMist?"

He studies the silver tube. "I suppose it does come in handy after all."

I pull out a dagger to cut Bunting free from the chair. "What are the chances that the school is bugged?"

"Most likely excellent."

He heads over to the file cabinet, but it is locked. I toss Van Brunt the key ring, and within seconds, he's got it open.

It's empty. There aren't even dust motes within.

A quiet swear escapes Van Brunt's lips. "They can't make this easy for us, can they?"

I rifle through the desk. There are no pens, no pencils, no anything that a headmistress would normally have. There is a gun, though, and a rather wicked-looking knife.

I slip both within my bag.

As Van Brunt reclaims his phone and taps away at the screen, I check the underside of the drawers as well as the backs. There has to be something here. Something to help us. I'm about to turn away when a fingernail snags on a small button just beneath the lip of the desk.

Excellent.

A click sounds beneath the desk. I bend down and find a new drawer has dropped open. In it is a file folder. I hold my breath as I open it . . . only to find it filled with white, empty pages of parchment.

Van Brunt peers over my shoulder. "Take it all anyway."

I add it to the collection in my bag.

A quick peek through the door shows an empty hallway on both sides. Even still, my daggers are out and readied as I push it wide open. Van Brunt hoists Grethel Bunting over a shoulder and then exits the door.

I always imagined him strong and capable, but I am impressed that he is so light and quick on his feet whilst carrying another person.

I have just opened the main doors when the A.D.'s voice fills the hallway. "Go! Go!" A mere split-second later, a different voice louder than life bellows, "INFIDEL!" The sounds of pounding feet and squeaking floorboards follow.

We do not have to be asked more than once. Van Brunt and I hurry to the car. The sky is white, it is snowing so much, and I can't help but worry over how we are to make a quick getaway in such conditions.

A child appears out of seemingly nowhere, his blackened teeth bared as he growls. Barefoot in the snow, his clothes ragged, he charges me as if running on burning coals.

"I'll take care of this," I tell Van Brunt.

The child leaps at me, but I'm quick enough to side step him. He does not sprawl, though—no, the little beast ducks and rolls before springing to his feet. If that weren't bad enough, a girl appears on my other side, also barefoot, her long blonde hair matted. In both hands are sais.

Oh, for goodness sakes. They cannot be more than six, perhaps seven, can they? Am I really to fight children? Or even so-called children?

The slam of the car trunk sounds. "Tick-tock!" shouts Van Brunt. Cheeky bugger.

I use the hilt of one of my daggers to knock out the boy when he charges once more. He falls to the cold ground, limp, just as the girl descends upon me. Snarling like a wild animal, she gnashes those blackened teeth at me as her sais swipe far too close.

She's got a bit of skill, then.

She takes off, running and flipping, the sais whipping fervently as she shouts in a language I do not understand. All of her showmanship is for naught, though, as the moment she is within striking distance, I manage to knock her off balance with a kick. Thankfully, her skill is more demonstrative than useful. When she stumbles, I use the hilts of both daggers in my hands to crash against the base of her skull.

It's utterly sentimental, but I cannot seem to find it in me right now to properly take care of the child as I ought to. Not now, not when I know she has been hypnotized by the Piper—or worse, enchanted.

The girl staggers and then drops onto the ground. She and her comrade will both have nasty headaches, perhaps even concussions when they wake, but they will wake. I snatch the sais from her open hands and sprint to the car. Van Brunt is already inside, switching on the ignition. Within moments, we are backing up and turning toward the road.

"What about the A.D.?" I ask mildly.

"Have no fear, Ms. Reeve."

A gunshot, then another rips apart the silence.

The backdoor is wrenched open, and the A.D. throws himself within. "Are you going soft, boss man? Why are you not further down the road?"

A third gunshot strikes a tree not ten feet from us. I turn around to find Pfriem with a shotgun, surrounded by a dozen or so screaming children.

"It's snowing," Van Brunt says, and then we are off, slush flying from the tires of the car. "That was a messy exit, Mr. Dawkins. Perhaps you are the one going soft."

"I'll admit it wasn't my finest." He smacks the back of my seat. "Just wait until I tell Finn that his father and his girlfriend were pretending to be married." The A.D. chortles. "I can only imagine how well that's going to go over with him."

I say, "How very mature of you," but silently pray that someday very soon, Finn will be able to hear such a story and laugh about it. But first, I must find this Wise Woman.

A fourth, more distant gunshot scatters the snow covering a tree behind us.

Van Brunt simply says, his eyes still on the road before us, "Report."

"It was hard finding the little buggers," the A.D. says. "Old Pfriem was locking them in their rooms, and they are quieter than mice, I tell you. I did manage to locate one, a boy, maybe thirteen or fourteen. Just standing in front of a closed door, unmoving. It was creepy, to be honest. I tried to approach him, see if I could maybe talk, but I didn't even know if the little bugger was breathing."

The car skids before Van Brunt rights it. "Did you take any photographs?"

"I took plenty, boss man. Even of the kid, who didn't bother blinking when the flash went off."

"What color were the child's eyes?" I ask.

"It's funny you should ask that, Your Majesty. They were just as black as Finn's. Also, Pfriem isn't following in that truck of his."

The child was in rapture, then. Rapture for what, though? I turn to Van Brunt. "The fact that Grethel knew nothing of the patterns is troubling."

The car slides to the left, toward a rather large tree, but Van Brunt quickly rights it. "Agreed."

The A.D. asks, "Did you guys find out anything useful from the hag?"

"Indeed we did," Van Brunt says. "And once we get home, we'll know much more. It turns out we've just found ourselves one of the

Piper's lieutenants."

"Is she in the trunk?" From the mirror overhead, I can see the A.D.'s eyes gleaming wickedly. "Please tell me she's in the trunk."

"She's in the trunk," Van Brunt confirms.

His assistant sighs happily. "Why can't all missions be like this?"

FAIRY TALES

ALICE

"**T**ELL ME EVERYTHING YOU know about the Wise Women, specifically the thirteenth."

The Librarian glances up from the book she's reading. "I was wondering when you all would return. I take it your trip was successful?" When I say nothing further, she offers me a seat.

I choose to remain standing. We're in her office in the Museum; I'd chosen to come directly here once we returned whilst Van Brunt and the A.D. situate Grethel in the interrogation room. "I searched for the term on my phone on the way back. There were nearly thirty-two million results, so I must ask you for further clarification."

"It depends on the story, of course."

I slide out my phone and hold it aloft for her to see. Both 1812GRI-

CHT and 1816/18GRI-GT are visible.

"Ah." She tucks a piece of dark hair behind an ear. "Those are collections of fairy tales by the Grimm Brothers. The first one is *Children's and Household Tales,* if I'm not mistaken. And the second is *German Tales.*"

"The Wise Women," I repeat firmly.

She removes a pair of white cotton gloves from a drawer in her desk before standing up and rounding the desk. Still resting upon the polished glass and quartz table are the stacks of fairy tale books from before. She selects the one marked *Kinder- und Hausmärchen* and delicately flips through it. "What do you know of the Grimm's tales?"

"Very little." I pocket my phone and come to stand by her side. "Except that they are fairy tales."

"Many consider them to be the epitome of the genre. Jacob and Wilhelm Grimm made it their mission to collect folktales throughout their lives. This volume," she holds aloft the cover for me to view, "is their crowning glory. In English, it is called *Children's and Household Tales,* although many people today merely refer to it as *Grimm's Fairy Tales.* In this first edition, there are around two hundred and twenty-nine tales, although twenty-nine of those were later removed from future editions." Her face is somber as she glances down at the pages. "With so many tales and so many characters and objects, you can imagine how daunting it is to try to access such a Timeline. That said, these stories have become the basis for many of the so-called fairy tales people embrace in today's world, although most have become watered down from their often violent or gruesome originals."

"Grethel Bunting claimed she was from this Timeline."

This has her pausing. "Did she now?"

I must admit, I'm a bit taken aback that she did not seem to inherently know this. "As soon as the SleepMist wears off, Van Brunt plans to question her further."

"And you are here, inquiring about Wise Women." Her smile is faint. "In most fairy tales, a prince or princess saves their counterpart. How very timely, do you not think?"

"I am not a princess."

"But you are a queen, and that makes you ripe for such a quest. Ah. Here we go, just as I thought. The Wise Women are featured in a tale called *Little Briar-Rose,* otherwise known as *Sleeping Beauty.* And herein lines another problem with our accessing Timelines. This tale is not only one the Grimm's recorded, but a variety of other authors. The earliest known specific version of the *Sleeping Beauty* comes from a man named Charles Perrault, nearly one hundred and twenty years prior, yet even that one has its origins in a medieval tale. And *that* story had its roots from Germanic mythology. It's a muddled mess, really, and terribly difficult to accurately assign a true designation to. In fact, legend says that the Grimm Brothers nearly left *Little Briar-Rose* out of their collection, as it was their policy to do so with French tales, but once they discovered its Germanic ancestor, they chose to include it." Her bright eyes meet mine. "Do you know of the tale?"

"It sounds familiar," I admit, "but I cannot recall the specifics. I assume there was a sleeping woman who was quite beautiful. Probably named Briar-Rose."

She ignores my sarcasm. "In a nutshell, the story tells of a princess who is cursed with enchanted sleep. A prince wakes her with a kiss. Some versions claim it to be specifically true love's kiss."

"Am I to take it that the Wise Women are the ones who cursed this princess?"

"In the Grimms' version, yes. In other versions, they're fairies. And it's not so much the entirety of the Wise Women cursed her, but one who had been excluded from a feast to celebrate the princess' birth. There are thirteen of these women, all gifted with magic. Twelve were invited, as there were only twelve places at the table. The thirteenth—the one you mentioned—felt slighted and decided to take it out on the baby. Luckily, one of the Women had not yet bestowed her blessing, so she was able to alter the terms of the curse and allow the princess a chance to wake under specific conditions from what could have been an eternal sleep."

"She cursed a child over such a slight?"

"Wars throughout the Timelines have been born from less, I'm afraid."

Isn't that the truth—or at least it is in Wonderland. I peer down at the words on the page. They are written in German, typeset in calligraphy. As with Latin, German is yet another language I never seemed to pay too much attention to during lessons as a child. I suppose my tutor would find much satisfaction in my frustration with not being able to effortlessly read the text. If he was here, he would surely say, *"I told you to pay better attention, Alice,"* for while I can read and understand the basics, I would not go as far to claim fluent proficiency.

"If I'm not mistaken," I murmur, "you also said that the Piper was from a Grimm story."

"One of his stories, yes."

I motion to the book in her hands. "This one?"

"I'm afraid not." She shuts the book and sets it carefully back down on the table. "Interestingly enough, while the Pied Piper of Hamelin is an incredibly popular fairy tale, the Grimm Brothers did not include it in their most popular book." She picks up the two books entitled *Deutsche Sagen.* "It's in these."

Deutsche Sagen means . . . *German Tales.* 1816/18GRI-GT refers to such.

"Grethel Bunting claimed that the children at John and Paul were from both 1812GRI-CHT *and* 1816/18GRI-GT. She referred to the latter as a connected Timeline. Do you think this possible?"

If I've surprised the Librarian, she does not allow it to show. "You of all people know that anything is possible, Alice."

"The obvious connection between the two is the authors." I rub at my temples; a dull headache has settled in, perhaps from lack of sleep. "Do you know of any other Timelines connected by authors? Perhaps the Janeites?"

Her head cocks to the side, as if she's amused by my suppositions. "All of the Janeite council members have pens that allow them to edit into each others' worlds. None possess the natural ability to move between Timelines without help, but then, it's a rare ability throughout the worlds."

"My books are connected, though. As are all of Finn's."

"They were part of series that go together, yes."

I motion toward the books in her hands and those on the table. "And these? Are they part of a series?"

"I suppose, in the loosest term, one might say they are, but those found in *German Tales* are typically described as historical legends. Some are even based on historical accounts, including that of the Pied Piper. The brother that spent the most time working on them, Jacob Grimm, considered them to be more scholarly than any found within *Children's and Household Tales.*"

"What do you mean, the Piper's tale is based on historical accounts?"

She waves one hand around her head. "Here. In this world. It is said that many children really went missing from Hamelin, Germany, in the late thirteenth-century." She shrugs lightly. "Then again, an Alice Liddell lived here, too. The fact that something occurred in this world does not prevent it from happening in another."

I want to scream in frustration, it's all so maddening. "Fine. Then what could be the connection between the two series of collections, if not the author? There has to be something that ties them together. Does either share the same story, perhaps, one that's told in both collections?"

She says nothing, but the amusement on her face aggravates me. I ought to have known better, coming to the Librarian, expecting clear answers.

Think, Alice, think.

"What about . . . characters? Are any featured in both collections?"

Her lips twitch a bit higher. "As a matter of fact, there is."

When she adds nothing further, I prompt, my voice tight, "Who is this person or character?"

"Her name varies a bit, especially when in concern to origins found within this world, but the brothers referred to her as either Mother Hulda or Holle."

Why must one have to pull each morsel of information out of this woman? "What kind of person was she?"

"A magical one, as is expected within such tales."

It is not much information to go on, but finally. A connection is made. "How many tales are in these *German Legends?*"

"Well over five hundred."

Between the two collections, that makes nearly eight hundred. The Grimm's fairy tale world must be enormous, and chances are, the Piper could be anywhere within them—or any Timeline, really.

Then again, there is much to be said about Pliny the Elder's old saying: *Home is where the heart is.*

I have nothing to base it on but intuition, but it seems only reasonable to assume The Piper might be hiding within this immense, complex world the Grimm Brothers wrote about. Not only is the villain I hunt most likely there, so are the Wise Women. The Librarian said that while the thirteenth cursed a child, the twelfth was able to lessen the severity. If the thirteenth Wise Woman cursed the sword that cut Finn's flesh, I must go see her.

"Alice, a word of caution."

I look up to find the Librarian carefully stripping her white gloves off. "Only one?"

My thinly veiled sarcasm only seems to entertain her. "It ought to be noted that the stories found within the Grimm collections are . . ." She taps on her chin. "Well, let us call them dark. While happy endings occasionally come to pass, so do gruesome ones. Children are eaten by animals, eyes are pecked out by birds, queens die by dancing with hot iron shoes upon their feet. Good often trumps evil, but that does not mean evil is always thoroughly dispatched. Intent makes all the difference."

I take a long, measured breath as I study this enigma of a woman. Then I ask, clearly, slowly, "Are you from one of the Grimm's stories?"

She laughs delightedly. "You are a curious little thing, aren't you? But I fear I must disappoint you. I have never been to any Timelines associated with the Grimm Brothers."

"Someday," I say, "you will tell me where you are from, and who you really are."

"Today," she responds lightly, "is not that day. Now, you have much work and planning ahead of you, and I have much research to delve into." She turns away, back toward a bookshelf next to her desk. "Try not to anger the Wise Women, will you? Sometimes you can be a bit . . . prickly."

I suppose it would be unbearably rude to throw one of her books at her head, wouldn't it?

I have just crossed the threshold of the office when she calls out. "Oh, and Alice? Remember who you are at all times."

I walk away without another word.

Once I make my way through the myriad of security mazes and measures and am back upstairs, I immediately head to the interrogation room. Inside, I find Van Brunt and Mary situating a still-sleeping Grethel Bunting into a chair.

"She'll wake up with the worst crick in the neck," Mary says cheerfully as she straps the woman's arms to the chair. She obviously has gotten some sleep herself.

I tell Van Brunt, "I'm going to edit into 1812GRI-CHT."

He looks up from the Piper's lieutenant to meet my eyes. "One of the Grimm Timelines?"

"According to the Librarian, it's where I can find the Wise Women." I briefly recount what I've learned. "While it appears Finn is not following the same trajectory of others inflicted with the transformation enchantment, I cannot stand by, simply waiting to see if he will finally succumb. I do not think we can fight his infection with mere medicine. If magic is what has done this to him, we must assume that it is magic which may cure it."

He says quietly, "Agreed."

"If 1812GRI-CHT and 1816/18GRI-GT are, in fact, connected as Bunting claims, then such a trip would also provide an excellent opportunity to hunt the Piper on his playing field. It's not ideal, but there it is."

Mary frowns. "But, in a land that is home to hundreds of fairy tales—"

I tell her, "Nearly eight hundred by my estimation."

"—wouldn't searching for the Piper be akin to hunting for a needle in a haystack?"

I turn to Van Brunt. "Has anyone in the Society ever edited into a fairy tale world?"

"None of our active agents have, no." He runs a hand through his dark hair. "That said, it isn't as if none of us have ever interacted with Timelines associated with collections of stories. I, myself, hail from such a Timeline." He glances down at the unconscious Grethel Bunting. "If Ms. Bunting's experiences are anything like those of yours, we still have hours before she wakens. Perhaps we can go to the conference room and discuss this further."

"I will go, whether with Society permission or not," I say.

"I would have it no other way."

On the way to the conference room, Van Brunt expands upon his previous revelation. "The truth of the matter is, growing up, I was not aware of the other stories and characters much. Some, yes—King James I of Scotland, for example. But most of the others . . ." He shrugs, tapping away on his phone. "The others within the collection that comprised *The Sketch Book of Geoffrey Crayon, Gent.* were quite diverse, I'm afraid. There were humorous tales, those which were melancholy or picturesque, or those that even served to terrify, like mine. Together, they helped build a world much like any other. If the fairy tale worlds are anything like mine, it's quite possible that the people you encounter in certain regions may have no knowledge of the others, no matter how popular their tales may be to us in this day and age. Ms. Lennox does have a point. It may be difficult to track one man amongst so very many others."

"How many stories originate in Hamelin, though?" I press.

"An excellent point, Ms. Reeve."

"We should still hunt for the Piper on multiple fronts, though," I say. "As he has been sighted here many times, we must take that into consideration. But it seems too coincidental to ignore that he has hidden away his library, doesn't it? Libraries do not simply disappear. I cannot help but think he would hide it somewhere he wouldn't think we could find it. Somewhere like in Timelines such as 1812GRI-CHT and 1816/18GRI-GT. If he's truly been infiltrating the Institute, he might very well know that we've yet to ever go to such a place."

"Another excellent point."

The conference room, by the time we get there, is already filled. Interestingly enough, though, the Librarian is absent. Van Brunt makes his way to the front. "This meeting will be short. Hopefully everyone has received the communiqués I sent while on the way back from our trip to Connecticut."

A quiet murmuring fills the room.

"By now you know we have captured what may be one of the Piper's lieutenants. She is still sedated, but once she is coherent, she will be thoroughly interrogated under the guise of truth serum. No stone will be left unturned. Our hand has been forced—the time for gentleness has passed. The risk of further catalyst destructions is too great."

The murmuring grows louder, more appreciative.

He turns to a pair of men sitting on the right side of the table. "Mr. Holgrave, Professor Lidenbrock, assemble a team. You are needed to journey to whence I just was, as John and Paul School for the Exceptionally Gifted has been officially associated with the Piper. While we still do not have concrete proof that the Pied Piper of Hamelin and Gabriel Pfeifer, née Lygari, née Koppenberg are one and the same, I do not hesitate to have us working under that auspice. There is a man there named Mr. Pfriem, one that Grethel Bunting claims is from 1812GRI-CHT. Find out everything you can about him, but be warned, he has a rifle and is not afraid to use it. Mr. Dawkins will send you all the photographs taken from our trip, alongside the building blueprints. I want it searched and its residents identified to the best of your ability. We must know the extent of their capabilities. Please remember that they were able to infiltrate the Institute and weaken us through some kind of hypnotism."

"Of course," Professor Lidenbrock says. If memory serves, Finn has informed me that this man is a great adventurer. Such a mission must surely be ripe for his interests.

"Mr. Blake." Van Brunt addresses another man, this one much closer down the table. "Have we had any luck tracking down either F.K. Jenkins or Rosemary Lovett?"

"Not yet." Franklin Blake taps his pen against the conference table. A man who loves a good mystery, Blake has always been one of the Society's better riddle solvers. "And there's been no sign of either returning to the Ex Libris bookstore."

"Keep searching." Van Brunt turns to Marianne. "Can we be assured that the Institute is clean?"

She looks up from her laptop. "Indeed. We thoroughly searched the entire building. Once I obtained a live bug, I was able to manipulate a tracking signal to detect the others. Nearly forty others were located, including one in your office and one here in the conference room."

His face darkens.

"All were destroyed save a pair set aside for studying. One was neutralized with liquid nitrogen for the time being. The other is carefully being deconstructed by one of my assistants. Anyone in the lab is under strict instructions that there is to be no speaking of any truths or legitimate Society business during the examination, or any communication of any kind until I return. It's taking longer than I had hoped to trace the signal, but I am most determined to solve this riddle."

"As am I." He coughs into a hand before falling silent for a moment. And then, standing a bit taller and looking all the more fierce for it, the leader of the Society says, "In the coming days, we must remain vigilant. Treachery the likes we've never seen before has come to darken our doorsteps. Our sanctum has been invaded, our secrets stolen, our people compromised. Lives and Timelines have been lost, and there is no guarantee we can stem the bleeding before another is taken. Make no mistake about it: we are at war. We fight not only for ourselves, but for those who will never meet us, who will never know our names. I am asking much of you all. When you joined the Collectors' Society, you probably could not fathom that someday you would be asked to put your life on the line for those you will never know. And still, I will ask that you stand with me and do so. If you feel you cannot, please do not jeopardize any of our missions or assignments by coming along only to renege when adversary appears. Our goal, as always, is the protection of Timelines. For many years, we have been able to fulfill this by collecting catalysts. Today, though, we must go above and beyond that. We do not have armies at our disposals, nor do we have local law enforcements. We are the only defense many of these worlds have."

The A.D. says, "To quote the Bard, 'We happy, chosen few are a band of brothers and sisters, and will be kicking arse on St. Whatever-The-Bloody Day it was'."

"It's St. Crispin's Day, you heathen." Mary regards him blandly. "That's not even close to the original quote. Your Shakespeare is terrible."

He smiles impishly. "Why, thank you."

"Now hush," she says. "I'm rather dazzled here by Van Brunt's Henry-ish fortitude."

Van Brunt's glare could wither the Queen of Hearts' roses, it is so heated. "As I was saying, there is a man who appears to not think twice about eradicating Timelines. He has underlings who follow his tenants, vicious ones like Todd who thought nothing better than torturing and killing for pleasure. There are children who may be children in appearance only, who possess the ability to hypnotize and murder. There may be people and beings we have not even dreamed of, waiting and ready to stop us."

When the door creaks open and Victor appears, no one turns to look at him, they are so focused on Van Brunt.

"A possible link between 1812GRI-CHT and 1816/18GRI-GT has been found, one that leads back to the Piper. While several teams will still hunt for him here in this world, at the multiple places of residence we have for him, along with John and Paul School for the Exceptionally Gifted, it is clear that we must also search for him within those worlds. I will be putting together a team to be heading out to do so within the next three hours. No stone must be left unturned."

"What happens if we find him?" an older woman asks. I wrack my mind to remember her name. Josey . . . Josephine? No. She prefers *Jo*. Jo Bhaer. While we've had little interaction together during my tenure at the Society, I've always admired her outspoken feistiness. "Prior to today," she continues, "a live capture was preferable."

"It is still the directive," Van Brunt allows, "providing it can be done safely. If not, I urge each and every one of you to consider not only your safety but that of the Timelines. Remain aware that the Pied Piper of Hamelin is infamous for his ability to lull his prey into mindless obedience. So far, we've seen this happen with a set of pipes and have personal testimony from Mrs. Carrisford that recordings may have been in use. Furthermore, it appears he has the ability to install some kind of trigger into his victims, causing medical maladies if they attempt to discuss anything concerning him or his agenda. From what we can tell, Ms. Darling is subject to seizures when speaking of her assailant; Mrs. Carrisford to blinding headaches. If you forget that he has this power over any of you for even a second, you risk your downfall. On that note, be wary of any and all weapons the Piper's associates might carry, especially those that might glow. We have learned that at least some of them are enchanted and have the ability to transform people into what are called the Piper's Chosen."

"Is this what happened to Finn?" Jo Bhaer asks.

Van Brunt is silent a moment, his eyes tracing the length of the room until they fall upon his other son. "It appears so," he says without emotion.

Even now, even though this is what I already know as fact, my stomach plummets from great heights, only to be replaced with cold determination. The rest of the room explodes in anger and astonishment. C. Auguste Dupin asks, "How long until he turns on us? What are we doing to protect our—"

"Do not. Say. Another. Word." My words are cool as I force his attention to where I sit. "He has not yet *transformed,* at least not in the way that Ms. Bunting has described. And he won't, if I have any say about it."

It's enough to calm the room. But the fool has yet to learn his lesson, because the detective says, red-faced, "You can't—"

"Oh," I say frostily, "but I can. And if I hear about you even entering his room, you will sorely regret the consequences. That is a promise I readily can offer."

"Wendy Darling was placed into isolation!" Dupin snaps. "Are we to treat Finn Van Brunt different simply because he is Brom's son?"

I'm on my feet when Mary places a hand on my arm. "Wendy Darling sold out our secrets," she says, "whether willingly or unwillingly. Initially, she was placed in the medical ward due to the seizures overtaking her. Once she was assessed to not be a high-level risk, she was retired to her room to convalesce. The reason you do not see her at this table, you prat, is that when she regained speech, she specifically requested to not be present at any meetings until she could assure whatever has happened to her would not be an issue. Another agent is present with her at all times, as is the case with Finn. Speaking of, Finn has yet to do anything to jeopardize the Institute. Don't you think the pitchforks are a bit premature?"

Before the man stupidly opens his mouth again, Van Brunt says darkly, "I suggest you listen to the ladies."

It's finally enough to silence the detective. Still, it leaves me apprehensive. If I leave for 1812GRI-CHT, what is to stop a paranoid agent from attempting to neutralize Finn?

"Assignments will be sent out within the hour," Van Brunt concludes.

Marianne glances up from her laptop, waving her hand. "All communications will now be going through a new encryption program. An update will be available for your phones shortly. Do not neglect updating them, please."

When the majority of the audience files out, I say, "I will not leave him to the wolves."

Finn's father's mouth forms a grim line as he considers this.

Victor comes forward from his place in the back of the room. "I take it Alice is going to 1812GRI-CHT to hunt the Piper?"

"I will first be searching for the one who enchanted your brother, but yes, that is the plan," I tell him.

He nods, pursing his lips. And then he nods again, more resolute. "Then I have a solution. We'll take him with us."

My eyebrows lift high. Again with the assumptions of tagging along.

"Obviously Mary and I are going." When he looks to her, she smiles brightly. "Did you think you were going alone?"

"Of course not. I—"

"I know my father is probably chomping at the bit to go, but, Dad. Let's be realistic here." He turns to Van Brunt. "There are too many pieces in play right now. You can't just remove yourself to a Timeline, especially one we've never been to before. You're needed here to help coordinate everything." His lips twist ruefully. "I'm not Finn, Dad. Shite, both of us know this. He's the one who can run this place, not me. I'm the one that needs to go, even if . . ." He pauses, tapping on his head with alacrity.

Van Brunt may sigh quietly, but he does not argue with his son.

"Look." The doctor's attention shifts back to me. "Here's the thing. If you find the person responsible for doing this to Finn, do you plan on dragging him or her back to the Institute? Obviously, if they can enchant anything, we must reason that they're dangerous. As strong as you are, and as charming as you can be,"—he winces a bit saying this—"the Grimm stories can be pretty terrifying when it comes to magic. My mum used to read those stories to me and Finn, and not the watered-down ones. Which witch are you thinking did this? It's a witch, right?"

Sometimes, I fear I underestimate Victor too much. Especially now, when his eyes are glassy and his movements erratic.

"I cannot say if she is a witch or not. She goes by Wise Woman."

His brow furrows as he considers this, a foot tapping impatiently upon the floor. "Which story?"

"*Little Briar—*"

"Ah yes." He snaps his fingers. "*Sleeping Beauty,* right? Shite, Alice. That takes this to a whole other level." His exhale is loud. "Nonetheless, the more I think about it, the better it is if we simply take him with us. When we find the Wise Women and they miraculously do not turn us into toads or the like, we'll want to waste no time. If he's with us, and they agree to help, he'll be cured all the faster."

Son of a jabberwocky, despite his behavior, he makes a decent argument. Still, there are other considerations. "Is Finn not hooked up to your medicines here? A feeding tube?"

"We can take them with us. Well, not the machines, but the IV bags. I'll monitor him the entire time." And then, "I'm taking my meds, Alice. I—I can do this." He sucks in a deep breath. "I won't let him down again."

"I hate to be the Debbie Downer," Mary says mildly, "but how do you suggest we travel with a comatose man? It's not like he can walk or ride a horse."

"In a wagon, naturally."

"I'm just going to throw it out there that he would kick your arse if he knew you were trying to tote his comatose body around," Mary says.

"I would be happy for him to try, because it would mean he was up and moving again."

"What if these Wise Women live where no wagon can travel?" I ask him.

"Then I'll find a way to keep him on a horse. It won't be the first time in history that's happened. I'm not saying it will be easy, but I think it's necessary." His focus returns to his father. "Dad, you know I'm right. The people here, they're good people. I know they are. But if they see Finn as a threat . . ." He shakes his head, more agitated than before. "You know that if it was anyone else, we'd have the same thoughts. I hate to give that prick any credence, but it's true. Even if you're here, monitoring him, something could still happen when you weren't looking. This way, Alice and I will always be with him."

His father twists his neck until a small pop sounds, and then he sighs heavily again. "Fine. Mr. Dawkins will go with you as well. One never knows when a talented thief may come in handy."

The person in question, still lounging at the table, his feet rudely propped against the gleaming wooden surface, tucks his hands behind his head. "*Always* is the proper answer, boss man."

Jack Dawkins has, much to my reflected surprise, been quite the good asset of late.

"And me." A coughing sound emirates from the corner of the room. "A party of five is bad luck, Your Majesty. Six is better; even numbers always are."

Isn't that a lesson I've learned all too well.

"Oh!" Mary claps her hands. "Yes! Yes! Grymsdyke must come, too."

I incline my head. "We would be much appreciative of your protection."

The spider drops to the table and kneels before me.

Victor whispers to Mary, "Thank you for believing in me, especially when . . ."

She touches his face gently. "I'll always believe in you, darling."

Apparently Van Brunt is as much of a fan as I am of feet upon a table, because he deftly knocks his assistant's boots back onto the floor. "Then it's decided. You best go and see if Mrs. Brandon can find you anything appropriate to wear to 1812GRI-CHT. Afterward, I want you to collect your weapons of choice. Do not worry about being stingy. It's best to be prepared for anything."

"One last thing." Victor tugs out a dirty scrap of paper. "I found this on Todd's body. Don't know what it means, but . . ." His shrug is jerky. "It could be something."

It's blank. But then, so were the papers in Bunting's office. Van Brunt takes the scrap from him before dismissing us to get ready for our latest assignment.

THE WOODS

ALICE

A CART TRUNDLES PAST us, its wooden wheels bouncing in enormous mud-filled potholes, sending a spray of brown that nearly splatters us.

Mary grimaces as she watches the receding convoy. "This places smells."

I'd written us into *Little Briar-Rose,* figuring it was best to start where we had concrete proof the Wise Women had been. As the only place the story mentioned was a palace, I wrote us just outside the grounds specifically requesting a time period as close to the end of the tale as possible.

And what a palace it is—or rather, a castle. With rounded, creamy rock-laden towers tipped with gray spires jutting up into the foggy skies, it looms in the distance surrounded by a spurt of dense, emerald woods and plenty of briar. A singular main road leads toward the castle, and at the base of the road sits a quaint medieval village of white and brown buildings with moss-covered, thatched roofs. Gray smoke from fireplaces curls out of the structures, twisting up into the mist weighing down upon the village. Uneven, disconnected bunches of thorny, blooming hedges creep in between edifices, lending an ominous feel to what otherwise might be an enchanting vista. The area is bustling, though. Carts roll past us every few minutes, and there are plenty of villagers carrying about their daily business. I can't help but watch a group of children, who have most likely never seen nor heard of a bath, run through the muddy streets, tossing one another balls and hoops. Too many of them wear ragged clothes better suited for a burn pile.

Old habits die hard, because I yearn to do something to better their conditions. That said, I must admit, Mary has a point. The stench of urine is unbearably strong where we're sitting. And it's validated when, in full view of anyone caring to watch, a man across the way undoes his breeches and pisses into a puddle.

Frabjous.

Grymsdyke peeks through the hood of Mary's cloak. "The inhabitants here are barbaric. Even we spiders have special locations for defecation. Who does such things in broad daylight?"

Mary promptly urges Grymsdyke to tell her more about Wonderlandian spider societies.

Victor has gone off to acquire us a serviceable cart with gold he's brought along; the A.D. has no doubt weaseled his way into the nearest tavern, intent upon inquiring about the Wise Women. Mary and I have been lounging irritably on damp grass for the last half hour. Finn rests next to me, his head in my lap, as I stroke his soft hair. Victor was able to hide the IV bag still attached to Finn's arm within a rather large brown tunic we've dressed his brother in. I do not relish allowing the men in our group to go off without me, like I am some damsel in need of assistance, but Victor and I came to an understanding shortly before we left: one of us would be with Finn at all times. And as my

German is rustier than his, Victor was the one best to go haggle in the village. On a more positive note, it's given me a few moments to doze on and off. How the White King is used to existing on so little sleep still flummoxes me.

One of the children I've been watching comes closer, his gaunt face streaked with filth. In each grubby hand is a beautiful rose surely taken from the briar hedges infesting the village. He offers one apiece to Mary and me. Grymsdyke withdraws into Mary's cloak before the child spies him.

Mary accepts the rose closest to her and smells it. She says in stilted German, "What a delightful little boy you are. Pray tell us, what is your name?"

Apparently I am not the only one who did not pay close attention in German class. Mary's accent is terrible.

As I claim my bloom, glad it is a dusky pink rather than red, the child says, "Phillip."

"We thank you for your lovely gifts." I offer him a gentle smile. "It was quite thoughtful of you."

He tugs at his tattered tunic, shrugging shyly. He must be . . . six, perhaps. Still so young, with so much life ahead of him. It aches to imagine the conditions he must live in. Grayish, dried dirt patches spot his face and neck, with some appearing more like skin better suited for an elephant than a child. His hair is matted, his bones far too prominent.

The queen within me seethes to see such conditions. Not all those in my lands in Wonderland were prosperous, but none lived in such stark poverty. And yet here a boy is, offering Mary and me gifts and kindness.

"Tell me, Phillip, do you live in the village here?"

He points toward a row of smoking buildings. "With me mum and father." And then, proudly, "Me father is the apprentice blacksmith."

His accent is strange, his words formed a bit differently in his mouth than what I originally learned. Still, I beckon him closer. "How wonderful. Do you ever go to the palace, Phillip?"

He solemnly shakes his head.

"We are recently new to this kingdom, come here from lands far away," I continue smoothly. "Pray tell me, who are your king and queen?"

He rattles off a pair of names, neither of which is Briar-Rose.

I try not to show my frustration or disappointment. Briar-Rose had slept for one hundred years before waking and marrying the prince who found her. It's a terribly long time between curse and end of tale, leaving plenty of opportunities for the Wise Women to disappear or even pass away. This realization sends a chill of trepidation down my spine, for as the Piper's tale is nearly equally old, any swords or weapons the thirteenth Wise Woman might have enchanted could have been done so at a distant time in the past.

"Do you know of Princess Briar-Rose?" I press. "Or perhaps even a Queen Briar-Rose?"

His eyes alight. "She is the King's mother!"

Sweet relief fills me up. Time really does move differently in each Timeline. Just as I am about to ask him about the Wise Women, the A.D. reappears. "What do we have here?" he says in flawless German. "A little man trying to charm my ladies?"

Poor Phillip is stricken before the A.D.'s sly grin surfaces. To make up for his teasing, our colleague digs into his pocket and extracts a pair of coins. "Here you go, little man." He ruffles the child's hair. "Go and buy yourself something good to eat, hmm?"

"How surprisingly generous of you," Mary comments once the boy bounds away. And it is, very much so. I'd planned on offering a coin, but the A.D. went and gave two.

It's more than generous. It is . . . sweet. Uncharacteristically so.

The A.D.'s eyes soften as he watched the child. "I know what it's like to be little and so hungry."

Well, now. There seems to be quite a bit of depth to Jack Dawkins that he hides all too often from the rest of us. Why does he hide so stubbornly behind such a flippant demeanor?

He clears his throat, scratching the base of his neck. "Well, I have both good news and bad news. Which would you fine ladies like to hear first?"

"Start with the bad," Mary says. "It's always better to start there. It's like a bandage we can rip off. Get it over with and then apply balm afterward."

Grymsdyke reemerges so he may listen, too.

"Fair enough." He settles down on the grass next to her, wrapping his arms around his gangly legs. "The bad news is the men in the tavern are scared shitless of the Wise Women—all of 'em, by the way. None of them were willing to talk to me about these ladies, and threatened my manhood if I continued to press the issue."

Mary plucks the thorns off her rose. "Well, that is rather bad news."

"I can make them talk," Grymsdyke says.

The A.D. blanches. "By biting a fellow?"

The spider coughs. "If I use a small enough dose of venom, there is time to question a person before they perish."

"We will try questioning first," I say firmly.

The A.D. is oddly relieved by this. Who knew that a thief and criminal could be so squeamish at the thought of poisoning? "The good news is that they mentioned there might be one person willing to risk spilling the beans. Apparently, there's an old lady living in the forest that the others claim is a witch."

"Is their logic that all old women—or *witches*—hang out together? Or have a secret network amongst themselves?" Mary snorts in derision. "Misogynistic pigs." To Grymsdyke she says, "I bet spiders are not so terrible with their women."

"Hive mothers are revered," he admits.

"When it comes to human societies, especially that are *here,* let's be fair," the A.D. says. "These Wise Women might be the real deal if they can do magic and the like."

"We'll go to this woman in the woods." As I attempt to set the rose down next to me, one of the thorns pricks my finger. Blood is drawn, son of a jabberwocky. "We'll see what she has to say. On a related note, I'm sorely disappointed in you, Jack. You claim you possess charm the likes that few have seen and you can't even convince a bunch of medieval townsfolk to recount local legends."

Mary bursts out laughing.

But the A.D. . . . well, he simply stares at me, mouth ajar and eyes wide as I suck on my bleeding finger.

"Ogling so blatantly," I tell him sternly, "is rather rude."

"Shall I punish him, Your Majesty?"

I stay my assassin with a quick shake of the head. The A.D.'s voice is soft, uncertain, on the other hand. "You called me Jack again. It's like the third time in as many days."

Have I?

I am saved from addressing such awkwardness when Victor, atop a rickety cart led by an elderly, bowed horse, pulls up in front of us. "Did anyone call for a cab?"

Mary slips the dethorned rose behind an ear and stands up. "Oh, ha ha. It took you long enough. My bum has gone numb, it's so cold."

"And wet," the A.D. says. "It looks as if you've pissed your pants."

The sweetness we'd seen vanishes, replaced with the A.D. we know all too well.

As Mary lunges at him, Victor climbs down from the cart. "I'm sorry it took me a bit longer than I'd hoped. I also bought us some food for whatever journey we're about to embark upon."

The spider leaps from Mary onto the cart. Whilst Mary attempts to tackle the A.D., I tell Victor, "An excellent idea. It appears we'll be journeying into the woods first to meet up with an elderly woman who may or may not be a witch."

"Ah, another day at the office," he quips. "How's Finn?"

Nearby, Mary manages to trip the A.D. When he lands flat on his arse, she sneers, "Who looks as if they've pissed their pants now, huh?"

"Woman, if I had, it'd be in the front, not the back!"

I roll my eyes. Those two are utterly infantile together lately. "The same," I tell Victor.

He nods. "I figured. Well, let's get him into the cart. There's fresh hay in there, and a small stack of cloth bags." He peers up into the sky. "Hopefully it won't rain anytime soon. Moldy hay is the worst." He pats the old horse's head. "Plus, old Lightning here wouldn't like to eat it, would you, buddy?"

The horse's tail twitches.

Victor continues, "I wanted to find a merchant's wagon for us, but there were none for sale."

As I slide out from beneath Finn, I ask wryly, "Are you subject to moldy hay often?"

"Some weeks," he says solemnly, "it's near daily."

For a moment, the breath in my chest stills. Victor's countenance, his tone of voice feel all too similar to his brother's. And although the man I love is here with me, his skin beneath my hands, his head in my lap, I miss him so fiercely I feel like howling into the heavens.

Victor kindly does not question my sudden loss of humor. Mary and the A.D. cease their immature ridiculousness long enough to come over and help us—the A.D. up in the cart to lift Finn in, Mary to ensure the hay is covered and piled high enough. After our satchels and weapons are also stowed safely in the cart, I climb in, taking my place next to Finn. When I tuck his cloak around him, I can't help but notice how pale he looks. There is no sign of fever, no clamminess, just cool, pale skin.

I bend over to kiss his brow, whispering, "Hold on, love. We're almost there."

I almost could swear his eyelashes flutter at the sound of my voice.

"Are you alright, darling?"

I look down to find Mary with a hand on Victor's arm. The doctor is staring off into the distance, his eyes narrowed. He blinks at her words, though, shaking his head.

"I'm fine." And then, more resolutely, "I'm fine. Let's hit the road."

Together, they climb upon the seat in front. Grymsdyke settles into the corner between the cart and Finn's head. The A.D. lowers himself next to Finn's feet, his own touching mine, before huddling beneath his cloak. The space we occupy is small and cramped, but I suppose we can at least claim in such chilly weather shared body heat will not be an issue.

"Well, now." Victor cranes his head to look back at us. "Where is this supposed witch we're to see?"

"Woman," Mary stresses. "There's no confirmation she's a witch."

The A.D. points in the distance. "Head through the village, and then take the left fork. It'll take us straight into the woods."

"Do you think we'll find any houses made of candy?" Mary asks wickedly.

The A.D. frowns. "We better not."

"Houses made out of candy," Grymsdyke mutters. "What utter ridiculousness. You would never find something so undignified in Wonderland."

I am tempted to chortle at the look of disbelief on the A.D.'s face at this proclamation.

Victor slaps the reigns; the cart lurches forward. Now it is our wheels bouncing through the enormous potholes, leaving my teeth snapping with each jerk.

It may sound ridiculous for a woman who has grown up with horses and carriages, but I believe it's safe to say I've grown to much prefer car travel to this. Wonderland's roads were never so neglected, though, especially those in the Diamonds' lands. Shortly before I was forced into exile, workers had nearly completed paving all major travel routes. The White King had the same done to his lands, and with the two routes connecting, it allowed merchants in the two lands a much easier, safer, and quicker way to do business.

The A.D. must feel the same as me about our journey's conditions, for he yelps during a particularly nasty jolt. "I think," he murmurs, gripping onto the side's railing, "you and I got the raw end of the deal back here. We'll be black and blue in no time."

I don't say it, but I absolutely agree with him.

The ride through the village is uneventful, although it offers a much better view of the castle. Gazing upon it as I am leaves me a bit melancholy. My own castle in Wonderland is far more majestic than this, gleaming white with gold and silver accents, appearing in both weather fair and poor like a glittering diamond. Lush gardens filled with militant yet beautiful flowers surrounded it, and every day we were treated to a symphony of delights. It was whimsical yet stately, and my people were always welcome upon the grounds. The castle here, though, appears so forbidding, so . . . untouchable. Almost as if a princess still slept within, it's so still.

As Mary and Victor talk quietly amongst themselves, I decide to attempt to peel back the layers Jack Dawkins has chosen to wrap around him. "Have you read these stories?"

He tears his eyes away from a woman just about to cut the head off a struggling chicken. "Some. They're a bit too dark for my tastes."

"Is that so?"

Once more, he wraps his arms around his legs. "I prefer books that make me laugh. Or biographies. I very much enjoy those."

Is he funning me? But, no—he appears earnest. And this is yet another thing I would not have thought the infamous Artful Dodger to be, a reader. As he answered me honestly, I do the same in kind. "For years, most of my reading was more for work than pleasure. Histories, policies, the art of warfare . . ."

"Do you miss it?"

"Reading such books?" I shrug. "I never minded them. They were interesting and aided me greatly."

He shakes his head, his greasy blond hair falling into his face. "No. I meant being a queen."

Grymsdyke quickly takes offense to such an innocent comment. "Her Majesty is, and will be until the day she dies, the Queen of Diamonds of Wonderland. It does not matter if she is within its borders or not to still be a ruling sovereign."

"My apologies." The A.D. waves a hand in a rolling motion to mimic what would be a bow if he were standing. "I ought to have asked if you miss *actively* ruling. Day-to-day stuff, I mean."

And now he's peeling back my layers. I sigh as I turn my focus back to our surroundings. We're close to the edge of the village now; the buildings have begun to thin out.

I tell him, "I suppose I do."

We settle into silence as the cart slowly clatters out of the village, old Lightning proving his name a misnomer. Even Mary and Victor fall quiet as the journey progresses. The conditions of the road worsen, as if that was even possible, but the view around us attempts to make up for it. Meadows line the dirt path, lush ones filled with tall grasses peppered with red poppies, tiny white marguerite daisies, and cornflowers. I could easily imagine how delightful it would be to spend a lazy afternoon amongst such beauty, crafting daisy chain crowns and dozing peacefully under misty skies. But such fanciful daydreaming leaves me even more nostalgic.

If only these flowers sang.

Lightning reaches the fork in the road, and Victor urges him to the left. Nearby, a falcon swoops down and snatches a rabbit from the meadow.

Miraculously, I am able to doze just a bit—fitfully, but still. When I waken, the woods loom before us, dark and foreboding. Fog seeps out from between the branches and leaves, leaving the impression that the trees are purposely doing their best to block out the sun. They are not welcoming, not even the tiniest bit.

"How far into the woods does this woman live?" Victor calls out from the front.

I kick at the A.D.'s shoes to rouse him from his own attempts at napping whilst traveling a bumpy road. "'Bout half a league or so." He straightens a bit. "We'll see a big oak that looks as if it's screaming, and then the cottage will be about a kilometer past that. Should be set not too far off the main road."

Victor holds up his hand, forming a circle with his forefinger and thumb and raising the rest.

Once we cross from the meadows into the forest, the temperature noticeably drops. The air is still, the mist covering the woods like a heavy blanket. Precious few sounds other than the clacking of the cart's wheels or the plodding of the horse's hooves surface—no crickets, no birds, no crackling of branches. Grand oaks and beeches tower over us, their long, gnarled limbs stretched out like arms hungry for prey. The farther we move into the woods, though, the quieter it becomes.

I scan the trees, searching for signs. It's too still. Too silent. Such silence isn't natural. My hand reaches for the hilt of a sword I've brought. Nothing good comes from such stillness in a forest.

The A.D. watches this subtle motion warily. I give a slight nod and he, too, reaches for a sword of his own. I raise a hand, flashing two fingers before my eyes and then a single over my shoulder, toward the woods.

It's his turn to nod.

I search the view from whence we came; he searches the path on which we head. Unease I cannot assign reason to pools in the pit of my belly. The hairs on my arms stand at end.

Soon enough, I know why.

A split second before it's too late, I spot subtle movement in a tree to my left. I lurch to my knees just as a number of dwarves, each dressed in browns and greens and bearing sharp, thin swords, drop from the trees around us like ghosts. Quick as a flash, they all thrust their blades toward us.

Victor doesn't bother urging Lightning to outrun them. He merely pulls the cart to a stop. Mary quickly reaches back and grabs his sword for him.

The dwarf with the longest beard and most bulbous nose says, his voice like gravel, "Your kind is not welcome here."

"What kind is that?" The A.D. stands up in the cart, his sword readied.

The dwarves titter amongst themselves. "He'll eat you," the shortest of the lot gleefully announces. "And then grind your bones with his teeth. He's been hungry lately, too."

Victor also rises from his seat. "I suppose you're warning us from the kindness of your heart to turn back."

The dwarf whose beard is braided says, "Not before you pay the toll. These woods are not for you."

I very nearly roll my eyes from such overdramatic farcicality.

"What happens if we do not pay?" Victor asks, his voice as taut as his arm and sword. I realize he's spoiling for a fight.

The dwarf with the milky eyes cackles. "Then *we'll* eat you up. We're hungry, too!"

I draw myself up to my full height. "Then you best come and take your payment."

For a moment, they all pause, their beady eyes locked onto me. But then the dwarf with the red curls shatters the silence with a battle cry, and his compatriots surge forward quicker than one would think dwarves might be.

"Mary, with Finn!" I shout before leaping over the side.

The A.D. and Victor are on my heels, their swords flashing through the murky gloom. Van Brunt's assistant rounds the cart to attack the pair of dwarves on the right, Victor and I charge the five dwarves on the left. Pointed teeth gnash at us as they whip the thin blades, slicing through the air like the blades of a helicopter. I toss off my cloak just in time to send one sprawling with a well-placed boot to the chest.

His wretched little blade carved an ugly hole in my skirt.

Grymsdyke flies from the cart, landing on the top of the little man's head. Arms swinging, the dwarf attempts to dislodge my assassin, but Grymsdyke is too strong, too clever to allow himself to be knocked off. Within seconds, his fangs sink into the man's neck.

The scream that follows pierces the air.

Another dwarf lunges at me, his whiskers flying furiously about his face. I manage to dodge his sword just long enough to drive my elbow directly into his nose. A satisfying crunch precedes my sword's hilt slamming down against his temple. He collapses onto the ground before me, muttering gibberish before his eyes droop.

The dwarf with red curls picks himself up off the ground, shouting obscenities. It's my turn to rush him, my sword slashing. Nearby, Victor knocks the bigger of the dwarves off his balance shortly before grabbing his tunic and tossing him into the distance.

A duck and a dodge later, I have the red-haired dwarf pinned by the collar of his tunic to the tree.

"You wretched beast!" he shouts at me. "The indignity of it all!"

A punch to his chin ceases his babble.

"Alice!" Mary shouts. "Your daggers!"

I turn just in time to catch the blades. The dwarf with braids charges me like a bull, roaring the entire way. It's incredibly petty and poor form in a fight, but at the last moment, I jump to the side and stick a leg out.

He hits the litter of leaves on the forest floor face first. Within a second, I'm straddling him, the hilt of my twin blades slamming against the base of his skull. Nearby, Grymsdyke's victim shrieks inconsolably, his body now purplish and riddled with bursting blisters.

When I stand up, I'm forced to immediately step to the side as Victor kicks one of the dwarves in the head, sending him through the air like a rag doll. He smashes against a tree before dropping to the ground, unconscious.

The A.D. comes into view, dragging the littlest dwarf by his feet. He tosses him next to one of his fallen comrades. "There's another back there that Grymsdyke took care of. Little bastard bit me!"

Grymsdyke appears on his shoulder. "I did no such thing! I know who is comrade and who is foe, thief!"

"Not you! The bloody dwarf!" The A.D. pauses, as if he just now notices a massive spider clinging to his body. "But just to be safe, please do not bite me."

I look to the cart. "Mary? Is all fine?"

She yawns. "It took you four long enough."

Victor lets out a breath of laughter. "Sorry to disappoint, sweets."

The A.D. holds his arm out so Grymsdyke can climb back into the cart with Finn and Mary. "I imagine those left with a pulse will wake up with some bloody awful headaches."

I bend down and finger the rope knotted around the dwarf's tunic. "It's best to tie them up. Chances are, when they do wake up, they'll want a bit of vengeance for being bested so easily."

We work quickly, and before long, the deed is done. The A.D. stretches his arms in the air, bowing his back. "Do you think they were telling the truth about the woman wanting to eat us?"

"They could be talking about *any* woman," Mary says from her perch in the cart.

Victor wipes his sword on one of the dwarf's shirts before climbing into the wagon. "I believe they said he. *He* is hungry."

An unfazed Lightning is once more urged forward, but this time as we travel, I keep hold of my sword. After a while, the rare shafts of sunlight slanted through the leaves begin to wan.

Night is coming.

Thankfully, we finally arrive at the screaming tree, a visage well suited for a nightmare. Its branches barren of leaves, elongated holes forming eyes and a mouth in its trunk, it is a terrifying yet perfect edition for this forest. An owl hoots from within, causing a chill to tickle my spine.

Soon enough, we spy a cottage set just off the road.

I tell Victor. "I can walk from here."

"*We* can walk," he says, but I gently touch his shoulder.

"One of us always stays with Finn. Remember? You and Mary stay here. The A.D. and I will go."

"And me." Grymsdyke coughs his little spider cough that is so familiar to my ears. "I refuse to allow the Queen of Diamonds to go into such an unknown situation unguarded."

If the thought of going into the house of someone who potentially may want to feast on one's bones unnerves the Artful Dodger, or being told by a spider he is not enough protection for me is an insult, he does not show it.

Mary takes offense, though. "I most certainly am coming. If this is a witch, who knows what fascinating poisons she might have inside her home?" A gleam shines in her eyes as she hops down from the cart.

I forgo my sword for my daggers before I exit the cart, as well.

"If I hear you screaming," Victor says, "I'm coming in. Finn would understand."

Fair enough.

Together, the A.D., Mary (with Grymsdyke upon her shoulder), and I make our way through fallen branches and leaf litter toward the cottage. Leaning toward one side, the roof nearly completely covered in moss, the abode looks worse for its wear. No paint decorates its surface, and the door appears more raw log than anything else. Smoke twists out of a brick chimney; a faint glow comes from the singular window.

The A.D. asks quietly, "Have you met many witches, Alice?"

I haven't, actually. Wonderland is not home to such mystical beings, although we had plenty of other sorts whose abilities far out-shone the normal. I've faced many a fierce opponent, though, and have seen magic wielded in other ways.

The door opens before any of us can knock. Standing there, wearing a drab brown dress and a white apron, her auburn hair arranged neatly upon her head, is a surprisingly non-elderly woman. This is what the villagers deem *old?*

"You might as well come in," she says in a clear, lovely voice. "And those out there in your cart, too. It's about to rain soon, and I'd hate for you to be soaked to your bones, especially that one in the back. I've got room for you all in here."

She must be in her forties or fifties, I estimate, but appears to be fit and in good health. Soot smudges her chin, but other than that, there is nothing to indicate if she's been gnawing on bones or flesh recently. Intuition tells me she's not all that she seems, but that she's also not as dangerous as reported.

Still, none of us move quite yet. I say, "We apologize for intruding, but we have a few questions for you and then plan to be shortly on our way."

As if on cue, thunder cracks overhead.

Her smile is tempered yet rueful. "Unless you plan on traveling through the storm, I suggest you come inside." And then, a bit cheekily, "I don't cook guests up for dinner, no matter what the rumors in the village may claim."

Next to me, the A.D. starts.

"Let me guess. You had a run-in with the dwarves?" She shakes her head. "They are naughty boys, are they not? Always spoiling for a fight."

"They threatened to eat us," the A.D. exclaims.

The woman stands to the side of her door. "They might have nibbled on you, but chances are, they would have sold you off to creatures far less reasonable for gold."

"Well, doesn't that make all the difference?" he mutters.

Mary, on the other hand, steps into the abode. "It smells wonderful in here. What is it you do?"

"I'm a healer," the woman says, "and a bit of an apothecary. Is that not why you are here?"

A quick glance around the room beyond her shoulder seems to confirm this statement. Dried flowers and plants hang from the ceiling, bottles of varying sizes line racks and tables. Far cozier and well-kept than it appears from the outside, the house does seem welcoming. But it's the drops of rain that splatter on my face that make up my mind. Good or bad, we need shelter for the time being. I turn to the A.D. "Might as well go and help Victor bring Finn in."

The woman reaches out and touches his arm. "Have him bring the cart up near the house. The tree cover is better."

The A.D. looks to me, though, several questions in his eyes. I give a quick, assured nod in response.

He jogs back out to the cart.

I step into the house, warily savoring the warmth. It smells like fresh bread, and a whole host of other pleasant scents.

"If you don't mind me asking," Mary is saying, "why is it that a healer and apothecary lives so far out in the woods?"

The woman motions toward a pair of stools nearby. I remain standing, but Mary takes a seat. "I'm afraid I am not always so welcome within the village," she tells us. "There are always those who fear that which they do not understand."

"What is it they do not understand about you?" I inquire.

She says simply, "My gifts. I am Gertrude, by the way."

Mary makes quick introductions for the both of us as well as Grymsdyke. Interestingly enough, a talking spider does nothing more than stimulate interest from the woman. Nothing further is said until Victor and the A.D. bring Finn inside, and by the looks of their cloaks, the light splattering from just minutes before has turned steadier.

It's hard to see him like this. Infuriating, really. Victor and the A.D. are gentle with him, respectful, too, but the fact that he still sleeps, that he cannot walk in here on his own two feet, that he cannot choose whether or not to come along on this mission, leaves frustration nearly crushing my chest.

He deserves better. I will fix this. I must.

The moment Gertrude sees Finn, she says, "Let us put him by the fire." She shoves a stool out of the way and drags over a pile of hay that sits nearby. "Here, where he can be comfortable."

The urge to personally ensure my beloved's comfort is strong, but I know I must stay on guard lest Gertrude turns out to be anything other than what she claims. I urge my assassin closer to ask quietly, "Do you sense anything out of the ordinary?"

"Yes, Your Majesty." He bounds from Mary's shoulder to my own. "But I cannot sense if it is nefarious or not. It feels . . . more neutral, if that makes sense."

It does, actually.

Gertrude peers down at Finn once he's situated. "Is this why you are here? To see what can be done for your friend?"

"In a roundabout way," I say carefully, "we are."

She kneels down next to him, pressing her wrist against his forehead. "If I am to try to help, I must first know what ails him."

"He was stabbed." My words are blunt, unforgiving. "By a sword enchanted by the thirteenth of the Wise Women."

The surprise that flashes in her eyes isn't covered quickly enough. Interesting.

I press my hand. "Might you know anything about this woman, or any of the Wise Women?"

She slowly stands up, taking each of us in: Victor, his hand on the hilt of a sword, hanging on his scabbard, eyes gleaming with a bit of madness that just cannot seem to dissipate; the A.D., leaning against the fireplace, his muscles tense; Mary, head tilted, eyes narrowed; and myself, standing directly in the path toward the door.

"I might," she drawls. Something in her changes then—invisible walls of protection seem to rise about her. She is on guard, too. "What is it you want with the Wise Women?" Suspicion practically paints each of her words. "Is it your hope that the thirteenth will reverse whatever enchantment she has laid upon this man?"

"Do you know where they are?"

She tucks a stray hair behind an ear. "I do not advise anyone to make that trek."

"I am not just anyone. Neither are the rest of my companions."

Gertrude's sigh is quiet yet resigned in the warmth of the home. "No, you are not, are you? Nor is your spider." She moves to a nearby table, one filled with herbs and mortars and pestles. Several stalks are selected before her nimble fingers strip the dried flowers off. "That said, you might not like the answers I give."

"We won't know," Victor says from his station by Finn, "until you offer them."

The flowers are dumped into a mortar. "Do not say I did not warn you."

THE TALE OF THE TWELFTH WISE WOMAN

ALICE

GERTRUDE SLIDES A BOTTLE filled with tree bark closer to where she stands. "How much do you know of the Wise Women?"

She's testing us, I realize, but I am willing to play just a little. "There are thirteen, all presumed to have some sorts of magical abilities. Twelve seem . . . less nefarious than the thirteenth, based on a story we have heard."

The sound of scraping fills the space between us as she grounds the flowers to a fine dust. "Are you referring to the history of Queen

Briar-Rose?"

When I tell her yes, she continues. "For centuries, the Wise Women have watched over the people of this kingdom. In the beginning, their intentions were pure: they were impartial, fair in their gifts and guidance. Kings and peasant alike would journey to visit them, bringing offerings in exchange for whatever it was they desired. Many were turned away, those found worthy were blessed. Those who were not were punished. But time is not always a generous mistress. Time allows slow changes, the warping of beliefs based upon observations both common and uncommon. The Wise Women eventually became less cohesive as a group and more splintered in their beliefs. Petty jealousies arose, arguments over who and what deserved their insight and gifts. It all came to a head when the King held a banquet and bade the Wise Women to attend. It was not often they were summoned from their caves, and this alone prompted much anger and resentment amongst some. But the true difficulty lay in that the King specified only twelve could attend. One would be forced to stay behind.

"As you can imagine, the thirteenth was truly angered. She was already bitter and outraged over the summons, but to discover that one was to be excluded? It was not to be borne. Lots were drawn; the angriest of all was selected to remain. Rather than allow rationality to rule as it once had for centuries before, she journeyed behind her coven and ensured the King, and the kingdom, knew what punishments were in store for insulting the Wise Women. Whilst many of the Wise Women agreed with her, albeit silently, there was one who felt she went too far. It was one thing to punish the King for his insolence, it was another to destroy the future of an innocent babe whose threads of life were yet woven. It was she who altered the curse." Gertrude selects a bottle and pulls out several dried leaves. "The princess suffered, of course, as did the entire castle. But they were not alone in their punishments. The Wise Woman who dared to go against one of her sisters was also castigated."

A quick trip to a rack laden with tiny, herb-filled jars has Gertrude bringing several more ingredients to her worktable.

"What happened to her?" Mary asks.

"She was banished." Gertrude's mouth is set in a flat line as she pulls a dried plant I do not recognize from the jar. "Sent into exile by a majority of her sisters. As she left, the group then splintered further until the once mighty and just thirteen were no longer whole. Most went into pockets of seclusion, refusing help to the people of the kingdom. A few who let too much anger and greed into their heart turned toward darker intentions." She wipes stray hairs off her face with the back of her hand before motioning toward Finn. "Thus, an unfortunate situation such as this."

"Why are the villagers so afraid to speak of the Women?" Mary presses.

Gertrude reclaims her pestle. "Dark deeds are only favored by those with holes and blackness within their souls, are they not? I cannot say for certain, but it seems fair to guess that there is fear of retribution for speaking out against those far more powerful than they."

"Where do you fit into this?" the A.D. asks. "I mean, you seem to have quite a bit of details about how it all shook down."

Before she can answer, I say, "Isn't it obvious? She is the twelfth, now banished to the woods so close to the village."

Half of her mouth lifts as she regards me. "Aren't you a clever little queen?"

The corners of my lips lift up just a tiny bit before I ever so gently incline my head. *Touché.* Across the room, Victor's hand tightens on the hilt of his sword. The A.D.'s moves to do the same. Grymsdyke's grip upon my shoulder is a bit more assured.

"Have no fear." Her faint smile matches my own. "Had I wanted you dead or worse, I would have ensured such fates already."

"Do not dare to threaten the Queen of Diamonds," my assassin insists.

The Wise Woman says nothing to this. She merely gazes upon the spider as if he is the most fascinating thing in the entire room.

"Worse than dead?" the A.D. scoffs to no one in particular. "What can be worse than that?"

She does not respond to his idiocy. Instead, she says to me, "If it is your hope that the thirteenth Wise Woman will revoke her curse, then

I'm afraid you have journeyed here for naught. If you were to petition her for such, chances are, you would receive that fate your friend here seems unable to imagine."

Chances are, she is right. Reasoning with the cruel is tricky, indeed.

Still, my options are rapidly dwindling. I cannot allow Finn to go through the Piper's transformation. If he was to become anything like S. Todd or Rosemary . . .

No. I cannot allow it.

"What about you?" My tone is cool, my breaths measured. "You have portrayed yourself to us as a healer, and admitted that you altered a previous spell."

She tugs a small cauldron over and dumps the crushed and powdered herbs into it. "I will know nothing more about the spell until I examine him."

"You can't magically just . . . tell? Or know?"

Her eyes flit over to the A.D. He genuinely appears baffled. "I know a great many things," she tells him. "But magic is not always so easy to unravel, especially if it comes from another." A bit of liquid is carefully poured from a black jar, her attention shifting to me. "Nor is it always able to be freely given, even if well deserved."

I offer another slight incline of my head. If she wants payment, I will give it.

The door suddenly blows open, bringing with it not only a gust of wind and rain, but also a brown and white falcon. Its strong wings beat furiously, raising all our hairs, before it settles on a perch nearby.

"Just in time." As she grabs a wooden spoon to stir her mixture, Gertrude glances fondly at it. "Is all as it should be?"

A rather loud series of chirps erupt from the bird.

She chuckles and then, with a flick of her wrist and the spoon, the door shuts, surprising even me.

"The surviving dwarves are put out with you all." She tsks. "You'll need to be careful when you depart and steer clear of them. They can be quite vindictive if they have a mind to it."

"Noted," Victor says quietly, his eyes blankly staring at the darkness beyond the window.

The twelfth Wise Woman turns to face him. "You are a healer yourself, are you not?"

He blinks and refocuses on her. "I am."

Her head cocks to the side. "How very interesting you are. How deeply you struggle with the monster within."

He does not flinch at such a blatant description. Does not even allow one emotion to flicker across his face at these words.

"Offer me your assessment, healer."

Victor clears his throat. "Infection from the wound has been stabilized and the fever controlled. No organs were damaged; the blade went clean through one side to the other. After cleaning the area out, I stitched it up. He was coherent and functional for several hours after the stabbing before collapsing. Further examination has shown a drastic change to his eyes, alongside the area surrounding the wound."

"Your guilt does him no good," she says briskly.

Mary stands up, her face darkening. "Hey now—"

Gertrude points her spoon toward her. "Nor does your misplaced anger."

The spoon is enough to shut Mary up.

The Wise Woman hangs the pot over the fire on a blackened metal hook. "Let us see what my sister has done." She kneels down next to Finn and places her hand against his cheek. For many long seconds, she simply stares down at him, unmoving. And then, just when I think she'll speak, she closes her eyes for what must be nearly another full minute.

My patience is already thin. The wait is unbearable.

Finally, her eyes open—but it's not that they've turned a milky, clouded white that has me concerned. It's that her brow is deeply furrowed as she once more angles her attention toward his torso. She releases his face, trailing her hand down his chest. His tunic is tugged upward; nothing is mentioned of the IV bag taped to his unmarked side. When a knife slips out of her apron, I yearn to rush her and knock it out of her grip.

Forces I cannot see cease my ability to do so.

"Have no fear, queen." No longer the lilting voice from before, her words are now hollow, as if they are nothing more than dried leaves whispering through barren trees. The knife slices quietly through the bandaging circling Finn's torso, and once more, as I take in the oddly beautiful swirls and patterns decorating his chest, I cannot control the quick inhale of breath that overtakes me. How can something so beautiful, so delicate and mesmerizing, come from something so insidious?

She traces a finger across one of the more elaborate swirls, pale blue and shaped almost like a bird in flight. "This magic," she murmurs quizzically, "does not hail from the earth and blood and bone that I know."

"What does that mean?" Mary whispers.

Such a description is a punch in my belly to hear, leaving a buzzing in my ears. The Piper must have . . . layered the magic? Found someone else to add another enchantment?

The twelfth Wise Woman swivels those eerie white eyes toward me. "My sister's magic is here. I feel it in his veins. It is fighting to find purchase. But *this* magic . . ." She traces the lines perfectly, although her attention remains on me. "It is his saving grace."

I must swallow the egg that suddenly appears in my throat. Those lines, those beautiful lines . . . have been *protecting* him? "Enough to heal him?"

She beckons me closer. "It has guarded him, but my sister's spell is strong. There is so much darkness, so much anger. So much vengeance. He does not have much time, I'm afraid."

I drop to my knees next to her. "I will pay whatever it takes for you to aid him."

Without notice, she grabs my hand. With a flick of her blade, blood is drawn across my thumb. And then, before I can retaliate, she licks the red beading off.

The spider upon my shoulder hisses in outrage, but I stay his retaliation with my free hand.

The Wise Woman releases me. "There is a salve on the shelf, in the small wooden box. It will help."

Mary is the one to fetch it. I, instead, watch in perverse yet wary horror as she does the same to Finn's thumb.

The white oculi return to me. "You do not hail from these lands."

"I do not."

"Nor does he." She licks her lips. "Why is your blood in his?"

The question takes me by surprise. When I do not answer immediately, she turns to Victor. "Why is the queen's blood in his?"

Finn's brother is thoughtful. "Perhaps . . ."

It's so clear. I cannot believe I forgot.

Blood magic.

Finn saved me from the Queen of Heart's boojum through Wonderlandian blood magic. His blood is in me, and mine in *him*. One of the steps for the ritual is to spread a poultice in the wound. His finger was sliced open during that time, after he had offered lifeblood to enact the ritual. My blood would have mixed with his—not a lot, but it still would have happened.

"The boojum." I turn to Victor. "It happened when he healed me from the boojum, during the blood magic ritual."

Victor snaps his fingers. "Not only that, but the White King gave him some of his blood, as well. He claimed they thought it might protect you or Finn if you ever had to go back to Wonderland again."

There is Wonderlandian blood within Finn—mine *and* Jace's.

The twelfth Wise Woman licks Finn's finger once more. "Yes," she whispers. "Yes." Her eyes glow. "Blood magic is what protects him. Yours and the other's, given freely out of love. Love is the most powerful magic of all."

My vision blurs at all the implications this holds.

"Wonderlandian blood magic is truly powerful," Grymsdyke says. "Especially that which stems from its monarchs."

In a swift, graceful motion, the Wise Woman rises to her feet. As she glides over to a rack of bottles, I must clear my throat to speak. "Can you heal him? Or alter the enchantment?"

"Oh, my dear," she says in that hollow, unnerving voice, "you already did that yourself. Any enchantment I can do will never be as strong as yours." A new bottle is selected, one with what appears to be dried violet petals in it. "We must hurry. We will need the light of the full moon before the final stroke of midnight."

I am both numb and filled with hope.

"Are you saying that the pattern around the wound is not part of the sword's enchantment?" Victor asks. "That . . . Alice's blood has done that to him?"

When Gertrude confirms this, Grethel Bunting's confusion when we inquired after the pattern makes all the more sense.

My love has protected him. Our love protects one another.

I take the salve from Mary and apply it first to Finn's finger and then my own. Gertrude is sprinkling the violet petals into the mixture bubbling over the fire, stirring slowly, Mary peering over her shoulder with great interest. "What is it you're making?"

"A healing broth." A faint aura surrounds her hair. "One that also offers deeper protection. But it will not work alone." Her glowing eyes find mine once more. "Have you ever heard of true love's kiss?"

My fingers curl around Finn's. "Yes, of course. But I must admit to you, I've kissed him a number of times in the past two days."

"But did you kiss him with intent?"

I blink. There's that word—*intent.* How many times has the Librarian mentioned such a thing to me? Intent is always the key. *Intent makes all the difference.*

Finn's intent when he offered me his blood was true love. Jace's intent when he offered both of us his blood was for protection, also given out of love and respect.

"Alice," Mary says excitedly, "there are stories in this Timeline solved by true love's kiss. Snow White, Sleeping Beauty . . ." She squats down next to me. "Was it not the same in Wonderland?"

I shake my head. Had it been so, I would not be here now. I would most likely be in my home in the tulgey wood, alongside Jace. True love's kiss was a beautiful thing, yes, but it solved nothing. Here, though . . . can it be so simple? Can a kiss, given freely, given with intent and the depths of a heart, overcome such sinister magic?

Nearby, the Wise Woman uses a metal bar to unhook the cauldron from its place over the fire. "Quick, child," She motions the A.D. closer. "Take this outside and collect a few drops of the earth's tears."

He takes the rod from her, the pot dangling in the notch on the end. "Do you mean rain?"

She waves a dismissive hand. *"Go."*

He does as asked. The Wise Woman comes over to where Finn and I are. "Magic is not free, Your Majesty."

I take a deep breath. "Ask, and I shall give it."

"Your blood."

Both Victor and Mary explode with, *"What?"*

She waves them off, indifferent to their indignation. "Just enough. Just a jarful. But it must be freely given. Otherwise, it will do no good for me. It has been some time since I had lifeblood from a royal."

My blood for Finn's life.

There is no hesitation. I look to Victor, now glowering above me. "Can you do it for me?"

"Alice, you must know Finn would never want you to risk your health for his."

Finn, I've learned over the last year, knows better than to ever dare to forbid me to do anything. "Then I suppose it is a good thing he is unconscious. If I must, I will cut my own wrist to do so. But I figured it might be more efficient if you can do it."

Indecision fills his face, but finally, he sighs. "I have a few extra tubes and supplies in my bag, in case we needed to change out Finn's. I'll use those."

Mary quickly hands him his bag. As he rifles through it, Gertrude says to Mary, "Fetch the clear bottle on the bottom shelf."

As Mary is looking through the mass of empty bottles, the A.D. comes back inside. "Do you know how hard it is to only get a few drops of rain during a storm?"

Still, I cannot hide the deep appreciation in my eyes when I thank him. In return, he says in a quiet voice, "I will always try to help in whatever way I can."

I am coming to learn this is true of the man.

Mary approaches, bearing a glass jar nearly the size of a wine bottle. She says faintly, "Is this it?"

I would gladly fill five of these if asked.

When Gertrude confirms it is, Victor sits down next to me. "You'll feel lightheaded afterward, I'm afraid. It'll be just like giving blood at a donation center." He eyes the bottle. "Perhaps even a bit more."

"It does not matter," I tell him.

He motions toward Mary. "Darling, can you give me something to tie around Alice's arm?"

She tugs off the knotted rope around her waist and passes it over to him. As he readies my arm, I watch the Wise Woman carefully pour the mixture into two small cups.

I barely feel the prick of needle into vein. And while my blood sluices into the bottle, I focus instead on Finn. *Please let this work. Please.*

Soon enough, the bottle is filled. The needle is removed from my arm. After Victor ties a strip of clean bandaging around the dot of a wound, I take my gift and offer it to Gertrude. "My blood, freely given."

She caps the bottle and sets it on the table. A cup is proffered. "Drink."

I do not bother checking with Mary or Grymsdyke to see if there is anything poisonous in the mixture. Instinct, that feeling in the pit of my gut that has served me well the majority of my life, insists I will not perish here tonight. Instinct has rarely led me astray. I drain the contents in two swallows. It is bitter yet sweet, and surprisingly lukewarm for having bubbled over a fire so recently.

"He must drink as well."

"He's unable to swallow," Victor argues. "It's why I have him hooked up on fluids."

To me, she says, "Time is running out, Your Majesty."

Finn's brother mutters something beneath his breath, but he kneels down next to us. When he lifts Finn's head, the Wise Woman stays him with a hand. "No. This is for the queen. It is her magic that must save him, not yours."

I offer Victor a nod, and he rises to go stand with Mary and the A.D. His love wraps a comforting arm around him.

I gently lift Finn's head, placing the cup at his lips. Slowly, slowly,

I manage to dribble it between his lips so that barely a drop is spilled. I massage his throat and am rewarded by the slightest movement of a muscle constriction. *He's swallowing.* It takes many long seconds, but in the end, I have done just as she has asked.

The Wise Woman holds out her arm, and the falcon flies to her. "Lead the way, my friend."

It squawks loudly enough to leave ears ringing. The door blows open once more, and it swoops out into the rain.

"Come," she tells me. "We must go before the time has passed."

Victor and the A.D. move toward Finn to pick him up, but his body lifts into the air with no help from anyone. A collective gasp fills the room. "No, children." Gertrude smiles. "It is as I said—this is the queen's journey, not yours. Not even yours, brave spider. You will be safe enough here as long as you do not touch that which is not yours."

Grymsdyke is affronted, but when I nod my assent, he leaps onto the nearby table. Victor reaches out and grabs my arm. "Bring my brother back, Alice."

I do not hesitate when I tell him I will.

The Wise Woman flicks her hand and Finn's body floats toward the door. A faint white mist trails behind him. "Hurry, Your Majesty. We have a journey ahead of us. Bring your weapons. The woods are not safe at night."

"How far do you plan on going?" Victor asks. "She's just lost blood. She—"

"It's fine," I assure the trio.

He does not look so sure, but I cannot worry about that right now. I will be fine because I will accept no other outcome. Mary tosses me my cloak, and I throw it around my shoulders before following the Wise Woman and Finn out the door and into the storm.

THE CLEARING

ALICE

THE FALCON'S CRIES PIERCE the chilly air as we head into the wood beyond the house. We have no lanterns, no candles. Any light from the house fades quickly with each step we take. The rain beats down on us relentlessly, and within a few minutes, my clothes are entirely drenched.

Determined as I am, I am also enough of a realist to understand that navigating such conditions in the rain and dark will be difficult at best. This caveat is driven home when the toe of my pointed leather shoe catches a fallen branch and I nearly plunge headfirst into the leaf litter.

I right myself, though. Barely, but still. Before I can sharply comment on the complexity of our task—at least on my end, considering

I do not know these woods—a glowing blue orb materializes roughly six or so meters ahead. It bounces up and down, a sparkling wisp of a tail trailing behind it as it draws pictures in the inky air.

The falcon swoops down, its glossy feathers illuminated pale blue as it dances alongside the light. I'm mesmerized as I watch them, at how graceful and magical they appear. Before too long, though, the falcon lets out a series of chirps. The rustle of wings marks its departure.

The orb then darts toward Finn, its light pulsing softly as it swirls around him. I sense no harm, though, no nefarious intentions toward my love. Just . . . curiosity. Soon enough, it makes its way to me. Each pass ruffles the wet braids circling the crown of my head, each brush sends the hairs on my arm, even beneath the wool of my dress, standing at attention like a bit of static shock. I hold out a hand and it settles in my palm for the smallest of moments. Delicious, comforting warmth suffuses my body.

Perhaps it is madness to claim, but I could swear this light, this orb, has a consciousness.

It circles me several times, tiny sparkles of glittering light left behind in its wake, before journeying toward the Wise Woman. She lifts her hand in the air, as if she, too, caresses it.

From the moment on, we journey in silence. I cannot say how far into the woods we travel, but the rain becomes less punishing thanks to the thick leaves and branches forming an umbrella overhead. Darkness swarms around us, foreboding and thick, but still we push deeper into the woods. The lightheadedness Victor cautioned me about has now come into full effect, but I force myself to find my balance and to press on.

Focus, Alice, I tell myself when things around me threaten to go woozy. *You can do this. You must.*

Each time I stumble, the orb draws close and circles me, as if it is offering me support. Branches tear at my cloak and clothes, draw blood across my cheeks and arms. My shoes, pointed, bothersome ones suited more for a genteel lady in a castle than a walk through the forest at night, gradually begin to soften to where the tip becomes more of a hazard than anything else. I stagger more than once, those blasted shoes catching on the forest's skeletons lying upon its floor. And still, the orb urges me on, nudging my shoulder or brushing against my arm until I catch up with Finn. When we are finally side by side, it prods my arm up until I take hold of Finn's dangling hand.

The ground miraculously steadies beneath my feet. As if it was happy by such a connection between myself and my love, the glitter from the orb's trail magnifies tenfold as it swirls about us. Together, we continue to follow the Wise Woman until I'm certain blisters riddle and pop and bleed upon my weary feet, my bones ache, and black spots dance before my eyes. And still, I force myself to continue the journey, to continue taking one step in front of the other.

I won't give up. Not now, not ever. Not even if I must crawl to wherever it is we go.

But the ground does not stay steady for too long. It starts small, a faint tremor, really, before everything around us shakes. That is not what has me concerned, though. No, the sound of trees falling is of more concern.

The falcon screams from above.

I scan the trees around us, but outside of the orb, there is no light. From small slivers in the branches high up, I know the moon is silvery and full, but that glow is beyond me with such dense treetops.

I coax the orb closer. It is trembling, its light weak.

"Hide him," I whisper softly.

The blue light dims even further until it nearly winks out before the orb darts frantically around Finn's body. It does as I ask, though, and soon enough, both Finn and the orb melt into the darkness, away from the rumbling.

The Wise Woman has disappeared, too.

Frabjous.

The rumbling grows strong, the crash of trees more violent. A roar booms through the cold night air, sending birds screaming from their sleep. I cannot make out the words—the language is guttural and coarse—but it's obvious that whatever is being said is done so in rage.

Son of a jabberwocky. It's a giant, isn't it?

I draw my sword, readying myself. I've fought many an enemy over the years, but never a titan. Nevertheless, I cannot allow him to put a halt to my journey tonight.

I cannot fail Finn.

My assumptions were correct, because within moments, a giant does, indeed, burst through the grove to my right. Now that the woods surrounding the enormous fellow are felled, the moon gifts me with her light and allows me a good view of my opponent. He looks surprisingly similar to any other man in this Timeline, only much, much angrier. Dirty brown hair, dark eyes, a beard, and an ordinary nose, the only bit that truly distinguishes him from the men in the village is his size. His head nearly reaches the tops of the trees still standing around him.

I'm a bit disappointed, to be honest.

The giant thrusts a finger toward me; so heated are the words from his mouth, spittle flies from him lips. Thank goodness, none falls upon me.

I have no idea what he is saying, but logic dictates he is accusing me of something terrible. Trespassing, perhaps? "My apologies if I am trespassing," I say in German, "but I am merely passing through and will be on my way momentarily."

He roars so loudly, so strongly, that if my hair were down, it would shoot straight out behind me. Furthermore, I am close to gagging, the stench of the fellow's breath is so rancid.

Apology and explanations are apparently not accepted then.

A tree is plucked from the ground and snapped in half as he yells at me some more. When one of the splintered logs hits the ground, I nearly fall from the ripple borne from such brute force.

The other piece, now jagged and pointy, is angled aggressively toward me.

"I don't want to fight you," I tell him, "but I will if I must." Especially as it's painfully clear there would be no way I could outrun a beast such as he.

The titan has the audacity to laugh. So he *can* understand me. The brute then hauls back the log and swings.

I duck just in time, rolling deftly beneath the timber. He roars once more, his weapon swinging, but I manage to run toward the woods still standing nearby. All around me, trees crash and splinter, leaves and branches raining on me in a ferocious storm.

I have to get around him.

Angrier words are thrown at me at he continues his vile deforestation. Another swing comes perilously too close, and I'm forced to run partway up of the length of a nearby tree to give myself the proper velocity to flip backward over the log.

Son of a jabberwocky, that was too close. I have no idea how long it is until midnight, but I best be getting this finished already. I weave through the fallen branches and timber, finally under the cover of still-standing trees thick enough to hide me. A stray rock upon the ground is sent sailing back from whence I came, and the giant refocuses his destruction in that area.

Well, then. Added height does not equal added intelligence. All that seems to be driving the brute is an intense desire to kill me.

Another pair of rocks is sent for good measure before I silently creep through the woods to circle around to the opposite side. For a moment, as he pokes the log into the trees I've long vacated, I hit the open ground created during his overly dramatic entrance.

Suddenly, the falcon's cries once more pierce the air. In the light of the moon, I watch as it nosedives toward the giant, screaming in its attack. I use the advantage it gifts me by sprinting across the barren patch and into the grove of trees to the side of the brute. From there, as he swats away at the frighteningly fast and daring bird, I'm able to make my way to where I'm parallel with his feet.

I take a deep breath. Grip my sword a bit tighter. And then I charge directly into the clearing he's created.

The falcon shrieks as it dives for the giant's face. The titan does his best to brush away the bird, but it's too fast for him. Let us pray my sword is the same. Just as the falcon swoops in for another dive, I slash once, twice across the giant's left Achilles tendon, right where leg and foot meet.

The giant stumbles. A roar such as I've never heard in all my years shakes even the skies.

Blood spurts from the wound, splattering me. I dive back into the standing woods, ducking and rolling as his club nearly makes contact. The falcon wastes no time, its battle cry deafening as it rushes the giant. I'm off once more, intent on completing the circle I've created.

If the giant had been angry before, he's utterly enraged now. But more importantly, he's clearly in pain. My cuts were true. He is unable to put much pressure on his left leg.

The makeshift club is sent sprawling into the woods, tearing into young trees. The giant limps forward, ripping out any and all trees that stand in his way. The falcon continues its assault, and for a moment, when I glance up into the sky, I fear for its chances. The giant's fist comes far too close.

Thankfully, the bird is just a hair faster.

I'm finally parallel with his legs again. His back to me as he tears through the forest, I once more sprint as fast as I can to him. One slash, two, against his right Achilles tendon before I'm forced to retreat.

The last roar, the one that shook the skies, is nothing to the one now torn from his lips. And when he drops to his knees and then to his chest, blood erupting from both legs, my own arse hits the ground from the impact.

Get up, Alice. You're not done yet.

I'm into the clearing once more, my sword gripped tightly. He's already got his palms on the dirt, attempting to push himself up. My time is perilously limited.

Sword out, I charge his side, slamming the blade nearly to the hilt into where I estimate a kidney lies. I can only hope my blade is long enough to reach.

A third roar—more agony than anger this time—blasts through the air. His hand finally makes contact with me, sending me soaring backward a good distance. When I slam into a tree, the breath is knocked clean out of me. Blood trickles down my cheek. I see stars. Darkness does its best to welcome me.

I stubbornly refuse its invitation, even though inappropriate mirth burbles out from between my lips.

I blink furiously as I clamber to unsteady feet. The falcon screams, circling the fallen giant. The titan yanks my sword out, tossing it nearby, before struggling to push himself up, but it's no good. There's blood gushing onto the ground from my latest attack.

I once saw a man bleed out from a stab to his kidney on a Wonderlandian battlefield nearly two years back. It was gruesome, really. An awful yet fairly quick way to go.

The giant's struggles turn weak, and before long, they cease all together. The rise and fall of his chest comes to a quiet end.

I allow myself to sit back down and catch what little of my own breath I still possess. A hand to the back of my head is left sticky with a bit of blood. Not too bad, though. I must look a right fright, though: dress torn and filthy, hair bloody and a mess, cheeks scraped and hands and knees close to raw.

A cross between a laugh and a sob falls out of me. I have fought many a beast in my time, but none so large as this titan before me. *I wonder if the Jabberwocky would be as fierce of an opponent.*

The falcon swoops down toward me, landing on a nearby rock. It chirps softly and it cocks its head at me.

"You have my gratitude," I tell it. "Your assistance was much appreciated."

It hops closers, its sharp beak nudging me.

"Is Finn all right?"

Another nudge is offered.

"All right, all right." I force myself back onto my feet. "Can you lead the way to where they are?"

It chirps and lifts off. I reclaim my sword, wiping the blood off on the giant's tunic. There is no hurrying, though. My legs simply won't let me. But the bird of prey flies low, constantly hovering so I do not lose sight. Soon enough, though, darkness envelopes me once more as the moon's light is blocked out by leaves. I'm stumbling, relying on hands against trees to keep me upright. It feels like a good half of an hour passes before a familiar blue light surfaces. And then, Finn's body, still hovering over the ground, with the Wise Woman standing next to him.

"Is it done?" she asks.

"Do you mean, have I bested the giant?"

Her smile is faint in the dim blue light. "He was a bothersome creature. If anyone around here has a taste for human flesh and bones, it was him."

There's something in her tone, something that tells me she expected this meeting of queen and giant. "Was this a test?" I ask coolly.

"All quests have dragons that must be slayed," she answers equally coolly. "And magic is never free."

I paid her already, with a bottle of my royal blood. "Why didn't you rid the forest of the giant yourself if there was such a concern over his proclivity toward eating people?"

"One would think that you, as a queen, would know the answer to that." She reaches up and runs a finger alongside my cheek; red decorates the tip. Before I can say anything, with that finger, she draws something upon my forehead.

"Come. We still have a ways to go."

I wipe my sweaty, bloody hand on my skirt and reclaim Finn's. The blue orb dances closer to me, its light now soothing. Our journey is silent and slow, considering the state of my knees. There will be bruises for sure. There are most likely bruises now.

Finally, after what I guess to be another hour of walking, we arrive at a small clearing in the woods. Situated in the midst is large, flattened rock and nothing else. The Wise Woman flicks her hand once more, and Finn's body floats over to rest upon the stone.

Above us, the falcon cries turn plaintive.

The orb circles me until I am dizzy, until my vision is nearly entirely filled with trails of blue stars. My body tingles; the braids upon my head loosen until my blood-stained hair swirls above me as if I was sinking in the ocean, drowning. With no word from the Wise Woman, I am compelled to drift toward the stone. The bluish orb now hovers over Finn, and in its pale, lovely light, I can see his dear face. The muscle within my chest constricts so very tightly.

I love him, I think. I love his goodness, I love his soul. I love how he thinks of others first, and how he risks much to protect people he does not even know. I love how he trusts me, and of how I can trust him when I once feared I would never do so with another. I love the way he kisses me, I love the way I feel calm and yet electrified with him all at once. I found him when I believed love was out of my reach, and I am all the more better for it.

We are partners. We are equals. We are, as he is so often to remind me, binaries of the very best kind.

The sound of a deep, intoning bell fills the clearing. This far into the woods, I have no idea where it comes from, but the countdown has begun. *One, two, three . . .*

"We will need the light of the full moon before the final stroke of midnight."

I gently cup his face, staring down at the slope of his nose and the fullness of his lips. *Four, five . . .*

I love him, I think again. His story is not finished. *Our* story is not finished. I will save him as he saved me. I will do whatever it takes, even if it means slaying a giant.

Six, seven . . .

Slowly, gently, my mouth drifts to his. I whisper the depth of my heart a hair's breadth away.

Eight, nine . . .

Then I kiss my beloved with intent.

Ten, eleven, twelve.

Thunder cracks overhead. Lightning pierces the ground in the clearing, not once, but twice. The cadence of the orb's pulses grows stronger, brighter, its light cutting blindingly through the darkness. And then, miraculously, I am rewarded by blue-gray eyes slowly opening to look up in mine.

Blue-gray. Not black.

I press my forehead against his, shaking from the effort at holding back the torrent of emotions threatening to pull me under. I can no longer speak, I am so shaken. So I kiss him, kiss his dear, handsome face—I kiss his eyelids, I kiss his cheeks, his nose, and then his mouth over and over again. Eventually, hands, warm, strong, familiar ones, curl around my arms.

True love encourages you to live. Thank all the goodness in the worlds for that.

My name is whispered in confusion, and it is the best gift I could ask for. I wish I could tell him it's all right now, that we're going to be fine, that he's safe, but all I can do is simply hold on. I'm not even embarrassed that tears of joy drip down my cheeks and onto his face.

Eventually, Finn says, his voice husky and oh-so-welcome, "Why does it feel like there's a needle in my arm?"

I'm laughing. It's raining, and we're in the middle of a clearing, on top of a giant stone and there's a dancing, magical blue orb above us, and I can't help myself. I'm laughing, and he most likely believes I'm well on my way to Bedlam—or even the Pleasance.

"Because," I say, kissing him once more, "there is."

"We're in a rain storm."

"Yes." Another kiss. "I have a lot to tell you. So much. But for now, tell me how you feel."

"Fine. Tired, though. How did we get here?"

He's speaking. He's awake. I cannot help but wonder if I am the one whose feet no longer touch the ground. I am beyond intoxicated with happiness.

"We walked." Yet another kiss. "Or rather, you floated."

"What?!"

"Do you feel as if you're yourself?"

"You're not making any sense, Alice. Why—why are there cuts on your cheek? Is that—is that blood on your face? Your clothes?"

His eyes are not black. I must pray this is enough.

I help him up despite his protests toward self-sufficiency. The orb swoops closer, pulsing so bright I can see every detail on Finn's face. Perhaps my madness and exhaustion and emotions color my perceptions, but I could swear it is as overjoyed as I am.

Above us, the falcon cries. I think I might just adore that bird. He would be a most excellent Wonderlander.

"Alice?"

I touch his cheek. "Yes, love?"

"Will you at least tell me who the lady behind you is?"

A savior, I think. "The twelfth Wise Woman."

His forehead scrunches as he considers this. "Why does that name sound familiar . . . ?"

The woman in question moves closer. "We must head back. There are those in the woods who are best not to be met tonight."

I can't help but let out a weary laugh. "Worse than my last introduction?"

She's solemn when she tells me yes.

I take hold of Finn's hands. "Can you walk?"

It makes me deliriously content to watch him roll his eyes. "Why wouldn't I be able to walk? Alice, you're kind of worrying me here. Actually, you're worrying me a lot. You look like you've been through hell."

It was worth it. To see him here, awake, to hear his voice . . .

The Wise Woman approaches us, her eyes still milky white in the light of the orb. She says nothing but simply angles her attention toward Finn.

"Did it work?" I ask. "Is the spell broken?"

Finn's alarmed. "Spell?"

"He is safe," she tells me. "As long as you live, as long as your love holds true, he is safe."

In the near distance, a wolf's howl pierces the air. The falcon's cries grow more frantic.

"And if I fall?"

She does not answer.

"We need to go now." I squeeze Finn's hands before letting go of one. "I'll explain all once we arrive at where it is we need to go."

"The woods," the Wise Woman says, "have many ears. It is best to remember that."

Noted.

As before, we journey in silence. I do not let go of Finn's hand once, and I must admit, it's not so much for balance but more for assurance. He's awake. He's here. He hasn't transformed. My feet and bones, so achy earlier in the evening, are no longer a concern. I feel his hand in mine. The brush of his shoulder against my body. And although I know he must be utterly anxious for answers, confused as to what's transpired and why he awoke in a strange place, surrounded by sights he has most likely never seen before, but he does not press for them. The orb dances around us, its light so pure, so magical, it feels as if we're being blessed and guarded all at once.

I do not stumble once on the way back to the cottage. Neither does he.

No one is asleep when we finally arrive at the cottage. In fact, the group of four I'd left behind bursts through the door the moment we are within twenty feet. The moment they do, the orb winks out of sight. Victor reaches his brother first, throwing his arms around him. "Jesus, Finn!" The doctor's voice is thick. "Don't—don't do that again, okay?"

I go to release Finn's hand, to give him space with his brother, but he merely holds on tighter. "Okay? Except, I don't have a single clue what's going on."

Mary and the A.D. laugh, converging upon us until we are squished between their well-meaning arms. Even Grymsdyke scuttles back and forth between Finn and myself.

"Seriously, guys," Finn gasps from the middle of the circle. "Can someone explain just what in the hell is going on right now?"

Once we are inside, our drenched cloaks and clothes hanging before the fire, we do. Finn insists Victor check me over for the scrapes and cuts, but I wave them off. Finn needs to be examined first. As he looks over his brother, Victor begins offering our story, as he was with Finn in 1905BUR-LP. I use the moment to pull Gertrude aside.

I do not dare to touch her, but I wear my heart on my torn and bloody chemise's sleeve. "You have my deepest gratitude, even if you sent me to battle a giant."

Her eyes are no longer milky white. Instead, they are once more brown and warm, albeit haunted. "When I was banished from the sisterhood, I vowed to continue helping those I could, even if it meant acting as a local healer and apothecary. My goal throughout the ages has never changed, even if those around me have."

"The kingdom is lucky to have a champion such as you."

The twist of the corner of her mouth is rueful. "Those whose intention are not pure do not feel as such. All blades are double sided, Your Majesty."

Isn't that the truth.

I drift back over to where my friends sit; the Wise Woman hovers in the background, tinkering with her bottles of herbs and potions. Finn reaches out and takes my hand in his once more as we unfold all that has occurred in the days since he fell prey to the Piper's machinations. He listens quietly, absorbing it all. And then, in the end, when it is my turn to explain what has happened just this evening, I find I cannot quite do so in the presence of others. It feels too . . . personal, in a way. Too raw.

So I simply say, "I did what I had to do, just as you did for me."

He studies me then, his eyes so serious in the firelight. A hand comes to cup my cheek, and there, in front of the others, he kisses me.

"I love you, my north star," he murmurs against my mouth.

My lips brush his. "We're binaries, remember?"

His chuckle sounds like heaven. The A.D. makes a lewd comment about us requiring a separate room if we were going to continue with such mush, considering what he just had to go through with Victor and Mary, and it only prompts more laughter to spill out of the both of us. Grymsdyke threatens to shut his mouth, insisting the A.D. not make crude comments about a Wonderlandian monarch, and it only leaves us laughing all the more. Soon, Finn eventually gets his way, and Victor tends to my superficial wounds.

The Wise Woman eventually encourages us all to sleep. Dawn is coming, she reminds us, but there is more to her warning than the simple motion of the earth spinning in the sky. No, a reckoning is coming, too. And we must be ready for it.

We lay on the floor before the fire once Gertrude excuses herself to the other room. Within minutes, the A.D., Victor, and Mary are all asleep. Grymsdyke settles into a nice web already constructed in one of the corners of the cottage. I curl closer to Finn's body, soaking in the steady thump of his heartbeat beneath my ear. Curiosity gets the better of me, though, and I gently push his tunic up.

The pattern on his torso has faded a bit, less vivid but more silvery, but it is still there.

Now that I know what it represents, I trace my fingers alongside the swirls and designs. The bird—*my* bird, the one that flew on my banners. How could I not have noticed this? There are diamond shapes intertwined in the vines. Stars, too. All subtle, all laid out in a way that, upon first glance, one might not notice such details. But there it is—the representation of my love laid out across his chest and waist, like a giant tattoo.

"I wonder if it will continue to fade," I whisper softly.

He lays a hand upon mine. "I hope not."

THE QUEEN AND THE PRINCE

FINN

I T'S STOPPED RAINING FINALLY, but damp fog has settled in its place. I watch Alice lean against the wooden frame of the cottage's distorted window, staring out at the woods. It seems so still out there, so peaceful. But then, there's always a calm before the storm, isn't there?

I wish she'd tell me what happened last night, why she's so bruised up like she is. But all she'll say is that, when there's enough time and we're alone, she'll explain it all.

"Do you have to do this right now?" I ask my brother.

He presses his cold-as-hell stethoscope against the skin covering my heart. "As a matter of fact, I do. We really ought to go back so I can do a full work-up on you."

"Don't be ridiculous. We've got a man to hunt. Besides, you checked me over last night, remember?"

"And I'll check you over again today, and whenever else I damn well please."

His eyes are bright, an all-too-familiar look for him, but I personally watched him take his protocol this morning, so I know he's doing what's necessary.

Nearby, a rip of a snore tears from the A.D. I wish I had my cell phone with me, because he's drooling buckets. I didn't sleep at all last night, though. I've slept enough. I just lay there and tried to process everything they told me last night, or at least, all they could before everyone nearly fell over in exhaustion.

I cannot believe we're in 1812GRI-CHT.

"I'm fine." I brush away the stethoscope. "Seriously. You ought to go see what Mary's up to."

"She's interrogating the Wise Woman as they collect herbs, attempting to wheedle some of her potions out of her before we head out. Don't try to change the subject. Magic notwithstanding, you were also stabbed not too long ago."

I sigh. "It's not like it was the first time, you know. I doubt it'll be the last."

He flashes a tiny pen light at one and then the other of my eyes, temporarily blinding me. "You really don't remember anything after the alley?"

"It's like I said, just bits and pieces of London. No Sara, no Sara's house." I remember what happened in the alley, though. Vividly so, especially how it felt to watch Todd finally pay for what he's done—to the Timelines, to the innocent people who lived in the ones now lost, to my mother and my grandfather, to what he did to Alice. How I'd shoot him again if I could. But as for the rest . . . Nothing. Just snatches of carriages rumbling across London's roads, flower girls desperate to make a sale, and the unsavory feeling of wanting to puke.

It pisses me off, having these blank pieces in my memory. This is the second time I've been forced into some kind of uncontrollable sleep, and I'm pretty damn tired of it.

"I can't believe you hauled my unconscious ass all around hell's half acre, by the way."

"If we hadn't, you wouldn't be awake right now. Is there any pain at the site of the stitches?"

I refocus on my brother. "None more than I normally would have."

He grunts, but checks them anyway. "We gave you antibiotics once you were brought back to the Institute." A finger gently pokes at the neat, black rows of thread. "Seems to have gotten the infection under control. I have another dose in my bag, just in case."

"Stop. Just . . . Stop. You're acting like—"

"Like what? Like you were on the verge of death?" His eyes harden. "Like Dad and I were scared shitless that we were going to lose yet another person we love to this bloody war?"

It's enough to shut me up.

"Finn, he *did* think we both died. That arsehole destroyed the Timeline we were in. All that shite that was going down right before we edited out? The explosions, the lights in the sky, the earthquakes?" He shakes his head. "All those people that were around us are now dead. Gone. The Piper destroyed the catalyst in the middle of the Institute. Hypnotized our father, our colleagues. *Our family.* Nearly blew up Mary and Alice—both ended up in the hospital! *Our father mourned us.*" He shoves the light and stethoscope back into his bag. "I don't think he's slept more than a handful of hours since it all went down. The man is running on fumes right now." He angles his head toward Alice. "Her, too."

Sometimes, I'm a total asshole. "You're right. I'm sorry. It's just . . . I'm hearing what you're saying. I get that I was . . . out, asleep, ready to transform, or whatever the hell it was that was happening. But I promise you I'm feeling fine. Better than fine." I reach out and grab his shoulder. "Thank you, though. For taking care of me, even when I know it had to be hard for you to focus."

His eyes won't meet mine. "I saw him, Finn. Or at least, I thought I did. At Sara's."

He's not talking about our father. "You know it wasn't real. You admitted you were in the middle of an episode."

Painful, bitterly rueful laughter falls out of Victor. "It felt real. It *still* feels like he's here, following me. Watching."

My brother has never met his biological father's monster, has never seen anything outside of what Halloween and Hollywood has had to offer up in terms of vision and appearance. And yet, he's inexplicably dreamed of and feared the creature his entire life. I overheard our parents discussing it shortly after they adopted me, of how Katrina was legitimately worried what it all meant. *"You know this all started when he was four. How is that possible, Brom? How could he know of his father's creation? He never met Dr. Frankenstein, not even once. His mother was illiterate and knew nothing outside of his name of the man she spent a single evening with. Yet Victor knew the creature's description long before he knew how to read. It cannot be a coincidence!"*

My father had no idea what to say. Years later, none of us do. Not Victor's shrink, not our father, not our mother, not myself, not even Mary. But all this time, he's only ever dreamed of the creature—never seen. Not even in his worst, manic episodes.

Until now.

"You know he didn't die," Victor continues bleakly. "He only disappeared at the end of the blasted book. Floated off on some chunk of bloody ice."

It's a conversation we've had countless times. There is nothing I can say, nothing our parents have ever been able to say, that can assure him that the monster isn't coming for him.

And still, we try, and will continue doing so.

"Victor." My tone forces his eyes back to my face. "I'm not going to insist he wasn't there, considering I was out the whole time, but you know the odds that he was are slim to none. He'd have to first figure out that you exist. How would he do that? Your mother died shortly after Brom brought you home. I'm sure it wasn't like she bragged to a bunch of people that she bagged and then got knocked up by some psychotic doctor, you know?"

He lets out a tiny puff of rueful amusement.

"Nothing in the book indicates he was psychic. But even if he was,"—because we'd heard this theory from Victor before—"he'd have to figure out how to edit. You know the odds of him being able to do so naturally are tiny. And honestly, how would he know you were in 1905BUR-LP? We didn't even know where we were until after Todd was dead."

He bites his lip. "I know. I know. Dad said the same thing."

And still, it kills me that he still believes it all is a possibility.

I clear my throat. Change the subject, because allowing Victor to dwell too long on his asinine bio-dad's crazy-ass mistakes is tantamount to validating them. "Sara didn't admit anything to you while we were there?"

Victor rubs at his hair. "No. She had her hands full dealing with us. We fought a few times, but it was about stupid stuff." He lets out a puff of amusement. "Normal stuff for me and her, at least when I was coherent."

I cannot believe that Sara was a mole. It just—it's almost like a kick to the nuts to hear that. For years, she was like my sister, one of my closest friends. She was my partner.

The Piper is going to pay for what he's done. It's only a matter of when, not if.

"Is everything okay?"

I glance up at Alice. Her lower lip is tugged between her teeth; it's obvious she's still worried. But it turns out her question isn't to me but my brother, because he says, "Everything seems fine. When we get back, I plan on doing some blood work, but other than him needing to take it easy so he doesn't tear his stitches, he's in decent health."

She sits down next to me, taking hold of my hand. "Excellent."

A low groan comes from the nearby floor. "Do you two ever stop shagging in public? Did I do something in a past life, so that it was my punishment to be constantly surrounded by lovey-dovies?"

Well, there goes the quiet morning.

When Alice levels him with a scathing look, he winces. "Does this mean our own love affair is over, Your Majesty?"

Her exasperated sigh is quite loud.

His rubbery lips curve upward in response. "You adore me the way I am. Admit it." But his humor fades when Grymsdyke lowers himself from the ceiling before him.

"What I'll admit," Alice stresses, "is that it's troubling that there's a Wise Woman working with the Piper on some level. The enchantment, from what Bunting claims, is specific toward turning people into the Piper's Chosen."

"The fact that the angriest, most vindictive one of the lot has joined in with the Piper is pretty damn terrifying, if you ask me," Victor mutters.

More solemn from before, the A.D. pretends to shudder. "The team from hell is what they are."

"So many of the Chosen have been with the Piper for hundreds of years," Alice says. "We have no idea if he was able to hypnotize them into their current state of being or if it's a result of the thirteenth Wise Woman's spell."

"Or," Victor adds, "a combination of both."

"Is it even possible for the curse to be broken or altered?" the A.D. asks.

"It would be incredibly difficult," says a voice from behind us.

We turn to find Mary and the Wise Woman who was in the clearing with Alice and me last night, both carrying baskets filled with herbs. She unnerves me, to be honest. There's something off about her. Almost inhuman. Her movements, while graceful, aren't like anyone else's I've ever seen. Nor are her eyes. When she stares at you, she's cutting straight through skin, muscle, and bones. She hardly blinks and I'm beginning to wonder if she even breathes.

"The spell last night was altered because there was already an enchantment put in place." The woman who introduced herself to me as Gertrude sets her basket upon a table. "The queen's blood magic had been enacted prior to my sister's, and therefore offered some protection. But if you remember, I warned you last night that even this bit of powerful magic would not hold indefinitely. Sooner or later, my sister's enchantment would have overcome it."

"You say it's been altered," Alice says. "Not broken."

The Wise Woman considers my north star. "No. Not broken. I suppose it's a good thing you had giant's blood to aid you in such a powerful alteration last night, is it not?"

She'd told Alice, *"As long as you live, as long as your love holds true, he is safe."* Christ, just thinking of that has me in a sweat—not so much for my chances, but the threat it seems to pose toward Alice.

Wait. Wait. Back up a moment. *Giant's blood?*

"Do you know where the thirteenth Wise Woman is now?" Alice is asking.

The A.D. holds out a hand. "Whoa. What giant's blood?"

Exactly. What he said.

The Wise Woman fixes those unblinking eyes of hers on my father's assistant. "Why, the one the queen slew last night."

What. The. HELL?

"A giant!" Mary exclaims. "How wonderfully fairy tale-ish. Did it know you were an Englishman? Fi-Fi-Fo-Fum and all that?"

Before Alice can answer, I ask, "When was this?"

"On the way to the clearing." She's utterly unapologetic. "It seemed quite put out with me for reasons unknown, and picked a rather nasty fight."

Mary claps. "I swear, somebody needs to write this down. The queen, en route to save her, well, lover, with true love's kiss, battles a giant. Perhaps we can slip it into a new volume of fairy tales. A feminist one that proves ladies can kick ass and save men just as well as men can save them."

"The Queen of Diamonds has always been one of Wonderland's fiercest champions," Grymsdyke barks. "There are precious few who can best her in battle."

"You're neglecting that there are already are some stories where women save men," Victor points out to Mary. "There's one where a prince was turned into a stove. A princess saved him. Remember that one, Finn?"

He's right—that's not one of his hallucinations. It's a story we used to think was ridiculous. But, I'm still overly focused on the fact that Alice battled a giant. *A giant.*

Mary scoffs. "A stove? Goodness. How unromantic and rather embarrassing all at once." She comes over and pats Victor's face. "Try not to allow yourself to be turned into something so wholly undignified while we're here. I'm not a princess, you know. Chances are, I wouldn't be able to turn you back."

"What kind of land allows a prince to become a stove?" Grymsdyke mutters. "Stoves are not people."

"Are you okay?" I gently grab hold of both of Alice's hands. She's got scratches on her face. One cheek is bruised. Her palms are a bit raw, and she's moving slower than normal today.

"Victor tended to me last night, remember?" Her smile is faint but genuine. "I'm perfectly fine. Granted, I do not wish to face another giant in the near future . . ."

Alice fought a giant and kicked its ass. She's amazing.

"Yet, I'm afraid we digress. I was asking the Wise Woman whether or not she knows where the thirteenth of her sisters now resides."

Gertrude admits, "It has been well over a century since I have last seen her."

Alice is undeterred. "Have you ever heard of the Pied Piper of Hamelin?"

This gets her attention. Her head snaps sharply up with the name.

I remember the first time Katrina read me the story of the Piper. I was sixteen, I think. It was a rainy day in New York City, and she and I were sitting before a fire and working on my reading. While I had several top-notch tutors on top of the private school I went to, it still felt safer to work with her than anyone else. She never judged me. Never made fun of me about how badly I had to sound a word out or had no clue about a subject—not that she or Brom would have ever tolerated anyone else doing so, either, but still. Katrina equaled acceptance, love, and safety. And when we read together, even though I was sixteen and still more than a bit of a punk, I felt like everything might just turn out okay.

I had a mother, one who cared. One who wanted to read with me.

But that story . . . yeah, it was terrifying as all hell. I mean, some dude can come and kidnap all of a town's children out of revenge?

"Some people are downright evil," I'd told Katrina.

"Unfortunately," she said, *"that's true. But there is also so much*

goodness in others. Never forget that. Never close your eyes to the kindnesses in the worlds, even when you are faced with the worst of souls."

Sometimes it's hard to remember, especially when it turns out the same monster that prompted these words is most likely the mastermind behind her murder. Just thinking about it makes my blood boil.

"Yes," the Wise Woman is saying in response to Alice's question.

"Is he of your acquaintance?" Alice presses.

The Wise Woman is quiet for a long moment, as if she's weighing whether or not to answer. I love that Alice isn't afraid to ask such questions, though. A lot of agents might be scared shitless to press their luck with somebody who could turn them into a toad, but not Alice.

God, I respect her so much.

"We crossed paths once," the Wise Woman finally admits. She places a clump of moss from her basket on the table. "Long, long ago, before I left the sisterhood."

"We have reason to believe he might be in league with the thirteenth Wise Woman," Alice continues. "The sword with your sister's enchantment was wielded by one of his associates. May I inquire as to your opinion of the person in question?"

"His soul," the Wise Woman says carefully, "is not like many others.' There is a darkness inside, one that is not easy to understand."

Is evil ever easy to do so, though?

"We suspect that he is the perpetrator behind the extinguishing of many lives. During your encounter in the past, were you able to intuit any reasons as to why a man such as he would embark upon such terrible deeds?"

"When there is a gaping hole such as his, attempts are often made to fill it."

It isn't really an answer, or at least it isn't one that couldn't already be guessed.

"Do you believe in good and evil?" Mary asks.

"It is the foolish who do not understand that the world is built of many shades of both," the woman says simply.

Such painful truth.

"Your journeys will not be easy." When I refocus on our hostess, she's holding a large dagger, her eyes that eerie white from the night before. Her voice doesn't even sound human anymore. But more importantly, her hair is now floating around her head, her feet dangling off the damn floor. "There will be blood. There will be pain and grief. Nightmares will come to life. The impossible will be asked of each of you when light seems the furthest away. If you falter, if you give in, if you allow yourself to embrace the darkness that wishes to curl within and fill the holes inside you, there will be no turning back to what once was."

"How very specific," the A.D. mutters. I kick his foot and he quietly yelps.

But when I look at the woman again, her eyes are normal, her feet are on the ground. Her hair is looped in braids around her head.

She helped save my life and all, but damn, that woman is freaky.

"I feel as if we're practically sitting ducks amongst such evil, magical beings," the A.D. continues. "Sure, we've got Alice, Finn is back, and the rest of us can hold our own in fights, but it means very little if the Piper can just music away anything, or the thirteenth Wise Woman feels like transforming us during battle. I wish there were a way to protect ourselves, especially if we've now got somebody telling us we're basically walking into the mouth of hell."

Sometimes, the A.D. never figures out when to shut his trap. But, he has a point here.

"I will make a meal for you before you leave." The Wise Woman drags a wooden bowl over to where she stands. "You will not want to go as far as you must on empty stomachs." A long, wooden spoon is pointed at Alice. "There are chickens in the back. Fetch the eggs and then milk the cow. There is a basket and pail by the front door for you to use." The spoon swivels toward me. "Fetch the goose with the lame leg that rests within the coop. She is old and ready to sleep. I have held on too long out of sentimentality, but now is as good as time as any to honor her wishes."

Oookay?

When Alice and I reach the door, the Wise Woman is already issuing orders to the rest of the group, including Grymsdyke.

It's cold outside. Frost tips the leaves on the trees around us. The ground is soft enough to suck in our shoes, the wind cutting. Thunder rumbles in the distance, making sure we know that the storm isn't quite done with us yet.

Once, just once, I wish one of my assignments took me to somewhere like Tahiti or Hawaii.

I throw my cloak around my shoulders; Alice does the same. I say, "She's interesting."

Alice doesn't comment, but takes hold of my hand again and pulls me around the back of the house. A coop sits fifty or so feet back from the cottage, with a neat herb garden filling the space in between. Farther on back is a small barn of sorts; somewhere within, a horse neighs quietly.

Before I can say anything, she slides her arms beneath my cloak, tugging me closer. I return the favor, and for several long seconds, we say nothing as we stand there, holding each other as the wind howls about us. And then, she reaches up, both hands cupping my face as she studies me intently.

Somehow, her concern doesn't feel as claustrophobic as Victor's.

She didn't give up on me. Everyone else thought Victor and I were dead, but Alice refused to accept it. She came for me when no one thought it was possible. She figured out who it was that cursed the blade that stabbed me, tracked down the Timeline, and battled a giant. And here she is, here we are, and she gave that woman inside her blood in order to heal me.

She saved me with her blood. With true love's kiss. Her love is now written across my body. If this isn't a fairy tale, then I don't know what else to call it. Any kind of reasonable words, any kind that actually could express what I'm feeling inside, are way out of my current reach.

She rises to her tiptoes, her lips brushing against mine. My breath stutters in my chest, the muscle in my chest feels like it might actually burst out of my ribcage. I love this woman so much. I want her. Need her. Value her. She's my partner. My sounding board. My heart. How did this happen? How did she get so irrevocably under my skin and into my head and heart so quickly?

I kiss her then, slowly, meaningfully. Our warm breaths mingle in the chilly air. Soon enough, though, our foreheads touch as we try to catch those breaths. Her pulse races just as fast as mine.

I wish we had more time. More privacy. It's pitiful, but I tell her, "Thank you."

Her forehead settles in the crook of my neck as her arms once more loop my waist. "Would you like to hear another fairy tale?"

She told me one once, a Wonderlandian one. I think it's my favorite of all stories now.

"From you? Always. Will it be a feminist one like Mary wants?"

"You are a rapscallion, you know."

"I do my best. But please, go on. I'd love to hear it."

"Once upon a time, there was a queen," she says quietly, "one who had a wonderful kingdom that she loved very much. Her life was very full. She had goals and aspirations to ensure the people of her kingdom never had to want like those in so many others. She desired and hoped for more for them and was willing to sacrifice much to provide all that she could. While she ruled alone, it did not mean her heart was empty. A king from another Court loved her just as much as she loved him. For many years, she felt content. Blessed. Together, they combined their dreams and planned for the future of their lands.

"But seasons changed as they always do. The land and her people's needs altered, and the queen struggled with what was asked of her. But she had made a promise the day she received her crown: she vowed she would always do everything in her power to provide for those who relied upon her. Heart heavy, she gave up all that she knew, all that she loved, in order to fulfill her promise.

"The queen was lost afterward. She feared her purpose was gone, that her heart had closed. She raged, she howled, she tore her hair out. Grief consumed her. And yet, once more, the seasons changed. Those that were lost came to find her once more, only in different forms. Her heart bloomed like a bud after a snow thaw. A prince from a faraway land grew to love her just as much as she loved him. He was more than simply her love. He was her partner, her best friend. She trusted him, she valued him. So when a villain tried to take him from her, she wrote herself a new fairy tale, one in which the queen saves the prince. Because there is no one, and nothing outside of a prophecy, that will ever be allowed to strip away her purpose and love from her again—except if the prince's heart changes, of course."

I was wrong. I think *this* is my favorite story of all time.

I press a lingering kiss against her temple. "It would never happen. He'd be the biggest idiot in all the worlds if he ever did that. Besides, he sees her the same way."

Her bittersweet laugh is little more than a burst of exhaled air. "Can I tell you one?"

I feel rather than see her nod.

"Once upon a time," I tell her, "there was this kid who was really messed up. He didn't believe in fairy tales. Childhood wasn't filled with knights and princesses and castles—it was filled with empty bellies, no warm places to sleep, and lack of money. He was stupid—"

"Not stupid," she quickly inserts.

"Hey. I'm telling the story, remember?"

"*Not stupid,*" she stresses.

"Fine. Ignorant. Is that better?"

"Barely. You may continue."

"Thank you." I try not to laugh. "As I was saying, he was ignorant and didn't really know better. He got mixed up with some shady people and did a lot of really stupid, dangerous stuff. He feared people trying to change him. Fought against it. Raged against the machine—"

"What kind of machine?"

Okay, now I do laugh. "It's a saying. It just means I swam against the current. Rebelled against the norm."

"Ah. Sorry. Please continue."

"To make a long story short, it took the kid a long time to get his head screwed on straight."

She sighs. "I'm never going to learn all these twenty-first-century sayings, am I?"

"If I could, you can."

"You've had quite a bit more time than I have. My apologies, though. I keep interrupting you, when I wish so very dearly to hear this tale."

"The kid learned that he could be anything he wanted to be. He decided he was going to be that knight he so long refused to allow himself to imagine—just not in actual armor. He wanted to help others in any way he could."

"My favorite kind of hero," she whispers.

"As a knight, he met a lot of ladies—"

A bubble of surprised laughter floats out of her.

"And some of them were pretty awesome. He kept his options open, though. His work was pretty important to him. Then one day, the head knight told him he had to go find a queen. The kid—"

"Knight," she says.

"Right. Sorry. The knight looked and looked for years. He couldn't find the queen. It drove him crazy to not be able to find her. Just when he thought she was a ghost or urban legend, she appeared at his castle. And when he finally met her, he realized all those other awesome ladies he'd met were, well, still awesome."

Another bit of delicious laughter escapes her lips. "What a perfectly charming story this is, Finn."

"But the queen outshone them all. She was more than awesome. She was smart. Funny. Capable. Strong. Brave as all hell. She kicked ass and took names like nobody's business. She was the star in his night sky. Her gravity sucked his in, and he was pretty damn glad for it. It didn't take long before he knew he wanted to be her knight for as long as she'd let him. Forever, if he was lucky."

I'm a terrible storyteller, but there it is. My heart, laid out bare for her to read.

She twists bunches of my tunic around her fingers. "I like this tale. It's nearly as good as the one about Alice Liddell falling in love with Huckleberry Finn. Somebody needs to write that, by the way."

"Only nearly?"

She laughs quietly again. "Actually, I adore them equally." And then, more softly, "Forever sounds just about right."

I run my hands up her back. "Yeah?"

"Yeah."

"Listen to you, using twenty-first century slang like a champ."

"Finn?"

"Yeah?"

"I must tell you that one part of your story is incorrect. You are not a knight. By now, the heralds of both the White and Diamond courts will have announced you legally as a Diamonds' prince of Wonderland. During his brief stay in New York City, the Cheshire-Cat drafted the necessary paperwork; both the White King and myself signed it. You probably know by now that Wonderlanders are very set in their often strange ways, and that even though I am in exile, once word got out that you and I are attached, it became . . . necessary, I suppose, to legally define the relationship." She lets out a surprisingly nervous breath of a chuckle. "This happens occasionally with other monarchs throughout the ages, even if they have a co-ruler. Princes and princesses are often the children of kings and queens, yes, but they are titles that may be granted for consorts, too. Your situation was just a bit different in that I do not have an officially crowned co-regent."

Holy. Crap.

"Furthermore, under such orders and requirements, and acting in lieu of my Grand Advisor, the Cheshire-Cat has ensured that a piece of land the throne holds has been transferred to your ownership, although it is highly doubtful you will ever be there to reside within the manor attached, considering my exile. Once upon a time, many, many hundreds of years ago, another Diamonds' prince oversaw the lands and it has been set aside for such use since. As my chosen consort, it is yours now."

I say, ever so eloquently, "What?"

I mean, the Cheshire-Cat had mentioned something similar when I was last in Wonderland. Everyone had kept calling me Sir Finn, and when I tried to correct them, he offered up some nonsensical explanation of how I was actually a prince. But I didn't really put much stock into it, as I was focused more on making sure the boojum was out of Alice as quickly as possible. I guess I kind of forgot all about it until now.

"Your legal title in Wonderland is now Prince Finn of Adámas. Although, I cannot see why it would not carry over into other Timelines as well." And then, more softer, "If it's all right with you. You always have the opportunity to reject it, of course."

Prince. I'm a prince. The dirty, scrawny, hick of a kid is now a *prince*. This woman, this queen who battles giants for me, saves me from fairy tale villains, granted me a title.

She is my fairy tale, come to life.

"If it means something to you," I tell her, my voice hoarse, "it means something to me." And it does, because me being officially granted a title—it has nothing to do with the name, really. It's all about her heart. Her choice.

"*You* mean something to me. *This,*"—she places a hand over my heart—"means something to me. It means everything."

My mouth finds hers, and soon my tongue. My focus narrows onto the woman in my arms and nothing else. I feel her. I smell her. I taste her. I want her. She folds back my cloak, her hands spreading across my chest, across the wide swatch on my torso that bears proof of her love for me. I cup her face, my lips trailing a path down the length of her chin, lower still to the base of her neck. Her quiet gasp only sets me further on fire.

Forever with this woman might not be long enough.

Her hands drift lower; mine do the same. Medieval dresses, though, are definitely not my favorite, because I have to fight through all the fabric just to touch her. Right before I think I might go crazy, she once more takes my hand. This time, she leads me into the small barn, surveying the lay of the land. There are four stalls within the barn: one with a horse, one with a cow, and the others empty from what I can tell. Off to the side is a small, rickety set of stairs; on cue, we both head toward it. Up above is a small area filled with a broken spinning wheel, several trunks, and, conveniently, several piles of hay.

Alice is once more kissing me, pulling me toward the hay. She's already working the belt around my waist, eventually tossing it to the side with a soft *thunk.* Her cloak is next, then mine. My boots, her shoes. Her dress, my tunic. Her chemise, my breeches. Bruises mar her beautiful body, all over her thighs and arms and belly. I run my fingers across the unmarred slices of soft skin. While I hate the thought of such bruises on her, of any pain she must be in, I cannot help but marvel at how they do nothing to diminish how beautiful she is to me.

My warrior queen.

Her fingers trace the lines on my torso, causing goose bumps to cover my skin far more than the chilly air in the loft. "This one, here," she whispers, her fingertip circling a space just to the side of my stitches. "Do you see it?"

I only see her.

"In Wonderland, you never saw my banners. But this . . ." Her voice grows husky. "This is the bird that my armies carried upon their flags. The one that hangs behind my throne. The one embroidered upon every piece of clothing I wore for years. The third time I came to Wonderland, my people claimed I was like a bird who flew away for the winter, only to finally return home. It became their symbol for me. When I left, people lamented that I was flying away for the longest winter."

I cup her face with a hand, tug her chin up so our eyes can meet.

"It's funny," she whispers, heart in her eyes. "But in reality, I flew to a new home, didn't I? One I belong in equally as much as the other. I flew to the Society. I flew to you. My winter is now spring. I found my forever home."

When I first came to the Institute, I asked Katrina if it was going to be my new home. She said, *"My mother used to tell me that home is where the heart is."* She'd turned to Brom and Victor before smiling at me. *"My heart lives inside these two men. I hope you let me have a piece inside you, too. In return, I hope someday you will allow a piece of mine in you. My home is with them and now you."*

She did get a piece of my heart—a large one. So did Brom and Victor. For a long time, I figured that was enough. Along with Jim, I'd let a precious few amount people in after holding so many others at arm's length. In the years since my mother's death, though, I've felt her heart within mine when I need it the most. And now . . . now there is another who holds mine and I hold hers in return.

Home is where the heart is. Home is with Alice. Alice *is* home.

Our mouths find each other, our kisses first slow and then unbearably hot. Soon, she's beneath me on the hay, our breaths coming out more as gasps than anything else. I'm careful of her bruises, she's gentle with my stitches. I kiss her clavicle, she kisses my ear. I kiss her breast, she licks the base of my neck. I worship her body, she worships mine. When I finally enter her, that, too, feels like coming home.

Somewhere below us, a horse neighs. A cow moos. Outside, birds sing mournful, beautiful songs. We move in unison, this queen and I, and with each thrust, I hope she feels the strength of my love for her. When an orgasm claims her, I watch her face with awe. She's gorgeous, yes, but it's what lays within her that attracts me the most. Her strength. Her heart. Her past and her hopes for the future. In this moment, when ecstasy pulls her under, so much of her vulnerability shows, and it's utterly captivating.

And when I shortly follow her over that cliff, into an ocean of pleasure, she cups my face and whispers over and over how much she loves me, too. I willingly drown in the feelings threatening to tear me apart, because no other option can be valid for me.

THE GOOSE'S GIFTS

ALICE

THE HENHOUSE IS TINY—Finn cannot stand upright in it. It's fairly comical to watch him attempt to maneuver around the gaggle of hens clucking and darting around impatiently, as if they expect us to feed them. He was the one who milked the cow, claiming he'd done so a number of times as a child when he'd stolen milk from various farmers. I ached hearing this memory, despising the thought of him being so lost and hungry at such a young age, but it also increased my respect for the man he's become. So many who harken from difficult beginnings do not find it worth the trouble to reach for the stars. Finn did, though. He fought through years of sporadic schooling, homelessness, hunger, and more to become the upstanding man he is today.

My heart flutters, watching him now.

I ought to collect eggs, but I cannot seem to tear my eyes away from him. Yesterday, he was asleep, his eyes black. Today, he is here with me, in a fairy tale.

Life is so very unpredictable.

Finn easily locates the goose the Wise Woman sent him to find. Sitting in a lonely nest off to the side of all the others,' one leg sticks out to the side of the poor thing's body at an awkward angle, the webbed toes gnarled and curled unnaturally. A scar runs the length of the goose's face, from milky, shattered eye, all the way across to the tip of the beak. Finn squats down before the little fowl; she does not run or attempt to flee like the others in the coop. She simply stares at him expectantly, her head cocked to the side. "Gertrude sent me to fetch you," he tells her.

She makes a soft honking sound before attempting to stand. She struggles terribly, unable to fully rise, and it's painful to watch. It must be for Finn, too, because he quickly picks her up before she falls. The little thing snuggles in the crook of his arm, a soft series of honks replicating purring coming from her chest.

I wander over to them. "Looks as if I have a bit of competition."

He laughs quietly, if not a bit ruefully, as he runs a hand across its back.

I gently stroke the goose's nearly bald head. Tiny, wispy feathers stick out at funny angles. "Outside of her obvious adoration for you, the poor thing appears miserable."

The goose chatters a series of quiet honks.

"There was a gaggle of wild geese that live on the land around my castle," I tell him. "They were excellent guards, really. One of the larger females, her name was Bathsheba, had a terrible temper. She bullied the poor gander that attempted to lead the group until he was clearly outmatched. But if you brought her tarts, she was such a dear. I rather miss her."

The goose looks up at me and honks knowingly.

"Geese as guards, spiders as guards," Finn says, smiling. "You had quite the menagerie going on there, didn't you?"

"Allies are allies. The brave come in many shapes and sizes, and all were welcome in the Diamonds Court."

As I collect eggs, I watch Finn and the goose out of the corner of my eye. Her honkish purring is quite loud now as she contentedly snuggles in his arms. It's silly, really, but I find the whole sight entirely endearing.

Finally, we head back to the house, our task finished much later than expected. Only the Wise Woman and Mary are within, kneading two lumps of dough.

I set the pail of milk down on the table before passing Gertrude the basket of eggs. "Where are the others?"

"I sent them out to acquire a few things." The Wise Woman smacks flour off her hands before coming closer to where Finn stands with the goose. "She likes you."

I cannot seem to contain the small snort that escapes me when Mary says, "Finn, is that what took you so long out there? You were charming the goose?"

I find it even more endearing that he blushes.

The Wise Woman takes the bird from his arms, kissing the little thing's head. "Old friend, are you sure about this?"

The goose honks loudly, passionately, at great length.

Our hostess exhales heavily. "I understand." To Finn and myself, she says, "Before she passes, there are a pair of gifts she wishes to give you for your bravery and kindnesses. You'll need them in the coming days. It will take a bit before they're ready, though."

She sets the goose down upon some of the straw by the fire. The poor thing grunts, nearly toppling over when she can't tuck her leg beneath her. Her owner wanders over to her racks of bottles, sorting through them.

Mary beckons us over before wiping a floury hand across her face. "I've never made bread before. It's oddly soothing."

"Pretending you're punching someone in the face is soothing?" Finn asks as she pounds against the dough.

She laughs. "Someone? Try Victor."

He really should have known better than to engage.

"You look good," she tells him. "Better. The black eyes just weren't doing it for you."

"Mary Lennox, ladies and gentleman." He holds a hand out, as if he is introducing her. "Keeping it real since 1911."

She smiles winningly.

Finn leans in, picking a strand of straw from my hair. "You don't think we're going to have to eat the goose, do you?"

I glance over at the fowl sitting by the fire. "I certainly hope not."

"I don't think I can." He also stares at the bird. "Actually, I know I can't."

I get to work helping Mary with the bread, even though I have never made it myself, either, and Finn is sent outside to chop firewood.

Victor, the A.D., and Grymsdyke show up shortly after the dough has finished rising and is just about to be placed into the ashes. Each man, with wet leaves decorating their wind-whipped hair and clothes, and mud smearing their faces, carries several large brown sacks stained a rusty color. And . . . is that blood? Lots of blood, actually, just hidden behind even more mud, I fear.

Even my assassin is covered in blood.

The A.D. drops his pairs of sacks. "We cannot get out of this forest fast enough."

The Wise Woman takes one of Victor's from him. "Was there any difficulty in the task?"

"None at all."

"For the doctor, maybe." The A.D. grimaces. "He's already good with a scalpel. Some of us have never sawed apart a body before. Or, in this fellow's case,"—he motions to the spider—"crawl inside a dead person looking for specific things."

What is this?

"There is always time for a first." The Wise Woman peers within Victor's bag. "Oh, your work is excellent. This will do quite nicely."

Finn makes his way into the cottage right as she dumps the bag's contents onto a clean table. I do not think it would be an understatement to say that he, Mary, and I are completely taken aback at what we're looking at. Various bloody chunks of what appear to be freshly cut-up pieces of flesh and organs now decorate the table.

"What in God's name is that?" Mary's whisper is strangled.

"You ain't seen nothing, yet," the A.D. mutters. Nearby, Grymsdyke quietly agrees with him.

"The queen paid two prices last night." The Wise Woman sifts through the pieces. "Although, she may not have known so until now. While it was my hope that we would encounter a certain fiend who has plagued the forest and village for far too long, it was certainly not a guarantee. The giant demanded sacrifices for years, ate those who dared to breach the forest, and destroyed many homes and families. We required a hero, a champion, and last night, that is exactly what we got. A queen slew the giant. In return, his blood provided her added strength to fight my sister's enchantment. Today, his meat will aid in another enchantment, one cast by me." She uses the back of her freshly bloody hand to wipe stray hairs from her face. "I cannot completely shield you from any of the Wise Women's enchantments, just as they cannot shield anyone from mine. None of us can destroy the others'— we can only alter. But if you are right, and the thirteenth sister is in league with the Piper, I must do what I can to help balance the scales. The payment for such an enchantment was the giant's death."

"Why did you not take care of the giant?" Mary asks.

"We do not intercede unless asked, and no one, in the many years I have lived here, has ever come to request my aid with the giant."

"But, if you cannot intercede without a request, how is it you are able to offer us one?"

"But you did ask." The Wise Woman turns to face the A.D. "He did, just this morning. He wished for a way to protect your group. And as the queen gave me extra payment, I will honor the request."

The confused and yet fairly pleased *Who, me?* look on Jack Dawkin's face is comical.

"And as he and the healer went to fetch the necessary pieces to aid in my spell, alongside others for future use, I have now received three payments. Your protection will thusly be two-fold."

The A.D. whistles. "Well, hot damn."

Gertrude drags over another of the bags and dumps the contents of that one out upon the table, too.

The smell, I must admit, is utterly foul. Any appetite I might have had from the comforting scent of bread baking evaporates without a trace. As if she can sense this, the Wise Woman deadpans, "Perhaps it will be best for you all to eat outside. The rain has stopped for now."

It is a very good idea. Still, once we are all outdoors, none of us has the desire to consume anything in the basket Mary brings. Instead, we use our time to plan. Victor pulls out a map of Germany he brought and spreads it across the stump of a fallen tree. "According to the Librarian's notes, we're here." He taps on a dot labeled *Sababurg.* "Hamelin is here." He taps another dot, this one marked *Hameln.* "By the way, here's the actual Koppenberg Mountain." He taps a dot way over in Belgium. "I think we need to consider that, hypnotized or not, it would be difficult to march a hundred and thirty children over three hundred miles—therefore, we ought to focus in on Hamelin and its surrounding environs. From what I can tell, it's about ninety-five kilometers, or roughly fifty-eight miles between Sababurg and Hamelin. Not so bad in a car, but we don't have a car."

Finn's nose scrunches up. "On horseback, or in a carriage . . . That's probably eight, ten hours? If the roads are good. We don't have either. We've got a cart with a single horse pulling five people. So we'll want to tack on quite a bit of extra time, too, because the horse won't be able to deal with it all." He pauses. "Or we can simply edit there once the Wise Woman's enchantment is done. Do you guys expect the Piper to be there?"

I touch his shoulder. "It's worth a try. Your father is investigating the residence Sara told us about, but chances are, as with his other abodes, it will be empty. A team is also searching the school he was associated with. When he left the Institute, he walked through a doorway. He edited, Finn. And he did so into the library at Bücherei."

"Are you sure?"

I nod. "While his music befuddled me, and I was utterly disoriented from the explosion, I recognized the room quite clearly. Wherever he went, the library was there, waiting. And as it is no longer in New York, I cannot help but think he hid it away somewhere else, somewhere one must edit into."

"You think he's come home."

"I think it's a very good possibility, yes."

"We have to assume the arsehole was able to get information out of Sara," the A.D. says. "She mentioned having holes in her memories. Wen, too. If he was listening in on us this entire time, he probably knows that the Society never interacted with fairy tale Timelines. Having a home base in one would be the perfect snake hole to hide in."

Grymsdyke peers down at the map. "Agreed."

Finn says quietly, "I can't believe she bugged the Institute." His muscles tense beneath my touch.

"I doubt she had a choice." I lean my cheek against his shoulder. "In the end, she sacrificed much in order to try and keep you all safe from herself."

Mary scowls. "I can't believe you're defending her. She attacked you!"

Victor places a hand on her shoulder, but it does little to tame the anger. And I fear I stoke it, because I admit, "Nevertheless, I believe her."

She plucks a wildflower out of the grass, her lips puckered. The waters between her and Sara, whatever they may be, must run deep.

"I do, too." The A.D. coughs into his fist. "I'm pissed off at her, but I believe what she told us. Mary, you didn't see the pain she was in. She was bleedin' from the nose, for crying out loud. The blood vessels in her eyes burst. She was a right mess, sitting in a puddle of piss and who knows what else, doing her best to spit out what she could to Alice and me. I basically had to carry her to a nearby motel. Her legs had given out. When the door was shut behind us, there were bruises all over her neck, forehead, and arms that weren't there before. She looked as if the best boxer in the world used her for his punching bag."

My God. "Why didn't you mention that in debriefing?"

"She didn't want me to. Said it made no difference, claimed she'd made her bed and now she had to lie in it." He pauses, his eyes turning painfully serious. "She heard that music when we were there, Alice. The one she told us about." He scratches the back of his neck. "I had to tie her up. Well, not so much to immobilize her, but she asked me to ensure she had enough length of rope to get her to the loo and the shower but not the front door, and it was her choice. She was bloomin' terrified of what she would do. She made me take the phone out and put a Do Not Disturb note on the door. I gave Marianne her whereabouts before I left, so she could go check on her. Dunno if she'll still be there or not."

Mary ceases the plucking of petals long enough to hold out a hand. "You're telling us that you tied up Sara Crewe like a prisoner in some low-rent motel and then just left?"

He nods. "One she thought nobody would come and check on her in."

Finn sends a rock he'd been rolling in his hands flying, a quiet curse escaping his lips. And then he turns and walks straight into the woods. Victor takes a step to follow, but I block him. "Let me."

I find Finn nearly five minutes later, his back against a tree. I say nothing upon approach; I simply come to stand next to him.

Another good sixty seconds pass before he finally speaks. "She's a good person, Alice."

I tuck my arm in his, once more leaning my head against his shoulder.

"Did she really attack you?"

Quiet wind rattles the leaves around us. "Yes." I won't lie to him. "To be fair, I was already deeply suspicious of her when I arrived. Remember, Mary and I had come to question her over the photographs we found in the Piper's Manhattan flat. After I heard Victor, well, I must admit I was ready to fight my way upstairs to find you if need be. She told me later she feared I was affiliated with the man she knew as Gabe Koppenberg."

His soft breath of a laugh is more bittersweet than anything else. "She's never been the best in a fight."

"She's gotten better."

His head tilts toward me. "Are you saying she was actually a match for you?"

My own laugh is derisive. "Certainly not. But she was desperate—and I think we both know how desperation can allow a person to source strength they may not have known before."

"Were her eyes okay?"

"Do you mean, were they black like yours were?"

A moodiness settles over him when he nods.

"Be assured they were green."

He leans his head about the tree, staring into the branches above us.

"We'll find him. It's only a matter of when, not if."

"Todd was only a cog in this damn Piper's wheel, wasn't he?"

"It appears so." I wish there was something better to say, something more meaningful. Sweeney Todd—or at least, the man who was made to believe he was Sweeney Todd—destroyed so very many Timelines, including that of Finn's mother. Todd is now dead, and yet, the threat to catalysts and Timelines remains.

The family's vengeance is not fulfilled. Neither is mine, yet. Although I have Finn back, I cannot risk anything further happening to him or anyone else. I will ensure the Piper is taken care of, and then I will exact justice from the Queen of Hearts for her treachery.

"Did he . . ." His swallow is audible. "Did Todd touch you? When he captured you?"

The memory of waking up in an unfamiliar room, in my chemise, with Todd's hands running up and down my legs settles on this moment like a lead balloon. He had touched me, yes—but I was spared from true horror when he'd muttered something about, *"I can see why he likes you."* The fiend then proceeded to pleasure himself next to me, and it was altogether one of the foulest, most frustrating moments of my entire existence.

And here Finn is, inquiring about it. He sounds so . . . stricken, guilty, and furious all at once. As if it was his fault that Todd was a psychotic pervert.

I tell him flatly, "Yes."

He covers his face with his hands for several seconds before pulling me into his arms. I tell him the rest, lest the no doubt lurid images in his mind go to places best not met. And still, it does little to abate his anger. How did he learn of it? Did Todd taunt him shortly before his death?

"Finn. Love. I do not wish to dwell on what Todd did, not now. Not when there's so much more to do."

He holds me tighter, and I welcome it.

"You and I," he whispers after many long seconds, "have had the worst courtship ever."

A tiny laugh escapes me. I suppose, when one really thinks about it, the beginnings of our relationship have not been idyllic. "I would not wish it away, though."

"Me either. I'm just saying—you deserve better than this."

I poke at his back. "As do you."

He kisses the side of my head. "I'm so glad to have you in my corner, Alice."

There isn't any other place I would wish to be.

Despite our lovemaking not too long ago, our mouths meet once more, and for long minutes, there they stay. Eventually, though, we know we must return to the others. They are still waiting outside the cottage, staring suspiciously at the greenish smoke that pours from the chimney.

"Everything okay?" Victor asks. He appears cleaner, as if he found a bucket of water to help wash away the blood and dirt from his morning autopsy. Thankfully, the A.D. and Grymsdyke have also freshened up.

"Yeah, sorry." Finn rubs at his hair. "It's just a lot to take in. Wendy, Sara . . . Mom." He shakes his head. "I want that son of a bitch taken care of."

"There's no need to apologize." Victor leans forward and hugs his brother. "It's a lot for all of us to take in. And you're not alone in that wish. If we're lucky, it'll happen very soon." His smile is bitter. "Apparently, I've inherited my bio-dad's skills when it comes to removing body parts. The Piper's head on a platter sounds just about right, doesn't it?"

"I'm glad one of us inherited such skills, because holy hell, hacking apart that giant was that disgusting." The A.D. pretends to shiver.

"Try crawling into its heart," Grymsdyke offers sourly.

This only has the A.D. shuddering more visibly.

The green smoke from the chimney bursts into bright blue flames, only to quickly morph into a series of shimmering lights. The door opens unexpectedly, bringing with it the Wise Woman.

"Your Majesty, Your Highness, a word, please."

"Your Highness!" Mary exclaims. "Whom is she talking about?"

Neither Finn nor I say anything, nor do we question how the Wise Woman knew of such a thing. I simply take his hand. I allow Grymsdyke to explain to the others Finn's new Wonderlandian title as we make our way into the house.

The door shuts behind us, with nary a breeze to do the deed.

"Whilst my enchantments will help protect all in your fellowship," the Wise Woman says, "there are two additional gifts I must offer that are for you two, and you two alone."

My eyes move to the pile of hay closest to the fireplace. The goose no longer rests within. Finn must notice this absence as well, for his hand tightens around mine.

"But first, I hope you will indulge me in a small tale."

"Of course," I tell her.

"Many, many years ago, I met a king and a queen who were desperate for a child, as many are. As payment, they offered me a very special goose they had, a golden goose. Feathers of pure gold, it was quite valuable and coveted throughout their land. Much trouble had been brought about by those who attempted to steal the bird, though, so it seemed to the king and queen that offering me such a prize would not only be good for me but would provide the goose, whom they were quite fond of, protection from the greed that plagued its safety. I accepted the payment and gave shelter to the fowl.

"Years passed, and as you probably know, birds molt and this one was no different. As the goose aged, golden feathers became nothing more than plain ones. She was fiercely independent, though, and would often wander despite my warnings. I, too, became fond of the creature, and did not want to stymie its character. Wolves and foxes attacked the goose, but she was strong and clever. She was a survivor.

She fought many a predator and won when other birds would have found themselves in bellies. She battled for her friends, and for innocent animals she did not know. All nearby cherished her valor. But years are not always so kind, and soon, after one too many skirmishes, even the goose realized that she was not strong enough to keep going as she once did." Her smile is brittle. "Not even I can hold back death."

A pile of nearby feathers catches my eyes.

"My friend asked for an ending of her choosing several times. She did not wish to die in an undignified manner. Affection always left me hesitating—and it was cruel and selfish of me, but there it is. Last night, she heard of the queen's victory over the giant. Once or twice, it and the goose had battled, only to leave my friend with broken wings and legs. But when she heard you were able to best the giant . . . my goose knew her spirit could live on in the two of you if I would only finally acquiesce to her wishes. This morning, when you showed her much kindness, her mind was resolute."

She removes a small, bloodstained cloth from the table. There, gleaming in the sunlight from nearby windows, is a handful of small, golden feathers.

"It's not much. Any gold left was always hidden beneath the white. But my friend wished these for you, to help pay your way."

Finn and I both simply stare at the unbearably generous offering.

"I received a gift myself. An egg, the only one my dear friend has ever laid. If I am lucky, I will soon have a new friend." She glances away, but not before I notice the sheen present. "The goose also offered up its strength to aid you in the coming days." Another cloth is removed, revealing a pair of cups filled with a glittering dark mixture. "It is, of course, up to you whether or not to accept such gifts from a benevolent, courageous soul."

Finn and I share a meaningful look before reaching, in union, for the cups.

My love holds his out. "To the brave and generous."

I quietly offer the sweet goose a Wonderlandian song for safe passage to the journeylands before I clink my cup against Finn's. Together, we drink the bitter contents.

The Wise Woman pushes the feathers toward us. Finn slips them into his pocket as she heads to the door, calling the rest in. Once all are present, she situates us in a circle and hands Victor what appears to be a bottle of wine. "All must take three swallows. No more, no less."

"Even the spider?" the A.D. inquires.

"Even he."

"As mentioned before, anything I do today cannot be erased by another of my kind. That said, if you are cursed, as was the prince with a sword of my sister's, the intentions will be altered. Her intention was to change the prince from what he was to something else, something whose soul was dark and riddled with holes. The queen and I have now altered that so he is safe as long as her love remains true and breath enters her body. It will be similar for any of you—if my sister's magic reaches out to you, it will not affect you as intended."

"But what will happen?" the A.D. asks quietly.

Her eyes do not blink. "You will be given hope to overcome that which will change you. What you do with it will be up to you."

"And what of the Piper?" Mary asks. "Will we be protected from his music?"

"As with the magic of my sisters, his, too, will be altered from its original intentions. More than that, I cannot say, as I do not know specifically what it is that they will try to do to you."

As the bottle makes its way around the circle, the Wise Woman chants something in an unfamiliar language. Green sparks and smoke fly about the room, swirling between our bodies and through our hair. Mary helps Grymsdyke take his sips before passing the bottle to me. Much like the goose's offering, this drink is also bitter.

The last of our group finishes the contents of the bottle. The green smoke billows until I can no longer see the people next to me, let alone in front of me.

An explosion fills the room, sending us all flying backward.

THE INN'S SPECIAL

FINN

'M SITTING IN A cart, Alice next to me. At my feet is the A.D.; upon one of his propped knees is Grymsdyke. A quick turn of head shows my brother and Mary in the front of the cart, Victor's hands upon the reins of a grazing horse. All eyes are open, yet unblinking.

There is no house nearby, no barn, no chicken coop. There is nothing but trees and wind and squirrels.

I blink rapidly, completely disoriented.

Grymsdyke crawls off the A.D., over to where I am. "I was wondering when one of you would snap out of it."

"How long have we been asleep?"

Alice's head swivels to face her soldier. Her brows furrow as she also blinks hard.

"I do not think it was sleep." The spider hops onto the cart's ledge. "I do know that the cart has not moved, though. This is where it has been parked since we arrived at the Wise Woman's cottage."

"How in the bloody hell did we get into the cart?" my brother asks from where he sits nearby. "Weren't we just inside the house?"

"More importantly," Mary mutters, "*where* is the house?"

I ask Grymsdyke, "How can you be sure we're not somewhere else?"

A hairy, small leg juts out. "That tree there is the same. See the whorl just below the largest branch to the left, the one shaped like an owl's face? I observed it both last night and this morning. It is not something I imagine is on too many trees."

Alice says, "I recognize it, too."

"I miss New York." The A.D. grips the side of the cart. "I miss magic being a thing on the telly."

"Well, here's a perk." Mary holds aloft a bag that was sitting by her feet. "The Wise Woman may be gone, but she left us with a bag of food."

All of the rest of the bags the team brought are accounted for, too. My brother must have been optimistic about them finding a cure for me, because two of my guns were packed, along with several clips. No extra sword, but I suppose these are better than nothing. More importantly, Victor brought enough of his protocol and medicine to last a few weeks. I hate knowing he spiraled so far away from himself, to that monster that haunts him. I hate that Alice was left trying to find a cure for me, that I failed her as a partner. I hate that my father believed his children were dead, like his wife, and I hate that the Piper grabbed the upper hand when nobody was looking.

It changes now. He's going down.

"Maybe we should try editing to Hamelin," the A.D. says. "Would take a hell of a lot less time than this old thing."

Mary rifles through her bag, but then softly curses. "The Grimm's books aren't here."

"Let me look." Victor takes her bag and sifts through it. Finding nothing, he also swears before asking me for his bag. I pass it up, but just as with Mary's, there are no books inside.

Alice and the A.D. immediately search through theirs only to come up empty handed. All that are left are the Institute books.

"What does this mean?" Alice asks me. "How can these volumes simply go missing?"

But I have no answer to that. None of us do, except to assume that the books disappeared along with the cottage. But what would the Wise Woman want with them?

"I guess we're getting to Hamelin the old-fashioned way," the A.D. says mournfully.

Fantastic.

I offer to drive, but Victor insists on the first shift. He's riding a high right now, with his latest dose of protocol not too long ago. With nothing left to do here, we pull onto the road, heading north. I wish I had my phone with me, anything that allows me to review everything I'd missed since that Pan kid (or whoever he really is) attacked me, but nobody thought to bring it (or, hell, theirs). It's disorienting, being the person least in the know for once. So I can't help but drill everyone to go over everything again, in excruciating detail. Thankfully, no one gives me shit over it, but still, I loathe the gap of missing time over the last few days.

Frustration percolates in my veins. Anger, too. Lots and lots of anger.

"You said your mother read you the stories from this Timeline?"

I turn to face Alice. "Yeah, to both me and Victor. Why?"

"Did you recognize the story that the goose hailed from?"

The A.D. is instantly interested. "You mean the goose that laid the golden egg?"

"That's not a Grimm's tale," Victor calls from the front seat.

"I think it was called *The Golden Goose* or something like that," I tell Alice.

"And what of the giant? Did he hail from a story you know?"

"*Jack and the Beanstalk?*" Mary suggests.

"Still not Grimm's," Victor says.

"Well, aren't you the epitome of the fairy tale knowledge base?"

she snaps affectionately.

"I can't remember what it was called," I admit, "but there was one where a kid was raised by a giant and thereby became one himself. He liked to hit people he worked for in lieu of payment."

"I remember that one!" Victor says. "It made no sense. Then again, so many of them didn't."

Alice is thoughtful for a long moment. "It's interesting how closely intertwined so many of these tales are here in this Timeline. A Wise Woman, from *Little Briar-Rose,* has a golden goose from another tale and tricks me into battling a giant from another. All within a small span of land."

"Well, Brom did say that his tales were connected in his Timeline, too," Mary offers.

"What if we were wrong?" Alice asks. "We assumed that all of the Piper's minions were the children he kidnapped, brainwashed or subject to the transformation spell to become one of the Chosen. And while that must hold true—after all, how else can we explain Sweeney Todd and Nellie Lovett—what if some of the characters are from the stories that make this Timeline? Grethel Bunting told us that she has always been Grethel. Perhaps she is *the* Grethel from this Timeline, now in the employ of the Piper."

It's a good point, and a bit of a terrifying one, too, because it opens so many more rabbit holes.

"Pfriem, too," Victor points out.

"Bunting and Pfriem did not have blackened teeth," Alice muses. "Nor did Jenn Ammer at the library. All of the other associates we've come into contact with have."

"Or F.K. Jenkins." The A.D. adjusts his smudged glasses. "His teeth were just a disgusting yellow from smoking a hundred packs of cigarettes a day."

I nearly forgot about that misogynistic asshole.

"How *does* he fit in?" Mary asks. "All of our background checks on him were thorough. Birth records, schooling, parents, grandparents, addresses . . . He didn't just appear one day. He was born somewhere in the Midwest. As far as we know, he isn't from any other Timeline."

I rub at my hair. Jesus, the playing field is way too complicated and crowded. "Is he still missing?"

"Yes. He and Rosemary both." Alice's lips press together. "When the Piper's minions attacked the Institute, both were freed at the same time as Todd. While we know Todd came to the museum to confront us, or at least aid in the Queen of Hearts' exit, security footage shows the other two going through a separate doorway to parts unknown."

"Nobody could see any details beyond the doorway?"

"Marianne did her best to clean up the recording, but the glare of the door was too bright," the A.D. says.

One of the wheels hits a large pothole, jerking us all so hard I can pretty much guarantee our asses are bruised.

"Sorry 'bout that," Victor calls out.

"What about this Jenn Ammer?" I press. "What did you guys learn about her?"

"Alice, I completely forgot to fill you in about that," Mary says. "Whilst you and Brom were storming the school—"

"I was there, too!" the A.D. says indignantly.

"—I did a bit of digging into her background. Outside of a pair of college degrees from small, private institutions I've never heard of and couldn't track down and a questionable Social Security number, there is very little else to prove Jenn Ammer exists. One of the techies hacked into the library's databases and found her job application conveniently missing. Fingerprints were taken by the police, but I have no idea what came up when they were run through the database."

"Did anyone contact Bianca Jones to see what she could offer on the matter?"

"I know it will come as a terrible shock," Mary says, "but Ms. Jones was rendered speechless by the turn of events."

"Be nice," Victor murmurs.

"She said she thought I was best matched with my cousin Colin! Can you imagine?" She grunts. "Colin. Really, now."

Victor says, "Good point."

It is, actually. I'd met Colin once and wanted to punch that punk in the nose.

"Thus, Jenn Ammer is still an unknown," Alice is saying. "At least she is in the authority's custody."

"Did she say anything to you that could be a clue?" I ask her.

"She knew who I was." Alice brushes stray hairs away from her bruised face. "Mary, as well. And she sang the same tune that Rosemary serenaded us with prior to interrogation."

"What did the Piper say to you, right before he destroyed the catalyst in the Institute?"

Alice clears her throat but then says nothing for a good ten, twenty seconds. "He rambled on about how sacrifices must be made in order for objectives to be met, even if it pained him to do so."

But . . . what objectives does he strive toward? "Anything else?"

She turns her head away to stare at the trees surrounding us. "He indicated that certain Timelines are even resented by those who originate from them, as if that validates a reason to destroy them." Her voice softens. "He was playing his pipe then, and I must admit that it is not the easiest to remember all of his words so clearly. It wasn't until he walked through the doorway and it closed behind him did clarity return."

"Mary, do you remember.anything?"

My brother's girlfriend's shoulders tighten. "After the explosion, I don't remember anything. I flew back and hit my head."

Victor leans over and kisses her cheek before placing a hand on her knee. Miraculously, she does not push him away.

I turn back to face those with me in the back of the cart. "What about you, Grymsdyke?"

The spider coughs from where he rests on my knee. "I was in the Queen of Diamonds' room, guarding the crown as ordered. I heard nothing other than the dissonant music played by an unknown girl."

"Why do you think the music didn't affect you the same way?"

He offers a spider's equivalent of a shrug. "Perhaps it is because we do not have ears and hear differently than you do."

"You bit her?"

"Yes. Her blood was foul and tasted unlike any else I've experienced. It was most disagreeable."

I turn that over a few times. "So, we can assume that whatever makes someone Chosen cannot be passed on through bodily fluids like a disease—meaning it has to be done through an enchantment or an enchanted object like the sword that stabbed me."

Alice grabs my hand, hard. "And of course, there's the Piper's music to contend with. We now know that he is not the only one who has the ability to hypnotize others."

"Please tell me someone remembered ear plugs," Mary calls over her shoulder.

The A.D. perks up. "Believe it or not, I did. Marianne found some in the lab that Wendy had been working on. Dunno what all they do. Marianne didn't have time to test them and there were no notes attached, but they can't hurt to try."

I ask, "How many pairs?"

His face falls. "Well, there's the rub. There were only two pairs."

And five sets of ears that would need them. Grymsdyke is a lucky bastard, I guess.

After that, we all fall into moody silence. The A.D. eventually dozes, as does Mary up front. Even Grymsdyke is snoring away.

I squeeze Alice's hand. "You should nap, too."

"Gertrude mentioned the dwarves might be of concern. I ought to keep watch."

"That was before she enchanted us with some kind of protection spell, remember?"

Her smile is wry. "From the dwarves?"

I shrug. "You never know." I tug one of my guns out of Victor's bag. "But, just in case, I'll be ready."

She hesitates, but she can't hide the exhaustion in her eyes. I wrap my arm around her shoulder and she leans in, her head against my chest. "Promise me you'll wake me if you see anything of consequence?"

That I can easily agree to.

From that point, it's a good hour before we finally emerge from the woods. No dwarves appeared—or, for that matter, anyone else. It was like the forest was empty of all life except that of animal and those here in the wagon, and I was fine with that. Victor and I didn't talk much ourselves, preferring instead to remain vigilant in our watches, but when we did, it was all about the retribution we both covet. Another hour or two passes before signs of a nearby small village appear.

Mary is the first of the group to rouse. "Maybe we can stop and eat, stretch our legs out a bit? Nose around to see if anyone has heard of the Piper?"

It's a good idea.

By the time Victor pulls up to an inn's stables, everyone is ready to do just what Mary suggested. My legs are cramping from the small quarters, and I know I can't be the only one uncomfortable. Grymsdyke offers to remain with the cart to ensure nothing is stolen. "I haven't hunted in some time now," he adds. "A nice rat will do quite nicely for lunch, as long as it is only a rat."

The A.D. looks horrified at such a suggestion. Mary, on the other hand, is fascinated.

As Victor hands off our horse to a stable hand, Alice tells the spider quietly, "We will not be too long."

"Be on your guard, Your Majesty. You will be at an odd number with me here in the barn." He coughs his weird little cough and scuttles off the cart.

"Is that a spider thing?" I ask her. "Like, a Wonderlandian thing?"

"Crawling?"

"No. The coughing. I've noticed he does it a lot."

"Ah." She tightens her cloak around her. "Only certain breeds of spiders do it, but I suppose yes, it's a Wonderlandian thing. One of his comrades informed me once that their throats are lined with hairs similar to those on their legs, so that whatever prey they ingest will feel the effects."

I like Grymsdyke, respect him even, but damn, if that isn't awful. I'd felt those hairs once, and they'd burned like hell.

"I imagine having such things in one's throat would tickle frequently, don't you?"

She makes a good point.

I pull aside Victor. "We're going to have to either trade in the cart for something better or resort to horses. At this rate, it's going to take us a few days to make it to Hamelin." I motion toward where our horse, sagging and exhausted, sweat dripping from his back, slurps from a pail of water. "He's not going to cut it."

He jingles a pouch tied to his waist. "I've got a bit of gold left."

I dig out one of the golden feathers. "I happen to have some, too."

His eyes widen. "Where did you get that?"

I tell him, and he nods appreciatively. "We'll be on the hunt after lunch."

The inn is surprisingly busy, but we manage to find a table. The kitchen wench is a buxom girl whose cheeks indicate she might have imbibed in quite of bit of wine already today. She informs us that the Fleet and Baker Inn is newly renowned for their meat pies, asking if we'd like the special. We decide to get one to split after Mary's inquires inform us it is mutton. Several tankards of ale are also ordered. I stay the wench a moment to tell her, "We were recently robbed, and our knives were taken."

"You poor things!" She leans down, giving a rather pointed view of her more ample assets. "We have a few extras I'll bring round to you."

"Knives?" the A.D. asks after she leaves.

"Eating knives," I tell him. "Most people are expected to have their own in this time period."

Once the drinks are brought round, my father's assistant stands up. "I think I might have a look around."

"Aren't you going to eat?" One of Mary's eyebrows lifts high.

He practically leers. "Don't you worry about me. I'll be just fine. I'm sure there will be some lovely ladies and gents who are willing to share what they have with me."

His implication isn't lost on anyone at the table. "You're disgusting," she snarls.

To that, the A.D. offers her a grand bow.

"I expect you to check in within the half hour," I tell him.

He nods and slips into the crowd. Within minutes, we can see him sidling up to a pair of lovely, giggling girls who quickly offer up their own tankards of ale.

Mary taps a finger against the side of her drink. "I swear, he's like a chameleon, isn't he?"

Victor takes a sip of his ale before tugging out the map and spreading it across the table. "By my estimates, we're here."

Mary traces a path from where Victor points up to Hamelin. "It's still quite a ways to go." Her lips quirk upward. "I bet you're a fan of cars now, eh, Alice?"

"We still have no idea how the two Timelines connect together. Is it continuous?" Victor asks. "Is there a doorway? A path? Do we need to track down the woman that's featured in both 1812GRI-CHT and 1816/18GRI-GT?" He shakes his head. "Shite. I can't remember her name right now."

"Mother Hulda," Alice murmurs. "Or, the Librarian said it could also be Holle. She apparently is also magical."

Of course she is.

"Well, I say we try heading straight to Hamelin." Mary taps her fingers against the table, but immediately pulls back, frowning. "It's utterly vile in here. The table is sticky. Anyway, as I was saying, if we can't get through, then we will track this Hulda down, but until then, it's best to go on as planned."

It isn't long before the food is brought alongside some crusty bread. The kitchen wench presses up against Victor as she slides the food onto the table, inspiring Mary's ire. After she leaves, Victor gets an earful for doing absolutely nothing but sitting at a table.

I swear, those two.

I pull the pie toward me and cut it into slices. Plates are distributed as well as knives. We're just about to dig in when Alice bursts out, "Wait!"

I set down my knife. "What's wrong?"

Her eyes are wide as she rotates her plate toward me. Shifting a bit of the crust with her knife, I get a good view of what has her so agitated.

It appears to be a slice of a human eyeball, blue iris glaring out at us.

Mary nearly chokes. Victor grabs the plate and slides it toward him.

"Finn." Alice grips my sleeve. "Sheep irises are different than ours. They are more oval, or rectangular."

My brother uses his knife to extract the piece. Roughly one-fourth the size of a normal human eye, its edges are jagged, as if it'd been minced. There is no doubt, though. The blue iris and rounded pupil are definitely not those of a sheep.

"It could be pig," Victor murmurs. "Their eyes are quite similar to ours."

"The waitress clearly said they were known for their mutton pies." Mary shoves her plate away. "Not pork!"

I glance around the room. Nearly everyone who is eating is indulging in meat pies. And then it hits me. Meat pies. *Human* meat pies. Mrs. Nellie Lovett. *Rosemary Lovett.* It cannot be coincidence.

I'm off the bench, scanning the room before I find the door the wench is coming in and out of, the one that must lead to the kitchen.

"Go and find us some new transportation," I tell Victor and Mary. "And try to track down the A.D. Chances are, we're going to be leaving sooner rather than later."

Alice also stands up. "You're thinking Rosemary is here."

I love that she's already on the same page as me.

We make our way to the door through a rowdy crowd drunk on ale and feasting on pies. Nobody says anything when I push it open, nobody tries to stop us when we pass through. A small, smoky, dark hallway opens up before us. As if on cue, familiar voices surface.

"You're such a stupid fuck! I said mince the meat, not cut it into strips!"

Rosemary.

"I'll mince you if you don't shut up, you ugly bitch!"

F.K. Jenkins. Well, now.

Rosemary cackles; a loud thunk followed by a series of curses follows.

I quietly tug out my gun, Alice does the same with a pair of her daggers. Thank God my brother saw fit to remember my silencer.

"I don't see what we're still fucking doing in this shithole," the former proprietor of the Ex Libris bookstore bellows.

We inch down the hallway, weapons readied. Rosemary snarls, "We're waiting for Todd, you sack of shit! Just like we've been told to. So unless you get back to work and mince that meat, you're going to find yourself in one of my pies!"

They don't know he's dead.

"You think he's still coming?" Jenkins' laugh is ugly. "It's been too long—"

Another thunk sounds, like that of a knife meeting wall or wood. A yelp precedes, "I'm going to fucking rip your throat out, you evil bitch!"

Discord is good. Discord means every man for themselves.

"We stick to the plan!" Yet another thunk. "As soon as Todd gets here, we'll head to the mountain and meet up with the others for the convergence. There's still time."

Alice and I share a meaningful glance. I hold up three fingers and she nods.

"Yeah? Well, that plan fucking sucks! We should go there now—"

One finger down.

"—because you know he's going to be pissed off at us for taking so long!"

Two fingers down.

"And I'm not looking forward to him being pissed off any more than he already is. I mean, maybe you are, but—"

Three. Alice and I burst around the corner, my gun out, her daggers ready. Rosemary has a butcher knife angled toward Jenkins; the bookstore owner, his back to us, has a cleaver angled toward her. Both are drenched in blood and guts.

The moment she sees us, she hisses, *"You."*

Jenkins whips around, shock coloring his face. "You're—you're supposed to be—"

I point my gun right at him. "Chosen? Yeah, that didn't happen."

Suddenly, a shriek sounds from behind us. A quick glance shows the inn's wench charging us, eyes crazed.

"I'll take care of her," Alice says grimly. "Subdue the others."

The chaos gives Rosemary the perfect opportunity to send the knife in her hand flying. I duck and shoot, striking her arm just before Jenkins rams me. I manage to hold onto my weapon, though, knocking the sonofabitch into a wall. Rosemary hurls another knife, barely missing me and hitting Jenkins in the leg instead.

He rips out the knife, tossing it to the ground before he roars.

I fire at her again, hitting her throwing arm closer to the elbow. She howls in rage, grappling for another knife. How many of those things does she have in here, anyway? Before she can throw it, Jenkins grabs hold of one of my legs and knocks me off my feet.

Oh. Hell. No.

My fist smashes into his nose; blood squirts everywhere. His teeth gnash as he grapples for some kind of hold on me, but another punch leaves his head snapping back onto the ground. Nearby, the wench sprawls on the floor, several long slashes leaving trails of red ribbons across her gown. Seconds later, when she slams into the brick surrounding the fireplace, she does not get up.

Alice is already halfway across the room, in hot pursuit of Rosemary. I jab the barrel of my gun up against Jenkins' forehead. "You're going to tell me exactly what I want to know, and maybe, just maybe, I'll kill you quickly."

"Eat shit and die," he snarls. But his fists against me are weakening.

I haul my arm back and hit him so hard he finally stills beneath me. And then I'm up, my gun angled once more at Rosemary. She and Alice are locked together, but my girl has the upper hand. Weakened by the two bullets I've put into her, even her desperation is no match for Alice's tenacity.

And still, I yell, "Pivot!"

Alice deftly sinks both daggers into Rosemary's waist, yanking her around. I send an angled shot straight into her back, just above where her heart lies. A scream doesn't follow—it's a gurgle. And when Alice removes her knives and kicks the bitch backward, right against the medieval oven she's been baking human pies in, she falls and does not get up.

Alice is immediately on the ground next to her, though, one of her daggers at the woman's throat. There's a strange smile of sorts on her face, a gleam in her eye, and for a moment, I can truly imagine what Alice was like when she was mad in Wonderland. "You mentioned a mountain, Rosemary. Which one are you referring to?"

A wet laugh hisses through Todd's paramour's lips.

A quick survey of the room around me leaves my stomach churning. There is a human leg on the chopping table, its bone splintered. On the ground in the corner is a partial ribcage, deep groves in the bones. Intestines fill a basket; what appears to be a pile of fingers sits next to a pot.

"Todd is not coming for you." I point my gun at Rosemary. "I killed that sonofabitch several days ago."

She struggles weakly against Alice's grip. "Liar!"

"I shot him right between the eyes. And then I shot him in the heart. If I could do it again, I would."

The sob that chokes out of her is filled with anguish.

"You're not going to leave this kitchen alive," Alice says. "We cannot allow you to do so, Rosemary. You must be held responsible for the deeds you have done."

The insane pie maker fumbles desperately for something, anything nearby, but I kick it all out of her reach.

"Now." Alice presses her blade more firmly against the woman's neck. "Tell us about this mountain you were to rendezvous at."

The smile that curves Rosemary's bloody lips coupled with the gleam in Alice's eyes make a pretty damn terrifying sight, if I'm being honest.

"Is it perhaps . . . Koppenberg Mountain, just outside Hamelin, which is approximately sixty kilometers north of here?"

Ah. Alice has surprised her, because the smile dims significantly.

"Who was it that informed you that you must meet there with the others?" Alice continues. "Was it the Pied Piper of Hamelin?"

Rosemary's face loses all color. "How—how do you know—"

"Tell me, Rosemary. Do you remember anything of your family

in Hamelin?"

Tears well in the woman's eyes. And still, I refuse to point my gun anywhere else but right at her head. She helped Todd find catalysts, she helped destroy them, including that of my parents' Timeline.

"You told me once that your earliest memory is of a time sitting in a London orphanage," Alice is saying. "I wonder if that is still true."

Strength that was not there seconds before surges through Rosemary's veins. She lashes out, struggling against Alice like a rabid dog. "He's going to kill you all! You think you are safe? He will kill you! You are impure abominations!"

Alice drives her dagger into Rosemary's heart and then ducks. My bullet meets the space between her eyes.

Behind us, Jenkins stirs, emitting a low groan.

"The wench is obviously working with them." Alice dusts off the folds of her skirt as she stands up. The only glance spared for Rosemary is filled with disgust and a bit of satisfaction. "And I would hazard to say the innkeeper, too. It would be difficult to imagine a person being so wholly unaware of such atrocities happening beneath their roof. How far does the Piper's reach stretch? It's a terrifying prospect to consider."

Rosemary and Jenkins had been in the wild now for less than a week, and they'd already managed to continue along their path of destruction and murder.

I make my way over to where Jenkins and the wench are lying. A quick press of fingers against the girl's throat tells me her heartbeat is weak at best. The others have always been so impervious to pain during a fight, so maybe, just maybe, she's a new recruit. But Jenkins, well . . . he's a whole separate issue, isn't he?

We quickly hogtie his feet and hands with twine found upon the butcher's table. Then I grab a pail of bloody water from nearby and dump it on Jenkins' head. He sputters, blinking behind his smudged glasses, struggling to move but finding it impossible.

I squat down next to him. "Her, I get." I motion toward Rosemary's body splayed out next to the oven. "She's been involved in this shit for centuries and probably never knew differently. But you?"

I shake my head. "You're from Nebraska. How in the hell did a man like you get hooked up with the Pied Piper of Hamelin?"

His face turns just as white as Rosemary's had. "Are you a fucking moron?" Jenkins pauses, swallows. "It's only a matter of time before . . ." He swallows again. And then, in a choking whisper, "They always get what they want."

Alice kneels down next to him, just out of reach. "They?"

"You two fuckers better promise me you'll kill me before you leave. You can't leave me behind, okay? I'll—I'll tell you what you want. You just have to promise to kill me. Anything they'll do to me for this failure will be far worse."

What?

"Is it a deal?"

"If that is what you wish," Alice says flatly.

He coughs, but it's more like a gurgle. "You want to know how I was recruited? I don't fucking know. It was shortly after I got the last round of rejections from agents for a book I submitted. I was pretty despondent, and considered shooting my brains out because I was such a fucking failure, but then one day I found an envelope on my desk with money and a small note that said, 'Your services are required.' I didn't know what the hell it meant, but . . ." He coughs again. "It was a shit ton of money. After that, I just woke up knowing things, knowing what I was supposed to do, like it was ESP or that weird psychic shit. Eventually, I started getting emails and phone calls. Those freaks Todd and Rosemary showed up at the bookstore with a note saying I had to let them live with me. That they'd be my team. I was to do the research, they were to go and find the stuff I dreamed up."

"Did you know what you were doing?" Alice asks harshly. "Did you know that you were allowing them to find and then destroy catalysts, thereby murdering countless souls?"

"I didn't give a fuck." His laugh is cruel. "I knew. I didn't care. I wanted to care, if it's any consolation, but I didn't. Couldn't, wouldn't, whatever. It was like that part of me that actually could give a shit about anyone's life was taken out of me or died."

"Why didn't you tell the Society this when we were interrogating you?" I ask.

He attempts to shrug, but it's difficult, being hogtied and all. "I wasn't allowed to, not even with your damn truth serum."

They played us. The whole time, *they played us.*

"Did you know it was the Piper you served?"

"I'm not a moron, you know!"

"No," she says coldly. "You're a murderous fiend who deserves no mercy."

He blanches at her arctic tone. She means business, and I think he's finally understanding that.

"How is it you're able to tell us now?" I press.

Blood trickles from the corner of his mouth onto the dirt floor. "They want you to know." His laugh is now ugly. "They want you two, you know. They'll do whatever it takes to own your souls. You'd be like the fucking cherries and nuts on top of their sundaes."

"You keep saying *they,*" Alice prompts.

I didn't think it possible, but Jenkins turns even whiter, his body shaking. "Yeah," he whispers. "The king and queen of the mountain."

Alice's eyes meet mine. "How much do you want to bet the queen is the thirteenth Wise Woman?"

It makes a hell of a lot of sense.

"Is it Koppenberg Mountain?" I ask.

"Nobody will be able to tell you where it is." His coughing is far wetter now. "Almost everybody has forgotten about it—or at least, those who know what's good for them. Hell, it doesn't even really exist except for them and their needs."

"What does that even mean? How can anyone forget a mountain, let alone have it exist solely for a pair of people?" Alice asks incredulously.

"What is this convergence you were talking about?" I ask.

Spittle mixes with the blood trickling from his lips. "The Chosen have been summoned home."

"Can we get to it from here?" I press. "The mountain, I mean? Are the Timelines really connected?"

Suddenly, the wench lurches to her feet and darts across the room, claiming a knife that juts from the wall. Just before I can shoot her, though, she whispers, "Fear not the blade of death," and then slashes the knife hard across her throat. Blood sprays everywhere.

"Dear God," Alice murmurs. Both of us stare in shock as the girl crumples to the ground.

"I've told you all I can, all that I know." Jenkins tries to scoot closer. "Now, fulfill your end of the agreement. Kill me! Don't let them get their hands on me!"

"Not before you tell me whether or not the Timelines are actually connected."

"As far as I know, yes! I never heard about any other doors. Please, do it before it's too late!"

He genuinely sounds scared shitless. Even though the bastard deserves no mercy, I put my gun against his temple and pull the trigger.

Alice gets up and makes her way back over to where Rosemary lies. She pushes the woman onto her belly, ignoring the large, messy hole in the back of her head. She tugs down the dress and chemise, staring down at Rosemary's shoulder.

"A rat," she says emotionlessly.

I come closer to see what she's pointing out. Sure enough, what looks like a birthmark shaped like a rat marks the pie maker's shoulder.

"She was one of the children, I am sure of it." Alice stands back up. "One of the ones he stole all those years ago."

Neither the wench nor Jenkins have the mark, though.

The two of us are a mess from the fight. Blood and dirt from rolling around on the ground cake our clothes and skin. I fear there is brain matter on me, too. We spend several minutes quickly cleaning ourselves up the best we can before heading out.

I dip a rag in the only clean bucket of water we found in the whole kitchen and gently wipe it across Alice's face. "Are you okay?"

Her hand cups mine. "We need to find them, Finn. They have to pay for what they've done. We cannot stop until every last one is neutralized."

"I know." I can't help it—I lean forward and kiss her. The horror of the room is just too much to bear. It's like a slasher film in here, and the two of us are left shell-shocked. "We will."

She whispers, voice taut as a string pulled across a violin, "They knew you were supposed to be one of the Chosen."

"I'm not. You saved me, remember?"

She steps into me, arms wrapping around my waist. "It will never happen. Never. I will not allow it."

Jenkins said they wanted us both, though. They want Alice, and I'll be damned if I ever allow that to happen.

"I know you won't." I kiss her newly clean forehead. "That's one of the perks of being in love with a kickass queen."

Her laugh is bittersweetly quiet. "You are quite the charming prince, Finn."

"There is such a person in the fairy tale world called Prince Charming, by the way."

"Well, then." She touches my cheek. "We truly are living a fairy tale then, aren't we?" And then, more softly, "Are you all right, my love?"

She's still on the same page with me. She knows that, once more, I just put a bullet through two of my mother's murderers' heads.

To answer her question, though, I don't know. I don't know how I feel right now. Numb, I guess.

I reluctantly let her go. "We should probably get going." I reclaim my gun and shove into the back of my pants. "It's a miracle nobody else has come in, but sooner or later, somebody's going to find this mess. When they do, we need to have road between us."

She wipes her daggers on the rag we used to clean ourselves. "Agreed."

We end up finding a back door to the inn and slip out that. Miraculously, the others are already waiting in the barn.

"Was it Rosemary?" Victor asks.

I nod. "And Jenkins."

The A.D. looks us up and down. "Are they dead?"

"Yes."

"Good." Mary's outburst is fierce. "She was a monster who deserved to die after all that she's done. First the catalysts, and now killing innocent villagers and turning them into meat pies?" She shudders. "She was a psychopath."

Alice says, "No one is in danger of Rosemary's evil ever again."

I turn back to my brother. "Any luck on finding us a new carriage?"

He shakes his head. "None around here, but I did find a man who is willing to trade us the cart and horse, alongside some gold, for five of his horses."

It'll have to do.

I pass over one of the golden feathers to Victor, who heads out with the cart, horse, and Mary to meet up with the man. The A.D. takes one good look at both me and Alice before saying, "Let me go nick you some new clothes. You look like you've been to hell and back." He holds his arm out to Grymsdyke. "Mind coming along? Turns out this village is a bit more dangerous than I first imagined."

After they leave, Alice says, "I think he's got that wrong."

"You don't think the village is dangerous?"

"No, about us having already been to hell. I'm afraid we haven't seen true hell yet, but we will all too soon."

We stand at the entrance to the barn, facing north. The path to hell lies in that direction, leading to a mountain that has been forgotten.

THE WELL

FINN

BY THE TIME WE reach the next inn, the sun has long set. Our horses are exhausted and in need of water and food. And still, despite pushing them as much as we could, we've only covered about fifteen miles of ground. During the long ride, the A.D. told us how the Piper's name struck fear into the villagers' hearts, as did any mention of the thirteenth Wise Woman. Many made the sign of the cross before turning away from him. But there was one young lady, two tankards of ale into their acquaintance, whose lips were looser than many of her neighbors. Behind the inn, after several kisses and who knows what else they did, she admitted that Hamelin was the devil's town, and no one willingly went there unless they wished to lose their soul.

Alice and I, in turn, told our tale of what we learned from both Rosemary and Jenkins.

"How do we find such a mountain?" Grymsdyke asks from my shoulder.

It's a question I don't have an answer for yet.

Despite the price we paid for the horses, we still have plenty of money left over. Apparently the golden feather was worth a hell of a lot, and famous, too. Victor claimed that the buyer nearly wet his pants, he was so excited to receive one. So when we check into the inn, we're able to get three of the best rooms available. We eschew the local dinner, though, instead opting for the food the twelfth Wise Woman packed for us.

After several hours of discussion, the A.D. once more heads out for information, taking Grymsdyke with him. Victor insists upon yet another check-up, during which I force myself to bite my tongue and allow him his way—that is, until he insists that I call it a night and take it easy.

"Bullshit. I ought to be going out there and—"

"Finn." He's uncharacteristically serious as he claps my shoulder. "You were in a fight today. You've been awake for only a little over twenty-four hours. Can you just humor me and not push it?" He gently touches the fresh bandages on my torso. "Hell, you tore open your stitches during that fight, both front and back. I warned you about that, didn't I? Who knows what kind of infection you could have gotten in that blood bath of a kitchen? For your sake, let's hope the dosing of antibiotics you had this week is strong enough to keep your immune system in check. I need you to hang tight and let yourself heal tonight. You're no good to us if you aren't in decent health, and you know it."

A loud crash sounds beyond the door. Victor jerks, his eyes widening until we hear the laughter and jeering from downstairs.

Alice touches my hand. She doesn't say anything, but her agreement with Victor shines in her eyes.

"Fine," I tell my brother. "But you'll come and get us if you need us, right?"

"Of course, although, at this late hour, I don't think it'll be necessary." He tucks his medical supplies into his bag. "Let me know if the tenderness around the stitches increases or if you're feeling light-headed or unusual pain. We might have to do another round of antibiotics." To Alice, he says, "Keep an eye on him, please?"

"I doubt he'll be leaving my sight." Her smile is wry.

Victor finally leaves to go find Mary, shutting the door behind him.

Alice comes to sit next to me on the bed. "You're a terrible patient."

"You should talk."

Her laughter is quiet. "We're not discussing me. We're focusing on you. Your brother is right, though. Your good health is incredibly important. I need you by my side in this battle."

I take her hand and kiss the base of her knuckles. "There's nowhere else I'd rather be." Another kiss follows. "But I have to admit, I'm kind of surprised you're not itching to go out there tonight, too. The Alice I know isn't one to stay back."

She crawls onto my lap. "Perhaps I have a different itch that requires tending to."

Did she really just say that? Holy crap, can this woman turn me on like no other. Maybe the twenty-first-century is influencing her more than she thinks. Yet still, I can't help but tease her. "You're only saying that to make me feel better since we've been sidelined for the night."

She lightly drags her nails across my chest. "Finn?"

"Yeah?"

"Shut up and kiss me already."

I do as I'm told. My mouth meets hers and every nerve in my body explodes into vibrant life, even though it's only been a short time since we were last together like this. Alice curves her hand around the back of my neck, tugging me closer until our tongues are practically at war with one another. She reaches down and cups me, and I gasp into her mouth. We're on the road to hell, but heaven is right here, right now, in this small room. She unlaces my breeches, folding back the flaps of linen. Her cool fingers curl around my heated skin, and I just about lose all rational thought.

And then she pulls away.

"I'm entirely overdressed, don't you think?"

God yes, she is.

Slowly, slowly, I peel off the rose-colored dress the A.D. found her in the previous town, tossing it onto the floor next to the bed. She stands there in an entirely too thin chemise, and for a moment, she's stolen my breath away.

I gently trace the curves of her hips, her breasts, with my hands. She shivers beneath my touch. Once more, my mouth teases hers as I take my sweet time lifting the chemise up and over her head. I love that her body isn't hard, that her muscles aren't perfectly defined. I love that she feels real beneath my hands, that she owns the body she's in. I've been with other women who make a point to work out every single day, hone every piece of their body into what they feel society says it needs to be, but none of them have anything on Alice. She's strong, she's smart, she's capable, she's gorgeous, she's beyond sexy.

She's the real deal. My fairy tale queen come to life.

We stumble back to the bed, Alice tugging me down after her. I spend many heated moments tracing each piece of her delectable skin, following each touch of finger with my mouth and tongue. There's nothing that I ignore, not the backs of her knees, not the soft curve between her legs, not the slope of her neck. She squirms beneath my exploration, her breath and heart racing in tandem. And when she can't wait any longer, when we're both to the point we're nearly insensible with need, she pulls me up for another kiss, allowing me to enter her in one swift push.

I let her set the pace. Soon, we're moving in an age-old rhythm, lost to music only we both can hear. I reach a hand down and rub her clit, and I swear, her moans are the most erotic thing I've ever heard. I'm shaking from holding back my own orgasm until she breaks apart, my name a cry from her lips. I follow just seconds later.

I roll us onto our sides, and she curls into me, her skin slick with sweat. And it's in this moment, this exact one, where we're in a fuzzy bliss, our hearts hammering like drums against one another, when I realize I will gladly take whatever this woman has to offer me. Her heart, her love, a home. A future, a child, a family. I knew it before, on some kind of superficial level, yes, but now I can't deny it's a bone-deep desire. I want to be the person she turns to, have her be mine.

I didn't lie to her when I told her my fairy tale. I've been with other women, some of them really amazing people. I'd thought once or twice that maybe I'd found the one, but now I realize lust and love are two very different things.

I kiss the top of Alice's head, wrapping an arm around her waist. She, in turn, presses a kiss against my chest. As her breathing slows and steadies, and my eyes droop shut, I realize that being sidelined isn't such a bad thing after all.

I WAKE TO THE pounding of a door. Alice is still next to me, her bare body warm next to mine. I'm tempted to ignore the noise until I hear my brother call out my name.

Alice murmurs something, tugging the blanket higher. I quickly slip on my breeches and open the door.

Victor's face is drawn. "The A.D. and Grymsdyke have returned, and one of them looks worse for the wear."

Fantastic. "We'll meet you in your room in a few."

Alice is already awake when I shut the door, reaching for her chemise. "I really look forward to when this is all over," she says quietly, "and we can not worry about waking early to unfavorable news."

Her and me both.

Minutes later, we converge inside Victor and Mary's room. The A.D. is sitting on the bed, holding a wet cloth to his face. When he sees us, though, he lowers the rag enough to give a nice view of a black eye and a split lip.

"What in the hell happened? You said you were going to nose around last night, not get into a fight!"

"Yeah, well," he says to me, wincing with each word, "apparently the Piper has cronies in every little town."

"Allow me to speak, thief." Grymsdyke descends on a thread from the ceiling. "You have done enough talking for one day."

The A.D. nods before pressing the cloth back to his face.

"The first stop we made last night was at a tavern," the spider says. "The thief was able to charm one of the wenches into fornicating behind the building—"

"Hey! No need for *all* the details!" the A.D. cries out indignantly.

The spider pays him no heed. "She imbibed in many drinks, which eventually loosened her tongue. When questioned about the Koppenberg Mountain, the girl went still, as if she was a statue, for a long time. Her eyes turned black shortly before she attacked the thief."

Mary snorts. "Wait—wait. The tavern wench did this to you?"

"Not all of it, she didn't!"

"She sang as she did so," Grymsdyke continues. "When the thief could not shake her, I eventually dropped onto her back and bit her. Her blood was foul, like the girl in the Queen of Diamonds' room, only it was different. Less . . . old. She did not scream, though. Not like most my victims. She sang until her last breath."

Alice asks, "Did you recognize the song?"

The A.D. nods, his cheeks flaming. "It sounded like one of those that Rosemary used to sing."

"After that," the spider says, "the thief hid the body and we continued on our quest. The next woman he fornicated with—"

My father's assistant is nearly beside himself. "Will you stop with that already?"

"—actually admitted to hearing about an unnamed mountain years before, but claimed it was a story told to scare children into compliance."

Huh. "Did she tell you the story?"

Grymsdyke coughs. "Children who go there never return, for their souls are forever claimed by darkness. Relating any more than that was too terrifying of a prospect. She left quickly. But the third woman the thief fornicated with—"

"My God," Mary says wickedly. "You ought to start charging

women a stud fee for your services!"

The A.D.'s face morphs into a tomato right before our eyes.

"She told a story of how she lost a sibling to a mountain," Grymsdyke continues. "Her father went searching for the boy years ago and never returned. According to what she had overheard between her parents prior to his departure, a proper sacrifice must be made to the Weser River before the mountain's name or location can be revealed."

"What kind of sacrifice?" I ask.

"She didn't know," the A.D. says. "No one did."

"So if the first woman isn't the one who caused that black eye," Mary asks, "who did?"

He winces. "The fourth lady's husband. He found us and wasn't happy about what he saw."

Mary chortles loudly. Both Victor and I stare at Jack Dawkins like we've never seen him before. Damn, he's got game.

Alice merely sighs. She's probably used to seeing this sort of stuff with the Hatter back in Wonderland, come to think of it.

"Did the fourth woman actually have anything to add?" I ask the A.D.

"No," he mumbles. "She was just quite lovely to look at."

"What about you two?" I look to my brother and Mary. "Did you find anything out last night?"

Mary says blandly, "There were plenty of interesting things discovered last night."

And now my brother blushes. Action was had by the entire group, it seems.

"There was one thing." Victor tugs on his collar. "Turns out that there is supposedly a well close to the next town that is associated with a Mother Holle."

Hot damn, isn't that convenient.

"Why a well?" Alice asks.

"If I'm not mistaken," I tell her, "the tale says a girl fell down the well and ended up in a new land. She found a woman living in a nearby house, and in need of shelter and food, offered to work for her, doing various chores. The woman was pleased with her work and kindness after a while and rewarded her with riches and a way back home. Her step-sister was jealous, so she took a trip down the well, too, only instead of riches, she got tarred for being lazy and cruel."

"Step-sisters always get the raw end of the stick," Mary says mournfully.

"You were never a step-sister, love. Just a cousin. That said, your summary sounds about right, Finn," Victor says. "Katrina always liked that one, remember? She said Holle was not only a fairy tale character, but also one of the supreme goddesses of yore. Something to do with death and birth all at once."

"And this is the woman that connects the Timelines," Alice says thoughtfully. "A goddess who can both hand out blessings and judgments equally." She lets out a deep breath. "Well, then. If sacrifices are to be made, who better to inquire about them to than a goddess who deals in death?"

"Wait—you want us to go down some kind of mystical well and hope that some woman will just offer up an answer for us?" the A.D. asks.

One of her slim eyebrows lifts up. "Do you have a better idea?"

He doesn't, of course. None of us do. In the end, Alice and I agree it's best that we go to the well, leaving the rest to stay with the horses in the next town over and try to find anything else about the Piper, his minions, or Koppenberg Mountain. Grymsdyke insists on coming with us, and I'm not opposed to him having our backs at all.

A NONDESCRIPT WELL SITS next to the road on the northern outskirts of the latest village, a number of spindles and offerings of flowers surrounding it. It's already midday, and we're tired from the hours upon horseback. It felt good to stretch our legs and walk here, but now that we're at the site, I can't help but wonder if we're wasting time with this side trip.

Alice peers into the well, but as it is filled with water brimming close to the top, there's very little to see. "The Librarian said Mother Holle was featured in two stories, one in 1812GRI-CHT, and one in 1816/18GRI-GT. Do you happen to remember anything of significance for the second story?"

I shake my head. "A lot of the stories in 1816/18GRI-GT are either really short or fragmented. Katrina didn't bother reading many of those with us."

"How is it we're to find Mother Holle?" She dips a finger into the water. "You mentioned a girl fell into the well?"

"It's been over a decade since I last heard the story, but I think that's what happened. Fell or jumped."

"Your memory is excellent." She smiles up at me.

"Spiders do not swim," Grymsdyke says from his perch on my shoulder.

"I do," Alice says. "I'll go first. If I do not come back up within a minute or so, you'll know that it worked."

The spider coughs. "Your Majesty, many wells are deep. If you plunge in, searching for a bottom to spring back from, you may not reach it in enough time to return."

"Have no fear, old friend." She takes a deep breath before holding my gaze. "We are in a fairy tale, and sometimes, in fairy tales, you must have faith that magic will hold strong."

Strong.

The goose gave us its courage, its strength. Alice is banking that whatever magic imbibed the goose now protects us, too.

"Don't forget," she adds, "we come from Wonderland, where the impossible is quite possible. I tumbled down a rabbit hole and slipped through a looking glass and found a new world. Who is to say that the same is not true for a well?"

I lean forward, pressing my mouth against hers. "See you in a few?"

Alice cups my cheek, her words infused with assurance and conviction. "Yes, you will." She climbs upon the stones surrounding the well and then, without another word, jumps in. The water bubbles around her as she sinks.

"Can you bite me but not inject poison?" I ask Grymsdyke.

"All spiders can. Why do you ask?"

"I need you to do that right now. I need some of my blood in you. Can you do it fast, so we can follow Alice?"

"Venom or no, my bite is painful," the spider warns. "It will be most unpleasant."

"That's fine." And I mean it. "Just do it quickly."

He doesn't hesitate any longer. His large fangs sink into my neck, and although he warned me about it, I fall straight to my knees, because holy shit. He was not kidding about the pain.

"Did you . . ." The muscles in my neck and shoulders cramp, causing me to gasp. "Did you get enough?"

"Your blood is now in my belly, Prince Finn."

I can't wait for digestion. I have to pray that this is good enough. Several deep breaths are required before I can make our way over to the well. The water is still, the bubbles long gone, and Alice has yet to surface. I wait another twenty seconds, my heart pounding the entire time. I trust her. I trust my mother's stories. I trust the goose and the twelfth Wise Woman, even though I have no valid proof they deserve it. After all I have seen, after all I have done, I, too, believe in the impossible.

On unsteady feet, I climb upon the stones. "Crawl down in my shirt and find a way to cling on to me the best you can. Hold your breath."

"My hairs will irritate your skin," he warns. "I cannot control them in such close quarters."

It's the least of my worries right now. As soon as he's done what I've asked, and a wildfire breaks out upon my back, we follow Alice into the well.

WHEN I OPEN MY eyes, I'm in a sunny meadow. Birds fly overhead, rabbits skip by, and grasses sway in a gentle breeze—and a spider scratches at my face.

"You nearly squashed me."

I let out a laugh at his genuine outrage. "My apologies. It wasn't intentional."

A warm hand touches mine. "How do you fare? Grymsdyke informed me he bit you."

I turn my head—slowly, as my neck aches from the bite—to find the most beautiful woman in all the Timelines sitting next to me. "I didn't know if he'd survive without the goose's strength."

She gently touches the holes in my neck. "There you go again, proving yourself to be the most generous, most noble of princes."

"You're obviously biased." It feels like I've been through the ringer when I sit up. I tilt my neck, stretching it, but it does little to relieve the pain. "Does it look like I was bit by a vampire?"

The spider scoffs. "Vampire! What utter nonsense. Everybody knows that no such things exist."

So says the talking spider in a magical land we had to jump into a well to find.

Alice helps me to my feet, pointing into the distance. "I saw smoke coming from that direction."

Then I suppose that's the direction we head. Grymsdyke climbs upon my shoulder, and we set off. Amazingly, none of us are wet, despite jumping into a well filled with water. We walk a good distance, past a random, cold oven, before a small house appears. The moment we come within striking distance, the shutters fly open and an old woman peeps her head out.

Make that an old woman with incredibly large, sharp teeth.

"A queen, a prince, and an assassin, all blessed by one of the Wise Women, upon my humble doorstep!" She squints at us. "What is the world coming to?"

Alice drops into a reverent, low curtsy. I follow suit and bow. "Greetings, Mother Holle."

The old woman disappears from the window, only to reemerge once she opens the door. "I see we all know who the other is, then. Come in, children. You will be all the better for it."

Her tone is kind, her face even more so despite her nightmarish smile. Neither Alice nor I hesitate to do as she requests. The inside of the cottage is fairly neat yet cool despite the mild weather outside. I wrack my brain to remember how the story went, the one that my mother read to me.

Chores. The girl in the story did chores for Mother Holle and was rewarded for dutiful behavior.

"Would you like me to build you a fire?" I ask the old woman.

Her smile brightens, showing off those terrifying teeth of hers. "That would be quite nice of you, Your Highness."

Grymsdyke leaps off my shoulder, onto a nearby table, before I make my way over to the fireplace. No firewood is stacked nearby, but there is an axe.

I head outside.

A grove of trees sits behind the house, with many branches and fallen trees already on the ground. I spend a good half hour dragging pieces back and chopping them up, working up a good sweat that eventually loosens the muscles in my neck, before reentering the house. Alice is inside, shaking a mattress so hard that flying feathers mimic snow. Grymsdyke, on the other hand, has a pile of freshly dead mice and rats lining up next to the entrance. They must have remembered my story well, too.

Once the fire is lit, we get to work on making a meal. The entire time, Mother Holle sits in a wooden chair with her spindle, stretching wool into thread. While the meat is boiling, Alice and I dust and clean the house while Grymsdyke continues to ensure it is vermin free. At one point, when I pause to wipe my brow, I find him upon the old woman's lap, being petted like a cat. There is a smile upon Holle's face, as if the coarse hairs that set my back on fire feel to her like the softest of fur. And I'll be damned, the spider is purring contentedly.

Dinner is ready by the time the sun sets. The spider feasts on a bit of raw meat Alice set aside, while the rest of us enjoy the boiled meat. When all plates are empty, and I am cleaning them with a bucket of water and a rag, Mother Holle finally says, "It is not often one finds royalty so willing to serve a woman such as myself."

"We are most happy to do so." Sincerity rings in Alice's words.

"It has been some time since I have had guests, and as much as I would delight in your continued company, I am also aware that you are here for a purpose. But it is not for the gold so many others seek, is it? Speak, child, and tell me what it is you wish for, for a job well done."

"We have no need for gold, that much is true," Alice tells her. "All we desire is information, if it is yours to offer."

The old woman grunts thoughtfully. "Some secrets are worth their weight in gold."

"That they are," Alice agrees. "And there is a good chance that the secret we wish to be uncovered may be worth even more than that."

"Ask then," Mother Holle says, "and we shall see if you are deserving of such a reward."

Alice bows her head briefly. "We are told that, in order to learn the way to Koppenberg Mountain, we must offer a sacrifice to the Weser River, only we do not know what kind of sacrifice is required."

For a moment, the old woman says nothing. She simply rocks in her chair, her hands folded neatly upon her lap. But then she says, her words filled with incredulous awe, "You seek the Piper."

"We do."

Her rheumy eyes swivel to me. "He has tried to claim you."

"Tried," I say, "but failed."

"Yes, yes, I can see that now. There is strong magic within you, more than just the Wise Woman's blessing. You are blessed by . . ." A smile curves those thin lips of hers. "True love." She turns now to Alice. "The blood of the other flows within you both—true love at its strongest and yet most fragile magical state." She nods knowingly. "True love saved you both so far. Time will see if it will save you when it is most needed."

Neither Alice nor I know what to say to this.

Mother Holle claps her hands together. "You asked if I knew what must be sacrificed in order to find the forgotten mountain, and the answer is lifeblood. To each that wishes to travel to such a damned place, they must offer blood to the river. But it must be done so with intent, and with full knowledge that precious few who go there ever return as they once were, if they even survive at all."

Alice leans forward, taking hold of the old woman's hands. "You have our deepest appreciation, Mother Holle."

Our hostess looks to me once more. "You have another question, do you not, Prince?"

I don't know if I will ever get used to that title. "I do, actually."

"Then ask it."

"The Piper has been responsible for the destruction of many worlds, for the deaths of countless persons—"

"Including those who mean much to you."

I nod. "My mother and my grandfather, amongst others. He has manipulated colleagues of ours, destroyed lives. He has stolen children and changed them, turning them into murderers. For the life of me, I cannot figure out why a person would want to do such things."

She stares at me with those shrewd eyes of hers for nearly half a minute before she responds. "He does it for the same reasons all others have done so in the past and will do so in the future. He does so for power and what he believes to be true."

I rub at my hair. "But it has to be more than that. Power, I can get. But . . . to actively seek out to destroy worlds and murder people he doesn't even know, ones whose lives have nothing to do with his—"

"That is his question to answer more completely, unfortunately, and not mine."

Alice asks quietly, "Is it true that the thirteenth Wise Woman is allied with the Piper?"

The old woman reclaims her spindle from a basket at her feet. "True love works in mysterious ways, does it not?" Before either of us can say anything, she adds, "It is too late for you to return to your friends tonight. There is a barn in the back; in the loft, there is a bed. You may sleep there. Do not worry; the barn is far warmer than you might imagine. Be prepared to depart at first light." She motions to Grymsdyke, who had been perched on a nearby table. "I have need of you in here tonight, little assassin, so we might have a discussion."

He lowers himself into his spidery equivalent of a bow.

Effectively dismissed once a candle is passed over, Alice and I make our way into the barn. Mother Holle was right—it's warm inside, and the bed is surprisingly soft. I'm sure Victor will be pissed off that I worked so hard today, but the ache in my muscles feels good.

I'm itching to get back on the road, though. The sooner we can figure out where this mountain is, the sooner we can take down the Piper.

After we take off all our clothes and climb in beneath the blankets, Alice rolls over so her head lies upon my chest. "She loves him, then." Her voice is soft, sad even. "The thirteenth Wise Woman, I mean. She does what she does out of love."

Which just might make her even more dangerous than he is.

SACRIFICE

ALICE

HAMELIN IS QUITE POSSIBLY the most unsettling village I have ever come across in my entire life. Eerily quiet to the point bird or cricket songs do not even fill the air, its buildings are wrapped in thick cocoons of fog and mist. Villagers go through the motions as though they are automatons, their movements slow, their eyes vacant as they move to and fro. No one speaks, no one laughs, no one makes eye contact with any of us when we ride into town. A peek into the local tavern shows a handful of men, silently drinking their ale whilst staring off into space. Orders are not placed; the wench brings drinks whether or not they are wanted.

There are no signs of children to be found anywhere.

I search the horizons for any signs of mountains or hills, but the fog is too thick.

As our horses slow when we reach the heart of the Hamelin, Grymsdyke leaps from Finn's mount to my own. He scuttles up my leg, perching on the front of the saddle. "Your Majesty, there can be little good in such a hollow place."

It is a sentiment I wholeheartedly agree with.

He remains with me whilst we make our way through the streets, vigilant as he constantly surveys our surroundings. For those we encounter, we must steer our horses around them lest they are trampled without care or thought toward their own personal safety.

The Weser River is on the southwestern edge of the village, its waters a murky yet placid dark gray. We dismount our horses, tying them to the trees that dot the banks. As I'm finishing my knot, a small boat slides by, a man staring forlornly into the distance as he clutches his unmoving oars.

"What in the bloody hell happened here?" the A.D. murmurs.

"Grief," Mary says quietly. "Loss. Devastation." She blows out a hard breath. "The Piper."

And, quite possibly, the thirteenth Wise Woman.

Since the trip to Mother Holle's, I cannot stop thinking about her response to my questions. Love, true love, has certainly influenced many decisions in my life over the years, whether intentionally or not. I risked much to love the White King of Wonderland, and he the same. And when my beloved land asked much of us, we bled and broke until we gave it what it wished from us. And I have risked much for Finn Van Brunt, to ensure his safety and our love—and I would risk even more if necessary.

True love is exactly what she warned us it would be: strength and fragility all at once. True love can fortify a person or it can shatter them mindlessly. We who experience it, truly feel it in the depths of our bones and the strands of each hair, often allow it to color our field of vision. If the thirteenth Wise Woman truly does love the Piper, then her actions will reflect it. She may fight just as fiercely for him as I will for Finn, and she may be willing to pay whatever price is asked to ensure their love holds true.

I wonder, though, if the same can be said for the Piper.

When we first met, there was a flirtation, a false heat born of liquor and (on my behalf) a need to drown. Nothing sincere or meaningful happened between us, but that had been my choice, rather than his. I can look back on those moments now with a clearer eye, one that understands his actions and persuasions were more manipulative than genuine. He also romanced Sara Carrisford for months, wooing her with attention and affection. She believed herself in love, believed him to be, as well. Who is to know how many times he has done the same to other women? The art of deception is one he has long mastered, whether it be toward luring children from safe homes or seducing a lonely, desperate woman to believe she meant more than she actually did.

Mother Holle mentioned the thirteenth Wise Woman's love, but I am not so certain that the Piper's is as genuine. Perhaps he has found yet another woman, lonely for affection, and found a way to use her and her skills to suit his needs.

"Are you sure this is what's needed?" Victor is asking his brother.

"So said the woman our mother claimed was a goddess."

I turn to Grymsdyke, hiding my smile. "I have yet to inquire of you what Mother Holle wished of you the night we were her guests."

"She wished to speak to me of my role as your assassin and protector."

How very curious.

"I am to give lifeblood here, as well, Your Majesty."

I must admit, I hadn't even considered such a thing. "Are you certain?"

"Mother Holle was quite insistent. It will be difficult for myself to do the deed, so I must beg help from you."

It feels wrong, somehow, to bleed such a magnificent soldier. "Perhaps Victor will be best, as he is a physician and skilled at ensuring precise cuts."

"No, Your Majesty," he says gravely, followed by a cough. "It must be you who takes my blood."

As he has done so much for me over the years, I cannot deny him this.

Our group meets at the edge of the grassy banks. Victor has his small medical kit from his bag out, and from it he takes a slim scalpel. "I wish I could just take some blood from each vein with a syringe, but I get the feeling that won't cut it, this being a sacrifice and all." A rueful, quiet laugh escapes like a sigh. "Sorry, what a terrible pun. That said, I brought a few alcohol wipes with me to sterilize the blade between cuts. After being stuck in 1905BUR-LP with nothing, I wasn't going to risk not being prepared again."

Finn lays a hand on his brother's shoulder. "It wasn't your fault. You know it wasn't."

"Still." The doctor's smile is thin. "I've got thread for stitching, a bit of antibiotic ointment, and some extra bandages for afterward. Do you know how much blood is required?"

Finn shakes his head. "She didn't say. Just that we had to offer it up with intent."

The A.D. smacks his hands together. "You mean, like . . . we intend the river to tell us where the damn mountain is?"

Mary rolls her eyes. "I think it's meant to be a bit more finessed than that."

"It's probably whatever intent we have," Finn muses. "My intent for giving my blood will be to know the location of the mountain so I can go and stop the Piper so no more catalysts and Timelines will be destroyed. I think it has to be honest, though."

"It might be nice to do it all at once," Mary says. "Perhaps the intent there would be more meaningful."

It's an excellent idea.

"I initially considered cutting into the palms," Victor says, "but upon reflection, a cut-up hand will not help any of us in a fight."

"Chances are," I add, "once we find a way into the mountain, there will be many fights."

The doctor nods. "As I can't merely draw blood, I'm guessing our best bet is to have a small, horizontal cut on whichever is your non-dominant wrist. It—"

The A.D. jerks back, gripping a wrist with his other hand. "I am not going to commit suicide in this bloody Timeline!"

Victor sighs. "Any cut like that, shallow as the one I will make, would coagulate before any true harm can come. And I'll be stitching us all up afterward—although Mary will have to sew me. Even I cannot sew myself up one handed."

His love's smile is a bit sad when she presses a gentle kiss against his cheek.

"I sharpened my scalpels before coming, so if there is even a scar afterward, it would be faint."

"He's excellent at stitches." Mary lets go of Victor so she can dig out some of the bandaging from his bag. "They're always quite neat." She passes a strip to each of us, explaining that as soon as we have offered our blood, we're to press firmly against the wound until it can be stitched.

"Are you sure you do not want Victor to make the incision?" I ask Grymsdyke.

"I am positive." He jumps onto a nearby, tall rock. "I do not have veins, not like you. I will bleed differently." He rises on several of his feet, baring his abdomen. "A small, shallow cut, just north of the mid-way point will do."

I must admit, I am terrified of the prospect. My talent with a blade is as a fighter, not a surgeon. What if I cut too hard? Crush him? He has been so loyal to me over the years. "Will you at least concede to Victor stitching you up?"

I think if he could smile, he would. "Your Majesty, I possess an exoskeleton. A bandage will do."

"Let us do him last," Victor says. "I'll talk you through it, okay?"

He begins with Mary, and then the A.D., with strict instructions that they hold their arms above their hearts until we are ready to make our offerings. Finn is next, and then me. When it comes time to cut Grymsdyke, my love gently cradles the assassin in his hands, ensuring a safe place for me to work.

Victor passes me the smallest scalpel he's brought, pointing to the area the spider indicated. "Here. You'll want to put enough pressure to break the exoskeleton, but not too much to go in deep. The length should be a millimeter, at most."

I already feel the *drip, drip, drip* from my own wrist. Yet it does not matter, not when there is such a delicate matter before me.

I will my hands not to shake. I take a deep breath and remind myself that I have been able to throw a blade across a battlefield and meet my target. That, when I put my mind to it, nothing is impossible. Not even cutting a millimeter length upon a spider whose venom would kill me in less than a minute.

Grymsdyke stills. He trusts me to do what is right, even though the thirst for vengeance burns in my throat.

I lean forward and take one more steadying breath. And then I gently, yet firmly, drag the blade across his abdomen. A bubble of blue blood surfaces.

"Excellent," Victor whispers before drawing the larger scalpel across his own wrist.

Now that we all bleed, we all hold out our wrists over the water, allowing the blood to drip into the gray depths. Finn holds Grymsdyke's body out alongside his own wrist, so that the spider's blood mixes with ours. I do not know about the rest, but I close my eyes and offer my intentions to the river.

I intend to assure the safety of millions of souls I have never met, so that they do not simply cease to exist one day without warning.

I intend to find the Piper and exact justice for what he has done to those I love and those I do not know.

I intend to ensure the friends with me here—and each is truly my friend, my *family*—walk away from the forthcoming battles and return home.

I intend to do exactly what it takes to achieve these ends, even if the meal the Caterpillar warned me about aches within my belly.

The wind picks up, whispering past us with a mournful sigh. Tiny ripples form in the water from each drop of lifeblood we sacrifice, and I do not think I am imagining it when I see the river is eating up what we have to offer.

After a while, Victor urges us all to press the bandages against our wrists as we wait for him to stitch us up. Grymsdyke is taken care of first with simply a dot of antibiotic cream and a bandage. While Victor is sewing up Mary, whispering loving words that leave the A.D. and Grymsdyke surreptitiously moving away, Finn takes me aside.

"I love you, you know."

How is it that, each time he says this to me, feels just as magnificent as the first? "I love you, too."

He ducks his head, pulls me behind a tree. "Mother Holle said that true love is what saves us. What may save us in the end."

I touch his cheek, already knowing where he is going with this. "It is a good idea."

His eyes, filled with so much concern and sincerity, widen in surprise. Silly man.

"Your blood saved me." I lean forward and brush my lips against his. "Mine saved you. We are about to head into the bowels of hell, with no knowledge of what is to meet us there. It cannot hurt for us to ensure a bit more of each into the other as we go into battle. You're my north star, Finn. My binary. "

Mother Holle wondered if true love would be enough to save us in the coming days. Instinct tells me it will—it always will. How could it not, with feelings as strong as these?

Finn's forehead comes to rest upon mine. "I swear, sometimes it's like you read my mind."

"And you mine."

"I know it's actually unhygienic—"

I cannot help but laugh quietly at his sweetness.

"—especially in this day and age . . ." He pauses. "Well, okay. Not *this* particular day and age, but—"

"I know what you mean."

I can practically feel his own smile growing, his mouth is so close to mine. "On a lot of levels, doing something like this is kind of kid-like—"

"Kid-like! How so?"

"You've never heard of how sometimes kids prick their fingers so they can hold them up against each other and become blood brothers or sisters?"

My lips tug up. "Not at all."

His laugh is not much more than a breath. And then, more seriously, "I can't stand the thought that anything could happen to you when we finally find him, Alice. They've threatened you more than once."

Just as I cannot tolerate any further attempts on his person.

Standing beneath that tree, we press our bleeding wrists against one another. The flow has slowed, thankfully, but there is enough to mix together.

Not all fairy tales have happy endings, this much is true. There are times when the innocent suffer, the good are defeated, and evil and wickedness reign supreme. I refuse to allow such an ending to this fairy tale, or my own. I cannot fail in this quest. None of us can.

"ANYONE?" THE A.D. THROWS a rock into the river. "Anything?"

Mary yawns, rubbing at the white bandaging sticking out from beneath her sleeve. She is seated between Victor's legs, her head resting against his chest. "It's not as if a map was going to appear in thin air."

"Why the hell not? We're in fairy tale land! Shite like that happens all the time."

At least three-fourths of an hour has passed since the last of us was sewn up by the doctor. I must admit, I can understand the Artful Dodger's frustration, as it's percolating within my chest, too.

"Maybe we should go back," he's saying to no one in particular. "See if the Society was able to track him down in New York."

"What the hell, man?" Finn snaps a twig and tosses one of the pieces onto the ground next to him. "You don't get an answer at the snap of your fingers and you want to tuck your tail between your legs and call it a day?"

"We're running in circles!" The A.D. grabs chunks of his greasy blond hair. "Who knows if that bastard managed to get his slimy hands on another catalyst while we're picking our noses, trying to find a bloody mountain that probably doesn't even exist!"

"It does," comes a voice from the tree above us.

But the A.D. has worked himself into a lather, for he continues, "For all we know—"

"Jack?"

He looks over at me, eyes wide.

"Cease your ranting."

His mouth appropriately snaps shut.

I glance up into the branches. My assassin climbed up earlier, searching for a bite to eat. "You were saying, Grymsdyke?"

"There is a mountain beyond the river, Your Majesty. It is swathed in fog, but I see it."

Everyone leaps to his or her feet. Both Finn and Victor immediately grab hold of lower branches and pull themselves up to where the spider is. A minute or two passes before Victor calls down, "I'll be damned! He's right! There's a mountain across the river, to the west!"

"The base is probably a half-day's ride," Finn offers. "Maybe even less."

I'm already scanning the length of the river to locate a bridge. And there, like a miracle, one appears in the far distance.

The river came through for us after all.

Our horses are reluctant to leave behind the grasses they've munched on, but we are soon making our way down the length of the waterway, toward the bridge. And from there, toward Koppenberg Mountain.

THAT WHICH WAS LOST IS NOW FOUND

FINN

ONCE WE CROSS THE river, our view of the mountain sharpens. Not so tall that any adventurer would seek it out for glory's sake, it still manages to loom in the distance like a gray and green prison. We soon find a small, neglected dirt path that moves in that direction, but the horses are forced to go in single file to fit through the trees. The woods are nearly as quiet as Hamelin had been, with precious little proof of insects, birds, or animals, and for some time, the only sounds to be heard are those of the horses' hooves. None of us talk much—if I had to guess, I'd say we're all considering the intentions we offered up to the river earlier.

We have no solid plan of attack yet, having no clue what the lay of the land is. It's not the first time any of us have gone into an assignment blind—hell, that's practically standard at the Society. But it feels distinctly different this time, as if we don't get our shit together the very second we reach Koppenberg, it'll be our doom. That pathetic sack of shit Jenkins claims there is a king and queen of the mountain, and I didn't get the feeling he was being metaphorical. A king and queen typically need somewhere to rule, and instinct tells me that whatever cave the Piper dragged all those kids he kidnapped so long ago into is probably just the place we need to find. Jenkins also mentioned some kind of convergence, and if that's going down any time soon, it's going to complicate matters.

Outside of stealth and no prisoners, there's not much more we can even expect.

It takes us far less time to reach the base of the mountain than I thought it would, maybe three hours at the most. A thorough survey of the area presents a small path that appears to climb up into the trees and rocks.

Victor squints as he traces the visible path as far as he can upward. "What do you think?"

I don't know what to think, to be honest. It could be a decoy, leading to who-the-hell-knows-where. But it could also be legit and take us exactly where we need to go. Time is running out, though, and our options are dwindling. Chances are, the Piper's got his hands on a new catalyst by now. He might have even destroyed one while we've been making our way through 1812GRI-CHT and 1816/18GRI-GT. Hell, we don't even know if this is where he is, except for the dying ravings of a mass murderer.

And still, I tell my brother, "We'll have to take the risk."

After the pace we've set for them over the past few days, the horses are exhausted once we dismount. We cannot just tie them up, though, not when we have no idea when or if we'll actually come back out of the mountain. There's always a chance we'll hike up there and find nothing. There's also a chance we'll find that cave. It's best to let them go now.

While bags and weapons are collected and situated, and canteens checked for water filled from the river we offered sacrifices to, I tell the group, "Obviously, having spent several days out of it, I have no idea what the Society's latest policy is right now. For all I know, Brom and the others expect us to drag the Piper's ass back to New York for interrogation. We all have a ton of questions, sure, but I gotta tell you, I'm not expecting any of you to risk anything to subdue that bastard. If you have a shot, take it. This monster has done too much damage to risk anything other than certainty."

"Damn right, I'm going to take a shot," the A.D. mutters.

"We know he has well over a hundred children he's been manip-ulating for centuries. If they're anything like Todd or Rosemary, you need to remember to remain vigilant at all times. I don't know if they can be redeemed, to be honest, but what I do know is that none of them are going to take kindly to us storming their hideout." I rub at my hair. "Provided there *is* a hideout up there. It sounds callous, but they're not my concern right now. I'm concerned about Timelines that have no idea about this bastard and his cult, and the millions of people within each who might just disappear because he thinks it's within his rights to choose whether or not they die."

"Do you think it possible, if the Piper is taken out, the others might revert to their original states?" Mary asks. Grymsdyke is perched on her shoulder at the moment, listening quietly.

"He was not the only one who has manipulated them," Alice says in a flat voice. "If our suspicions are correct, we will also have the thirteenth Wise Woman to contend with. We cannot take our chances with either of them, not when the stakes are so high."

"And she's a wild card," Victor muses. "Outside of that blade, we've had no contact with her so far. We don't even know what she looks like."

"We know she's dangerous," I say. "And we know she has the ability to transform people into whatever the Chosen are. We may have the twelfth Wise Woman's enchantment and blessings, but you guys heard what she said. We're still at risk. Don't ever forget that. It may come from a blade or her lips, but someone like her can do a hell of a lot of damage."

"Plus, there are the pipes," Mary says. "And from the surveillance footage, we've learned that there are quite a bit of children who know how to play them just as effectively as the Piper. We're just as much at risk for falling under that spell as any other up there."

That reminds me . . ."You said you have two pairs of ear plugs?" I ask the A.D.

He digs in his bag and produces a small metal case. "No idea what Wen meant them for, but yeah. Two pairs."

"Considering you're able to slip into a lot of places unseen better than the rest of us, you ought to wear one of them. We're going to need your eyes to find out whatever you can."

He nods, but it's uncomfortably done, like he knows I've just given him a huge cushion most of us will not have.

"I think Mary ought to have the other pair," Victor says.

Her eyes widen. "Why me? Shouldn't it be someone who is a better fighter?"

"Because I happen to know, having rooted around your bag a little, that you brought a nice little set of poisons with you. We may have need for them, and if you're hypnotized away, they won't do us any good."

"Agreed." I clear my throat before turning to Grymsdyke. "I've never asked you before exactly how much venom you have."

The spider twitches. "As much as required."

"I meant, can you bite more than one person within a certain time period?"

"My fangs are strong."

I try my best not to roll my eyes. I like the guy, but sometimes, getting answers out of him isn't always the easiest.

"Everyone on board?"

All I see is acceptance and eagerness to get this show on the road. And so we do.

We've been hiking for a couple of hours, and despite the cool, misty weather, I'm sweating. Nobody is complaining about being tired, though, not even the A.D. The path, if you can even call it that, is uneven, filled with rocks and holes, and has quite a bit of vegetation creeping across it. Some parts have been steep, others not so much. And as we make our way up, all I can think is: *Thank God this isn't Everest.*

Just when I fear we're less than an hour from the top, I see it. Winding off to the side, maybe a few hundred feet away, with trees bending around it in unnatural angles, is the mouth of a cave.

I hold up a hand and then motion a pair of fingers in the direction. Everyone stops and looks.

The A.D. fist pumps. "It's about damn time."

There are no visible guards to consider. And still, my hand goes to one of my guns. Behind me, the hiss of a blade cuts through the air. A light press against a shoulder tells me Alice is here, she has my back.

I send the A.D. to scout the area, ears plugged, grudgingly impressed at how he always manages to disappear in any kind of environment when he wants to. I maintain a watch on the entrance. From what I can see, there's no movement. No indication that this is anything other than a cave on a mountain—only logic tells me it's a hell of a lot more than that.

Hairs prickle on the back on my neck. Something feels off, something I can't put a finger on.

He returns a quarter of an hour later. "There's nothing, no one. There are also no animals, Finn. No birds. No insects. And there's a ring of dead plants low to the ground, about twenty feet back from the entrance. I can't say for sure, but the shriveled berries look like those from the belladonna plant."

"Did you get a view into the cave at all?"

"Just inside, to the left, there is a lip that narrows the entrance by well over half." He shifts his weight from one foot to the other. "Outside of that, all I saw was darkness."

We have no flashlights. No cell phones. No candles, no lanterns. We literally are going in blind.

Or not, because Mary says, "Hold on a sec." She squats down, rifling through her bag. "I might have also nicked something from the lab. I can't believe I forgot about it until just now. Where is my head?" Within a few seconds, a handful of the Society's special glasses are held aloft.

Bless that sneaky woman.

"What about the ear pieces?" Alice asks.

Mary shakes her head. "Wasn't sure if the wireless signal would work here. Obviously, we're also not going to be able to use the view function on these outside of individual camera shots, but there's a night vision function."

Victor high fives his lady love before kissing her. "Have I told you lately how astoundingly awesome you are? Because you are, Mary Lennox."

She smiles winsomely.

The glasses are passed out to everyone save Grymsdyke, who informs Mary he already has excellent night vision. Nobody points out that they wouldn't have fit him anyway. When she offers me my pair, I say slyly, "Mary Lennox, the optimist? Bringing me some even though it wasn't a guarantee I'd wake up? Did you go into one of those body snatcher Timelines and not tell any of us?"

"Oh, ha ha, you ungrateful lout. Just take your damn pair." She glances at the woman standing next to me. "In all honestly, I've come to realize that Alice's determination gets her just about anything she wants." She pauses. "Except, well, remaining in Wonderland and marrying that hot king of hers." Another pause. "Sorry about that."

Nope, I was wrong. This is most definitely the Mary Lennox I know, not some kind of changeling or alien.

Alice says nothing to the callous remark, but her smile is tight.

Glasses on with the night functions activated, weapons drawn, we make our way slowly up the winding path to the cave. I take the front, Victor carries the back. The closer we get to the mouth of the cave, though, the more those hairs on the back of my neck tingle and stand on end. The air feels charged, leaving my skin itching uncomfortably.

We really are descending into the mouth of hell, aren't we?

I hold a hand up as soon as we reach the ring of deadened plants.

The A.D. was right—these are definitely poisonous belladonna. Clustered tightly together, the blackened line they form is a stark contrast to the green of the trees looming overhead. I grab a nearby stick and poke at the space just beyond the plants, but nothing happens.

Why all the dead belladonna?

Mary quickly collects a number of the berries and leaves, stuffing them in her satchel.

Stick tossed aside, I take a deep breath and step over the crumbling plants. The air's charge becomes a hundred times stronger, so much that my eyes water behind the glasses.

This is not good. This is not right. And still, I take more steps forward.

The entrance is exactly as the A.D. described it. A jagged lip juts out, blocking much of the view. I slowly allow myself a peak around, but in the green of my glasses, I see nothing more than a thinning tunnel that eventually will only allow one body through at a time. A faint glow emanates from beyond the space. There are no sounds, though, no indications that there is anyone lying in wait behind the bend.

Gun drawn, I make my way around the lip, Alice directly on my heels. Several feet into the cave, my ears begin to ring from a growing pressure I can't find a source for. Discomfort turns to pain.

Well, hell.

A hand against my shoulder has me pausing. Alice leans forward and whispers, "I know this place."

My eyebrows lift in question.

"When I went to Bücherei, to try to find the Piper shortly after the attack on the Institute. There was nothing there, just . . . just a cave. A tunnel. The rocks here are the same." She reach out and runs a finger alongside a ribbon of sparkling quartz. Similar lines run through the entire tunnel, up and down the walls. "This cannot be a coincidence."

A quick glance behind us at Mary and A.D. shows confirmed recognition.

"The rock bled," she breathes into my ear. "When I hit it with my war hammer. Look here." She points to a rust-stained section of one of the rocks.

How can that be, though? How can a cave in 1816/18GRI-GT be in New York, too, without a doorway or editing?

However it is, though, it's further confirmation we're on the right path and that we need to keep on going. Soon, I reach the point where the cave slims to just roughly two feet across. The light from the around the bend grows brighter. A peek through shows the tunnel sharply veering to the left and widening to . . .

I blink. Holy. Shit.

I slip through the space and stare down a torch-lined tunnel. No longer filled with rough stone and quartz, there are frescos and tapestries decorating the walls filled with familiar scenes. *Fairy tale scenes.* A girl, in a red cloak, escaping the belly of a sliced-open wolf. A woman, lying on the ground, a partially eaten apple just inches from her open hand. A witch in an oven, burning, as children nearby watch. A glass coffin. A griffin. Dwarves. Fairies. Giants. Princesses. Princes. Women with mutilated feet, their eyes pecked out by birds. Castles. Birds. Gnomes. Each descriptive, nearly all brutal in nature. They're all here, all of the Grimm's tales my mother used to read to me.

And while the tunnel stretches a good distance, the pièce de résistance is on the far wall at the end, shortly before another bend. Stretched from floor to ceiling, at least twenty feet wide, is the depiction of a man in a colorful outfit playing a pipe in the foreground, while a group of children led by the same man march toward a mountain and cave in the distance.

There can no longer be any doubt. We are in the lair of the Pied Piper of Hamelin.

Alice grips my arm, her eyes narrowed meaningfully. Angrily.

I nod, my sentiments the same.

We make our way slowly through the macabre monument to the stories of 1812GRI-CHT and 1816/18GRI-GT. Every face in my group shows horror at what they see. These are not the happy endings one imagines for fairy tales—no, what is depicted is the worst of each tale. When I get to the Piper's fresco and turn to the right, I'm shocked into pausing once more.

It's Bücherei—the first one I went to, when I was sent to acquire books for the Librarian.

I turn around and find the outline of a door that looks very much like the one Alice and I first entered the Piper's mansion. We're in a small foyer—complete with electricity—that leads to another hallway. There is no doubt in my mind what lies at the end of that one, and when I turn the corner, I find out just how right I am. Massive carved and painted doors with golden knobs loom before us.

The hidden library is here, in the forgotten mountain.

I flip up the screen for my glasses, switching the night vision function off as I take in my surroundings. This—this cannot be. I've been in here before, in New York. This exact place. How can it come to be here, in 1816/18GRI-GT, in a mountain of all places?

My brother comes to stand next to me. His whisper is barely audible as we stand there, staring at the monstrosities before us. "Is this what I think it is?"

It is. I don't know how, but it is.

I motion for the A.D. to scout the astoundingly long hallway to the left of the doors and beyond. He nods and is off without a single word.

Alice slowly approaches the door, running her hands over the sides, as if she was searching for something. When she doesn't find it after several minutes, she grips one of the golden doorknobs and turns.

It's locked.

Frustration fills her face when she turns back to me. "If memory serves, the mechanism was complicated, but the key was simple. Do you think our thief could pick it?"

Before I can answer, the man in question appears, his face pale. "Did you find anything?" I ask.

He tugs out an earpiece. "Yeah. I found a whole hell of a lot that you need to come see."

I turn to Victor. "You and Mary stay here." I glance at her, and she pulls out one of the earplugs. "I know you're pretty damn good at locks, too. See what you can do?"

She nods and squats so she can rummage through her bag.

"I will come with you," Grymsdyke says from Alice's shoulder. Together, we follow the A.D. down the hallway, past several locked doors, and up a gilded staircase. At the top, a wide veranda of sorts spreads before us, surrounded by elaborately designed wrought iron. There are chaises up here, plants that appear healthy despite the lack of sunshine. Fur rugs spread across a marble floor. A large fountain is showcased in the middle of the area with an emerald-covered frog perching atop it, water spitting from its mouth down toward carved lily pads and lotus flowers crusted in more jewels, gold, and silver.

Apparently, this bizarre scene in the middle of a mountain is not what we're to see, though, because the A.D. holds a finger up to his mouth and motions to the edge with another finger. Alice and I creep over to the side, hovering as close as we can to the wall closest to the stairs.

My breath falls away.

I can only best describe it as a sumptuous chamber, complete with two massive carved and painted thrones holding court at the head. Tapestries line the walls; gold-lined marble fills the floors. Behind the throne is yet another replica of the fresco I'd seen in the tunnel, of the Piper and the children. Resting on an elaborate golden stand in between the two thrones is an enormous, closed book. An elaborate chandelier, made of crystal and antlers, hangs from the high ceiling above the space. But none of this is what shocks us—no, it's the crowd of people, both children and adults, standing completely still as they face the thrones. There must be at least a hundred. At *least.* And all are armed with some kind of weapon at their side. There are guns, swords of all flavors and varieties, sais, daggers, bows and arrows, crossbows, machetes, axes, war hammers, pikes, and maces.

He's made an army. And by the looks on the others' faces, I can tell they're just as taken aback by this turn of events as I am.

I scan the crowd but cannot find the man I know to be the Piper anywhere.

Alice whispers, "Finn. The woman who attacked Mary and me at the library, Jenn Ammer. She is there, just to the left of the bookstand. The last I saw of her, she had been taken into New York police custody."

The A.D., who has so far stayed close to the stairs, says tightly,

"You'll want to look about halfway through the crowd, dead center."

I do so and my heart nearly drops out of my chest. I can only see the back of her head, but there is no doubt in my mind who it is. Standing there, a gun in her hand, is my former partner Sara.

I'm on the A.D. immediately. "You said you left her in some sort of motel, that you locked her up!"

Alice places a hand on my arm, warning me to keep it down.

"I did!" the bastard whispers. "I swear I did! Even took the key back with me to the Institute! It's sitting on me dresser!"

"Is Wendy present?" Alice scans the crowd. "Did you find her in the throng?"

"No." Still, the A.D.'s words crack. "No green hair. But I'd know her even if it were brown or any other color. Wen isn't in that crowd."

But it doesn't mean she might not be here. I want to smash something, I'm so pissed off.

"Our odds," Grymsdyke says, "have greatly decreased with so many opponents."

No shit. Six of us, including him, against hundreds of fighters who, if they're like any of the rest we've faced, will do whatever they must to take us down? And there are the pair of a Wise Woman and the Piper? I'm good in a fight—so is Alice. Victor, too. The A.D. can hold his own, as can Grymsdyke. With her back up against a wall, Mary always pulls through, but her strengths have always been elsewhere.

Wait. Mary's *strengths*. Of course. Could she have brought any of Wonderland's SleepMist with her? Or anything else that can wipe out a crowd's potential, thereby restoring our odds?

I'm down the stairs, hurrying back toward the library doors. I turn the corner to find Mary behind Victor, eyes wide in terror, a hand on his arm. He's staring down the hallway leading to the foyer, sword in his hand, all the blood drained from his face.

"No," Mary cries. "It—it can't be. *No.*"

"Mary, run. Run to Finn and Alice." Victor holds out his sword, hand shaking just as badly as his voice. When she doesn't move, he says more firmly. *"Go."*

"I'm not leaving you!"

But he shoves her, as hard as he can, in our direction. And I'm right there with Mary when the person they'd been staring at appears, because this cannot be happening. This cannot be real. Thick, lustrous black hair falls around a sallow face with skin so tight, it appears as if it's stretched over bones. Stitches form rings around the neck, the hairline, his wrists, and other places. He's tall, his body fit beneath the rags he wears.

My God. It's my brother's nightmare, come to life.

It's real.

The monster holds out a club, pointing it at my brother. "A family's sin is a stain that cannot be washed away!"

Alice and I bolt down the hallway. I fire my gun, striking the creature in its neck. It doesn't even flinch, though, because the bullet bounces off like it was made of Styrofoam.

The monster swings its club; Victor's sword readily meets it.

"You will not get away now," it bellows. "Not until retribution is mine!"

Mary screams his name, and Victor pleads with her to stay back. Alice catches hold of her, and my brother's girlfriend is rabid in her attempt to get away.

I fire again, hitting it right in the back, right where I know its heart to be. The bullet bounces once more off the monster, slamming instead into the nearby wall. It lunges for Victor, its club too fast for the blade. Victor hits the wooden library doors, his sword clattering on the ground next to him.

Mary screams again, his name falling over and over from her lips.

I shoot again. And again. *Nothing makes contact.* The club swings once more, crashing down upon one of Victor's arm. The crush of bones is so loud it echoes in the hall.

It's my turn to yell my brother's name.

"Get Mary out of here!" Alice yells at the A.D. And then, to me, "Finn!"

I catch the sword she tosses me. In turn, she tugs out her daggers.

Victor grapples for his fallen sword, his crushed arm hanging awkwardly at his side. As he rolls to duck another swing, he roars in pain. Alice and I converge on the monster, our blades flashing, but no blood is drawn in our initial attack. Grymsdyke leaps off Alice's shoulder, landing on the creature's neck, but just as he readies to sink his fangs in its neck, the spider is sent flying with an ungodly strong swat of a stitched-together hand.

Alice immediately doubles her attack, but it manages to catch her shoulder with its club. I watch in horror as her back slams into a wall. My fist swings and smashes into its face during the distraction—and for a blinding second, I wonder if I've struck a brick wall rather than a pieced-together monster made of man parts.

Its club swings at me now, sending me flying back a good three to five feet.

Victor struggles to his feet, his newly reclaimed sword pointing at the monster. "Leave them alone. They have nothing to do with this! This is between you and me."

It bellows once more, "A family's sin is a stain that cannot be washed away!"

Victor charges him just as Alice and I regain our footing. Club clashes against metal, and for a moment, it appears as if my brother's desperation has the upper hand as they fight their way back down the hallway toward the foyer. Alice and I grab our swords to follow, but then—I swear to God—the hallway grows right before our eyes, stretching farther and farther with each second.

"Victor!" I'm frantic now, my gun once more in my hand, firing as many rounds as I can get out. "Victor!"

My brother's sword makes contact, driving straight through the monster's heart, into the wall behind them. For a moment, everything around us calms even though Alice and I sprint down the lengthening hallway. The monster gasps, its head sagging before stilling completely.

A smile of disbelief curves Victor's lips. "I—I did it." He turns to face us, still so far away. "I—"

The monster's head snaps up. With a howl, it tears away from the sword, smashing a fist into my brother's head. Victor slams into the wall behind him just as the monster pummels him relentlessly.

"VICTOR!" All of my bullets continue to deflect off the monster as the hallway continues to stretch them farther into the distance. Even Alice's thrown blades merely bounce off, the sharp tips which I know to be striking their marks not cutting through cloth and skin. "VICTOR!"

My brother is no longer moving. Blood cakes his face, his hair. It soaks his clothes.

"VICTOR! GODDAMMIT, WAKE UP AND FIGHT HIM!"

But he doesn't. The monster grabs a leg and hauls him up, dragging him to a door I hadn't noticed before. Before it goes through, though, it turns to face Alice and me, smiling like the cat that ate the canary.

Its teeth are blackened shards within its mouth.

Another bullet whizzes through the air, aimed at the space between its eyes. It laughs at me, deftly entering the room with my brother in tow. The door slams shut just as the bullet passes by.

No. No. *NO.*

The hallway stops growing, and Alice and I finally gain ground. My fists pound against the door, she tries the knob. I step back, ready to kick the damn thing in, when the door fades away. It just . . . vanishes without a trace. The hallway is once more the size it was before, and we are in the foyer at the front of Bücherei.

I grab my hair, pulling at it as I spin around, searching for any kind of door. It's gone, though. There's no doorway, no monster, no brother.

What the fuck just happened?!

"Finn." Alice grabs hold of my arm, but I try to shake her off. "Finn. Look at me."

"He's gone." My heart thunders in my chest. "It took him. Just like he always fucking feared it would!"

"Who did?" She grabs hold of my face now. "Who was that monster supposed to be?"

Bitter, nearly hysterical laughter falls out of me. "That's just it! *The* monster. *His father's monster.*"

"No. Love, listen to me." But I can't. I'm—this has to be one of the Piper's tricks. Hallways don't grow. Doorways don't disappear. But my Alice is stubborn, though, refusing to let me fall apart. She yanks my face to ensure I'm looking at her. "Finn. Whatever that thing was, I do not believe it was any creation of Victor's father's. You must have seen its teeth. They were just like Todd's and Rosemary's. Wholly blackened and rotted. Its eyes were completely black, too. It was just another creation of the Piper's!"

It doesn't matter if it is or not. Victor is gone. I let that thing take my brother.

"We will find him." Her eyes bore up into mine. "Do you hear me? We will find him. But we must first go back and ensure that the others are all right. Once we do, we will begin our search."

"Alice." My voice is a whisper now. "He's dreamed of that monster his entire life. He always feared it would come for him, but we always promised it wouldn't. He told me he saw it at Sara's, standing beneath one of the windows, watching the house. I . . . I didn't believe him." I shake my head. "He was right. The whole time, he was right."

She tugs my head down and kisses me gently. "We will find him. Together."

The A.D. and Mary are at the top of the stairs, his arms around her as tears trickle down her pale face. Sitting next to them, one leg more crooked than the others, is Grymsdyke. The moment my brother's love sees me, and not him, she leaps out of the A.D.'s grasp and runs down the few steps.

I don't know what to say to her. How to even explain what just happened.

Justifiable anger fills her eyes. Her fists pummel my chest. "Where is he? Where is my Victor?"

My chest is hollow. All I can say is, "Gone."

She slaps my face, hard. "How could you let it take him? HOW COULD YOU?"

I don't stop her assault, not even when it nearly knocks me backward. Alice does, though. Alice grabs hold of her friend, wrapping her arms around her. "We tried, Mary. I vow to you, we did. It was impervious to our weapons—"

"Liar!" Mary collapses against Alice, quietly sobbing.

"I wish I were." Alice's eyes meet mine. "I believe in the impossible, Mary, but what was just experienced . . ." She shakes her head. "It is beyond the fantastical."

The peal of a music box sounds in the near distance, softly first, and then insistently. The A.D. crawls over to peek over the railing. When his mouth flattens and his eyes narrow, I absolutely know why.

I make my way up the stairs, cold fury replacing the shell-shocked in my veins. At the top step, I reach down and gently pick up Grymsdyke. He doesn't say a word; he just settles on my shoulder, his good legs digging into my tunic and skin.

I make my way over to the railing, not bothering to hide. Alice and Mary come to stand beside me; the A.D. rises to his feet. There, sitting upon the thrones, is the Piper and a woman dressed in a multi-hued dress much like the garb depicted in the tapestry behind them.

"The time has come," the sonofabitch says, his damn lips curved in a faint grin, "to talk of many thing: of thieves—of assassins—and prince and princesses, of poisons—and desperate folk, and why they think coming here means anything at all."

None of the hundreds standing before him say anything, let alone move.

"I want to welcome our guests. It took them far longer to arrive than I initially hoped for, but they are all here just the same. Although, I must admit, upon reflection, it's rather fortuitous their arrival occurred during the convergence. I was worried I might have to send some of you to fetch them. We wouldn't want them to miss out on the festivities, do we?" His eyes, and that of the woman's next to him, drift upward to where we stand. The woman then places her right hand upon the closed book between them.

In unison, every man, woman, and child turns to face us.

I do not shout, nor raise my voice. I do not threaten. I merely say, "I'm going to kill you."

His smile widens. "Children, they think to stop our work. How do you feel we must respond?"

The mass of armed soldiers in the room bursts to life in a flurry of motions and battle cries.

Alice immediately pulls Mary back. "Jack, I need you and Mary to go and try to find a way to get that book. I don't know why, but instinct insists it's important to them."

I grab one of my guns, snapping out the empty clip. "Mary, did you bring any SleepMist?"

Her tearstained eyes swivel back to me. "Yes."

I insert a new clip of bullets. "Get to work on figuring out how to neutralize these bastards so you can get the book." To the A.D., I say, "Get Sara. She's coming back with us, understand?"

He nods.

"I am staying with you two," Grymsdyke announces.

I won't say no to him. That said, I tell the A.D. and Mary, "Once you do get the book and Sara, edit back to the Institute right away. Show it to the Librarian and Brom."

"I refuse to leave Victor behind!" Mary vows harshly. "We're not leaving you."

"Yes," I tell her just as harshly. "You will. Because right now, this shit is bigger than us. You get that damn book back. Did you take any pictures of this place with the glasses?"

"Yes, of course, but—"

"Good. If the Society chooses to send people back, you know where to edit into."

The sounds of a multitude of feet pound on nearby stairs. I search the veranda and find a set of doors in the far back. "Go. There's a door back there."

Alice adds grimly, "We will take care of this."

"But . . . Victor!"

I tell my brother's girlfriend, "I will find him. *Go.*"

The A.D. grabs both his and Mary's bags, and together they sprint across the length of the room to the door. Thankfully, it opens on the first try, and with small waves of their hands, they disappear from view.

I take a deep breath. Look at Alice. "I love you, my north star."

"Don't say it like that." Heat fills her eyes. "Our story is only in the beginning chapters. We still have many, many to go before the end.

And we're binaries, remember?"

"I love you," I say again.

She grabs hold of my arms and crashes her lips against mine. "I love you, too. Do not dare to undo all the trouble I've gone through to ensure your safety, do you hear me Huckleberry Finn Van Brunt?"

My laughter is nothing more than a whisper. "Yes, Your Majesty."

"We have true love. It will save us as it has before. It will always save us. I believe that, Finn. You must, too."

Grymsdyke transfers from my shoulder to hers, and I'm glad for it.

We move to the middle of the room just before black-eyed men, women, and children bearing weapons swarm from staircases on either side of the veranda. The moment they see us, screaming so loud I fear my ears are bleeding commences.

No prisoners. No mercy. These are not really children, not like they look. They're older than I by centuries, trained to be murderers whether willingly or unwillingly. I can't subdue them all, neither can Alice.

We have to fight.

I begin shooting; Alice starts hacking away with her sword. Some of our assailants are better than others, but there are a lot in the initial wave that we're able to kick away. Grymsdyke leaps off Alice's shoulder, attacking those who come too close. The ancient kids, as ferocious as they can be, can't knock him off as easily as the monster did. And while my gun and Alice's sword slow them down, his bite stops them altogether.

The Pan kid reappears, flying above us, his skin sallow and eyes sunken. Alice chops away at him, and he laughs as if it's the funniest thing ever.

Despite the three of us cutting down as many as we can, more of the Piper's soldiers pour into the room. Bodies are dropping like flies in our paths, but they're relentless, like they don't have a care in the world that they're heading to their doom. Soon, the veranda is completely filled with children bearing deadly weapons.

And then . . . the music box sounds again, and everyone stops.

Just . . . stops. Weapons readied, facing us, they form a veritable wall.

Alice and I freeze, too. We're both bleeding, both breathing hard and wary as all hell. We press our backs up against each other, circling around to survey the mass of fallen bodies and the horde of still-standing persons all around us. Grymsdyke quickly scuttles off his latest victim, darting back over to where we are.

"What is happening?" he asks. "Why have they ceased their attacks?"

"I don't know." And I really don't.

I take a step forward, toward the ring of children in front of me, and their ranks close in unison. There isn't enough space between any of them to slip through, no way to even get close to the railing to find a way down into the throne room. They're all smiling now, like they know they've got us cornered. A ripple of laughter and excitement sounds through the vibrating crowd.

Maybe we can—

It's then I hear it. Softly, but I hear it.

No. No. Not now. No.

Alice reaches back, her hand gripping my arm so tightly I am sure she will leave a bruise. The music swells, growing louder by the second. It's a haunting melody, one whose roots dig deep beneath my skin, into my bones and the pink folds of my brain.

I stumble; so does Alice. We fall to the ground, dazed.

My head swims, my vision blurs. I grapple for Alice, for her face. "Look at me," I insist. "Focus on me."

Her fingers dig into my arm, but I can barely feel them. "Love you," I think she says. And then my name, more loudly and yet distantly all at once.

The melody fills the room until it's all I can hear. I tug Alice closer, unsure of where my gun is, where her sword might be. I can't—I can't even find Grymsdyke. All I see, blurry and beautiful before me, is Alice.

Soon, I don't even see that. I sink into the black river below me, unable to fight my way back to the surface.

HOME

ALICE

MY BODY CONVULSES, FINN'S name spilling from my mouth. I reach out and find . . . a soft, warm, bare body.

I am not on the veranda, surrounded by the Piper's minions. I am in a bed, and there is a man lying next to me. He curls closer, his arm wrapping around my waist—my *bare* waist. "Shh," he mumbles. "Just a dream."

I jerk upright, yanking the sheet higher. Faint, golden sunlight spills in through dark curtains nearby, slanting rays upon the room I'm currently in. I know those curtains. I . . . I know this bed. I know the painting on the wall before me.

I look down at the man next to me, now pushing himself up into a sitting position. I know him, too.

I whisper, shaken to my very core, "Jace?"

He curves a hand to cup my face, pressing his lips against my cheek. "Another nightmare?"

What is happening right now? How . . . how can this be? Where is Finn? Grymsdyke?

I'm out of the bed, across the room in an instant to throw the door open. Before me is a familiar hallway, filled with familiar paintings and doorways.

Soft feet pad across the room, gentle hands wrap around my waist. "It's okay. It was just another dream. You're okay. You're at home, my love."

A . . . dream? Yes, that's it. A dream. The Piper—he's . . . his flute. We were surrounded, and he was playing his music and—

And Jace is tugging me back toward the bed. My bed. The bed I commissioned to be made just for us. "I know you keep refusing to do so, but, Alice, I think it's time we talk to the Caterpillar about these nightmares. They only seem to be worsening. Tell me about this latest?"

I pinch my arm hard. Jace immediately grabs my hand, pulling it back. "You're awake. I promise you're awake. There is no need to continue to maim yourself."

My skin, reddening and throbbing, stings. Up and down my bare arms are bruises. How is this possible? Just minutes before, I was in the Piper's lair within Koppenberg Mountain, fighting, and now . . . now I am in my bedroom in the tulgey wood?

Where is Finn?

As the White King pushes me down onto the mattress, I grab the letter opener resting upon a stack of correspondence on the stand next to my bed. Jace attempts to snatch it from me, but he's not quick enough. I slash it across my palm a split second before he knocks it away. I wince as blood wells in thick beads.

I . . . I must be dreaming, and yet . . . I can feel pain. I'm bleeding. There is no bandage on my wrist, no fresh row of stitches.

I have to get to Finn. I cannot let the Piper have him. I can't.

The White King of Wonderland has a handkerchief out and is

wrapping it around my hand. "Alice, please! You must stop this. Dammit, I could have sworn I took that out of here last night."

Stop . . . what?

He must see my quizzical look, because he flips my other palm up. There, now scabbed over, is a nearly identical line. And then, across my thigh, yet another line.

"I'm worried about you." He pulls me into his arms. "This cannot go on. Today, when our Grand Advisors arrive, I will speak to them whether you wish it or not. There must be a draught or something they can offer to help you sleep more serenely."

"The Caterpillar . . . is alive?"

He pulls away just a bit so he can look down at me. His handsome, dear face is filled with so much concern. "Did you dream he was not?"

I glance around the room. It seems so . . . real. It cannot be, though. The prophecy banished me from Wonderland. The White King and I are no more. This home now sits empty, a silent memory of our love, hopes, and dreams.

I turn to face him, my hands cupping his face. His dark hair is askew from sleep, his pale eyes, so light they are nearly colorless, are just as I remember them. There's a tiny scar cutting through his left eyebrow, one made when he was a child, practicing swordplay with his squire. There is another scar, much less noticeable, just beneath his chin, created from the clumsy hand of youth while shaving.

He looks exactly as he always has. I feel his skin beneath my own. I feel the heat of his body next to mine. His smell is so familiar, his voice even more so.

My eyes well with tears. Confusion, so much confusion, muddles my thoughts. "How are you here?"

He leans forward, his lips brushing mine. "This is our home."

Our home.

"Are you real?"

Another brush of his lips against mine, and I stiffen in disbelief. "Do I feel real?"

He does. And that is the problem—*he does.*

"How . . ." I swallow. "How did I get here?"

"We arrived three days ago via horseback."

Three days. "This cannot be real." I shake my head. "I was . . . I was in . . ." I cannot remember the designation. One of the Gram—no, *Grimm's* Timelines. "The prophecy—"

"What prophecy? Was this part of your latest dream?"

I suck in a breath at the implication of what he is saying.

He smoothes the hair around my face. "Talk to me, dearest. Tell me about this prophecy you dreamed of."

He feels so real. He sounds so real. I can feel him. Smell him.

I lick my dry lips. "The one that banishes me from Wonderland."

Surprise fills those haunting eyes of his. He genuinely seems taken aback by what I've just said. But how can that be? This prophecy not only tore apart my life, but his, too.

"Why ever would you be banished from Wonderland? You are the Queen of Diamonds."

"Because the Courts are unbalanced." I search for any recognition in his eyes. "Because there is no King of Diamonds."

A small bit of understanding appears in his eyes. "I knew you were worried about the transition, but—"

Transition?

"All will be fine." His smile is reassuring. "The Cheshire-Cat and the Caterpillar have assured us that the legal issues have all be rectified, remember?"

I—I don't—

"Dearest, we saw the Oracle just two days ago, remember? She said Wonderland itself embraces our union. Until our deaths, the White and Diamond Courts will be unified."

I don't know if I am even breathing right now. This *must* be a dream. A long, cherished dream I was forced to lie to rest that somehow the Piper has brought forth to trick me.

"If you are still worried about the White Queen, please do not. She has agreed to the conditions and signed the necessary documents in preparation for the ceremony the day after tomorrow. The Cheshire-Cat sent word last night that he had them in hand and would be bringing them today for us to co-sign. Although, isn't it just like her to wait until such a late hour? I suppose it could have been worse; she could have made us wait whilst standing upon the altar."

I hold up my left hand. There, upon my ring finger, sits the most beautiful white diamond I have ever seen. I reach up and find a golden H dangling from my neck.

"Is that what the dream was about last night? A prophecy saying you must leave Wonderland?"

I am shaking in his arms, so very, very confused. This cannot be real. This must be a trick of the Piper's, or of the thirteenth Wise Woman's. "I fear I am dreaming right now."

"What can I do to prove to you that you are not?" A hand curves around the back of my head. His lips hover over mine, a bare hair's width away. "You are not dreaming, Alice." His mouth touches mine, once more shocking me into stillness. "You are here, with me, in our home, exactly where you belong." Another kiss, more meaning full now. My heart hammers so very terribly hard in my chest, and while my body sinks easily into the passion his touch inspires, something else surfaces, too, something far more powerful.

Guilt. Oh so much guilt.

I . . . I love this man, yes. Desperately. This was my dearest dream for so long. Him, me, here. Our union, our joining of kingdoms. But I'm also in love with someone else, someone who I willingly gave my heart to. One who I feel inside my veins right now.

My true love. My north star.

When Jace's tongue touches mine, though, my body ignites in such bittersweetly familiar passion and need. He tastes the same. Feels the same. I feel him. His hands, his wonderful hands that are now worshipping my body, do not feel like a dream. I would know—after my expulsion from Wonderland, I dreamed of this more times than I ought to admit. None of those felt real, though, and that was the problem. I dreamed of kisses, imagined our lovemaking, and all of it was hollow and intangible.

I feel him. He's—he's here. This is not a memory, it cannot be . . . can it? I've bled. I felt pain. I feel him here, now, his body pressing against mine as we lay down upon our bed.

And still, I pull away, my head turning until our mouths no longer touch. *This doesn't feel right.* "We are to wed in two days' time?"

There's surprise in his eyes, a bit of hurt, too. "Yes. Providing you still want to go through with the small ceremony."

I never wanted a lavish affair. He and I had always only planned on an intimate ceremony, despite our royal statuses. We reasoned a large celebration afterward, complete with plenty of food, drink, and revelry, would be enough for our peoples.

Instinct, for the first time in so long, fails me. I cannot discern if this is truth or the Piper's work. "Are you really here, Jace? Am I?"

A knee gently spreads my legs open wider. "Yes, my queen. You are really, truly, absolutely here."

I scoot into a sitting position, clutching the sheets to my chest. Confusion swallows me as Jace stares at me, stunned by my actions. "The prophecy said we could not be," I whisper. "That—that our love, the shuffling of the decks, would cause Wonderland's people much pain."

He pauses. "Is this the same one which banished you from Wonderland?"

I nod warily.

"It was a dream, nothing more. I vow to you this."

The White King's word has never been suspect. And still, I whisper brokenly, "I left. I left, and it shattered both our hearts, but I did it."

He takes my hand, the one that is not wrapped in his handkerchief, and places it against his heart. A steady, familiar beat thumps beneath my fingers. "I am here," he says quietly. "You are here. My heart is, as it always has been, yours. It is not broken, but rather, fuller than ever before."

Hazy images flash through my mind: the Pleasance Asylum, the Institute in New York City, the Collectors' Society, Van Brunt, Mary, Victor, Wendy, the A.D., the Librarian, Marianne, Todd, Rosemary, a playbook, my crown, the Piper, and Finn. Finn Van Brunt. Huckleberry Finn Van Brunt. He—I love him. Am in love with him. He and the others are in the mountain, too. I slew a giant to save him.

I love him.

I stare up in Jace's eyes. There is no subterfuge in them—not that he ever has been dishonest with me before, but all that shines back at me in the growing light of dawn is love and concern.

I no longer know what is real and what isn't. He feels real. This feels real. He claims I have been having nightmares, vivid dreams. There are bruises up and down my arms, no doubt from pinching. There are cuts.

Cuts. I have had more than one recently, haven't I?

"Is there a mark on my lower back? One at the base of my spine, caused from stitches now removed?"

Gentle hands trace a path down my back until they reach the spot I've just described.

"I feel nothing."

I reach back, my hand searching for where the boojum was removed. But there is nothing. No tenderness, no raised bump of a line to show where the Queen of Hearts' duplicity happened.

I hold back the sheet and peer down at my bare body, searching for the fading bruises from the battle with the giant. There is nothing. The only ones that I can find are small, the product of pinches. Could the Piper do this? Or the Wise Woman?

"What of the Piper?"

"Who?"

"The Pied Piper. The one destroying catalysts and Timelines."

"Was he also in your latest dream? What are catalysts and Time-lines?"

Could Jace be right? Could it all be nothing more than a dream? A nightmare? Could all of what I thought I experienced over the last year be nothing more than a figment of my admittedly very overactive imagination?

Could I be foolish enough to believe myself in love with nothing more than a dream?

I turn my head away from Jace, shaken.

"Shall I go make you some tea? Get some of your favorite bis-cuits? They might help you wake up a bit more."

The Piper had never been able to access Wonderland, which is why he could never find the catalyst. He could not have known what my house looked like, or my bed. He could not know that there is a painting of Jace and I, in the Field of Daydreams, hanging on the wall. He could not know that I always keep a vase of flowers—the non-person kind, of course—next to both sides of our bed. He could not know these things. He could not know of the scar on Jace's face, the one that cuts through his eyebrow. He could not know that Jace more often than not brought me breakfast in bed.

Grateful for a reason to distance myself, I tell him I would very much like that.

He presses a kiss against my cheek before rolling off the bed. I watch as he tugs on a robe, one with the seal of the White Court of Wonderland embroidered on it. He pulls open the heavy curtains to reveal the most perfect kind of morning: golden light, skies so azure they almost hurt to gaze upon them, clouds curling into intricate patterns as they paint the sky, trees swaying gently in a light breeze. The flowers in our garden are already singing their morning choruses.

He slips the letter opener into a pocket. "I'll be right back. Go ahead and rest. The others won't be here until midday."

I nod and then he leaves.

For a good minute, I lay in our bed, stunned. The Piper—he—
Wait.
Wait.

I cannot clearly remember the Piper's face. He was . . . tall? No. Medium build. I shake my head, desperate for the memories, but they feel like sand between my fingers. He had . . . a musical instrument. There was a hill. A mountain? My fists knock against my forehead. Why can't I remember? *I must.*

Finn.

I yank at my hair. His face, in my mind, is blurred. No. No. I cannot let him go. No. I must remember him. He's—he's my heart. My partner. Isn't he? I must find him. I must—

I pluck at my hair. *Focus, Alice. Focus.*

Everything swirls about me. I rush over to the looking glass, peering at my back. There is no cut there, no sign of stitches . . . but there is a small smudge of blue and purple lines. Could they be . . . bruises? I crane my neck further. No—not bruises. But what are they?

A minute later, I'm tugging on my own robe. A robe that has a bird on it, *my* bird, the one carrying a diamond in its beak. Drawers are opened and searched, the closet the same. Everything inside is just as it ought to be. My things. Jace's things.

I am home.

I sit down at my vanity. My hairbrush lies before me, strands of my hair in the bristles. I stare into the looking glass—the Queen of Diamonds stares back at me. There are darkish circles beneath my eyes, my hair is braided. Nothing is amiss.

My vision blurs before refocusing. Why am I concerned that anything might be so? How very silly of me.

By the time Jace returns with a tray of tea and biscuits, I am back in bed, looking over papers from the stack on the nightstand. There is also a gift of a small cluster of white heather. A smile curves my lips. "You are so good to me."

He sets the tray down and joins me on the bed. "Feeling better?"

"Much." A small laugh falls out. "All this drama over a dream. I fear I am such a mimsy. This will teach me to not drink any of the Hatter's juice before bed."

An empty bottle of the wretched yet delicious concoction lies on the floor next to two goblets.

Jace kisses my shoulder, and I force myself not to flinch. "I still think we ought to talk to our Grand Advisors about what's happening."

"Nonsense." I take his hand and squeeze it. "What we need to talk to them about are these." I rattle the papers in my other hand.

A sigh follows a quick glance that darkens his handsome features. "Well, that's the Red King for you."

"The arena games are barbaric, and the fact that he is now using prisoners for blood sport is appalling. Some of these people are merely debtors, too poor to pay their taxes. Some have been imprisoned for stealing a loaf of bread to feed their hungry families. They do not deserve such a fate. We must put a stop to the games."

"We will." He lifts our hands to kiss the base of my knuckles.

"The White Queen will back us in this. My envoy to the Hearts' Court claims he believes the King of Hearts will also lend his support. That will give us a majority."

I let out a bitter laugh. "Not the Queen of Hearts, though."

He rolls his eyes. "She probably has offered up her own prisoners."

At the thought of my fellow royal, anger simmers in my blood. Although I am typically annoyed and revolted by the woman, searing rage such as I feel now is not so common.

"Has she done anything more despicable than normal lately?"

"Hearts?"

I nod.

He tears a piece of a biscuit off and pops it into his mouth. "None of our spies have reported so. Why?"

"Instinct," is all I can tell him.

"As your instinct is nearly infallible, let us send word for another report."

I pour us cups of tea into china marked with an elaborate white diamond embellished with a J&A. "On a related note, I am gobsmacked that White agreed to our conditions."

"She saw the writing on the wall. The people are behind our marriage; they crave for the stability of unified kingdoms. Even she would not risk an uprising."

That is debatable. I offer him his cup. "When does she arrive?"

"I am sure she will arrive no less than absolutely possible before the ceremony. She'll want to make a scene."

The tea is delicious. Jace has always known exactly how to brew it right. I savor the warmth of the cup by wrapping my fingers around the delicate china. "When doesn't she?"

He laughs over his tea. "Yes, but this time, she'll want to do it doubly so. The benevolent, magnanimous White Queen of Wonderland, standing back and watching her co-regent marry her equal in the Diamonds Court? She'll ensure all will know of how she's sacrificing much for her people. Chances are, her agents will whisper suggestions to villagers of sainthood."

Agents. Why does that word feel so . . . important? Meaningful?

I shake my head. "Chances are, you are right."

"I suppose it's one of the prices of happiness."

I lean my head on his shoulder. "It's a fair price."

Once breakfast is eaten and we have dressed for the day, we go for a ride. Just beyond the eastern edge of the tulgey woods lies the Field of Singing Wildflowers. Their songs are particularly lovely this fine day, melodious harmonies swelling in the air. It feels good to be upon my horse, to have the wind in my hair as we race through the field. Calls of, "Greetings, Your Majesties!" follow us until we find the great willow hovering over the burbling creek that waters these fields. This tree has always been a favorite of mine—tall and graceful, its leaves silvery green, it acts more like the field's guardian than anything else.

Wonderland is at its best today, filled with magic and beauty so wonderful that it leaves me drunk on pleasure.

Jace pulls his horse up next to mine. "What has you so pleased?"

"It sound silly, but it feels as if I haven't ridden for pleasure in so long."

He urges his stallion a bit closer so he can lean over to kiss me. And this, too, feels good. Better than good, despite how my muscles tense with each touch between us.

I'm happy. Content. Above us, the clouds twist into our initials.

Once we dismount, and our horses are munching on soft blue-tinged grasses nearby, we lounge beneath the tree. Tiny Rocking-horse and Snap-dragon-flies buzz merrily in the warming air around us. "Do you remember the last time we came here?"

Heat fills his eyes. "How could I forget?"

I climb upon his lap, my arms circling his neck. I was so cold to him this morning, so distant. I have never felt that way toward this man before, and it concerns me. "It was a perfect afternoon."

"Any moment with you," he says so wonderfully, beautifully seriously, "is perfect."

Our mouths find each other's once more. Our kisses are languid—there is no rush right now. Wonderland is at peace. We are to be married, our kingdoms unified. Soon, we will be able to launch our educational programs that we've worked so hard on. The worst trouble in the land comes from the Red Court, and even then, we will have very little trouble overcoming them. If anything is a dream, it is this, here, now. It is what we have worked so hard for, what we have always wished for.

Eventually, the layers of my skirt are sorted and pulled to the side. His breeches are loosened. Heat fills our kisses, our touches, until I feel as if I've consumed a full glass of the Hatter's juice. My heart jackrabbits in my chest, his does the same. Our touches have always been able to do that to one another. Just before I am about to position myself over him, though, an uneasy feeling tickles at the back of my consciousness.

It's . . . guilt. A sense of wrongness. And it grows stronger with each second that passes by. This—this isn't right. I shouldn't be doing this.

This isn't the man I want to be with.

"What's wrong?" His hands come to cup my face, his breath is hard. "I feel like you are a million miles away all of a sudden."

I blink, my eyes refocusing on the man beneath me. "I . . ." Yet I do not know what to say. To explain the insidious feeling of betrayal scratching away at my happiness, as if . . . as if this here, the two of us together, is wrong. That I am meant to be elsewhere, with someone else.

I desperately try to remember the man from my dreams. Who is he? Why does he feel so important? Because Jace and I . . . We are not wrong. We cannot be wrong. Wonderland is on our side. Wonderland has sanctioned our union.

Nonetheless, I cannot make love to this man with such feelings haunting me. My stomach cramps, tears sting the backs of my eyes. I shift back slightly, shaken. Our lovely moment slips past my grasp. "Maybe we should talk to the Caterpillar."

He leans forward, cupping my face to kiss me once more, only this kiss is meant to be soothing. And still, I am entirely unsettled. My muscles tighten beneath his hold. "I'm glad you think so." Earnest concern etches his face. He is gentleman enough not to call me out on my change of heart. "Speaking of, we ought to be heading back to get ready to receive him and the Cheshire-Cat."

I nod, but as we adjust our clothing, I cannot help but feel more than a bit ridiculous that I've allowed irrational feelings from a rapidly fading dream to ruin this moment for us. I can only rouse snatches of the dream to memory, and even those are fluid and increasingly out of reach. And yet, the sensations of importance, of relevance, refuse to lessen their grip on me. The entire ride back to our home, I am fixated on trying to piece together any and all bits of the nighttime imaginations that would inspire such emotions within me.

I fail, though. By the time our horses are tended and put into their stalls, my focus returns to where it ought to be: preparing for the merging of two of Wonderland's kingdoms in as many days' time.

WHEN THE PAGES TUG down the ramp from the carriage bearing the White Court's shield and hold open the door, I am inexplicably tempted to reach for Jace's hand. I do not, though. I assume the pose that my mentor and Grand Advisor taught me early on: back straight, feet together, hands primly folded together in front, a serene yet aloof smile upon my face. The Cheshire-Cat appears first, his length growing with each paw padding down the ramp. By the time he touches dirt, he is the size of a pony. Brownish fur sleek, golden eyes glowing, he regards us with an impish smile. "The old canker is in a frightfully nasty mood—"

"I heard that, you blasted flea-ridden beast!" comes from inside the carriage.

The Cheshire-Cat continues without a beat, "Therefore, I hope tea is ready and waiting."

I turn to a lady-in-waiting, now exiting the carriage behind that of the Grand Advisors.' "Please ready the table in the garden."

She curtsies. "Yes, Your Majesty."

As she departs, the White King welcomes his Grand Advisor. "I hope the journey was comfortable?"

The Cheshire-Cat yawns. "Tolerable, I suppose." He motions to a nearby page. "Fetch a bowl of cream, boy. Make sure to add a dash of juice."

The page, arms loaded with trunks, dashes into the house.

The carriage groans and shakes before the Caterpillar sticks his head out of the door. Half-moon spectacles are perched halfway down his rather bulbous nose, a small beret rests upon his head. More importantly, he wears his typical sleepy frown.

My vision momentarily blurs for reasons I cannot understand.

Each of his leather-clad feet patters against the wooden ramp as he descends. A small tilt of his head precedes, "Why you two continue to insist upon dwelling in such a remote location continues to boggle my mind."

"I refused to allow him to smoke in the carriage," the Cheshire-Cat says. "I'm afraid it left him even more unfit for decent company than normal."

The Caterpillar ignores him, instead focusing on me. Eyes narrowed, he sniffs. "You appear rather fatigued. It does not become you."

I take no offense. "Let us go and enjoy some refreshments in the garden. Perhaps that will help ease the effects of such a weary journey."

"I hope you have instructed those flowers of yours to keep their petals shut while we're out there. They're frightfully off-key."

They had, in fact, been practicing a song before Jace and I left to go riding. Begonia, the lead Rose in the garden, has vowed on multiple occasions to produce a performance that will finally earn the Caterpillar's applause, but it seems today may not be that day.

"I have done no such thing," I say calmly.

He sighs heavily before instructing another page to bring his hookah along with us.

The house bustles with the added staff that the caravan has brought with it. The garden is no different, and as predicted, the flowers burst out in a symphony of choruses the moment we walk through the gate. The Cheshire-Cat makes a grand show of his delight, purring so loudly he might as well be part of the show. In direct opposition, the Caterpillar plops down upon his tufted velvet pillow with a distinct groan of displeasure.

Jace waves away a page and pulls my chair out himself. Once he is seated across from me, we share an amused, knowing look. Some things will never change.

Soon, the Caterpillar's hookah is set up and he is puffing away at an alarming rate. His nerves are calmed enough to allow two of his many feet to actually offer the weakest, tiniest of claps when the flowers finish, though, so there is that.

Begonia nearly withers in shock, she is so delighted.

The Cheshire-Cat swishes his tail as he motions for his cream. "My seneschal has brought the White Queen's documents as requested. May I just say that dealing with the Tweedles is exhausting. I very nearly clawed the both of them before it was all said and done."

"Where was the Sheep?" Jace inquires.

The Cheshire-Cat shrugs in his cat-like way. "Mostly likely off doing the White Queen's nefarious bidding as usual."

"I am surprised she would not have her Grand Advisor there to ensure such important papers were proper," Jace muses.

"Oh, have no doubts. The Sheep, Caterpillar, and I spent many long hours in the days beforehand poring over the documents. But even she could find nothing amiss in the wording. She signed the documents prior to teatime yesterday."

"Her absence meant she was most likely readying her network of spies to inform the White Rabbit, the Walrus, and the Carpenter of the contents." The Caterpillar blows a perfect smoke Sheep, bonnet and all, morphing into the White Queen. "Never mind that we already had envoys ready to deploy with the same news." Another figure is blown, that of the Sheep with her legs in shackles. "Of course, the possibility that the White Queen had her jailed for daring to sign the decree is to be considered, too."

"I certainly wouldn't put it past her," I mutter. "It isn't as if she hasn't jailed her Grand Advisor countless other occasions for lesser offenses."

"It astounds me that the White Queen brought in the Tweedles in lieu of the Sheep." Jace frowns. "She often rails of their buffoonery in Court even when they come in victory."

The Cheshire-Cat looks up from his bowl of cream. "Yes, well, they are loyal buffoons, aren't they? And dangerous, if not valuable, ones to boot. They have gone to hell and back for Her Majesty, have assassinated countless people both innocent and guilty, and still have those inane smiles upon their faces."

"To follow blindly," the Caterpillar says languidly, "is to yield possession of your own compass."

If there were anyone that this could ever describe, it would be the Tweedles. Chances are, the White Queen has found a way to extract their souls and sew them up within a pair of her many dolls she collects within the White Court.

"Nonetheless," Jace says, "the contracts are signed." He lifts his cup of tea, a special blend made by the Hatter for us that is far more potent than any wine. "To the White and Diamond Courts unifying."

The Caterpillar and I raise our cups, too. The Cheshire-Cat mimics the action, as his bowl is too large to lift.

Biscuits are consumed, much tea is drunk. Everyone is in fine spirits, even the Caterpillar. His rhetoric tones down into something almost cheery. Faint praise is offered to Begonia: "My ears did not bleed this time, Madam."

A petal drops, she quivers so strongly with pride.

Jace and the Cheshire-Cat excuse themselves to the library to look over documents. I am ready to follow when the White King leans down and says quietly, "Talk to him?"

My defenses go up. "There are more pressing—"

He lifts my hand and presses a gentle kiss against my wrapped palm. And then he leaves.

The Caterpillar lifts an eyebrow, smoke hazing around his head. "What are you to talk to me about?"

His hearing, unfortunately, is quite excellent. "I am apparently having—"

"Apparently?" He tsks. "Queens do not use improper or unreliable wording."

I sigh quietly. "When I awoke this morning, I was disoriented and believed I was in a dream. I was quite insistent about it, I'm afraid." I proffer my wounded hand. "I required proof that I was awake."

His pipe stills. "What kind of dream?"

"That is the thing. I cannot quite remember what it was that I dreamed about during the night that led me to believe this was not real. I can only summon tiny slivers of memory, of pictures, but the sensations remain."

"What sensations?"

"That . . . this is wrong. Me, being here, is wrong."

"You?" he asks. "Do you mean Alice? Or do you mean the Queen of Diamonds?"

"I do not know," I whisper.

"Do not whisper, Your Majesty." He sets his hookah pipe down. "It is not befitting of your status. Say everything you mean as you mean it."

But I do not know what I mean, and that is the problem. Because something within me insists that this here, me speaking with my Grand Advisor, is a bittersweet impossibility, too.

"I dreamed I am in love with another."

His eyes squint. "Does that sensation remain?"

I take a breath. "Yes, although I cannot remember why or for whom I have them for. They are strong, though. I feel them within my bones."

"Even when you are with your beloved White King?"

I do not lie. "Even then."

"Dreams are tricky," he says. "Some tell of the past, some of the future, some of the present. Some tell us nothing more than imagination or horrors, some are representations of our dearest wishes. Is this the first time you have woken to such feelings?"

"The White King insists that this has occurred several mornings in a row. I have no memory of them, though."

"How very curious." He is contemplative for a number of long seconds. "What is it you ask of me?"

"I cannot allow myself, as a ruler of Wonderland, to continue to wake disoriented each morning." I cannot allow myself to feel guilt or wrongness when I am with the man that I love, either—for him, or for our kingdoms once they are unified. "Is it possible there is something to remedy this situation?"

He strokes the few long hairs jutting from his chin with one of his many hands. "There are sleeping draughts, yes. But they are only masks for what ails you. Perhaps we can . . ." He grunts quietly. "It would be best to dig out the roots before we extract the problem. Give me a few hours with my poisons to see what I can concoct."

A small grin tugs at the corners of my mouth. "You brought them here, to my wedding?"

"My dear queen, I do not travel anywhere without my poisons. On that note, I have a present for you and His Majesty. I have come into possession of a nice heir potion that will increase both your fertilities by tenfold. There is enough for two doses, if you wish, although why anyone would want multiple spawn is beyond me."

"How thoughtful of you to keep our fertility concerns in mind," I say mildly.

"Not that it isn't going to be a nightmare when your children come." He waves a pair of dismissive hands. "Will they be of the White Court? Diamond? Both? Titles may have to be created for the future prince or princess. The logistics are bothersome, Your Majesty."

"I am quite certain that you and the Cheshire-Cat will figure it out." And still, the thought of having a child with Jace both saddens me and aches, as if it is more a dream put away rather than a certainty in the future.

Why is it that I continue to harbor hopes for my present and future with someone else?

I wish I could remember the man from my dreams. Why can't I? Why can I *feel* him yet not recall his face? It's as if magic is at work, refusing me my answers.

The Caterpillar stretches. "Go and look over the documents with the others. Ensure you read them carefully, even though the only changes have been the ones that the White King and yourself have sanctioned. Be sure to sign each copy."

He says this as if I have never signed a decree in my entire reign. I do not allow myself to be insulted by this, either.

The Caterpillar's advice, prickly or no, has always been spot on.

AT SUPPER, MY GRAND Advisor asks, "Are you still wishing for a solution to your nocturnal problems, Your Majesty?"

This piques Jace's interest immediately, as well as the Cheshire-Cat's for entirely different reasons. "What nocturnal problems? Is there something I am unaware of?"

Jace hushes him. I offer the Caterpillar a nod of assent.

"After meditating upon the problem, I realized the wisest course of action would be for you to return to those dreams which have plagued you."

"How exactly can Her Majesty return to a dream she cannot even remember?" Jace inquires.

"We will have to force it with poisons, of course." The Caterpillar turns his beady eyes toward me. "It will be as if you are stepping into the dream world as a separate person. It will be disorienting, Your Majesty. You most likely will discover another version of yourself."

I ask, "How will this solve what has been happening to me?"

"To break it down into simplistic terms, you will take an object into the dream world with you. A symbolic item. When the time is right, you will destroy it and therefore destroy the dream world. When you awaken, whatever influence your nightmares have had will cease. That dream world will no longer exist for you. All you will have is this."

Jace's eyes meet mine. There is hope in them, understanding, too.

I temper my own hope, though, and try my best to fight through the alarm and guilt continuing to claw at my insides. Something— there's something I'm supposed to remember, but cannot. As if I'm missing something. As if wishing to destroy the dream is the wrong choice, a dangerous one.

But I cannot allow such misplaced feelings to affect what is happening now. Wonderland, at least a good chunk of it, is on the brink of unprecedented peace and prosperity. My people deserve every effort their queen can give toward ensuring this fate. The only choice that matters is this one. "Can it really be so simple?"

"Of course not." It's the Cheshire-Cat who answers. "Dreams are terribly problematic. And if the old bug is thinking of what I'm thinking—"

The Caterpillar glares at him.

"Then the poison required is a difficult one to find."

"I have the ability to create it," the Caterpillar sniffs. "There is no need to attempt to find a dose on the black market."

"Do you now?" The Cheshire-Cat leers. "Am I to take it the Jabberwocky simply offered up a spare scale to you?"

"No," the Caterpillar says calmly. "But it may to the Queen of Diamonds, if she asks. Particularly if she has her vorpal blade with her."

The Cheshire-Cat bursts out in surprised laughter. "It will do no such thing! It is a beast beyond reasoning. Countless soldiers, adventurers, and fools have died before its feet over the centuries."

The Caterpillar merely looks to me expectantly. I, in turn, look to the White King.

He grins. I do, too.

"Well then," I say. "As the wedding is in two days' time, I—"

"*We*," Jace corrects.

My smile grows wider. The White King's curiosity has always been as strong as my own. "We will head out at first light to find the Jabberwocky. How long does the poison take to create?"

The Caterpillar shrugs. "An hour at the most. I have access to all other pertinent ingredients."

"I would like this done prior to the wedding." My eyes meet Jace's once more. "I suppose we'll have to hurry, won't we?"

He laughs that delightful laugh of his. "I suppose we shall."

The Cheshire-Cat sighs. "These two and their love of adventures."

He motions to the Caterpillar. "When do you think we will ever convince them that staying home is a good idea?"

My Grand Advisor also sighs. "That, my hairy colleague, would take a miracle, I'm afraid. Or a prophecy."

"Good thing there is no such thing," Jace says meaningfully.

And still, something scratches at my brain. Something that rings true at the word *prophecy.* But I shove it aside, because tomorrow, there is a Jabberwocky to hunt—and a wedding in two days to attend.

A BIBLIOGRAPHY

Curious as to who was featured or mentioned within *The Forgotten Mountain?*

Here's a list of some of the people and the books they came from.

Abraham Van Brunt (AKA Brom Bones); Katrina (Van Tassel) Van Brunt
Featured in the short story *The Legend of Sleepy Hollow,* found within *The Sketch Book of Geoffrey Crayon, Gent.* by Washington Irving

Alice (Reeve) Liddel; Grymsdyke; the White King; the Mad Hatter; the Caterpillar; the Cheshire-Cat; the Queen of Hearts; various other Wonderlandian animals & peoples
Both from and loosely based upon *Alice's Adventures in Wonderland* by Lewis Carroll
Through the Looking-Glass, and What Alice Found There by Lewis Carroll
The Hunting of the Snark by Lewis Carroll

Briar-Rose, the Wise Women; the Golden Goose; Grethel; Mr. Pfriem; the Giant; the Dwarves; Mother Holle; various other villagers and peoples
Both from and loosely based upon characters found within fairy-tales in *Children's and Household Tales* by The Grimm Brothers, including:
The Blue Light
Clever Grethel
The Golden Goose
Little Briar-Rose (Sleeping Beauty)
Master Pfriem
Mother Holle
The Young Giant

Cat(s)
I Am A Cat by Natsume Sōseki

C. Auguste Dupin
The Murders of the Rue Morgue by Edgar Allan Poe
The Mystery of Marie Rogêt by Edgar Allan Poe
The Purloined Letter by Edgar Allan Poe

Franklin Blake
The Moonstone by Wilkie Collins

Gwendolyn Peterson (AKA Wendy Darling); Peter Pan
Based loosely upon *Peter and Wendy* by J. M. Barrie

Henry Fleming
Red Badge of Courage by Stephen Crane

Mr. Holgrave
House of the Seven Gables by Nathaniel Hawthorne

Huckleberry Finn; Jim
The Adventures of Tom Sawyer by Mark Twain
Adventures of Huckleberry Finn by Mark Twain
Tom Sawyer Abroad by Mark Twain
Tom Sawyer, Detective by Mark Twain

Jack Dawkins (AKA The Artful Dodger); Fagin
Oliver Twist by Charles Dickens

Josephine (Jo) Bhaer
Little Women by Louisa May Alcott
Little Men by Lousia May Alcott
Jo's Boys by Lousia May Alcott

Marianne (Dashwood) Brandon
Sense and Sensibility by Jane Austen

Mary Lennox; Colin; Dickon
The Secret Garden by Frances Hodgson Burnett

The Pied Piper of Hamelin; various children
Featured in the fairy-tale *The Pied Piper of Hamelin,* found within *German Tales* by The Grimm Brothers

Professor Otto Lindenbrock
Journey to the Center of the Earth by Jules Verne

Sara (Crewe) Carrisford; Mr. Carrisford; Mr. Groverley
Both from and loosely based upon *A Little Princess* by Frances Hodgson Burnett

Sweeney Patrick Todd; Rosemary Nellie Lovett
Based loosely upon *A String of Pearls: A Romance,* most likely written by James Malcolm Rymer and Thomas Peckett Prest

Victor Frankenstein Jr.; Victor Frankenstein; the Monster
Both from and based loosely upon *Frankenstein; or, The Modern Prometheus* by Mary Shelley

ACKNOWLEDGEMENTS

MUCH GRATITUDE IS SENT out to the wonderful ladies who helped to make this book the best it could be: my editor Kristina Circelli, my publicist KP Simmon, my assistant Tricia Santos, Victoria Alday for designing yet another gorgeous, perfect cover, Stacey Blake for her formatting wizardry, and Bridget Donelson and Jessica Zelkovich for their eagle eyes during proofreading.

Andrea Johnston, Jessica Mangicaro, Ashley Bodette, Kathryn Grimes, and Tricia, please know how deeply grateful for all the time, feedback, and love you've given to the Society. Van Brunt wants me to let you know you're all honorary members.

To the fab members of my street team, the Lyons Pride, I adore you all and hope you know how much your support means to me. (in alphabetical order) Amy, Ana, Andrea, Ashley, Autumn, Brandi, Bridget, Candy, Cherisse, Christina Lynne, Christina Marie, Courtney, Cynthia, Daniela, Enrica, Ethan, Eunice, Gina, Ivey, Jenn, Jennifer, Jennifer, Jennifer (love all the Jennifers!), Jessica, Jessica, Jessica, Jessica (love all the Jessicas, too!), JL, JoAnna, Kate, Kathryn, Kelli, Kelly, Keri, Kiersten, Lauren, LeAnn, Leigha, Lindsey, Maria, Martina, Megan, Melissa, Meredith, Nicole, Nikka, Rachel, Rebecca, Samantha, Sheena, Tracy, Tricia, Vilma, Whitney, Yvonne, and all the rest . . . you guys are the best.

A pair of special shout-outs to two fab ladies for their special support of these books: Daisy Prescott and Shelly Crane, I'm sending out big hugs and virtual cupcakes to you. Actually, let's have real cupcakes next time we see one another!

Jon, no book of mine could ever be written without you as my sounding board. I am so lucky you are my north star and binary all at once. Thanks and love are also sent out to my family for supporting me through all my crazy writing jags and long hours before my computer.

For everyone who has come along with the Society and their journeys, much gratitude is sent out to you, too.

ALSO BY HEATHER LYONS

"Each of us here has a story, but it may not be the one you think you know . . ."

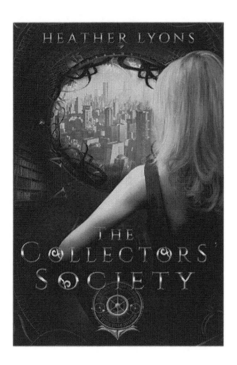

"The most unique, fascinating, wondrous book I've read in a very long time! I was glued to every page."

-Shelly Crane, New York Times bestselling author of Significance and Wide Awake

From the author of the Fate series and The Deep End of the Sea comes a fantastical romantic adventure that has Alice tumbling down the strangest rabbit hole yet.

After years in Wonderland, Alice has returned to England as an adult, desperate to reclaim sanity and control over her life. An enigmatic gentleman with an intriguing job offer too tempting to resist changes her plans for a calm existence, though. Soon, she's whisked to New York and initiated into the Collectors' Society, a secret organization whose members confirm that famous stories are anything but straightforward and that what she knows about the world is only a fraction of the truth.

It's there she discovers villains are afoot—ones who want to shelve the lives of countless beings. Assigned to work with the mysterious and alluring Finn, Alice and the rest of the Collectors' Society race against a doomsday clock in order to prevent further destruction . . . but will they make it before all their endings are erased?

The series continues with . . .

"This is not a series for fantasy lovers or new adult lovers. This is a series for all book lovers."

-Book Briefs

Sometimes, the rabbit hole is deeper than expected . . .

Alice Reeve and Finn Van Brunt have tumbled into a life of secrets.

Some secrets they share, such as their employment by the clandestine organization known as The Collectors' Society. Other secrets they carry within them, fighting to keep buried the things that could change everything they think they know.

On the hunt for an elusive villain who is hell-bent on destroying legacies, Alice, Finn, and the rest of the Society are desperate to unravel the mysteries surrounding them. But the farther they spiral down this rabbit hole, the deeper they fall into secrets that will test their loyalties and pit them against enemies both new and old.

Secrets, they come to find, can reveal the deadliest of truths.

*An enthralling mythological romance two thousand years
in the making . . .*

"Heather Lyons's *The Deep End of the Sea* is a radiant, imaginative romance that breathes new life into popular mythology while successfully tackling the issue of sexual assault. Lyons is a deft storyteller whose engaging prose will surprise readers at every turn. Readers will have no trouble sympathizing with Medusa, who is funny, endearing and courageous all at once. The romance between her and Hermes is passionate, sweet and utterly engrossing. This is a must read!"–*RT Book Reviews*

What if all the legends you've learned were wrong?

Brutally attacked by one god and unfairly cursed by another she faithfully served, Medusa has spent the last two thousand years living out her punishment on an enchanted isle in the Aegean Sea. A far cry from the monster legends depict, she's spent her time educating herself, gardening, and desperately trying to frighten away adventure seekers who occasionally end up, much to her dismay, as statues when they manage to catch her off guard. As time marches on without her, Medusa wishes for nothing more than to be given a second chance at a life stolen away at far too young an age.

But then comes a day when Hermes, one of the few friends she still has and the only deity she trusts, petitions the rest of the gods and goddesses to reverse the curse. Thus begins a journey toward healing and redemption, of reclaiming a life after tragedy, and of just how powerful friendship and love can be—because sometimes, you have to sink in the deep end of the sea before you can rise back up again

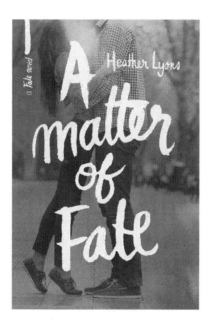

"Love, love, love this book! Such a fun and exciting premise. Full of teenage angst and heartache with a big helping of magic and enchantment. Can't wait to read the rest of this awesome series! Not to mention . . . TWO hot boys to swoon over."–*Elizabeth Lee, author of Where There's Smoke*

Chloe Lilywhite struggles with all the normal problems of a typical seventeen-year-old high school student. Only, Chloe isn't a normal teenage girl, She's a Magical, part of a secret race of beings who influence the universe. More importantly, she's a Creator, which means Fate mapped out her destiny long ago, from her college choice, to where she will live, to even her job. While her friends and relatives relish their future roles, Chloe resents the lack of say in her life, especially when she learns she's to be guarded against a vengeful group of beings bent on wiping out her kind. Their number one target? Chloe, of course.

That's nothing compared to the boy trouble she's gotten herself into. Because a guy she's literally dreamed of and loved her entire life, one she never knew truly existed, shows up in her math class, and with him comes a twin brother she finds herself inexplicably drawn to.

Chloe's once unyielding path now has a lot more choices than she ever thought possible.

Follow Chloe's story in the rest of the Fate series books . . .

"Heather Lyons' writing is an addiction . . . and like all addictions. I. Need. More."
—*#1 New York Times Best Selling Author Rachel Van Dyken*

"Enthralling fantasy with romance that will leave you breathless, the Fate Series is a must read!"—*Alyssa Rose Ivy, author of the Crescent Chronicles*

ABOUT THE AUTHOR

photo @Regina Wamba of Mae I Design and Photography

HEATHER LYONS IS KNOWN for writing epic, heartfelt love stories often with a fantastical twist. From Young Adult to New Adult to Adult novels—one commonality in all her books is the touching, and sometimes heart-wrenching, romance. In addition to writing, she's also been an archaeologist and a teacher. She and her husband and children live in sunny Southern California and are currently working their way through every cupcakery she can find.

Website: www.heatherlyons.net
Facebook: http://www.facebook.com/heatherlyonsbooks
Twitter: http://www.twitter.com/hymheather
Goodreads:
http://www.goodreads.com/author/show/6552446.Heather_Lyons
Stay up to date with Heather by subscribing to her newsletter:
http://eepurl.com/2Lkij

Made in the USA
Columbia, SC
07 November 2021